Praise for

The Lost Book of Eleanor Dare

"You do not need a deep grounding in colonial misadventure to appreciate Kimberly Brock's graceful work of speculative, historical fiction. This ambitious, indelibly Southern novel is told from three points of view—Eleanor, Alice, and Penn—in two timeframes. The storytelling is rich, lyrical, and garlanded with Spanish moss, with jewel-like passages that beg to be re-read. Brock, however, is just elliptical enough, and deft with her pacing, to keep the pages turning."

—*Atlanta Journal Constitution*

"Brock weaves a multigenerational story based on the supposed descendants of the real-life Eleanor Dare. I appreciated that the story was well researched as I read the pages from Eleanor Dare's viewpoint as she flees from Roanoke Island to points unknown. The characters are unique and carry their own human flaws that make them come alive and feel believable. I rooted for each of them as they strove to find their place in a complicated family history. Highly recommended."

—Historical Novel Society

"*The Lost Book of Eleanor Dare* is an intriguing, dreamy story about the impact of one unhealed woman who has yet to reconcile her past in such a way that lends itself to transparency with her young daughter . . . Author Kimberly Brock delicately balances mystery, family lore, and honoring one's forebears in sonorous language throughout a sweeping story with three points of view, two timeframes, and remarkably steady pacing. Weaving myth and legend with historical fact pertaining to an age-old American mystery, *The Lost Book of Eleanor Dare* is a spellbinding, beautiful story written by a graceful hand with just the right amount of mysticism."

—*New York Journal of Books*

"In this complex, compelling, and beautifully crafted novel, Kimberly Brock explores not only the enigma of the Lost Colony of Roanoke, but also the boundless mysteries of love, family, and the human heart. As Alice Young and her daughter Penn settle into Evertell, the crumbling ancestral estate they've just inherited, they discover secrets long hidden in the shadows there, keys to understanding their own veiled pasts. This is a story filled with many charms, both literal and figurative, and I guarantee it will captivate readers from the first page to the last."

—William Kent Kreuger,
New York Times bestselling author

"For readers of Patti Callahan and Kate Morton, this harrowing exposition on history and loss is a juxtaposition of love, hope, and the wisdom that binds women across centuries. *The Lost Book of Eleanor Dare*'s plea that we learn from each other, grow from each other, and empower each other is wrapped in an arresting, urgent voice that reads as much a rallying cry as a tract on the burden of women to suture the cracks of history. A magnanimous undertaking steeped in impeccable research, Brock offers a feast of a narrative that crackles with a resonant, binding echo of sisterhood across the centuries."

—Rachel McMillan,
author of *The Mozart Code*

"Kimberly Brock has crafted a luminous story, multi-layered and shimmering with beautiful prose, that deftly ponders the way of sacrificial love."

—Susan Meissner, bestselling author of
The Nature of Fragile Things

"Kimberly Brock's *The Lost Book of Eleanor Dare* is an immersive, engrossing tale about the lost colony of Roanoke, but even more significantly, about the relationship between a mother and daughter whose lives have been irrevocably altered by loss. Brock's writing is lush and captivating, and her characters are rich and complex. A masterful work by an expert craftswoman, *The Lost Book of Eleanor Dare* is not to be missed."

—Aimie K. Runyan, bestselling author of
The School for German Brides

"Compelling and immersive, *The Lost Book of Eleanor Dare* is the story of Dare's descendant Alice, who pushes away the pain of the past until her daughter Penn holds her accountable to the family story. Brock's lush narrative is rich in American and Virginia history with deep roots in the mysterious disappearance of the lost colony on Roanoke Island. As Alice and Penn seek answers, they rely on the enduring strength of their foremother Eleanor, who was determined to leave the truth behind so generations might walk in its light."

—Adriana Trigiani, bestselling author
of *The Good Left Undone*

"Amid the atmospheric backdrop of the Lowcountry, Brock stirs up a beguiling blend of family legacy, historical mystery, and generational connections, examining the unbreakable ties of mothers and daughters, the power of stories told and stories hidden, and the unquenchable need to understand those who came before us. A beautiful tale to curl up with and contemplate the intertwining of lives past and present."

—Lisa Wingate, #1 *New York Times* bestselling
author of *The Book of Lost Friends*

The
LOST BOOK
of
ELEANOR
DARE

Also by Kimberly Brock

The River Witch

The
LOST BOOK
of
ELEANOR DARE

KIMBERLY BROCK

HARPER MUSE

Published by Harper Muse, an imprint of HarperCollins Focus LLC.

Published in association with Browne & Miller Literary Associates, LLC, 52 Village Place, Hinsdale, IL 60521, www.browneandmiller.com.

Interior design by Emily Ghattas

This book is a work of fiction. The characters, incidents, and dialogue are drawn from the author's imagination and are not to be construed as real. Any resemblance to actual events or persons, living or dead, is entirely coincidental.

ISBN 978-1-4002-3427-1 (TP)

Library of Congress Cataloging-in-Publication Data

Names: Brock, Kimberly, author.
Title: The lost book of Eleanor Dare : a novel / Kimberly Brock.
Description: Nashville : Harper Muse, [2022] | Summary: "Based on real history and alternating between the story of war widow Alice searching for identity in the 1940s and excerpts from Eleanor Dare's Commonplace Book and the tale of her harrowing survival, The Lost Book of Eleanor Dare explores the meaning of female history and the sacrifices every mother makes for her daughter"-- Provided by publisher.
Identifiers: LCCN 2021053067 (print) | LCCN 2021053068 (ebook) | ISBN 9781400234202 (hardcover) | ISBN 9781400234233 (epub)
Subjects: LCSH: United States--History--20th century--Fiction. | Roanoke Island (N.C.)--History--16th century--Fiction. | Roanoke Colony--Fiction. | BISAC: FICTION / Southern | FICTION / Historical / World War II | LCGFT: Historical fiction.
Classification: LCC PS3602.R62334 L63 2022 (print) | LCC PS3602.R62334 (ebook) | DDC 813/.6--dc23/eng/20220112
LC record available at https://lccn.loc.gov/2021053067
LC ebook record available at https://lccn.loc.gov/2021053068

Printed in the United States of America

22 23 24 25 26 LBC 5 4 3 2 1

For the curious girls

They say there are no real mysteries left in the world;
no silver-scaled dragons of the air; no fantastic
lurking monsters in the deep, nor invisible people of
the wood. But Eleanor White could have told you
with certainty that these things were real.

Eleanor's Tale

The
LOST BOOK
of
ELEANOR
DARE

Prologue

The summer I turned thirteen, my mother took me into the forest to work a charm that was my right from birth. They say what happened there might have killed me. I think I might have killed her instead.

I thought I would be like her and all the women before me in my mother's family. For generations they'd come of age by inheriting a vision and learning of a myth, whispered from mother to daughter. But no vision had ever come. The charm that had been uttered for generations turned to poison in my hands. And when my mother died, the myth and all it meant went with her.

The story I was left with is one I've never told.

The truth is, things had taken a wrong turn even before the trail faded beneath the palmetto fronds, flooding out into swampy ponds as the light failed over the wetland. First, Mama lost her sense of direction. Then, in the night, she lost her mind. And while I'd slept beneath the hush of tall pines, secure in her love, she'd deserted me. It was a wonder, people later said, that I found my way home, surviving the sucking mud and the creatures that might have devoured me. And in fact, when I ran into the yard the next morning, some thought I was a ghost.

To my horror, so did my mother. She took one look at me and said, "Who are you, child? Tell me."

I had no answer for her.

)(

My mother taught me that a story matters not because it is true but because it's been told. I don't know if I believe this, but I've been trying to find a way to tell myself the story of that night with Mama my whole life in hopes that one day the ending will change. For while we both came home that day, the truth is, both of us disappeared.

Once there was a girl who went into the forest.

Until now I'd tried to forget what happened. I'd never planned to go back to that place. But that was before I had a daughter of my own. Now she looks to me with the question all daughters are bound to ask their mothers: *Who are you?* And I hear the echo behind that question. *Who am I?*

Even if I have no answer, I am still my mother's daughter. And so, I will give to my own daughter the only story I know—and hope that if I tell it well, she will find the answers she needs.

Once there was a girl who always took a dare.

Once there was a girl who went to sleep and awoke someone else.

Once there was a girl who could always find her way home.

Chapter One

Alice

"I'm telling you, we're not lost," I said, but my daughter looked worried.

Really, we were stranded with a dead battery a few miles south of Savannah. We'd traveled all day, over three hundred miles to cross the length of the state, from the mountains in the north. But my planning had been poor, to say the least. I'd underestimated the distance, then taken a wrong turn that had cost us time. Now, as dusk settled around us, I felt sick as we stared at my daddy's broken-down '38 Ford pickup truck.

Penn said, "What'll we do now?"

"It's fine," I lied, trying to sound more confident than I felt. "Come on. We can walk there."

We'd passed Hawkes's Feed and Seed about a mile and a half back, the only store on the road that might have been a help to us, although I dreaded walking into the place again. In any case, it was already closed up tight for the night.

The shadows stretched as the swampy air filled with a choir of indistinct insects and frogs, and I knew there were things in these wetlands that were dangerous. I reached under the seat for a flashlight but came up empty-handed.

I said, "I know this road. We're not far. We'll be there before it's really dark. We'll deal with the truck in the morning."

Penn pulled the strap of her satchel over her shoulder, looking around with hesitation. I shouldered my own thin bag. I hardly knew what I'd packed.

"I can't see anything. There's nothing out here," Penn moaned.

Clearly this was not the adventure she'd had in mind when we'd left home in such a rush late this morning. I'd shut Merely's, our family-owned service station, and told my stepmother, Imegine, not to open it to strangers. She'd rolled her eyes at what she deemed my unfortunate mistrust in my fellow man. I knew as soon as we left she'd be happily feeding hobos out the front door and they'd all love her for it. Imegine was honey where'd I'd always been turpentine.

"You wanted to come here, remember?" I teased Penn. "It'll be worth it. It's not that bad."

I was counting on it. I needed a way to snap her out of the dreamy, despondent state that had settled over her in the last two years, changed her from a daring daddy's girl to some shadow of herself. I feared where things were leading.

Three years ago, when she was only ten, Penn had become enamored with the Brenau Academy, the only all-girls college preparatory boarding school in Georgia, grades nine through twelve, a few hours from us. We'd just entered the war, but her daddy had enlisted immediately and gone overseas to fight. She was restless and worried and fed up with the dull education she was enduring in Helen, where local kids often dropped out around seventh grade to farm. Even though she wouldn't even be eligible until high school, she'd called the school for an admissions packet and started writing an essay with a determination that could have won awards, begging to apply early to ensure her chances of a slot. The waiting list was years long. But I'd refused. I'd made excuses. I had reasons that were personal, secret reasons that reached beyond the financial challenge or Penn's chances of acceptance.

But then I'd watched Penn forget her dreams. And her heartbreak was worse than anything I had feared. Last night, while everyone slept, I'd dropped her packet in the mail. Out of caution for her feelings, I wasn't sharing the extent of my plan until I knew for sure that I could pull it off.

It was now the spring of 1945 and my husband, Finch, had been killed in Italy two years before. The war had crept into the small rooms where we lived above the motor garage my daddy had owned on the outskirts of Helen, Georgia, a remote and failing logging community on the verge of becoming a ghost town with less and less traffic on the highway. The change was so quiet we hardly felt it at first, but with so few travelers, the need for our services was all but obsolete. Rations limited the food on our table and, although Penn didn't know it, the savings in our account.

We were like almost all the other families around us. The sorrow of neighbor women shone in the gold stars flying on flags outside our doors and we mourned the ordinary lives we once believed we would live. Mysteries were the meat on our tables. We didn't long for the unknown but fantasized about full pantries, dirty boots by the door, and the soft snores of sleeping men who would never breathe beside us again. Finch had been headed for a POW camp, but then the army learned later from an Italian POW who'd been present at the execution that he'd been shot and rolled into a mass grave in some farmer's field. The prisoner's memory surfaced only after Italy declared itself an ally in 1943, more than six months after Finch's capture, and amounted to only a vague location, no other details. When the news finally came by way of a very young officer standing at our door, we'd been given hope that at least they might find remains and he'd be brought home. It would have been better had Penn not had that expectation, for it consumed her, though it appeared less and less likely the more time that passed. Whatever his dreams had been for himself or his family, Finch had taken them with him, and hers, too, it seemed. His pension was all that was left now, barely enough for us to live on. Not that it was any excuse for the choices I was making, but I'd been working hard to be both mother and father to Penn, and I was exhausted long before we'd ended up on this roadside in southern Georgia at the edge of night.

The service station was all we had, and all Penn had of her father, and I knew what it was to lose your home. For a while, I'd bartered rubber patches for fresh vegetables and took in wash to get cloth for Penn's clothes. I'd made do every way I knew as long as I could. And I had been foolish enough to think our lot couldn't be any sorrier, but then my daddy had died.

The church had still smelled of leftover lilies from the service a full week before. Barely a dozen people had been there for us. Afterward, Penn and I walked alongside Imagine through town, filing into the bank to collect the contents of my daddy's safe deposit box. At first, everything was orderly, sorted, exactly what we'd expected from my daddy. There'd been no sentimental notes, no official will and testament to be read, only an envelope for each of us, containing short lists divvying up his scant belongings. Imagine inherited Merely's and what monies he had saved, enough to keep her comfortable into old age. For Penn, there was his truck. No surprises.

Only my envelope remained. What I found there hit me between the eyes—the deed to Evertell, along with the antique key to the rambling old estate. When I pulled out that paper, the key clattered to the floor. I'd grabbed it up fast, like I might have a sharp knife. It was maybe six inches long with an ornate handle and large teeth on the end of the shaft, and I'd closed both hands around it, my thoughts rushing back to the memory of Evertell. Days after they'd buried Mama, I'd whispered in Daddy's ear something to comfort him, sweet enough to make us forget. *"I'm nothing like her. I never want to go back."*

But now he'd left me with the choice. "I thought he sold it years ago."

"I guess it never was his to sell, Alice," Imegine said.

"You knew?"

"Of course not."

Imegine was the one I should have been comforting. Instead, she'd squeezed my hand as I stood there, dumbfounded.

"What's Evertell?" Penn had asked.

The unknown was powerful. It was the monster in the dark, the secret in the box, the poison in the wine. We'd kept everything about Evertell a secret, like so many things I'd never intended to tell Penn. But here was a question that would have to be answered. One she would never stop asking. I'd stared at the deed and felt my hands tingle.

"It's where my mama was from," I'd finally said. "Where I grew up. A farm."

There was a note scratched at the bottom of the document in my daddy's cramped handwriting, followed by the name of the estate's executor and an address for the man.

Upon my death, see O. Lewallen in Savannah, Georgia, for any business with this property.

"Savannah?"

"Yes, that's where the house is, on the river." I'd looked into Penn's face. If we stayed in Helen now, I feared I would watch her opportunities wither. Her fate would set hard and fast like the other girls without choices. Surely she was destined for an early marriage to whomever this war had left to her, saddled too young with the burden of a widowed mother and grandmother. And me? I'd end up a gas chiseler, caught out soon enough. Or I could take what fortune we'd been given without dithering over my conscience and change everything again, this time for Penn. Farmland in Georgia wasn't going for as much as some places, but I'd seen it listed for thirty-five dollars an acre. At that rate, I figured it up in my head, the property from my mama's family would bring enough to cover school and then some.

Imegine leaned in to peer at the deed and put a steadying hand at the small of my back. "You don't have to do anything with this, Alice," she said.

But already my mind was running ahead of itself, thinking of new clothes for the fall and a future to look forward to, all suddenly possible for my daughter because of this forsaken legacy I'd believed was a curse.

"We have to go there," Penn said. Imegine and I looked from the deed to Penn, then to each other. This was the first interest Penn had shown in anything in so long that we stood silent, as if we might scare away a wild thing. But she looked clear-eyed and eager, like herself. She had such confidence in her conclusion. I'd taught her that. Straight ahead. See for yourself. "I want to see it. I want to go."

"Not now," I said. "You have school." Penn rolled her eyes. She'd always excelled in her classes and I'd let her stay home more than I should this last year and she knew there were only a few weeks left in the school year. Her absence for a few more days wouldn't even raise an eyebrow from the powers that be, given she was a star student while other kids were dropping out left and right. All it would take was a note from me and Penn knew it. But she was thirteen, the age my mama had claimed was the year of visions for the girls in our family. The timing scared me. "Maybe sometime," I said, trying to placate her, ignoring her disappointment, seeing full well she knew I was lying. Knowing she would simply bide her time, grow up, and live for the day she could do as she pleased. I still thought I had things in hand.

But last week I'd sold a barrel of black-market gasoline out the back door.

Afterward, I'd run inside to vomit. Honestly, it wasn't the betrayal of my scruples that bothered me. I was fairly certain that in the scheme of things my pitiful crime wouldn't rate much, but these days people were quick to turn on one another to save themselves, and it frightened me that I'd compromised our fragile household. I couldn't bear the idea of being charged and separated from Penn. I'd been careful to keep the extra income secret and independent from the finances I'd managed for Merely's. But even as I'd stared down at the false numbers on the page, I was struck that this would be the account of my life. The only legacy I left to my daughter. And it turned out, that was the thing with which I couldn't live.

)(

Still, I wasn't here to lead my girl down the primrose path. Stark reality was my aim. Evertell was no fabled kingdom. It was worth everything if it could pay the way for what she wanted, but in truth I hardly knew what to expect after being gone so many years. I felt anxious and cranky, and it didn't take long before we both realized I was wrong about how far we were going to have to walk. We were starting to struggle to see the sandy path as the light diminished. The air was so slick it draped over us. For once, Penn was quiet. After a few moments she stopped short so I almost stumbled into her. "Is that it? Listen," she said. "I think I hear it."

"You can't hear the ocean. We're not close enough."

Penn had never seen the ocean and she was expecting it around every corner. I hadn't been able to bring myself to take her, to smell the salt or hear the gulls. She only knew the clear streams and high mountains of the northeast corner of this state.

"That could be it. I think that's it," she said. "What's that stink?"

"Fish. Mud. You'll see when it's light."

"Ew." Penn was getting nervous. I could hear it in her breathing. "Tell me again what we're going to do."

"We're going to visit so you can see where the other side of the family came from before we sell it. Then we'll put that money in the bank and you'll have a fat nest egg. Think of all the places you can go, all the things you can see, Penn. Travel, college." I'd said that before we left this morning and I liked the sound of it. Now I was laying out visions like sweater sets, waiting to see what she might choose. "What'll you do first?"

"I could go to Europe," she mused dully. I knew she was thinking of Finch. She'd once dreamed she would go to Italy and find him there. I tried not to worry she'd brought it up again. "But not until the war's over."

"Well, no, not until then. And there are plenty of places to see right here."

She sighed. "Tell me what you remember."

"Uh, well. Let me think."

10

I hadn't talked about my mama or Evertell in so long that at first the words wouldn't come to me, only brief images, like flickering photographs. There was a lot of ground to cover before we reached the estate, both physically and metaphorically. Some of it, Penn wasn't going to like.

"I remember a big white house on a saltwater marsh with a deep forest behind it, between us and the sea. It's old. The land was granted to our family by King George II."

"King?" Penn said, fully impressed. "Not really."

I nodded. I had to carry her back, gradually, through centuries of history, if I was going to get to the heart of our story. The house was only the beginning. "That's what I was told. Wars were fought over this land for years before our family came here, battles between the Spanish, the British, and the Creek and Cherokee. People are always loving and losing land. Makes the best and makes the worst of us, too, how we all want to call a place home and what we do to each other to have it. You'd think there'd be enough room on this earth for everybody."

This was a familiar idea for Penn, having grown up collecting arrowheads along the banks of the mountain rivers and streams near Helen and hearing of the Cherokee people being marched to Oklahoma on the Trail of Tears.

"Our family came in 1758 with a religious group from South Carolina. They'd been asked to settle here as part of the British effort to establish a nearby port."

"We're from South Carolina?"

"And before that, lots of places. Florida, even before it was Florida. Then Barbados, because of pirate raids."

"You're joking. Pirates?"

"Pirates. One woman and her daughter—Catarina and Marguerite—were captured in St. Augustine and sold into service.

11

Marguerite's daughter, Francoise, was born out of wedlock. Later, she was hanged as a witch."

"But was she a witch? Really?"

I shrugged. "It's what they called her. A word for a woman who must have caused trouble for somebody. But I doubt she rode a broomstick. Lucky for us, Esme, her daughter, was sent to South Carolina and carried on, even after all of that."

"I can't keep them straight."

"I memorized their names when I was about your age," I said. "Esme married a religious man, a Congregationalist, and when she was a very old woman, she came here with her daughter, Garnet Lee, and her husband. They built a little tabby cottage, a farm, a church, and a mill, and we've been here ever since. The first house was just one room, really, built before anything was anything. Evertell was part of a land grant from the English king. Of course, what King George didn't count on, I guess, is that the folks he sent here would all eventually join the Revolution, including our family. It's a bloody history."

"Here? The Revolutionary War happened here? In Georgia?"

I shuddered to think what they weren't teaching her in school. "Yes, here. During that war, this place was sort of a no-man's land, so Evertell went unharmed aside from being a sanctuary for men from both sides who passed through and took their rest. And later, it was the same with the War Between the States. Over the years, the house grew around those first rooms. You can count the years of Evertell like rings in a tree, my mama said, if you know where to look."

"She told you all of this? What else did she say? What do you remember about Grandmama Claire?"

"I remember watching her catch fireflies. She was beautiful. She believed in signs and fate. She had a book that belonged to the women in her family, passed down with the house. A kind of journal or scrapbook with poems and recipes and things. Their names are all listed there. I always wondered what happened to it."

"All of this is in that book?"

"Some of it. Some were just stories people told."

The book, like the estate, had passed from each lady of the house to her eldest daughter for centuries, making it an unusual legacy for unusual women, women who were both literate and property owners for generations. I recalled the evenings I'd spent with my mama, the ancient book open in her lap, the soft rustle of pages turning, the smell of her skin, vanilla and something sweeter, the perfume of jasmine blossoms. There'd been ink drawings of plants and constellations. There were entries about the weather and the changing seasons and the births of babies, all written in different hands by different authors over many centuries.

I took advantage of the dark when I wouldn't have to look at Penn. I'd raised her in a world of engines and oils, machines that could be repaired, men who predictably woke and worked. Stories were novel, coming from my mouth. But as Penn and I marched on, I found it was easier than I thought to let the old tale whisper its way back into the world. "But what we know about our family started even before Evertell. My mama once told me she knew the fate of a woman named Eleanor White Dare. She was part of a first colony from England that disappeared. They were called the Lost Colony of Roanoke."

"Oh, wait," Penn said quickly. "You mean like the message on that rock at Brenau Academy?"

"That's right." Of course she knew about the stone. "The Dare Stone, yes. Eleanor's part of the story." Penn knew everything about Brenau but nothing of our history with that stone. I spoke carefully, gently laying out the details. "It turned up in 1937. It was found in

North Carolina. Some man just tripped over it one day and it was a big discovery, all over the news. Everybody said it wasn't real, just a big hoax."

Penn looked puzzled. I could see she was trying to make a connection, waiting for answers. "Grandmama Claire knew about Eleanor Dare? We learned about her last year in class, about the actual history. A whole bunch of poor English people got left behind on an island in North Carolina somewhere. And nobody knows if they were killed or went somewhere else to live with the Indians, right? Nobody ever found them."

I took a breath, slowing my pace a little. "Well, people think different things about that. But used to be, that stone they have at the college was placed in the forest of our property here."

"The same one?" Penn asked, confused but suddenly more animated.

"I think so. The pictures in the paper looked the same. It was carved with the same message. It was supposed to be Eleanor Dare's message to her father, telling him what happened to her. And if you believe that, the women in Grandmama Claire's family are what happened after that. The book has a list of descendants, starting with Eleanor's name and all the way through the ones who built Evertell, all the way to my mama. If you believe it, it's our family myth."

"You're making this up." Of course she didn't believe me. How much easier it would be if I could pretend it was all a joke.

"No," I admitted. For once, Penn said nothing, only listened. "The way it was explained to me, the women in our family knew where Eleanor first put that stone, but Grandmama Claire didn't think we ever had any business moving it here. It was a message to say Eleanor had survived, but it was also a gravestone. It marked the place where she lost her family." I could hear my mama saying all this even now, an accusation, spitting it out like too much salt. I tried to tell it to Penn as I had been told. The names of the heirs marched through my head, and I did my best to keep the details simple for Penn.

"Bernadette Reece Telfair started it all," I said. She'd been the heir who had finally completed Evertell in 1799. But over the years, she'd become obsessed with a hand-drawn map in the common-place book, initialed EWD, showing Eleanor's journey. She sent some men to find the place where the journey began in the wilds of the new world, to retrieve the marker Eleanor had left for her father, inscribed with the terrible fate of his family. The stone was found just where the map said it would be and brought to Georgia, to our forest, to protect it from anyone who might want to steal or deface it.

"Bernadette thought she was correcting a wrong, that she was honoring Eleanor's legacy, bringing Eleanor home, I guess," I said. "The trouble was, this was never Eleanor's home, and it wasn't long before people got fed up with Bernadette and how highly she thought of herself after that. They got a bad taste in their mouth about that stone, started whispering things about it, that it was asking for trouble to have it here.

"So when Bernadette's daughter, Camille, had a little girl, then disappeared about three years later, just a few weeks after that stone came here, everybody blamed the stone. Maybe it was a co-incidence. Maybe Camille took off with some man. Nobody knows. But even Bernadette believed she'd brought a curse on our family."

Penn had taken my hand as we walked. "But Grandmama Claire loved Eleanor and tried to make peace with her. She visited the stone. She loved Eleanor's book and all the things the other heirs had drawn or written there, their secrets and dreams. She wanted me to love them too. She believed that was what Eleanor had wanted, for us to have the book. My mama said it was a book written by women, full of women's wisdom and mysteries."

Penn was listening intently. And I realized with a kind of wonder that I was enjoying being the storyteller, a disarming thought. "You won't find any of those stories in your history books, but I can tell you for sure that Eleanor Dare was a very real girl, just like you. Even if nobody knows what happened to her, just like nobody knows if the words on that stone were true or if we really are her descendants. That's why I said it's a myth."

"I want to read this book."

"We'll have to see. Maybe we'll look at it together. Girls read it after they come of age. Thirteen, like you. But it's not a game or a toy, okay? It's very old, something Grandmama Claire kept put away safe." I saw her ponder this. "Anyway, we left it all behind—the house and everything that went with it. There's no guarantee any of it is still there."

"Like the stone? If it was protected in our woods, how come they found it so far away? Did Pop give it away too?" she mumbled.

Here was the question I'd avoided. I meant to keep the answer simple. I didn't hesitate. "It was stolen."

It was my fault. All of it was. I lost your birthright. I lost so much.

"Why didn't you ever tell me any of this? When they found it? You don't believe in curses. I know you don't."

"No, I don't. But it had nothing to do with us anymore. And you were so little when it showed up again. Why would you have cared?"

"I wasn't so little. I was five."

"Five is little, Penn."

"Well, you could have told me anytime. You could have told

THE LOST BOOK OF ELEANOR DARE

me when I wanted to go to Brenau." She made a low sound of disappointment.

"Okay, I'm telling you now," I said too sharply, then took a breath and tried for a calmer tone. Just the facts. A shiver ran through me. Curses might be dismissed as superstition, but consequences were very real. "I figured I'd tell you one day if you were ever interested. That's all there is to it, really," I said, trying to dust the story off my hands. "And here we are. Now you know."

Even with all these revelations, I was holding back and Penn could sense that. I expected her to be angry. I expected her to feel like I'd lied to her or tricked her. She should have felt that way. But I didn't expect what she said next.

"Eleanor Dare would like this, wouldn't she? What we're doing here."

Penn's mind turned in original ways that sometimes surprised me. "What do you mean?"

"We're sort of the same as her, like you said. We have no idea what's around the corner, but we're going there anyway."

"Evertell heirs always know how to find their way home. That's what my mama said." I felt hopeful in that moment. Penn was still young enough that every ordinary day could feel like a dream. "And I'm sure that you are just like Eleanor Dare. And if I know anything about Eleanor," I added, "she'd have taken the cash on the barrel and never looked back. I am positive she had big dreams too. She ended up at Brenau," I said. "How about that?"

Penn asked, "Did you believe it was real? When you were here? When you were little?"

"Yeah," I admitted. "At the time, I did. There was the stone and the book and Grandmama Claire's stories. That seemed like all the proof I needed."

"But about Eleanor and the curse? Do you still believe any of it now?"

"I don't know." That was true too. "I don't know if it matters what I believe. Maybe it's just a story to tell you."

But there was still a lot of our story I didn't know how to tell. Or if I ever would. And it started with the story my mother had written for me in the pages of the commonplace book: Eleanor's Tale. If my mama was to be believed, Eleanor's Tale contained the key to our true inheritance, a kind of mystical vision. She'd called it our Evertell, the inspiration that guided each heir. But she'd gotten sick, and when she died, both she and the conclusion had been lost. She'd never shared the ending of Eleanor's Tale with me. No secret feminine wisdom had ever come to help guide my way. I was stumbling down this road in the dark, and my worst fear was that I'd never be the kind of mother to pass that kind of faith or magic to my daughter in such an uncertain world.

But the stories I did know seemed to satisfy Penn. She only slapped at a mosquito and said, "Can I have the key?"

"What?" I said, distracted.

"The key for the house, can I have it? When we get there, I want to be the one to let us into the house. I can't believe it has a name. Evertell, Evertell," she repeated.

I handed the heavy key over, an ache in my chest. The night seemed too quiet. "Listen, whatever we find here, if the house has fallen in, that's fine. Don't be too disappointed. It's to be expected, right? If we need to, we'll stay in Savannah for a few days," I suggested brightly. "Or go out to Tybee Island, to the shore. Would you like that? Give Grandma Imagine a little peace and quiet."

"Like an actual seaside holiday? We could do that?" I could hear the delight in her voice, but then hesitation too. "I don't know. I don't want to leave Grandma Imagine out," she said, sounding tired. "Not when she's so sad." She trudged along for a moment, thinking, then added, "I just wanted to see where you grew up. And maybe Pop's man you're supposed to see will know what happened to Eleanor's book. He might have it," Penn said.

"He might."

I couldn't pretend I hadn't already thought of that myself. The very idea that I might hold that book again filled me with both hope and dread. It had been foremost in my thoughts from the instant I'd learned Evertell remained my inheritance. But there were other possibilities, things and people I hadn't told Penn about yet. I worried what else might be waiting for us here. Penn had so many questions. There'd been a time when I was just like her, when I'd believed all stories had conclusions and all things might be known.

In the dying light, I could make out the look of consternation on her face. The best I could do now was walk beside her and help her find her way forward, so we could stop looking back. I'd never have come here otherwise. I believed that given the chance, Penn would dream wider and farther than this place. Maybe I would finally hold that book again and see what my mama had wanted me to see. Because there was truth to Eleanor's Tale in at least one regard: the fate of the world is often driven by the curiosity of a girl.

Ж

Soon enough, we came to a low concrete wall that led to a narrow iron gate hidden in palmetto fronds and a wild tangle of jasmine vine that scented the night air with a familiar sweetness I'd have known anywhere. The entrance was old, barely wide enough for an automobile to fit through. Fashioned into the iron were neat, clear letters. Penn touched them with her fingers. I didn't need to read them to know what they said.

Evertell.

"It's real," Penn said, pushing her way through.

"Completely real."

I followed her, my own eyes searching for a glimpse of the house. On the night breeze was the bitter smell of the yew hedges and the shrill call of tree frogs. Everything was cast in deep shadow with only a crescent moon to light the way. The long lane of crushed oyster shells crunched underfoot on the straight approach until we reached a curve at the end and still, Evertell was hidden. I remembered the grand porch and the wide, smooth lawns. The towering pines and oaks and the rustling sounds of the palm leaves in the sea breezes. Nothing like the home we'd known in the shadow of old mountains in Helen.

The main house had been stunning in Italianate style with white wooden walls that rose from the stone foundation and the dark greens, blues, and browns of the landscape. The house's crown was a dainty cupola, trimmed in lacy moldings, with a view of the fields that lay inland and the broad, glistening river and marshes snaking behind the house until they were hidden behind the deep green forest of oaks and palms that stretched to the sea. Once, Evertell had seemed enduring, but I feared the shape it might be in, presumably after twenty-three years of neglect.

"So real, I'm afraid we'll be lucky if we have a pot to piss in," I mumbled, growing more anxious with every step.

Only a breath later, Penn said, "There's something. Look." She pointed through the hanging moss and the low-growing limbs of the twisted oaks and I caught a first glimpse of the line of the roof and cupola.

I squinted, unsure if I was imagining things. Maybe it was a firefly. Or maybe it was something else, showing us the way, exactly as my mother had always claimed. My heart pounded beneath my ribs. Already I was entertaining fanciful thoughts. I blinked to clear my vision, but it was still there. A faint glow shone high in the lead glass windows. A light inside Evertell.

"Holy mackerel," Penn whispered. "Who do you think it might be? Maybe it's haunted. Maybe there's a ghost."

"We don't believe in ghosts," I said as we came to stand below the porch.

"I might." She giggled.

More of the jasmine vine grew up the railings and the side of the house, and the scent of the tiny white blossoms, like pricks of light in the glow of the moon, was so strong and sweet, I felt overwhelmed.

"Wait." All at once, I didn't know if I could take the last steps to the door. I thought of my last warnings to Imegine about strangers and realized I should have taken my own advice. "I should have thought better about this. We should have waited till morning to show up. It could be anybody squatting in there. Some old tramp. Some drunk with a gun."

Penn dismissed all of this the way only a teenager can in the face of danger. "Don't be crazy. You always think the worst. Nobody's going to shoot us. We just have to introduce ourselves. They'll see who we are. And we have the key."

Before I could stop her, she leapt ahead and stood on the porch, so I had no choice but to scramble up beside her. I fastened my hand on her arm, stopping her. I looked at the heavy iron key. "Give me that."

"But you said I could do it."

I pushed Penn behind me, shushing her. My hand shook as I fumbled to fit the heavy key to the lock. With a twist, the door easily gave way and slowly swung open on well-oiled hinges. The air from the dark hall met our faces, carrying the scent of old wood and abandoned rooms as we peered into the gloom. Whoever or whatever had cast the light from upstairs, there was no sign of them down here, but then I heard shuffling in the shadows of the stairwell. The sound bounced off the empty walls of the vast foyer and I stiffened.

"Who's there?" I called. "Hello? I've got a key so I've let myself in. Didn't mean to startle you. We didn't know anybody would be here."

When I looked, I could see only a small light moving closer, throwing shadows through the railings, against the walls. My own voice shriveled in my throat. Someone descended the staircase in a rush from the highest landing. One foot dropped heavily on each step, followed by a lesser scrape. It was such a burdensome effort that there could be no doubt of the determination it took for the person to reach us. I recognized the sound.

I knew it because when I lost Evertell and everything about who I'd once been, I'd lost him too.

Chapter Two

"Stopping by awful late in the day."

For a moment it seemed the house itself had spoken. But it was a man. I knew the shape of him, even if it seemed impossible that he would still be here. I clenched the key, jagged teeth pointed out, so tightly my hand ached.

"You got business here?" he asked.

"So the deed in my pocket tells me. At least for a few days."

"Weeks, you said," Penn corrected me.

Sonder lowered the lantern in his fist as he crossed the hall. He stood before us tall, thin, head hung low, shirtfront buttoned wrong, exposing a lean chest. His was a long face with deeply set eyes and his hair fell over his forehead. When he spoke, his expression turned to one of quiet delight. The cool breath of memory crept across the back of my neck.

"Alice Merely? That ain't you."

I hesitated before I coughed up, "Mrs. Alice Merely Young."

Penn spoke then. "She thought you were a tramp."

"I've brought my daughter with me. This is Penn," I said, giving the back of her arm a small pinch where he couldn't see. "I never said you were a tramp."

Sonder shrugged, then lowered his chin. He was enjoying watching me backpedal the comment. "That's one I haven't heard in a while. To be a proper tramp, a man's got to be on the move. Been here so long now I've just about grown roots down into the ground." He looked at me closely then. I felt such an immediate familiarity and the impulse to hug his neck, but that would have been wrong. "You know me, surely?"

"I knew a boy. Barely said boo to anybody."

"She doesn't believe in ghosts," Penn said, watching him closely.

"Way I remember it, your mama's the ghost around here. Did a disappearing act that's still got people talking." He gave me a slow smile and I remembered that too. He took no offense at being called either a tramp or a ghost. He liked being a mystery. But he'd been a bit of both, hadn't he? Turned up without explanation to work for my daddy only a few months before we left Evertell. I'd been drawn most to his quiet ways and the unknown past that had taken him places I couldn't guess—and taken part of his left leg, too, giving him that limp from his prosthetic. He'd let a lonely little girl trail behind him on the water and in the fields and let me wonder about him.

"Come on home for a neighborly chat, have you?" he mused. "After all this time."

"Come by," I said. "But just for a stop. Forgive us waltzing in. We didn't mean to surprise you. We thought the place would be empty."

He peered past us into the dark and addressed me. "Something's gone wrong for you? Traveling on foot at night, without your husband?"

"Finch? Oh no," I said. Of course he knew nothing of my

husband and Penn's father, but the name filled the empty night around us until I could add, "It's just the two of us. Our truck quit on us awhile back." I lowered the key by using it to gesture back down the drive. I wasn't ready to get into too many of the details. "Husbands are scarce these days. He was taken prisoner and killed in Italy two years ago."

He bowed his head. "Sincere condolences."

"Thank you." I believed him, which, in itself, was miraculous but unnerving. I had to turn away and pretend to take in the dark hallway.

I'd grown something like a callus inside to protect from the sickly sweet, well-meaning expressions of sympathy and shared grief since Finch's death and it had served me well, kept me somewhat sane when I looked at the kind faces of those who could not imagine the reality of what I conjured in my mind for his last moments. A callus I was grateful for that prevented me from screeching at them or suddenly spewing forth the details of dreams of mass graves, of the monstrous thing that had become of his long, pale body, of waking with the smell of death in my nose.

Finally, I said, "Look at this place. I can't believe I'm standing here."

But when I glanced back, Sonder's attention was directed at the stairs. He wore a worried expression. We were interrupting something. For an awful second I was concerned someone might be waiting for him. Then there was the faint sound of warbling voices and Penn's eyes widened.

"What's up there?" Penn asked, her eyes bright in the lamplight.

He handed her the lantern he carried, then took a step back, and then another. "That's my work."

"Your work?" I asked.

But the question went unanswered as he took the steps as

quickly as his prosthetic leg would allow, leaving us standing in the great empty hall. We were all missing something here.

When he reached the second floor, Penn whispered, "If he had a parrot, I'd guess he's a pirate."

"Shh. Stop that." I muffled a laugh. "He's Sonder. He's the caretaker at Evertell, or he was. I guess he still is."

I could barely believe it, even as I said the words. I turned to Penn, but clearly her thoughts were no longer on the unusual man. An expression of astonishment made her face seem even younger than she was as she gawked at the shadowy foyer. She'd barely stepped across the threshold and already she was in love. The air was thick and sweet off the river, even inside. I wanted to weep for the familiarity of it, a kind of unexpected comfort for my weary heart, as if I'd come to lay my head on the sighing bosom of the great house.

And yet, Evertell was a shell of itself, empty of the noises of a family, no rich carpets on the floors, hollow and cave-like without its heirlooms so that every sound we made seemed intrusive. The house might still be in my name, but someone had cleaned it out. I had the ridiculous thought that though I had dreamed often of these walls, this place no longer knew me. But the names of the women who came before flooded my memory. Familiar names with foreign sounds that tasted of a wilder, far-flung world. I remembered them all. Above our heads, I noted the absence of the audacious chandelier that had once hung in the entry. I paused to peer into the front parlor, shocked to see the lonely outline of my mama's small writing desk still sitting beneath the tall leaded window where I remembered the light had once poured in through pale blue glass. Here, with her indigo blue ink, she must have written Eleanor's Tale into the book, I realized.

This was the oldest part of the original house, the only room built of tabby concrete, the mixture of lime and crushed oyster shells so commonly used along the coast in those days. It had been my favorite room when I was a girl, always cool, and I'd spent hours discovering and tracing my fingers over decorative seashells that had been particularly embedded in the walls.

I moved deeper along the hall to the library, now empty, the lavish furnishings from my memory gone except for a small piano, waiting in silence. It made the room seem as desolate as the dining room with the long, empty table, which I could see just across the hall. I stopped to lean against the staircase banister, unwilling to see any more until morning.

"You didn't mean what you said about a pot, did you?" Penn urged at my elbow, hopping from one foot to the other. "I really need to use the bathroom."

"Back there." I pointed the way to the door at the end of the hall.

"You don't mean an outhouse?" Penn said, appalled.

I shrugged. "See for yourself."

She moved down the hall with the lantern while I pulled the front door closed. The house had once been famous for its early luxuries—a gravity-fed water system providing hot and cold water, and flushing toilets that had functioned as early as 1846. Acetylene gas lamps had illuminated the house by the early 1900s while the other homes along the coast had remained in the dark. My great-grandfather made and stored the gas on the estate, the same as miners used in their lanterns. All of this trivia I recalled dimly overhearing from the delighted conversations of visiting neighbors.

"You're messing with me," Penn called, discovering the toilet. "There's electricity too."

I heard the click of a switch and I peered down the hall to see light glowing beneath the door of the little room at the back of the house where I remembered there'd been a tub. Clearly a few updates had been made. I was relieved. The gas had been volatile, and it was a miracle no one had inadvertently sent the house up in flames long ago. I knew this was the reason a small kitchen house stood out back several yards from the main structure. With a stove for cooking and heating the water that was piped into the house, it had burned to the ground twice before I was born.

With Penn settled for the moment, I turned my thoughts to the more pressing matter of a man in the house.

"I'll just go see what's going on upstairs," I said, mostly to myself as I looked up into the dark. Creeping up the staircase, I stayed to one side of the thick runner, worn in the center, to avoid the exact places where a stair would creak, a pattern of steps I recalled without effort. I climbed to the top floor, then ascended a final, steep flight of steps to a small octagonal space in the rafters where the air poured through windows on all four sides. The cupola had been built for my grandmother, Calista Clerestory, a victim of tuberculosis. Once, I had looked out from those heights over the changing colors of the river and marsh and forest and I had belonged to this place. Tonight bright stars winked down at me like a thousand witnesses to my return, mine and my daughter's. I wondered how they would judge us.

The only light in the cupola now came from the dial of a short-wave radio. It cast a dim glow over the small space. Dark curtains covered most of the windows, but one had been pulled back by a few inches, giving a narrow view of the drive below, and I realized this was the source of the light we'd seen. Sonder hunkered over a small table with a bunch of blank postcards. His eyes were closed. He was wearing a set of headphones, completely still in his concentration. I couldn't hear anything of the radio conversation or the voices we'd heard earlier, but I took the opportunity to study him. His face was cleanly shaven, marked deeply with the lines of middle age. I guessed him to be in his forties now. A thousand questions filled my head. Had he married? He wasn't wearing a ring. He seemed the most solitary figure I'd ever seen. That much hadn't changed.

"Sonder Holloway," I said carefully, hoping I wouldn't startle him. Just speaking his name aloud sent a shiver through me. "I thought you left here a long time ago. After us. I should have tried to call ahead before busting in."

He didn't move. He didn't look at me. A cigarette burned in an ashtray at his elbow, the smoke wending its way upward. "There's no phone."

"Still?"

I reached a hand out and he offered me a drag. "Thanks. I can't believe you have these. We haven't been able to stock them at home for weeks."

"All going for the GIs. I've been doling out my last two packs."

I took one more drag and nodded. It wasn't a habit in general for me, but it certainly helped in the moment and my thoughts organized themselves. I watched him grind the butt out as I exhaled. I'd promised to call Imegine to let her know we'd arrived safely, and I needed to get in touch with the solicitor. When I was a girl, we'd walked to Hawkes's to make calls. I'd have to wait until morning, another thing to be sorted out along with the truck. "At least there's electricity," I finally said. "Penn found the switch downstairs. When did that happen?"

"In '33. They ran the wires out this way to Tybee Island, so the lighthouse operates on electricity now, if you can believe it."

"You're still using a gas lantern," I pointed out.

"Ah, old miner's habits. Except for the radio." He reached to jiggle the cord that ran to an outlet in the wall.

An awkward silence followed. Whatever he was listening to, his expression was blank. I fixed on a detail: he'd been a miner. For all I knew, he'd left here to work in a mine since I'd gone. I wanted to ask now, but it would have been wrong to begin an interrogation of the man. He certainly owed me no answers.

Then, without warning, he sat forward. He began feverishly writing on a small notecard. I watched all of this, intrigued. I couldn't help wondering what else he'd been doing all this time. Suddenly I realized what I was looking at and stated the obvious.

"POW messages? That's what this is? From the Berlin broadcast? I thought everyone knew they're just propaganda." I said all of this loudly so he could hear me. His expression made me regret the criticism. "I'm sorry. It's really none of my business what you do."

People were warned about enemy broadcast news coming over the shortwave and cautioned not to be victimized by unscrupulous persons attempting to sell such information. The government told us over and over that the names of our soldiers and the messages that were read over the foreign airwaves were merely bait in the Axis propaganda war, tailored to weaken the resolve of grieving, fearful Americans. The programs were laced with innuendo and conspiracy theories to undermine our patriotism and faith in the fight. I hadn't been able to stomach the thought of listening to them even when Finch was missing.

We'd gotten a postcard from the provost marshal general, informing us they had just received word from the International Red Cross that Finch was a POW in Italy, with a promise to check the accuracy of the information. Then we were told to wait for further word from them and not to trust civilian monitoring or any other unofficial source. Families were prone to send money as thanks to these volunteers, and we were told not to fall for a scam, that we couldn't trust a postcard like the ones I saw on Sonder's desk.

Sonder didn't respond to my argument, making it clear where he stood. I was made more aware of how little we knew of each other now and grew uneasy with the thought of him staying up here while we slept.

I quickly said, "Look, we're tired from the trip. Do you know how long you'll be? Or do you stay in the house?"

He pushed one of the headphones off his right ear and looked up. "Half an hour or so and I'll be out. I sleep at the millhouse, like always."

I nodded dumbly, recalling the room above the millhouse. Nervous, I blurted, "My daddy died. It's been two months now, but that's why I'm here. It seems out of the blue, but it's really not." He was watching me, not speaking. I could see my news wasn't a shock. He'd already heard. "Anyway, you'll have to tell me if he paid you, that sort of thing. I'm sorry to bring it up. I guess you should know straightaway that I'll be seeing his executor for the details on selling." It seemed wrong to keep my plans from him, but I certainly hadn't had time to think about what it would mean for him.

"It can be sorted out. Just stopping by, you say?"

"I'll have to see how things shape up."

"Right. All the same, I can move the radio down to the front room if you want use of it," he offered. "I've kept it up here be-cause the overseas broadcasts come in stronger, but you might want the news on the regular. Some folks like to listen to programs in the evening. Doubt you want to climb all the way up here. I can see you don't like the monitoring in general. Some people don't. But if you could see your way to let me carry on, I'd appreciate that. You can say you never knew a thing about it."

I quickly dismissed his concern. "Oh no, no. Really, you don't need to move it. It's just we'd prefer a little privacy once we've settled for the night. You understand."

He nodded in agreement and I thought he looked a bit relieved. "Sure. Like I said, thirty minutes and the broadcasts end."

"But do you really believe any of them are the real thing? How can you trust them?"

"How would I know? All the same to me whether it's bunk or some poor soul wants to let his mom and pop know he's still breathing and wishing he was sitting at the kitchen table eating pot pie. Just seems if somebody's bothering to send them, somebody ought to at least bother to listen. Ought to at least try to send the message along so it's not left floating out in the air for all eternity. That's what I trust, that it's just the right thing to do. Let somebody else sort out the rest."

I nodded, feeling overwhelmed by the forthright declaration and wishing I had the courage to see the world in such a way.

"I've got to tell you," he said, "this house is not accustomed to company these days."

I flinched. "I noticed. Good thing I'm not much for company."

He chuckled. "There's a little settee downstairs in the front room and the main bedroom still has furniture. Can't promise you won't be sharing the mattress with a mouse."

"Really, we're not expecting the four-star treatment." I almost asked if he knew what had become of the rest, of Eleanor's book. My tongue was pressed to my teeth.

Penn called from below, "Mama, where'd you go?"

Leaning over the stairwell, I threw my voice down to her. "Come on upstairs. We're staying in the front room."

"You've got a girl," Sonder said.

I stared at him for a long second and saw that the deep brown pond of his eyes hadn't changed. He pulled a pack of cigarettes from his shirt pocket and went about lighting a fresh smoke, taking a long drag and offering one to me. I shook my head. A single hit for the nerves was one thing, but better not start something I couldn't finish.

"I do. She already has ideas about you."

"Way I heard it, they were your ideas. What's your take now you've seen me up close?" He sat back in his chair, presumably to give me a better look.

Because I was embarrassed of myself, there was a need in me to get a rise out of him. I jerked my chin at the radio and his stack of cards. "I guess you look to me like a regular old spy."

"Think so? Not a ghost, then? Or a tramp?"

"Not really," I admitted. "But I've never seen a ghost, so how would I know?"

"Call it like you see it. You'd be right though. Just the messenger," he said, spreading his hands in a gesture of surrender. It made me smile.

"Good to see you, Alice. You've not changed a whit."

It was the saddest fib I'd ever heard, and I stood there suddenly feeling the weight of my age, my widowhood, and my responsibility to Penn in the full knowledge that he could see it all. I wished it was true that I could still be the girl he'd known, so certain of her opinions.

He was distracted again, one ear cocked to the headphone still covering his left ear, listening to catch whatever was coming across the air that I couldn't hear. He held the cigarette in his lips. "If you don't mind, I don't want to miss any of these."

I smarted at the dismissal. He'd told Penn I'd performed the greatest disappearing act, but my reappearance after all these years had barely rated a five-minute conversation and a drag on a stale cigarette. His compliment had been meant as a simple kindness, a little flattery. It was a thing he would say to any passing stranger. In it, I heard a meaning: *you might have come back, but you haven't come home*. This house might have been mine, but no one had saved a space for me.

)(

In the front bedroom on the second floor, Penn found a bare mattress on the big bed. I hated the idea of lying down on it and poked at the dingy ticking. At least there were no signs of mice.

"Which side of the bed do you want?" I asked.

Penn surveyed the space and perched gingerly on the edge of the bed. "There's a whole fireplace in here," she said, clearly awed and comparing the extravagance of such a thing to the tiny space we'd shared at Merely's.

"All the main rooms have them. There are three chimneys. It's how the house is heated. Or it was."

"I think we're rich, Mama. Admit it," she said.

"Oh yes," I said, giving the mattress a slap so the dust puffed up and made us cough. "Everything you ever wanted, mice and mildew."

"This furniture," she noted, "it's huge. I mean, like giants lived here. It matches Pop's wardrobe at home, doesn't it?"

"Yes, that awful thing."

"Was this your room?"

"No. Your grandparents'."

While Penn prowled through the furniture, I unpacked what little we'd brought with us and pulled the drawers open on a standing dresser. *No book.* I exhaled. It was spooky being back inside these walls, and I half expected to find my mama's clothes still folded there as Penn reached to run a fingertip through the layer of dust on the dresser next to the bed, exposing the shiny black walnut. It was a child's expectation, irrational and egotistical, as

THE LOST BOOK OF ELEANOR DARE

though the world inside this house should have frozen when I left it. Less than an hour back here and already I wasn't thinking straight.

"There must have been a ton of stuff in a house like this." Penn had an uncanny way of always seeming to read my thoughts. "What was it like before?"

"Full."

Penn frowned. I thought about the little desk, the lonely piano, the dining room table covered in dust. It was as if I were somehow existing between two realities. I reminded myself it was only a quick stop, a few nights here and gone.

"But where did it all go?"

"I wouldn't know. I never asked. Maybe Bridie Quillian. She had a resale shop in town that Grandmama Claire liked to prowl through."

"You should've asked. It was yours. You should have brought things with you. Maybe we can ask that man upstairs. Or the one you're meeting. What's he called?"

"The executor. Mr. Lewallen. I can ask, but whatever was in this house, it's long gone. And good for us we don't have to deal with that too. We brought the wardrobe. That's what Grandmama Claire wanted me to have. I guess Pop sold the rest."

"I wonder if we can get any of it back."

"We didn't come here for that," I reminded her. "And where would we put it? We hardly have room for the three of us at Merely's as it is. We'll look for the book. And that wardrobe is already yours if you want it. It comes apart, you know? It's built to be moved. It's a traveling wardrobe so it can go with you wherever you decide. Like that?"

"Sure," she said, still pondering. "Aren't we going to call Grandma Imogene? We said we would. She's going to worry."

So many questions. I reminded myself that this was what I'd

wanted, her interest, her attention. "I know. I've already thought about that, but there's nothing we can do tonight. We'll find a phone. There's a store that has one we can use. That's a can of worms that can wait until morning."

"Why is Grandma Imegine a can of worms?"

"Not Imegine, the man who runs the store. If he's even still there. He wasn't a friend of the family," I said. "No, Imegine'll be fine. She'll understand. She knows where we are, that things may be complicated at first."

Penn chewed on the end of her hair and watched me. Honestly, I felt completely drained and rather relieved to put off having to give Imegine a rundown on our misadventures.

"And what about . . ." Penn pointed overhead, only mildly concerned. "Will he murder us in our sleep?"

She was droll as a seasoned old maid. She'd grown up at Merely's where men were in and out of the service station all day long, and it occurred to me that it wasn't the typical life of a young girl, as I'd liked to believe.

"He's not a murderer; he's a messenger," I said, deciding this was as good a way as any to think of him. "He'll be gone in a minute. And he's harmless. He came to work for Pop when I was little," I said.

She got a look on her face and teased me. "So you're saying we have a servant?"

I laughed. "Hardly." But I knew the question was just the start of Penn trying to understand the complicated history of this house. "Your daddy worked for your pop. Was he a servant?"

Penn's mood shifted to somber. Just mentioning Finch and my daddy, I felt panicked and alone, astonished at what I'd done, running back here.

"But what's he really doing up there?"

I adopted a breezy tone. "Right now? He's recording POW messages off the broadcasts from Berlin coming over the shortwave. You know how people do? He listens in and writes down what he hears on postcards that he sends to the families."

"Wow. And you're going to let him?"

She was intrigued. She knew we'd never listened for Finch. She knew Americans were warned not to trust the messages. Now they were coming in right over her head.

"You know what I think about it, that people are gullible. They'll believe anything when they're scared and hurting, and those messages just take advantage. That's what the government says. The Germans aren't doing us a neighborly favor, letting prisoners call home to say hi. They're the enemy and it's a horrible trick. But it's none of our business what Sonder Holloway does up there. Let him listen. We don't have to. It's not hurting us."

"He seems nice."

"He is nice. We'll just live and let live while we're here. Maybe it makes him feel better to think he's really helping those families. Maybe it makes them feel better to think those messages are really from their boys."

"*A story doesn't matter because it's true but because it's been told.*" I heard my mama's words echoed in my own. But I really was telling Penn the truth where I could. I had no idea what had happened to the things in this house. Bridie Quillian would have loved to get her hands on every last stick of furniture in Evertell and I hoped she'd made a fortune off of it. Bill Hawkes was no friend to this family and I hated that he'd enjoy watching me sell the family home. And Sonder Holloway was a nice man in the attic.

I worked the window open before I flopped on the bed beside her.

"How can it be this hot?" Penn fussed. "We may burn right up in here."

"In the morning I'll find a fan. Do you think you can rest?"

"Who wants to rest when we're finally here with myths and ghosts and spies in the attic?"

She was happy about the mystery. I thought of Sonder's words: *"You've got a girl."*

I did indeed. She was all arms and legs at this age, especially coltish. Like me and all the women in my mama's family, Penn was tall so she stood out. She embraced this trait, determined to be unusual. While we shared the same propensity for height and thick, dark curls, mine were an unruly riot I was always pushing out of my face. Penn's hair shined and wound in coils over her shoulders. She was beautiful in a classic sort of way that drew the eye of other girls who envied her pale skin and fine cheekbones and of the boys who'd begun to stammer in her presence. She was unaware of this effect on people, something that worried me for her future. She insisted on wearing a pair of old black boots she'd found at a local rummage sale, mostly because I didn't approve. She could pick any lock in under a minute and hot-wire a car almost as fast, both tricks she regularly performed to the delight of the customers at Merely's. She irritated her teachers with constant questions about the curriculum. *Talks too much* was written in every report from school. *Won't stay in her seat.*

Life with Finch had been easy, uncomplicated. And I'd expected when I had Penn that we would be an island unto ourselves, insular and content, never needing anything more from the outside than the all-consuming love that came with motherhood. She was my world. But Penn was born reaching, and from that moment, like it or not, she brought the world to us. It had frightened me. But since Finch's death, she'd struggled, grown moody, withdrawn, alienated the friends she'd had at school, and I'd known true fear. She started to pretend illness, to beg off attending class. Instead of bouncing out to fill gas tanks or wipe down windshields while trading jokes with the customers who passed through the service station, she lingered in corners or crouched in the kitchen to be near Imegine. She'd seemed confused at times, often talking of dreams from the night before as though she had trouble knowing where her imagination began and ended. I started to see a family resemblance that chilled me, the shade of my mama. I'd brought her back to Evertell, hoping that what had been the curse might also be the cure.

"Did you believe what your mama said about us? Who we are?" she asked, shaking me out of my reverie.

"I don't know. Penn, I just want to rest my eyes," I said, trying to put the thing off, at least until morning when my head wasn't feeling so heavy, so full of memories that didn't all fit together nicely.

"You can talk with your eyes shut."

I threw up my hand and let it land on my face, but she wouldn't let it rest. I knew that much about Penn. I leaned up on one elbow to see her better, her sweet face. I hadn't realized how tired I would be.

"We'll talk about this for a few minutes, but then I want to get some sleep. We have lots of time to talk."

Penn nodded earnestly.

I sighed. "My mama had a disease that made her confused. She thought a lot of things about Evertell and Eleanor and who knows what. For one, she thought she was having visions. She thought we should all be having visions. She had a charm in the book, a way to help see the future, I guess. A future. I think it was mostly wishful thinking."

"Did she? Did you?" Penn asked, her voice slightly breathless. We were sharing secrets.

"No, Penn. No," I said, a little sad. "Of course not. You know better."

"So then she was just crazy?"

Penn looked down at her lap, drawing little patterns on her thigh with her fingertip while she listened, probably embarrassed to learn there'd been madness in our family.

"I think it was just the kind of person she was, fun and hopeful, and she liked living in her imagination." Here it was, the moment when I would lay out Mama's details like a dress pattern that would fit Penn just right. I kept my explanations crisp and impersonal. "But later, things changed. The doctors said she'd started having seizures in her brain. There was nothing anybody could do."

"But they tried?"

"They tried. We all tried. Nothing worked. When Pop put her in the hospital, she died from the medicine they gave her. It was an accident. A few days later, when he came to get me, Pop closed up the house and we never came back. That was it. She was gone and he couldn't stand to be here. Neither of us could. Honestly, I was so glad to leave, Penn. I didn't think I'd ever see this place again until we found that deed. I didn't want to see it."

"That's why the man upstairs said you were a ghost? Because you disappeared?"

"That's about the size of it."

"I know why you didn't talk about it. It makes me sad." She sighed.

"It makes me sad too."

"Does this mean—"

"No. No." I interrupted her before she could finish the thought, draw the wrong conclusion. I grabbed her hand. I needed her to hear me. "Nothing like that is going to happen to me. Or to you. We are perfectly fine, Penn. It's sad, but I've tried not to think about it, that's all. And now we're here, it's an unexpected gift. We can make something happy where it's been so unfair. We should try to think about the good things. What we have. About what the future will be for us. We should be planning something wonderful. Grandmama Claire would want that."

But Penn only looked as tired as I felt. Her eyes were dark now. "It's been a big day," I said.

"I want to remember the good things, like my daddy and Pop. And I like being a Dare descendant. That's who we are, right? We can believe it for right now, can't we? The good things? That's kind of an Evertell vision, isn't it?"

I didn't argue with her. "You're the best thing, Pennilyn Rebecca Young," I said softly.

After all, it was me who had named her Rebecca, for my mama—Claire Rebecca Clerestory, before she married my daddy. When I said Penn's name aloud, I witnessed the first glimmer of joy I'd seen in my daughter in many months. I felt an overwhelming maternal need to make it stay. I couldn't bear the thought of telling her what had happened in the forest, what it had cost my mama, the end of our story. Instead, I hoped we'd find Eleanor's book and an ending to her tale that would give us both the courage for a new start. A new dream.

A distant, wild call broke the silence of the night and Penn sat up straight. It came again and I groaned.

"What is that?" she said, startled. She hurried to the window and I joined her there. The call came again, even as I answered her.

"That," I said, "is a peacock." That was the sound of Evertell in my childhood. It was what I'd been listening for on our long walk, without even realizing it. A strange voice raised against the day or night, as if delivering an urgent message for the universe. *Eee-ooo-ii! Here I am!*

She turned her face to look at me, stunned, then burst out laughing. "You're making that up."

"I wish I was."

"There are peacocks here? Really?"

"One peacock. One hen. Or that's what was here when we left. Who knows now. The peacock makes all the noise. The hen is probably trying to sleep and cussing that fool."

Penn laughed. "Where is it?"

"In a tree somewhere, sounds like. They roost up there at night to keep safe. You'll see them in the yard, but they can fly up and perch on the roof too."

The bird's call came again, an eerie, desperate screech that floated down from some high place beyond the house. "This place is crazy," Penn said, but she meant she was fascinated.

"Crazy is what it will make you. Get used to it because that guy will do this all night. All spring. Good luck sleeping. When we moved to Helen, I had trouble sleeping without that sound. Like when people move away from train tracks and say they can't get a wink because they miss the racket."

"I love it. It sounds like we're in a whole different world. You don't like them?" Penn said.

"They don't like me. We'll have to watch out for them. They're not friendly birds."

"Well, I don't care. They're so pretty. I can't wait to see them. Nobody has peacocks, Mama. *But we do.*"

She was delighted. But she was tired. After a few minutes, the novelty of the bird's call wore off. Thankfully, Penn yawned and settled in beside me on the bed again. I stroked her forehead as I'd done when she was small, and in that effortless way only the young enjoy, Penn's breathing grew slow and deep, and, faster than seemed possible, she fell asleep. I can't say I wasn't relieved. I knew when she woke, she'd be full of questions, ready for battle. Laughing or crying, Penn never had hidden a thing she felt. It was one way I knew she was stronger than me.

I lay awake, hearing the peacock's intermittent call, and when that finally quieted, I listened for the soft, uneven descent of a man with a limp as he moved through the hallways and down the stairs. It wasn't long before I heard him. I slipped from the bed and moved to the window to catch a glimpse of Sonder Holloway, a shadow in the moonlight. I watched him cross the lawn, the sounds of the cicadas a chorus rattling in the trees, and remembered the girl I'd once been.

Once there was a girl who disappeared . . .

I hadn't been lying when I told Penn I didn't believe in ghosts. I couldn't afford to. But that didn't stop me from feeling like one.

Chapter Three

As hard as I'd tried to forget Evertell, like the insistent sound of that peacock in the night, this place had never stopped calling me home. I still dreamed of silver light on water. This morning the strong scent of evergreen lingered. It came from the chest of drawers in this room, lined with cedar, giving off the familiar bittersweet scent. As Penn had noticed, it was the match for the old wardrobe at Merely's.

Whenever I'd looked at the wardrobe, I'd only ever seen my mama's shame. My daddy had discovered inside it her stained dress and the sack of strange things she'd carried into the forest to work her terrible charm on me years ago. It was only because she had begged and clawed at him in her last coherent moments, insisting it belonged to me, that the wardrobe had come with us to Helen. It had followed us like a specter and, somehow, rather than belonging to me, it had become my daddy's burden. A magician's box.

But there was nothing magical about my daddy. He was only a broken man.

When he had been especially worn out from his work, he often liked to take his rest inside the old wardrobe. This strange habit was one more thing on a long list of the things we wouldn't discuss, but I took it for romance. I'd imagined him remembering my mama there, in that locked-away space where he could keep her contained, even if he couldn't remember her aloud. Imegine had been smart enough to leave him to it. She'd told me once that she wasn't going to complain if her husband preferred to spend the evening in a wardrobe large enough to hold a grown man rather than the local bar. She'd known my daddy wasn't perfect, but at least he'd been faithful.

I loved Imegine, but I worried that might not be enough. And after news came of Finch's death, I found myself wishing for a dark place of my own where I could curl up as my daddy had in the wardrobe, where I might be enveloped in my husband's familiar scent and hidden away. I supposed this was what Penn had done in her own way, hiding inside Merely's, inside her own mind.

In any case, the memory of wanting to hide myself was swept away when Penn's high, thin laughter rose up to my ear and brought me fully awake in a sweat. A fan, I thought again, was the thing that was needed. Something to stir the air and cool my head.

I stood at the open window to gulp fresh air. Seabirds cried sharply in the distance, replacing the minor key of the peacock's song from the night before. A low fog clung to the pale water of the slow-moving river below the house, creating a mirror of the vast gray sky. The fog would burn away when the sun was full and lift like a veil to reveal the richer colors of the marshes and sea.

My eye caught Penn standing near the far edge of the lawn, near the deep green of the tall oaks and pines and palms of the forest, in a large vegetable garden with Sonder. My mouth curled in a smile, something unfamiliar of late, and I touched my fingers to my lips.

Still in my clothes from the night before, I banged down the long hallway that led from the staircase to the back of the house, throwing open closed doors to the other empty bedrooms before making my way to the main floor. The portraits of Dare descendants that once hung on the walls of the stairwell and over the mantelpieces had disappeared. I recalled my favorite, an oil painting of my grandmother Calista. She'd worn a deep green dress and peacock feathers in her hair, crowning her with their brilliant colors and little moons. All that remained was a faded spot on the wall where the painting once hung.

In fact, aside from the very few things I'd seen the night before, every treasure, every oddity, almost every stick of furniture had been carted away. But we could sleep and eat here comfortably enough. I made a quick search of my mama's writing desk, but there was no sign of the book. Later I would check the old silo, a space she'd transformed into a chandlery where she'd made candles as a hobby. Maybe I would find Eleanor's book there. I felt my fingers twitch at the thought of touching things as she'd left them, something that would have seemed impossible to me only a few days ago.

At the end of the hall, the door to the bath stood open. The morning light filtered through a small window, barely big enough for a child to squeeze through. I knew that much from experience.

When I was five, Mama had left me in the bath to soak. I'd listened as she moved through the house before I climbed out of the tub, soaking wet, and stepped up onto the toilet. Then I slipped my slick little body through the window. Before she knew I was gone, I was far across the lawn and down by the water where the fireflies were out for one of the first nights of summer. When she found me there, feet muddy, hair tangled, naked and delighted, she didn't scold me. She joined me. Mama could be like that. She could recognize a moment for something more than a disobedient little girl's whim.

She had retrieved a jar with a piece of smoothly burnished

metal with holes punched in it, her favorite mold she used for her candles. We'd caught the glowing bugs and shut them in there. Later I'd lain awake in my bed, watching them light my bedroom walls.

"See there," she'd said, pointing out one of the lights. "That one's your grandmama Calista, shining on us. She loved the constellations. Worlds of possibilities."

I'd watched my mother's sleeping face that night, shining like a map of the stars. She'd believed in all sorts of fanciful things. Dare descendants, she said, were women who never needed a map and could always find their way in the dark. We carried a light inside. Our hearts were like magnets drawn to love, always knowing our way home.

I'd believed I was just the kind of girl with a light at her center who would never have to fear being lost, free to take risks no other girl would've dared.

X

I pushed past the fog of memories and through the French doors leading to a small patio. My eyes darted side to side, watching for any sign of the peacock or his hen, alert to any need to dodge the territorial birds. This morning, at least, the path was clear. The brick pavers were uneven, and I stumbled down several narrow steps to the shadowy yard beneath a stand of towering pecan trees. The shade was cool and quiet. I caught the sweet scent of the jasmine vine, and now I noticed the trumpet-shaped coral blossoms of bougainvillea and lilies in bloom near the porch, bright orange, forgotten perennials that must have returned year after year. The strangely statuesque bird-of-paradise flowers rising from thick, glossy green leaves that lined the edges of overgrown flower beds must have looked otherworldly to Penn. It seemed we had entered a garden that had been growing of its own accord since the beginning of time. But in the morning light, even the flaming color of the flowers couldn't mask the harsh truth of the exterior of the house for me, sadly on display. Time had done its worst here too.

And yet, in many ways, Evertell was as I remembered it. The estate was situated about eight miles east of the city's edges on what was essentially a peninsula. The farm overlooked the flat banks of the Savannah River, a wide blue plain of water and mudflats that shifted with the tides and stretched for miles past the farm until it emptied into the Atlantic Ocean. In the middle of the river lay a long, thin strip of land known as Bell Isle, and from the upper floor of the house the pretty white bell tower of the Evertell chapel could be seen. To the southwest stood almost a hundred acres of dense forest dotted with freshwater and brackish ponds. The main house was a tall, broad confection of Italianate architecture, one of the earliest pre-Revolutionary farms that had grown indigo and rice.

"Look!" Penn called. Her voice pulled me back to the present. "We have our own victory garden!"

Penn had no losses here, only gains to be made, I reminded myself.

"I see that," I called as I walked down to the garden to meet her and Sonder.

"We're eating breakfast," Penn proclaimed. Her mouth split into a wide smile, full of strawberries. "There's a milk wagon that comes every morning and I went out to meet it with Sonder. We told the man we'd need extra now."

She held a glass quart jar in her hand and offered me a drink, which I accepted gratefully. My stomach was empty, but it was more than the heat and need for a solid meal that made me unsteady. She held a half-smashed strawberry up for me and my heart turned over. She seemed brighter, with color in her cheeks. Her brown curls, like my own, blew back from her face, and I felt my hair lift away from my forehead, carried on the breeze off the marsh.

"Don't let us bother you. We don't want to put you out," I said to Sonder. "But I have to ask, do you think you could turn up an electric fan for our room?"

"Sure." Sonder nodded. "There's one at the mill. I'll bring it up."

"Good. Thank you. You'll be doing us a big favor. Now all we need is a phone." I hoped he'd have a recommendation that didn't send me to the Feed and Seed, but from his expression, I knew before he spoke that my options hadn't changed.

"You know where to find that," Sonder said.

I nodded and handed the last of the milk back to Penn, a little embarrassed that I'd consumed most of it so quickly. "Great. Thanks. And I'll pay for the extra milk." I didn't want to seem like a couple of hungry beggars, but a breakfast of strawberries and cream felt luxurious.

"I figure you're already paying for it," he said, then offered, "I can give you a ride this morning, if you like."

"Oh no." I made a weak gesture toward the ramshackle mammoth behind us. "I'm sure you've got plenty to do." I realized too late how rude it sounded. "I mean, we aren't going to put you out like that. We can walk. It's not like I don't know the way."

"I haven't seen the peafowl yet," Penn said, glancing at Sonder to see if she'd gotten the word correct. He nodded. "But they come to the barn for feed in the evening, and Sonder said he'll take me out on the water later too." Penn squinted in the sunlight. "Can I go?"

I recalled Mama's original pair of great, mean peafowl—Gustave and Babette. I had no notion as to how long a bird like that might live or if any of the birds we'd see here might be the same ones I'd known. I only knew that they'd lurked like guardians of my mama's little kingdom and I'd feared them. And I recalled, too, going out on the water with Sonder, the gloom of first light, the sounds of the marsh waking, watching for alligators on the banks. I wondered if he might be remembering the same. I flapped a hand at Penn. "You can go, but tomorrow morning. After we're settled. And to be clear, Sonder's busy. Don't be a pest."

I could feel him looking at me and I wished I weren't a too-tired woman who'd spent the night tossing and turning. I lowered my eyes and shielded my face with my hand, as if the sun were too bright. But it was Penn he spoke to.

"How about this? You want to do me a favor?" he said. "While you're up the road, maybe when you stop in for that phone you can pick up the mailbag. Bill's holding it for me."

I caught Sonder's eye. "Bill Hawkes? You're kidding. He's still running that place? Does nothing ever leave this place?"

"Sure." He grinned at me and I rolled my eyes. "Bill will be glad to see you drop in."

"No. He won't." I crossed my arms, already on the defensive, with Bill Hawkes all the way down the road. Sonder shook his head. Penn looked between us.

"He's not a friend of the family," Penn said, parroting my words from last night in an attempt to join the adult conversation.

I let out a sharp laugh. There were very few people anywhere near Evertell who would be glad to see me. But most especially Bill Hawkes. I'd accused his son, Charlie, of stealing Eleanor's stone.

⚭

While Penn and I walked the mile and a half back up the road to Hawkes's Feed and Seed, I was distracted from her chatter about the marsh. After passing the store last night, I'd half hoped it was no longer in operation. Now I expected Charlie Hawkes, my tormentor, to creep up behind me. *"Little Alice, better beware."* In my ear I could still hear his laugh. It had been a regular occurrence when I'd walked to the store as a girl. I'd been too sensitive and too young and a little afraid of him. I'd been the perfect target.

When a bus passed, coming in from the beaches that lay to our east on Tybee Island, returning to Savannah and leaving a cloud of dust, Penn coughed and grumbled. "You should've let Sonder drive us."

The familiarity of the road, the nearby marsh, the fields of tall grass, the buzz of insects, brought my childhood rushing back so hard I felt dizzy and I wished I'd had more to eat before we'd left.

"Just stay in the shade," I said when we reached Hawkes's. "It's a perfect spring day. I won't be long."

"But I could come inside. To help carry. I have to get the mail, remember? Don't make me stay out here."

"There's a good chance this man will throw me out the front door, all right?"

"Maybe he'll like me. Why doesn't he like you?"

"I didn't get along with his son."

"What does that mean?"

"I accused him of a crime."

Her mouth fell open. "Then I definitely want to come in. What did you say he did? The man's son?"

"That he trespassed on our property."

Penn looked at me like I'd never been so ridiculous. "That's all? Nobody cares about that."

"Just do what I'm asking, all right?" I could see I'd said the right thing about Charlie, even if it wasn't entirely true, because Penn lost interest in arguing and sat down in the shade beneath a tree to sift through the sandy soil for seashells.

Inside, the little store hadn't changed. It was dark and cramped and smelled of corn, just as I remembered it. The public phone hung on the wall near the back, and when the operator connected the call, Imegine sighed over the crackling line, telling me that she was lonely. The day before, she'd sent us on our way, looking so uncertain and small. She'd dusted her hands on her apron and I'd kissed her cheek on my way outside, where I'd watched my daddy's faded blue work shirts snap in the wind, and dried my eyes.

"I don't like leaving you by yourself," I said.

"You're a good mama and I'll always say it. Besides, what are you going to do here for me?"

"I don't know. Keep you company."

"There'll be plenty of time for us two biddies to peck at each other if you send Penn off to that school."

That school. Imegine did not approve. "It's Brenau Academy, not a reform school, and it's what she wants." I took a breath. "I dropped the application packet in the mail before we left. You'll need to watch for anything that comes back. They'll want an interview, I think, if she's got a shot. Let me know as soon as we get anything."

"Alice," she said, "did you at least ask her first? They require an essay, don't they? She worked on that thing night and day a few years ago."

"I know. I used it."

"Used it?"

"Used it. Tweaked it. Whatever you want to call it, I sent it in. It's mostly still her words, Imegine. She's smarter than she was when she wrote it and nobody will know any different. She's been telling us that this is what she wants for three years. I'm not going to argue with you about this over the phone."

Imegine did not argue. She was quiet so long I thought the line had gone dead, but then she sighed. "You do what you want."

"I hate when you do this."

"Do what?" She sounded offended.

"You're the one who said we should come back here. You're the one who said this was the opportunity we needed. You said Daddy had given us a gift and we'd better not squander it."

"I did say that. Why are you picking a fight?"

"I couldn't wait, Imegine. It takes years to get in and I'm trying to do this overnight. Did you think I'd get here and be all overcome with nostalgia and change my mind? You, of all people, ought to know why this is hard for me."

"Alice, you make things hard on yourself. You always have."

"Things can't stay the same. Not for Penn."

"Well, they most certainly will not if you go through with this," she said, then changed the subject. "I guess you've heard the worst has happened? It's all over the news. FDR's died from a stroke. Happened yesterday, down at Warm Springs. That Truman's in now and we'll just have to see."

I had not heard. I was too stunned to know what to say. I thought of our drive, Penn and me winding South through Georgia, not so far from the place where the president had lain dying. We hadn't felt the world shift, not even at such a passing. Sonder didn't mention it, but perhaps he hadn't heard last night. If he'd known this morning, he might have been trying to spare Penn. Now I would have to tell her. Imegine didn't dwell on this new loss and strangely, I felt detached.

"Storm's coming," Imegine said. "I need to get the wash off the line. Quick, tell me what you think. Is the house in as bad a shape as you worried it would be?"

Just one more in a string of losses now. Men came and went, and women brought in the wash. I took a deep breath and got hold of my temper. This wasn't easy for either of us. I knew Imegine didn't like the thought of sending Penn away, even the short distance to Gainesville, when we'd already been whittled down to the three of us. Now I dreaded the idea of telling Penn about the president. And I realized I was grateful we were here where she could think about the house, the ocean—anything but the war that seemed even farther away.

"The house is about what you'd guess. It hasn't been lived in for a long time. Somebody probably ought to just light a match."

"Oh heavens, that's not what I'd hoped, honey. For you and Penn, I mean. Is it that bad? How's our girl?" she asked.

"Good. She's perked up a little. Thinks we've been left a fortune and we need to go on treasure hunts for everything that's been emptied out of the house. Honestly, that ugly bedroom set that matches the wardrobe is about all that's left. I should've brought that awful thing back here while I had the chance."

"Your daddy loved it." She paused, then asked wistfully, "Do you think he's with her now?"

"With who?" I said. But in that same instant I realized what she meant. "You're talking about my parents? Are they together? Oh, Imegine, I don't know. I have no idea how it works."

"Well, if he is, I don't guess I'd be surprised. And I got some good years with y'all, didn't I? It's been something." The pain in her voice was plain, even over the crackling phone line.

"Don't talk like that, Imegine. We'll be home in a blink." I kept my voice low and leaned close to the wall of the phone box. "We'll take that wardrobe apart and sell it for firewood."

Imegine laughed, but it was a brittle sound. "No, honey. That spooky old thing belongs to you. I won't have your mama haunt me. To tell you the truth, Alice, I think you ought to stay awhile. Give Penn some time away from here. Maybe you just stay down there a little while, through the summer."

"What? The summer?" I gasped. "Are you serious? Penn wants to get back to finish up school."

"Penn does? Now, that's a lie. She knows good and well, same as you do, nobody's going to raise a stink over a couple of weeks right here on the tail end of the year. She's top of her class, meeting all requirements. That principal told you to take the time she needs. There's no sense rushing back. You ought to at least consider it."

Her words stung. "I thought I was considering you."

"Thank you, baby. That's sweet, but it's not you I'm missing. If you want to know, it's easier this way. Going through his things without you watching me act a fool."

I swallowed my arguments for the moment, but then she explained she'd already made a call to my daddy's old lawyer from Savannah.

"But why would you call him? I was going to drive into town and see him today," I said, annoyed.

"I just wanted to help. Anyway, he says he can't see you until tomorrow. He'll save you a trip and come by the house. He says tomorrow's better."

I felt I'd been railroaded somehow. Imagine couldn't stand not moving the pieces on the board. "You could have just come with us if you'd wanted to be part of this, Imagine."

"I don't want a thing to do with that place. But if you really want my opinion—"

"Yes, I want it," I said, interrupting her. "I've been asking for it."

"Then I think your daddy meant to slow you down so you'd think before you sold it. And I think Penn might want to stay now she's there and you all might feel different. I'm not saying you're nostalgic and stupid, Alice. I'm saying you ought to talk to her about it."

I felt certain then that Imegine had made sure I had some time before I saw Oscar Lewallen.

"I just don't see the sense in giving it all away at once. Maybe he'll have advice and you could break it up, sell it a parcel at a time," she said, her voice wheedling. "You're rushing is all I'm saying."

"Well, I'm not rushing now, am I?" I snapped. "I've got a whole extra day on my hands. I can't pay the tuition until we sell this place, not if we want to eat." I leaned my forehead against the wall. "And I miss you," I admitted. "I guess this gives me time to size things up before he gets here to talk me out of it."

"Now, that's not true. But I do believe we've caught poor Mr. Lewallen off guard. He seemed upset about your daddy. Nobody'd let him know about John's passing. He sends his deep condolences."

"All right." I felt eyes on me and looked up to see the man behind the counter watching me. His jowls hung so low his face seemed limp. I knew him for Bill Hawkes, older and paunchier, and could see from the look in his eyes that he was still trying to place me. I was wearing Finch's overalls and I found myself feeling satisfied as he scowled at my unbecoming wardrobe.

I turned so my back faced the counter and watched as an older woman with salt-and-pepper hair pulled tight to her head came through the door, swinging an egg basket from her elbow. She wore a cotton housedress that hung loosely off her thin frame and sandals with dark socks pulled up to her knees. I tried to get off the phone, hoping the customer would keep Bill busy while I got what I needed.

"Listen, there's no phone line to the house so I'm at the store down the road. There's somebody else here waiting to make a call." I lied so smoothly now, cupping my hand around the receiver to hide my conversation. "But I'll let you know when we'll be headed back. You don't worry, all right?"

"I'm not worried a bit. You know best. I just want you to settle whatever you need to down there, but I know one thing. You can't settle overnight whatever has had you and your daddy running scared all these years."

"Neither can Oscar Lewallen," I said, feeling exhausted by what should have been a simple conversation, just a quick check-in. But I should have known that nothing about this trip was going to be simple.

Imegine said her goodbyes and as I hung up, I thought about what she'd said about my parents and some otherworldly reunion, leaving her alone on the side of the road in the life my daddy had made to pass the time until he could slip his earthly bonds. I felt bad about being angry with her for trying to help, the only thing she'd ever tried to do for us. I thought of FDR dead in an instant. I should have told her I loved her again. If not for Penn, I'd have told her to take a sledgehammer to that old wardrobe.

𝄪

I'd no more than hung up the receiver before the woman with the basket was beside me. Bill, thankfully, had walked into the back.

"Such a sad day, isn't it? Did I hear you say Lewallen? It's just I think I know who you are. You're Claire's girl? Claire Merely?" She peered at me, waiting. After so many years of anonymity, it was strange to be recognized.

"Sad, yes," I agreed. The whole world would be shocked with the news. That much even strangers had in common. "I'm Alice Merely. Actually, it's Young now."

"We were so sorry to hear about your daddy. Sonder let us all know. John was a good man."

She seemed sincere and I felt my own grief raise its head. I lowered my eyes, unwilling to reveal too much. "Thank you."

"You've been out to the house?"

"Yes, we're staying there while we settle the estate, me and my daughter." I tried to give her a careful smile that would show confidence.

She shook her head as if she couldn't fathom such a thing. "Well, Lord. Is it fit to live in? Surely we can do something to get you better set up while you're here."

"Oh, that's not—"

"Of course we will. We're neighbors. Don't argue about it. I can at least manage some clean sheets and pillows for you. Maybe a few towels. Let me think what all's needed. You'll be living like a wild thing over there. Do y'all even have dishes?" I could see myself reflected in her rheumy light blue eyes, her gaze unwavering. "Just look at you, honey. I'm Doris La Roche. Do you remember me? It's plain you don't. That's okay. My husband and I've been tenants on Bell Isle for years." She smiled and waited.

"Wait. No, I think I remember you. You live on the estate?" Not only Sonder, but this woman and her husband too? I did remember her, or some version of her, a sweet woman who would come to the house to visit my mama. There were so many things I didn't really know about Evertell, things I probably should have, but I was so young when we left. I was relying on an immature perspective and suddenly understood I was at a serious disadvantage.

"We have the cottage out by the family chapel," she explained. "Well, it's just me now. My husband was a Selectman for years."

"Oh! I do remember him." The little island with its quaint white church came to mind, and the elderly couple who'd lived there. *Selectman.* It'd been years since I heard that term. An appointed caretaker for the church. He'd looked after the structure and the grounds like a lighthouse keeper, and I remembered watching him cross the river in his small boat to talk to my daddy on our dock.

A bald man, the skin of his scalp pink from the sun, small dark glasses to protect his eyes, a man living on an island for the dead. If they were old then, this woman must be a hundred years old now. It must've shown on my face because Doris La Roche smiled, showing a row of unexpectedly nice white teeth in her pale face, with spots from the Low Country sun.

"You had a son, I think. Is that right? Adopted after the first war. My mama helped with that?" I couldn't recall if I'd known him, or maybe only known of him. He'd been younger than me.

"That's kind of you to remember. Your mama was an angel." Doris gave a soft nod. I could see she was touched. "You come see me and we'll talk about old times."

It was a nice thing to say, but my memories were not something I wanted to rehash. However, Doris remembered my mama, that Claire Clerestory Merely was a different person than I had known. I tried to put her off, nodding and smiling while picking up the things I'd come for, a bit of cheese, some eggs, a loaf of fresh bread, and butter, filling a basket before moving to the counter to settle up. We'd need more and a standing order for while we were here.

Bill returned to round the counter and faced me as I placed my items in front of him. "What about that? Little Alice Merely coming back here after all this time."

"Bill Hawkes." Now he knew me. If Doris La Roche meant to welcome me, I didn't get the same feeling from the storekeeper. "How's your family?"

He didn't answer. "You got a nice load of hay put up over that way. At least four acres in field corn going in before end of the month."

I nodded as if I had some idea what he was talking about. Behind him hung a poster encouraging us to grow a victory garden. *Feed yourself. Be a soldier of the soil.*

"Fine garden, too, I hear," he went on. I thought he sounded nervous. It pleased me. "You should bring what you like out to the farmer's stand outside the store. My daughter-in-law runs it. I'm sure she'd be glad to have the help."

But then something else caught my attention.

In front of me on the sales counter sat a large hunk of iron. I shot a glance under my lashes at Bill and he was watching me. The size of a giant fist, the piece of metal wasn't easily identifiable as anything in particular, not exactly round, most likely a remnant of old farm machinery. Just junk. But here it was, displayed as if it were something of value. I puzzled over it.

It sat on a flat bottom. The top wasn't smooth like the rest but jagged. Still, none of that was the reason it caught my eye. Someone, probably Bill or one of his kith and kin, had scratched into its surface *Hawkes's Stone*.

"Is this a joke?" I said, aghast.

"No, no. This ain't no joke. This is historical memorabilia." Bill slapped a confident hand atop the thing, clearly pleased to have me bear witness. "You know what they say. One man's trash, another man's treasure. All in how you see it."

This was his way of showing anybody who walked through his door what he thought of our stone. The hunk of iron seemed insolent, immovable, as sullen as this old man's grudge against me, and I felt furious he'd made this ridiculous display of his feelings out of spite. I knew exactly how long he had been waiting for the day I'd walk back into this store, anticipating the satisfaction he'd have when he could gloat. There were dozens of sets of initials and dates, a few little cartoon faces, all over the surface of the iron object. I felt my stomach sour and roll.

"Now, stop it, Bill, with that silly thing. Look," Doris said, "Bill's our local historian."

Beneath the counter in a glass case, news reports were displayed. The largest clipping was from the *Atlanta Herald* and included a picture of the stone I remembered from our forest and a group of proud historians standing round it. After the call with Imegine, I was already on the verge of tears, and now this. Rubbing my nose in the fate of the stone, the great humbug it had become to the greater world. The last thing I wanted was to let this man see me cry. I leaned close to the grimy glass to read the article, taking deep breaths to calm myself.

New Clue in 350-Year-Old Lost Colony Mystery

January 30, 1938

Officials from Emory University report that a California man traveling through coastal North Carolina may have discovered an important clue in the 350-year-old mystery of the Lost Colony of Roanoke.

In August 1937, the man, whose identity is being withheld by the university, unearthed a large, flat stone measuring 14 inches long and 10 inches wide. The stone is vein quartz, much like an English ballast stone, and is covered in strange markings and writing that seem to be Elizabethan English, say officials from Emory University's history department.

Most American school children know the story: In 1587,

colonists sponsored by Sir Walter Raleigh settled the village of Roanoke on the North Carolina coast. They later disappeared, never to be heard from again. Archaeologists and historians have searched for answers ever since, but no theory has been proven.

Historians at Emory believe the stone found last summer may contain a message from Eleanor White Dare, daughter of Roanoke's colonial governor, John White. White departed the colony in August of 1587 for a three-year trip to England, but on return to the colony found everyone vanished—including his daughter, son-in-law, and granddaughter.

Writing appears on both

sides of the stone. It includes the following: the fate of 117 men, women, and children and the carved initials "EWD." University historians say this points to Eleanor, who may have been one of only seven colonists to survive a massacre, then be taken hostage by natives.

Emory University officials say they will authenticate the stone before revealing further details. "We intend to publish complete data on the investigation in historical publications before any popular interpretation is made," says Haywood J. Pearce Jr., professor of history.

Until then, the Lost Colony of Roanoke remains America's oldest mystery.

Other clippings were laid out, further reports of other stones that had turned up over the last few years, each of them inscribed with accounts of Eleanor or the other colonists, stories that sometimes matched the one my mama had told and sometimes didn't. They'd seemed ridiculous, even to me. Just before the war started, a reporter for the *Saturday Evening Post* had dismissed the lot of them as a hoax. I'd actually felt a sense of relief that people would lose interest and the stones would fall back into obscurity, along with Eleanor. At least she'd have some peace.

"People sort of took to knowing the stone had been here, in our forest. A point of pride for the community," Bill said proudly. "I always thought your mama would've liked that we carried on with the tradition."

"She might have," I admitted, furious. "Personally, I shut the book on fairy tales a long time ago. But to each their own. I hope you've all had a nice laugh. You always did. Nice seeing you, Bill."

The sounds of a bus pulling in, the motor idling, and the voices of passengers stepping off reached the store. A few of the people came ambling inside. I looked at my watch, as if the time mattered, my hands shaking. I took the basket on my arm, tossing money on the counter, not waiting for change.

"Here now," Bill said. He picked up a heavy cloth sack filled with pieces of mail, squinting as he handed it over to me. "That fella of yours, Holloway, he records messages from those Berlin broadcasts. The president himself advises civilians against monitoring enemy radio. Folks around here have their concerns about what's going on out there. Myself, I've had a word with him."

Nothing had changed here.

"Whatever he does, he's no fella of mine. I don't live here. I'd say he's your problem, Bill."

Doris La Roche looked at me with sympathy. "All Bill's saying is Sonder Holloway's a good man. People are scared of their own tail feathers these days. But I can understand. Your husband likely won't approve of such doings, monitoring enemy radio in the house."

"Luckily my husband is dead," I said flatly.

※

Once we were out of sight of the store, Penn and I dropped the bag and sat down in the sandy dirt to catch our breath. I felt anything but lucky, rattled to have come face-to-face with those stupid news articles and old neighbors. I was ashamed of what I'd said and grateful Penn hadn't been there to hear it. I tried to get over my temper before she could get a whiff of my soured mood.

"This is all letters from families who got Sonder's cards?"

"Help me roll it off the road here until we can come back with the truck."

"Wait. Just dump it? Isn't that some kind of crime?" Penn said, startled. "Leaving other people's letters out here like this?"

I thought of the articles in Bill Hawkes's cabinet and all those suspicious stones that had turned up, opportunistic stones scattered here and there just like his stupid Hawkes's Stone, waiting for some gullible girl like my daughter to stumble over them. She would take it all to heart and her heart was already so bruised and beaten. How could you tell what was the truth when the world was full of lies carved into solid stone and airwaves brimming with promises?

I pushed the heavy sack down from the roadside and my stomach lurched as an unexpected wave of horror washed over me. I thought of Finch and turned my face away from Penn. "We're coming back for them, Penn. We're not leaving anybody's anything." I'd have liked to have lain down on top of that mailbag and wept for my own husband and child.

I told her then of the news I'd learned. "Alright?" I asked. She listened solemnly, then started down the road, her expression resolute. What could a dead president matter to a girl who'd already lost her father and grandfather? I felt even more resolved to avoid listening to the radio while we were here. I was glad I'd told Sonder to keep the thing in the rafters, away from us.

When I'd met Finch, I'd looked much like Penn. About a year after he started working for Daddy, I waited out behind the garage under a persimmon tree for an hour. I knew Finch would finish his shift and find me there. I'd left him a note that I needed his opinion on an important question. He was out of breath when he came to me, rubbing grease from his hands on a rag, his hair hanging in his eyes. I didn't say a word but pulled his face down to mine so our lips met and jammed together. It didn't last more than a few seconds and there was nothing exceptional about us, just a boy and a girl sneaking a first kiss. But he looked at me then as if I were transformed before his eyes.

"I didn't know you were going to do that," he'd said. Then he took my hand and we were begun. Finch was simple like that. Reliable.

I missed that and thought on it while we walked the rest of the way to where we'd left the truck the night before.

Thankfully, when a car stopped to help, the driver had jumper cables. When he pulled away, Penn looked down the road, little more than a sandy track, toward the coast. I knew she was trying hard to imagine what was over the far horizon.

$\mathcal{X}$

As evening fell, I watched from the porch while Penn helped Sonder scatter Startena feed for the peafowl in a trough beneath the oaks. I remembered doing this very thing as a child. As the birds began to appear from the edge of the lawn, Penn and Sonder stood at a distance and I saw my daughter was thrilled at the four hens and the regal peacock with his royal-blue head and long neck, his blue-and-green train streaming behind him. Watching the birds have their dinner, I thought again of Imegine, my own little hen, who would have been Imogene had her mother not misspelled the name on her birth certificate.

She had been an unlikely stepmother. She was thirty-two and I was seventeen the first time she'd come home with me, the only guest I'd ever brought to the rooms above Merely's. Not that it had been my idea. She'd invited herself. Imegine was a substitute teacher at my school and had befriended me at a time when I was desperate for a woman's attention. Although she had been somewhat colorless, had a big nose and very thin legs, I thought she hung together in a way that made everything about her seem to swing in all directions when she walked.

We'd learned about the Dahlonega Gold Rush at school and I'd been eager to tell her my daddy had a five-dollar 1838 half eagle in mint condition. She took one look at Daddy flipping that coin up in the air like pirate's loot and said she knew she was meant to be a part of us. What she lacked in charm, Imegine made up for in baked goods. I'd always thought that for my family to have looked like such a catch, Imegine must have come from worse than a dog patch. After her mother died of sepsis, Imegine married my daddy, who was more than twenty years her senior. Soon enough, she'd taken the spartan rooms where my daddy and I lived and done what neither of us had been able to do since leaving Evertell. Imegine made Helen another home for us. Imegine made it easier not to look back.

And then later, it was Imegine who'd heard the thud when Daddy suffered his stroke and fell out of the wardrobe. She'd found him as he lay with his top half on the braided rug on the bedroom floor, his legs tangled in the tall wooden compartment, the sharp scent of the cedar paneling strong in the air like all his heartbreak, exposed.

Nothing had shocked Imegine, not even that horrible moment. But she'd have been appalled now, I thought, to see me making a supper of scrambled eggs and saltine crackers and Coca-Cola while a pretty pile of fresh asparagus, green onions, and a ruffled head of lettuce languished in the sink.

Still, when Penn came bounding inside the kitchen house looking enchanted and we sat at that little table, she looked happy enough.

I filled a big tin basin with the icy water that flowed from Bell Creek through the pipes to the kitchen sink. We carried the tub between us and then soaked our feet while we sat on the wide porch of the house, the heady scent of the jasmine vine enveloping us, looking out over the river as long as we could stand the mosquitos. The peacock had not started his evening serenade yet, and we were quiet a long time before Penn's voice startled me out of my thoughts.

"Tell me about Sonder. When did he come here?" She must have been thinking about him since this morning and even more since we'd brought the heavy bag of mail home with us. She was anticipating going in the boat with him come morning and I hoped I wasn't making a mistake, entrusting her to a man I hadn't known in decades. But when I reflected on the boy he'd been, I couldn't believe he would have changed so much he wouldn't be kind to her. He was a good man. Doris La Roche, and even Bill Hawkes, had said as much.

"I made him up," I said. "Or that's what I thought. It was the year before your grandmother died. You know from what I've told you, she wasn't well." Penn nodded. "By the time Sonder came, she'd already been in the hospital here in Savannah for her seizures, when things got low. Or worse, when she was wound up too tight. They called it hysterics, and that's the kind of day she was having by then. The latest stay at the hospital hadn't really changed anything and they were already talking about sending her away to the state asylum for treatment. She'd only been home a few days and things were going right back like they'd been. When it got like that, I knew to make myself scarce."

Penn scowled and I decided I'd said enough about that.

"There's a walnut tree outside the old silo where my mama made her hobby shop, a chandlery, a place where she made candles. She went there to keep her hands busy, she said. She only let me come inside once or twice. But I could climb the tree and look down inside the one window and see her working there. It was one of my favorite secret places when she was in a mood. But that day, when I went to spy on her, I saw someone else instead."

"It was Sonder," Penn guessed.

"I forgot all about what had sent me running to the woods so upset." But now I remembered like it had been only days before. "He was just outside where the chandlery backs to the forest, pull-ing wild onions up from the ground and sitting there like he didn't have anywhere else to go. I couldn't imagine who he was or where he had come from. But I was excited. I could barely breathe."

"That's how I felt when we came here."

"I know," I said. I smiled into her eyes and admitted, "I didn't want him to know I was there. I wanted to watch to see what he would do next. He was such a lonely thing. He was older than me, not a man yet, but old enough to be exciting. Old enough to know more than me."

"How old?"

"I don't know. Maybe twenty-five. I had no idea, really, just that he was old enough to go places I'd never been. I'd always had a fantasy, an imaginary friend, and I thought I'd wished so hard that I'd made him real."

Penn sat rapt as I told her how the evening had grown cool that day as dusk settled over the edge of the forest. The boy gathered a knapsack. But even after he went inside the chandlery, I didn't move from my perch for a long time. Finally, when it seemed safe, I hurried down the tree to peer over the edge of the window. Inside, the room was lit by the great fireplace where he had dared to start a fire, and he sat before it, his face glowing in the warmth. My throat tightened at the scene. I worried who might see the smoke and discover him, but he sat completely still, gazing into the flames as I stared at him. I determined I would stay there and defend him if anyone should come to run him off in the night.

Hours later, it was the light of a full moon playing over my face that woke me. I sat up gasping, jumping to my feet, ready to run home. In a rush, my first thought was that I must have fallen asleep outside the chandlery. But when my panicked eyes focused, I discovered my bare feet standing on the braided rug of my own room, not the forest floor. The clock on my bedside table said two

68

in the morning. Somehow I'd been safely tucked in, just as I should have been, spirited home.

And I knew it was the boy who had done it. And then I thought maybe I'd dreamed the whole thing, and that made me cry.

"But he was real," Penn said. "He wasn't your imagination. He carried you home."

"He did. I went out early to see if he was still in the chandlery, and when it was empty, I was so disappointed I was sick to my stomach. But he was real," I said, confirming her conclusion, and she smiled. "And that was better than a dream. He'd already gone to see Pop and been put to work for us. I learned he'd been given permission to stay the first night in the chandlery until a better place could be sorted out for him. After that, he had the room upstairs in the millhouse."

"But then he was your friend, just like you wanted. A real friend. Better than if you'd made him up."

"Better than I knew how to make up," I admitted.

Later, after we'd settled for the night and Sonder had come and gone from his monitoring with only a polite word to us, I fell asleep thinking of the chandlery and the night I found him there, and I wondered if I climbed the walnut tree tonight what I might see.

Chapter Four

Morning bloomed over the foggy river in pale pinks and purples like layers of chiffon. A girl could dream anything in a place like this. I climbed to the cupola to look out. In the distance large ships carrying freight on their way out to sea cruised the deeper water beyond Bell Isle. The sounds of their horns were like throaty echoes. But what might be cruising below the surface along our coast, silent and deep? Sea monsters? Or the U-boats of the enemy? How different were they, really?

Walking the dock, I listened to the cicadas throb in the trees, their love song to the building heat of the day. The salty air off of the marsh and the river and the sharper scent of pines from the forest made my stomach knot with nostalgia.

I stood on the lawn to survey things, looking for a place to start. A cloud of gnats hung in the damp air. I shielded my eyes as I passed through them, my feet remembering the farm, taking in the lay of the land, as Daddy would have said. The temperature was already climbing with the sun barely over the horizon, and walking this fecund ground, I could readily see the ways nature was taking back every inch of the estate.

Evertell had real trouble with the roof, made undeniable by the stains on the interior ceilings and floors. Holes were visible near one of the three chimneys on the house. And then there was the chimney itself, which was obviously buckling away from the roofline. I cringed at all the peeling places on the trim and termite damage. The whole house looked as if it might crumble at the slightest breeze.

"Some vision," I mumbled. I had a sinking feeling at the seemingly impossible amount of work to make this house habitable, much less appealing to a buyer, and made my way to the wide porch to sit and look out over the river.

Just then Penn rushed out to find me. "He's already here," she said in a flurry. "You didn't wake me up."

I looked and caught sight of Sonder coming up from the direction of the millhouse, an old stone structure tucked out of sight from where we stood, situated on Bell Creek, the rippling tributary that ran along the west border of the lawn. Water ran through Evertell like veins. Sonder had said that to me once.

I raised a hand to wave good morning.

"Aren't you going to eat something?" I asked Penn. She was bouncing on the balls of her feet, ready to take off for the boat ride Sonder had promised.

"No time. I'm not hungry anyway."

"You will be."

She ignored me, shoving her sock feet into a pair of my sturdy brown dress shoes. Surprised to see they very nearly fit her growing feet, and that she'd abandoned the sad old boots, I clamped my lips shut, regardless of how inappropriate they were for her outing. She was wearing a pair of shorts and a cotton top too nice for a morning on the water, but she'd rolled up the blousy sleeves and left the buttons at the neck undone. Clearly she meant to impress Sonder, and I had to admit he did cut a romantic figure on his approach. She smiled and waved to him, and my heart clenched. It was so good to see her enthusiasm. It reminded me of watching her greet Finch when she was small. I wanted to believe that was the only reason for the feelings that stirred inside me. Certainly I was no longer the little girl in the walnut tree.

"Did you know he has pigeons too?" she said.

"What?"

"A whole barn full of them. It's pretty huge."

"When did you see that?"

"Yesterday. Before you came out to the garden. Before we went to get the truck. He showed me."

"You didn't say anything."

She shrugged. "He calls it a loft. You should see all the birds. They're not free-range like the peafowl though. They don't fly outside. There's a bunch of net over what he calls a yard that keeps them from getting out. I think that's like prison to them. I'm going to get him to let them fly."

"I guess they're his birds and he knows best."

Penn clearly didn't agree, sighing deeply. "He said I could help feed them and stuff. Pick up eggs. But I missed it. He's already done all that this morning. I should have been up earlier."

"Try again tomorrow."

She rolled her eyes at me. "If he even lets me now. I should have been there. He's really serious about them. I had to promise to keep the door to the loft shut. He showed me about half a million times how he does it and checks himself so it never gets left open. He's kind of nuts."

Sonder was almost within earshot of our conversation. "Don't say nuts like that. Sonder is a careful person."

"You should go see them." She was too excited to argue, struggling with the shoes and yesterday's blisters. "There are so many. It's amazing. This place is amazing." She ran out to meet Sonder then and took one of two bulging gunnysacks he carried over his shoulder.

When they reached the porch, I said, "I hear you've branched out from peafowl to messenger pigeons now. Too bad they can't carry these enormous mailbags for you."

He shook his head at my poor attempt at a joke. "They refuse on principle. And this isn't mail."

I laughed, watching as Penn opened one of the bags and began pulling out sheets, a pair of quilts, and towels.

"But where did you get pigeons?" I asked Sonder. "Why?"

"Doris La Roche saddled me. Thinks I need more to take care of. She says people need to be around life to be alive."

"She couldn't just get you a dog?"

"I wouldn't subject a dog to that peacock."

I had to agree with that. "I can't believe you didn't just eat it."

I reached for the second bag. Inside, I found kitchen sundries and a set of four dishes and chipped teacups wrapped in an old apron. "What's all this?"

"Housewarming from Doris," he explained. "She said you'd be expecting it."

"Expecting a lunch basket, sure. But this is too much."

"Could've been pigeons."

"Very funny." I stood there, stunned by the kindness after the way I'd left the store, and realizing, too, that there was pity in this gesture. "How am I going to thank her?"

"I thought she might send the book if she had it," Penn said, holding a small copper pot and sounding more than a bit disappointed.

Sonder looked to me and asked, "That book of your mama's?"

I shrugged, pretending it wasn't all that important. "We were hoping it would still be here, but so far it hasn't turned up."

"Pay Doris a visit—that's the best thanks she'd like. Gets lonesome over there by herself." Then he addressed Penn as he stepped off in the direction of the dock. "You're looking for an old book, about this big?" He spread his hands in exaggerated shapes. "Lots of women's business in there? Recipes, pictures, pretty ribbons? Charms to give boys warts?"

He was charming. Penn was falling for it. She wrinkled her nose. "Stop it."

"Never seen it," he teased. "But you drop in on that chapel while you're over there. See what you don't find on that big podium right down front. Seems like it might be the thing you're looking for."

Penn was thrilled. She bounced over to hug me. "When we get back. It won't be too late, right?"

I was breathless with the idea of the book so close. Before I could answer her, Sonder said, "We'd better get on, if your mama says you're good to go. Daylight's burning. Fish don't wait. You'll have plenty of time to see Doris when we get back."

"Thank you," I finally said. He gave me a gesture as if to tip his hat, had he been wearing one.

With a giggle, Penn handed me a copper kettle she'd pulled from one of the bags. "What's funny about this?"

"What?" I responded.

"Now we have a pot to piss in." She grinned, then bounded after him, and all I could see was the girl I had been when I'd believed in my own magic.

X

Left alone all morning, I found memories surfacing sharply, some of Eleanor's book and what I might find inside its pages.

Knowing the book was waiting, I wanted to see two things out here while I was on my own. Beyond the wide lawn to the back of the house and the victory garden, I made my way past a large freshwater pond. I headed for the barn, navigating muddy ruts, the results of heavy farm equipment.

Sonder's loft was just as Penn had described. The pigeons' cooing was peaceful and I felt my heart calm. There was the sweet, familiar smell of leather and grease from farming equipment. Harnesses still hung from the walls for a team of horses and a mule, now long dead. I stepped around a small tractor, obviously still in use for cutting hay or planting and rotating crops. I did a quick inventory and made note of milled boards, hammers and nails, a gallon of white paint, and a bucket of paintbrushes. This was how Sonder had made his life in my absence, or at least a living. And the way I remembered Daddy. It wasn't so different from the ways and spaces in which I'd spent my own days at Merely's, and yet there was a warmth to this work, the elements of it, the encouragement of a thing to grow, not just function. I looked to the birds above. There was something to the idea that we need to be around life to be alive, maybe even dozens of tiny heartbeats, to keep us company. It was messy and organic. It couldn't be entirely shut up for the night. It required more than the sum of its parts. I hadn't even known I missed it.

On impulse I dragged out an old crab trap. Later, I would clean it up and drop it off the dock. Finally, I found a heavy crowbar to pry up the rotten porch boards, and my thoughts turned to the reasons we'd come back to Evertell. The house was only one of mine. I left the crowbar on the porch for later.

I followed the crushed oyster shell path to the mysterious stone tower just at the edge of the forest, with its solid walls and soaring ceiling: my mama's chandlery. While I had rarely been allowed inside, there had never been a lock on this door. Still, I hesitated, as if I still needed permission.

"I'm coming in now," I said to nothing but empty air and pushed in. I was greeted with silence of the cool air. It still smelled of fire and earth.

At least a century ago, the chandlery had served as a silo that held rice harvests. But rice had ceased to be a cash crop not long after the founding of Evertell, and the building had been abandoned for many years before Mama had seen its potential and claimed it for her own purposes. Daddy had added a small window for light, along with a chimney and a wide hearth, all at my mama's request.

With only the one window, the light was dim. There were tapers still hanging from dowels. The sense that I was trespassing slipped away and I could see that Sonder had kept the room aired and the cobwebs at bay. There was a stack of dry wood and kindling ready for use, but the hearth was clean with no sign of ash from recent use. A quick glance around and I found dozens of raw blocks of wax, forgotten here despite the war rationing, covered in dust.

In my memory this room had always been full of magic while Mama worked out her miseries and joys. On one of the shelves a half dozen of her favorite pillars sat in a row, their sides etched by a special mold. I ran my fingertips over the raised image of tall pines and a distant horizon beyond a wide sea. *Evertell.*

I used a heavy pair of scissors to clip the wick. I found a box of matches and lit it, surprised when the honeyed scent of the wax blanketed the room in comfort. The small flame danced, casting a glow over the stone walls so their craggy surfaces appeared to shift like water.

This was my mother's work. She was an illuminator. She liked to put a shine on everything. What did she want me to see?

I'd listened to her as she read Eleanor's Tale, but I'd never heard the end of that story. Perhaps I had hoped the conclusion would transform me into something more than myself. But I'd never received my Evertell vision as a girl because I had already outgrown whatever simple wisdom my mama had managed to give me. And that transformation had come a different, more inevitable way: I'd grown up without her. And now there was no undoing the past. I'd gone dark too long ago.

No, what I hoped to find in those pages of the book had changed from what I'd been seeking as a girl. I wanted the house, the book, the secret to Eleanor's Evertell light for my own daughter. I wanted to light her way.

The rumble of a car motor nearing the house interrupted the tender glow of the chandlery. With a start, I hurried to blow out the burning wick, taking the pillar with me. Smoothing my hair, I closed the door and stepped into the bright daylight to scurry around the house. The dreamy mood conjured by candlelight dissipated on sight of the homely man who stepped from his automobile.

He wore a sorrowful look on his face and I felt my mood sink with the reality of his visit. He took off his hat, swiped his thin hair back with the other hand, and leaned back to peer at the house as he greeted me. "Alice Merely, I expect?"

"Yes. But my married name's Young."

"Oscar Lewallen," he introduced himself.

I offered my right hand after shifting the candle to my left, and he took it before withdrawing to wipe his palm. I smelled of wood smoke and my fingers were grimy with beeswax, but I offered no explanation, only smiled politely at his tight mouth.

"So glad to meet you. Please, come in. I appreciate you coming out."

"Of course," he said.

I helped him navigate the more solid boards of the porch as his grimace deepened and I pretended nothing was amiss. Inside, he looked askance at the empty hall and I hurried him into the dining room. I'd spread the deed open on the long table and I offered him one of the three chairs. In a matter of minutes I was left with no doubt as to the ownership of the estate.

I let my breath escape in a slow stream. Oscar Lewallen congratulated me with a bit of chagrin. It was a lackluster moment, for he apologized as he handed over the papers.

"I'm afraid most of the assets were liquidated when your daddy bought the service station in Helen, the furnishings and whatnot. Most everything has already gone from the house, as you can see for yourself."

"Bridie Quillian's resale shop?"

"Yes, I suppose that'd be right."

I was looking at the papers, touching Mama's frail signature. Mr. Lewallen looked up at the ceiling as if he expected it would cave in at any moment.

"Now, the good news, Mrs. Young, is that you've arrived in time to pay your property tax for the year," he said.

"Taxes? You're serious? I'd actually like to talk to you about selling."

"Yes?" He seemed surprised at this. "Well, I don't expect this to be a problem. With farms such as yours, the property tax is generally paid out of the harvest profits. That'll need to be settled first before you can sell."

"Okay. When will that happen?" I cleared my throat and looked him straight in the eye, the way I'd been taught to deal with customers at Merely's. Mr. Lewallen seemed a bit surprised. "How much are we talking about? Maybe I could pay them up front. What would you estimate the property is worth now? I've seen reports that people have gotten thirty an acre, maybe more for good farmland," I said, exaggerating a bit.

He paused a moment. "Well, that's hard to say. I'd only be giving you my best guess, you know. In total you have 236 acres, including the marshland, Bell Isle, the working farm, and the forest. Along with the house, there is the millhouse, a barn, and an old silo, not of much use in its current condition. There's also the chapel and the Selectman's cottage. But none of these structures are worth a substantial sum, aside from the mill, you understand, which might be considered a source of income."

"That would go to Sonder," I said. "The mill. That and a few acres, anyway. He lives there. It's his work. And Doris La Roche. I'd need to consider her."

"I guess you'd be keeping Bell Isle, the family cemetery," he said.

I hadn't even thought of it until then. "That's right. I couldn't sell that." I smiled with some effort. "But I want to sell the house and everything else. My daddy sent me to you because he trusted you to give me assistance. Can you help?"

"Well, you'd just put a sign out, post an ad if you like. You don't need anything from me. As I said, the property is yours to do with as you like once those taxes are settled." He hesitated. "But out of respect for your father, I'm going to tell you, at the moment, that's a terrible idea."

Another obstacle. "Why's that?"

"First off, you're a smart woman with eyes in your head. You can see what you have on your hands is hardly in any shape to bring a good price. You're looking at major repairs, just to take care of the obvious. You've got wood rot, and there's evidence of water damage," he said, rolling his eyes up to the stains on the ceiling. "Which means you've got plenty of trouble with your roof. The cracks you see in the plaster there," he said, gesturing with hat in hand at the thin, diagonal line running from the top of the door frame to the molding at the ceiling, "and running through the brick outside—those are signs of trouble with your foundation."

"But surely the money is in the land. Not this." I gestured widely.

"Even if things looked better, Mrs. Young, nobody's selling," he said flatly. "Because nobody's buying. This is wartime. Farmers around here are leaving the fields to go work in the shipyards. Truth is, I'd advise you to wait. Right now you'd get paid more as a welder down at Southeastern, if you had the inclination."

I chuckled at the ridiculous suggestion before I realized he was quite serious. And rude. But I noticed that his suit was shabby and fraying at the edges. It made me want to trust him in spite of his terrible counsel.

"I'm not a greedy woman, Mr. Lewallen, or frivolous or completely without sense. I need the money for school fees." With not a little pride, I explained, "I hope my daughter will be attending Brenau Academy in the fall."

"You changed your mind?" asked a small voice. I looked to find Penn at the door, her expression drawn. I hadn't heard the farm truck arrive, too preoccupied with what Lewallen was saying, but she'd returned from her day with Sonder, hair tussled, face pink from the sun. She looked to the lawyer and back to me, waiting for an answer.

"Mr. Lewallen, this is my daughter, Pennilyn," I said. "Future scholar." My voice took on an enthusiasm that made the man uncomfortable. He ran a hand over his jaw. "We knew what we were getting into when we came here. We'll take what we can get. I thank you for everything."

He shrugged. His jacket was far too large through the shoulders.

"Does he know where the rest of the stuff is?" Penn asked quietly. "Did you ask?"

Lewallen looked as ready to go as I was for him to leave. He didn't understand Penn's question, or didn't feel it was his place to offer an answer. Instead, he stuck out his hand to me and I shook it. "It's a beautiful farm you've got here, Mrs. Young. Beautiful home for a family," he said, his tone full of regret. "The rest of us should be so lucky. I remember some nice times here. Beautiful dinners. Some lovely mornings when the bells from the chapel would ring after harvest, people would come have a meal together, a homecoming. Haven't seen such as that in a long while now, since this house has been empty. Don't expect I'll see it again."

I handed Mr. Lewallen his hat to send him on his meddling way.

"That's not true. We're home now. You could come have dinner with us," Penn said. "Sonder can come too. We have a lot of room here."

He looked stunned. He glanced at me. There was no graceful way to refuse, for either of us. Penn looked at me with a guileless expression, but I understood this was how she would punish me for keeping a secret. She'd inflict company on me. I thought of the birds in the barn, the heartbeats, the need for life to be alive. I thought Doris deserved to have a seat at this table too. So I nodded.

"Sunday dinner then? For old times," I said meekly. "A nice way to thank you for making us so welcome, and a fond farewell, I guess."

"Absolutely," he mumbled. "Thank you."

When he'd gone, Penn looked at me from the corner of her eye. She'd expected me to object.

"You're right, I don't like it. But it was thoughtful. Imagine would be proud of you," I added.

I could see the old shadow had fallen across her expression.

"I'm sorry if it's a shock about the school. I wanted to surprise you. I thought I should wait to say anything. Give you a little time to see this place. And Pop hasn't been gone that long. I thought it might feel wrong to be in a rush for something new and good. And to be honest, I didn't want to say anything until I knew for sure we'd have the money, which we still don't. But you should know I dropped the application packet in the mail before we left. So we'll just have to wait and see. I used your old essay, but I polished it up. I think it's real good. Are you too upset with me?"

"No," she said quietly. "It's okay."

It was not okay. I could see that.

"But it's going to be good news, I know it. Pop would be happy about this, for you. And I love giving this to you. It's the perfect way to pass on Evertell's legacy." I was talking too fast, forcing things. I took a breath. I had to give her time. "Honestly, there's a lot of work to keep us busy while we're here, so we don't have time to even worry over hearing back from the school. But look, I'm glad you know. I'm relieved. I don't like keeping something from you. And we can talk about everything now. Imegine knows I put in the application, and she said I should have talked to you first."

"Grandma Imegine knows?"

"She wants what you want, Penn. We both do."

She was quiet. I knew the news had overwhelmed her. After three years of no, here was her yes. But when she looked at me, she seemed so much less excited than resolved and my heart fell a little.

She said, "I want to go see the book, like we said. That's what I want right now."

With one hand, I reached for hers. In my other, I was still holding my mama's candle. Now I had an idea what to do with it.

"Okay. And we'll take a little something for Doris. You can ask her to dinner too. Why not?"

Chapter Five

Bell Isle, the small island directly across from the main house, sat in the middle of the river. The white bell tower of the Evertell chapel was easily seen in the thick green vegetation, and I kept my eye on it as Penn and I crossed in the bateau. With the river less than a mile wide and only two miles long, it was a short ride from the dock at Evertell. But my exhausted arms reminded me how long it had been since I pulled an oar through the water.

Penn talked of her morning with Sonder, of a great blue heron on the wing, the shining perch she'd caught with his fishing rod and how she'd carried them back on a string.

Her reflection played in the background of my thoughts right up until we reached Doris La Roche's front door.

"You look just like your grandmother," Doris said. She held the screen door to her little cottage open to us. She wore the same simple cotton housedress she'd been in when I met her at the store, and her socks slid down uneven and loose around skinny ankles. I wondered when she'd last changed into fresh clothes.

"You think so?" Penn asked, obviously thrilled by the friendly observation.

Doris turned and walked inside. Over her shoulder, she answered, "I was talking to your mama, little one."

Penn pulled up short and shot me a glance. She seemed even more pleased, if possible. She whispered, "You look like Grandmama Claire's mama?"

I shook my head. Doris La Roche's opinions on family resemblance meant nothing, but I was already trying to call to mind the austere portrait of my grandmother, Calista, that had once hung in the library. She'd died of tuberculosis, an old woman under the stars in the cupola, trying to catch her breath. I could still hear her coughing in the night, naming her constellations, when I thought about it. When she died, my mama grieved herself sick and that had been her first serious treatment. Doctors sent her for a week at Central State Hospital, hours away from Evertell. This was before Sonder came to us, when I'd spent days on my own in the lonely house. I remembered the fear that my mama wouldn't come home at all, that she would die too.

"Come on and let me get you something to drink," Doris said, bringing me back to the moment.

Doris's house was pleasant enough, a small tabby structure to match the oldest parts of Evertell, but without the pretty seashell patterns. It sat in deep shade beneath a canopy of oaks, surrounded by tall banana and palmetto trees that made the air cooler by several degrees. Situated adjacent to the cottage was the chapel, as empty as the main house, and beyond it, a wide sloping lawn where we could see the shapes of headstones.

The windows inside Doris's living room let in a warm light. But there were old newspapers and magazines piled on the floor and across every surface. Dirty dishes were stacked on a small table near a chair that had been draped in a thin blanket where it appeared Doris spent most of her time. It felt lonely, as was the nature of the small island, and I wondered what made a person choose to live on such an isolated spit of land with no one but the dead for company. She most certainly wasn't taking her own advice. If anyone could have used a pet, it was Doris La Roche.

We followed Doris into the kitchen where she rummaged through a pantry and came up with nothing but a little bread and butter. She pulled a can of loose tea from the cupboard. I moved to put a little water in a kettle on her stovetop. She wasn't doing much better than we were in the hospitality department. She gestured rather apologetically, and Penn and I both took a seat at the table.

"Don't think it's a luxury," she said, noticing my concerned expression. "No telling how long that tea's been there. I'm a thrifty woman. Not much call for tea when there's no visitors."

"I could come by," Penn said.

"Could you, now?" Doris dropped into the chair adjacent from us.

I spoke up. "I wanted to say thank you for sending those things to the house."

"Come to stay, I hope. Be good to have you for neighbors."

"That's nice of you to say, but I'm afraid we'll only be here long enough to get the place in shape to sell."

"Sell Evertell?" She seemed abashed. "But your girl don't want it?"

I put a hand on Penn's shoulder. "Not Bell Isle, of course. I couldn't do that. But the rest will be parceled out. I'm hoping to find one buyer, to keep things simple and quick. I don't know. You've seen the house. Either way, Penn's inheritance will go in a trust," I explained. "She wants to see the world, don't you, Penn? We have high hopes she'll be attending a very fine girl's boarding school this fall." I looked at Penn, careful to add, "If she wants."

"Well, that's not the same thing, is it? Money in the bank? Never been anybody at Evertell but your family," Doris said. "It'll sure take time for folks to get used to change like that."

"I think folks will manage," I said dryly. "Anyway, I guess it won't be too hard to get used to since we haven't been anywhere near here for two decades. It might be harder to get used to *us*. But I wanted to assure you that your situation on the island will remain as it's always been. If you'd like to stay, that is."

"Oh, that's fixed." She flipped her hand at me. "Your mama let me have this house as long as I can stay in it. That was what was worked out after my George died. If you'd come here to fight over it, I guess I could take you to court. Glad I won't."

Taken a bit aback, I only smiled. It was her home, after all. Maybe I'd only just learned the place and these people were still here, but she'd lived a lifetime in those years.

Our cups were dusty and the tea was bitter, and indeed stale, but I was proud of Penn, watching her take small, polite sips. "What are you baking? It smells like cinnamon," she asked, sniffing the air.

"It's in the walls. That old oven's not seen use in years. Who would I cook for over here when there's nobody at this table? Too much trouble."

"We came to invite you to dinner," Penn said. "Like old times. When neighbors used to sit around the table at Evertell."

Doris frowned, an odd tension in the room, and abruptly stood from her chair with some effort. She shut an open cabinet door but then seemed directionless. She chewed on her tongue and I searched my mind for something pleasant to say to fill the awkward silence. In the front window, a candle burned. Doris noticed it had grabbed my attention. "Oh, you'll recognize that," she said.

"That candle. One of your mama's. I like to keep one burning. I started it after my son died. But you know about that. The accident at the still?" I shook my head. "My boy Jacob was killed in that explosion."

"I'm sorry. Daddy and I must have already been gone." But I did recognize the candle. I pulled the engraved wax pillar from my bag and set it on the table next to the misshapen candle, so close to guttering out. "I didn't know, but I was going through some things this morning and found this. I thought it would make a small thanks for everything you sent over to us."

"Well, what about that? There's nothing nicer than this."

Penn looked on, curious, and Doris seemed genuinely pleased.

"Why don't you two come take a little walk with me, if you've got the time? I'll show you something." She held out a hand to Penn and led us outside.

"Are we going to see the chapel?"

"Well, sure. And you can come by and see that anytime. It's your family chapel, honey. I'm glad to hear you won't be selling that."

I ignored the remark.

Penn thought about this, then said, "Sonder said the book was there. Can we take it with us, or does it have to stay in the chapel?"

"The book, huh? That's what you want?" Doris looked at me. "Belongs to your mama. She can decide where it goes. Sonder brought it over not long after y'all left and it's been there ever since. That little chapel holds a lot of memories, I guess."

I was holding my nerves at bay with the book so close at hand. Nothing was going to stop me opening its pages. My insides churned. It took every bit of my will to follow this old woman instead of darting across to bust into the chapel and get it over with.

The tea must have given our neighbor a kick in the pants because she looked more focused. We followed her across her back lawn toward a shed near the tree line. She pushed the door open, and we blinked in the shadows of the cool interior room where she reached for something on a tall shelf on the back wall. I recognized the scent: a block of beeswax. My fingers wrapped around the cool, smooth, solid weight of a bar and I brought it close to my face to inhale the sweet scent. My emotions were too close to the surface. My eyes burned, trying to start tears. "I remember this," I said.

"Nothing like a familiar smell to bring a memory washing over you. The beeswax always brings your mama back to me. Never alone out here so long as I'm burning one of her candles."

"You gave her the wax, didn't you?"

"That's so." She reached to take a jar down from the same shelf and gave it to Penn, showing her how to hold it up to the light so it was illuminated.

"Honey!" Penn smiled, holding up her jar like a prize.

Doris laughed, a strangled sort of sound. "Put some on a piece of cake. That's my favorite."

I watched as Penn turned the jar this way and that and the honey oozed slowly from one side to the other. Doris was watching her too.

"I heard about your daddy, and now your granddaddy. That's a lot of people to lose. I'm sorry about that," Doris said to Penn and then turned to me. "It's hard when the people we love pass. Although I may think a little different than most people do when it comes to the dead, living with them so close here. I talk to George and Jacob on the daily. It's probably a good thing nobody's out here but me or they'd think I was off my rocker."

I could see that Penn was enthralled. "I'd be nervous, living by a graveyard."

Doris smiled. "You ought not be nervous of a grave. They're peaceful places. I spent most of my life dealing with the beginnings of life, but living out here's made me comfortable with the endings too. Jacob's down there, not far from your granny Claire."

She pointed toward the cemetery where we could see the stones, then she gripped my hand tightly, surprising me. She looked to me and her eyes were moist. "It was a turpentine still. Whole thing blew sky high. Nobody knew my boy was out there at first. But Sonder found him."

"I'm glad he found him," Penn said, as somber as I'd ever seen her. Doris reached and squeezed her hand softly. "Sonder took me fishing this morning."

"Oh yes. Jacob was always trailing after Sonder, too, pestering him. He wanted to learn Sonder's tricks."

"What kind of tricks?"

"He's a diviner, you know."

Penn lit up, immediately interested. "Like with those little sticks? He finds things?"

Doris nodded, then continued her story. "He came out here to tell me about the accident. Came walking up my yard and I knew it before he even said it out loud. Knew Jacob was gone. He'd expected to find Sonder divining a new well at the still. But Sonder hadn't made it out there yet, I guess. He wasn't looking for a little boy. Just the good Lord's timing. But it might as well have killed Sonder too. Killed us all some way or another. But it was nothing but an accident," Doris explained. "And it's been years now. My husband's there, alongside Jacob. It's my only comfort. I know he was waiting for Jacob, so they're not alone."

"That's a nice way to think about it," I said to Doris. I glanced at Penn's face beneath my lashes, to see if she was okay. Doris mistook my pained expression.

"Oh, don't feel bad asking me. I don't get much excuse for talking about Jacob or George. I don't mind it."

Penn's face was pensive. I tried to change the subject. "George was a Selectman for the chapel, you said?"

"What's that? A Selectman?" Penn asked.

Doris smiled. Her pride in her husband was obvious. "He managed the chapel when they used to hold meetings. There were meetings here since they built the chapel for a wedding for one of the Evertell girls, in 1818, I believe. I'd have to check to remember her name. George took care of the family records, the grounds, and the bell. A Revere bell, you know. You could hear it all down the creek. George was awful proud of it. They put a stop to that after you all left. Not heard it ring in a long while now. That was old times," she said to Penn. "I guess this is new times."

"I'd like to hear it," Penn said. "Just to see how it sounds. We could ring it before our dinner."

"Penn, it's not a dinner gong," I said, making a rather lame attempt at humor to dismiss her request. I had no interest in hearing that bell again.

Doris didn't appreciate it. She shook her head. "Baby, lots of folks would like to hear it again, but it won't ring. Hasn't since that last homecoming."

"Mr. Lewallen said he remembered that, a homecoming."

"Oscar Lewallen told you?"

Her tone was sharp and made me uneasy. I muttered an explanation, although I wasn't sure why I owed her one. "He was at the house this morning to talk to me about arranging the sale."

She looked to Penn. "If you want to know about homecomings or any little thing about Evertell, you ask me. I've lived here a long time. I've seen what comes and goes around here."

"Mama never tells me anything."

"Penn, I think we're wearing out our welcome. We didn't come here to put you out, Mrs. La Roche. We just wanted to drop by on our way to the chapel to see about the book."

Doris looked to me then with a puzzled expression. Her mouth drew into a thin line. "Well, there's nothing to hide about any of it. Used to, every year there'd be a big day for a harvest when folks from all over would come back to Evertell. The work would be done and when the sun rose the next morning, they'd ring the bell, ring in a new season. George would ring it. He rang the bell for any occasion here, like a wedding or a funeral, a baby being born, Easters and Christmastime. The bell was always something we looked forward to hearing. But homecomings are what I remember most. That big lawn under the trees over at the house, full of people, if you can imagine it."

"I think I can imagine," Penn said. "Who came? Who were they?"

"The family, everybody around here. People who worked here or lived here over the years. Cousins, they were called, even though they weren't all blood relatives. Probably a hundred showed up that last time. Alice, you remember? They'd have a big dinner and some music and it was good times. People miss such as that. But there's been two wars since then. No telling when this one will finally end, but soon enough, I hope. A lot's changed."

"What if we could fix it so we can ring it?" Penn suggested. "I have my daddy's tools."

"You think I could climb up in that tower?" Doris snorted. "I'm afraid we're both duds now, me and that old bell. That thing lost its inside parts, what hits the dome and makes the chime. No good without it."

"Penn," I said, shaking my head. I looked to Doris and made excuses. "She grew up in a service station. She thinks she can fix anything."

"What? I could do it," Penn said, suddenly stubborn.

I looked at her, annoyed, then interested to see her digging in her heels over something, anything. "Why are you so interested in an old bell? I think we're going to have plenty to work on around here without adding that to the list."

Doris took my side in this, at least. "Nobody but Sonder and the bats goes up there now to mess with it. He just sees it don't come crashing down out of the rafters."

"What happened to the inside parts?"

"Your pop had Bill Hawkes disassemble the thing after he and your mama left here. Bill took a hacksaw up in there. It's a big, heavy thing, and he had to cut it up in two pieces to get it down. First, he cut the end off, that big ball, but if a wind got up, the arm that was still hanging would clang around something awful. So he came back and cut that out too. It knocked a big place in the floor when it fell. You can still see that. I guess it's probably still leaned up back of the chapel, or maybe Sonder's put it someplace. Bill's got the round piece sitting up on his counter down at the store, if you want to have a look. Your mama's seen it."

I scowled, remembering the hunk of iron.

Penn furrowed her brow. Her chest rose and fell and I could see her mind working the problem. She'd heard something in the story of the homecomings and the bell that had her attention. Maybe because after Finch's death, Penn had gone quiet inside just like that bell. It wasn't hard to see why she would identify with it. She looked toward the chapel and said, "Pop stopped it because Grandmama Claire died?"

"It was a long time ago," I said, before Doris could volunteer anything further. "We can talk about this later." I wasn't willing to let anybody else tell this part of the story. "Come on. The sun's

THE LOST BOOK OF ELEANOR DARE

going to go down on us in a few hours. If you want to see the chapel, we'd better get on before we lose the light."

We walked back to the front steps of Doris's house and I thanked her again.

"Go see about that book and step around the side and visit your people," she said, her tone softer than before, speaking of the dead. "I need to get back there and clean off the headstones, but it's a nice, peaceful little spot. And don't worry. Your daddy will find his way straight to her on that far shore. No doubt about it."

"Thank you," I murmured, struck by the words after hearing Imagine wonder the same thing. To me, the sentiment seemed to leave Imagine so alone.

"And you come back and see me," she said to Penn. "We don't need any bell to have our own little homecoming. Might do me good to talk to somebody besides myself."

⋊⋉

The thick tropical vegetation of Bell Isle seemed to breathe around us as we walked the short path from the Selectman's house to the Evertell chapel, a sweet little structure that matched Doris's cottage. Weekly church services had stopped before I was born, the congregation preferring to worship in Savannah, but I knew that a congregation had met here for at least a century—the main family, but also neighbors and those who worked for the estate, including slaves. Before the Emancipation, the slaves sat in a high, hot balcony. It was likely stifling up there today. Later, the chapel had still served Evertell as a community house for celebrations and gatherings. I'd only ever been inside when it was empty and I had climbed over the pews. Now, high above, the bell hung silent. And my mama's book reportedly lay in wait for us just inside.

Penn gave me no chance to change my mind. She pushed the door open. Without the slightest hesitation, she marched up the aisle toward the podium. I took a few cautious steps inside. The space was hushed and smelled of old paper from the hymnals that sat in the racks on the backs of the pews.

"It's here," Penn said, her voice ringing out in the eaves. "Sonder was right. I think this is it. It looks really old. I don't know, but, Mama, come see."

But I knew. I knew. "It's Eleanor's book," I said, my throat gone dry. "A commonplace book."

I stepped up beside her to stare at the heavy old book that was bound in dark leather. I recognized it immediately. I put a hand on the podium to steady myself. The tool work of some long-ago engraver decorated every inch of the cover, front and back, with curling vines and lush leaves that crowded and stood out from the leather so they seemed almost real. Astounded, I said, "It's here. I guess it's been right here the whole time."

"I knew it," Penn said, thrilled. "Mama, we found it! Or maybe it found us," she whispered.

"I can't believe it."

She lifted the cover and the pages crackled.

"Careful," I urged. The pages were yellowed with age and damp.

Penn's lips moved as she began reading silently, flipping through the entries that seemed to have no clear progression. But I was looking at the faded blue velvet ribbon that marked a page deep inside the book, marking a story Penn knew nothing about.

"Look, there are words I can't read," she said. "It's a whole different language, I think. Maybe French or Italian." She tried to sound them out and the strange words felt like an incantation. I felt a chill. "But look. Somebody else wrote it in English."

"Wait. Let me see," I said, unable to keep the edge out of my voice. I leaned in to read the translation: *Tomasyn Cooper's Fish Stew.*

I laughed at myself. "Yes, an old recipe."

"What did you think it would be?" Penn asked, suspicious.

"Nothing," I said, dismissing her curiosity. "I'm just excited, like you. See, it looks like Tomasyn Cooper put it in the book and later someone else translated it. The later ones wouldn't have known how to read Old Norse, so it must have been one of the first descendants. Tomasyn was Eleanor's mother. She was from the islands," I said, starting to relax a little. It was only a book. Something I could hold in my hands. Pages I could choose to turn, or not. "The Old World, they called it. That's the only thing my mama ever said. I think it's all we ever knew. She said the women who came from there had hair that smelled of evergreen."

"How old is it, really? Can you guess?" Penn asked. I could see her trying to work it out.

"Maybe around four hundred years." My voice quivered.

We were both fairly overcome with the thought. "How does it still exist?"

"It has been treasured. Love makes things last."

That was another impossible thing Mama had told me, but to find the book lying here on the simple podium in the chapel seemed its own kind of miracle. It felt sacred that Penn and I could lay eyes on the words and images put there so long ago, and yet it was as if they'd been thinking of us when they'd recorded them, just as we now thought of them.

"It's like a journal," Penn said, reading from the front page. "'The Book of Eleanor Dare.'" She continued to flip carefully through the pages, turning them with reverence. My heart hammered and I reached to stop her from going further.

"Look here," I said, carefully opening the book to the final page, to the list of names with birth and death dates beside them. Penn ran her fingertip down them until she came to the last name, my mama's name. "There's Grandmama Claire."

We gazed at the names of the women who had come before us and I had the strange sensation that the descendants gazed back, waiting to see what we would do.

"I feel like it could fall apart." Penn lingered only a minute more before gingerly closing the book. "Let's wait. We'll take it with us. So we can look at it all." She surprised me and hesitated to pick it up. "You carry it."

"Mm," I said. "All right. We'll be careful."

The truth was, I wanted to know the secrets of that book as badly as Penn. I wanted to open to Eleanor's story and run my eyes over the beautiful blue swirling penmanship inscribed there in my mama's indigo ink. But I wanted that moment for myself. It was private, the last word between us.

Penn's attention was drawn toward a narrow door. It gave a squeak when she opened it, the only reason I looked up from the beautiful leather cover, and I saw her peering inside a small closet. Built into the wall was a ladder, presumably leading up to the bell tower. She looked back with a question in her eyes, her face lit with excitement.

"No, not that," I said, shaking my head. "You heard what Doris said. It's not safe."

She scowled and groaned and peered up into the dark opening. She reached her toe inside to scrub at the floor. "It's there, like she said. A big chunk in the floor is knocked out, where the part from inside the bell fell down. But I don't see the piece anywhere. I can't tell if it's in there." She continued to lean in, her eyes searching the dark corners for any sign of the heavy arm.

"That's too bad," I said. "Are you sure?" But I was grateful she was distracted. My heart pounded as I fingered the frayed edge of the blue ribbon at the heart of the book. A ribbon I remembered. My mama had put it there to mark the pages where she'd written Eleanor's Tale.

"Time to go," I said. "I think we've got what we need."

※

For the remainder of the afternoon, I hugged the book to my chest as if I were cradling an infant and I brooded over the conflict inside me. Beyond the chapel, an overgrown lawn stretched down to the banks of the water. The spreading arms of the giant trees shaded the gravestones and overhead, gray moss swayed softly. I'd never imagined my mama at rest in this kind of stillness. She had always been such a force, tearing around in my imagination. But the headstone that marked her grave was small and tilted at an angle as though it had been there a hundred years. Penn found it, brushing aside the grasses so we could read the letters of her name.

"Why isn't Pop buried here?" Penn asked.

I blinked hard in the sun. Another choice about Evertell that Daddy had left to me. "Grandma Imegine should have him nearby. He's at home there."

It shouldn't have made me sad to stand over a grave he'd never visited and question my decision.

"Are you crying?" Penn had every right to be stunned at the idea. I never cried in front of her, if I cried at all.

"A little."

"I think you should cry a lot. I can't believe you had to live at Merely's when all this was here. Does it make you miss her?" Penn asked gently.

"Imegine?"

"No, your mama."

"It makes me miss a lot of things. But I've never really thought about Mama being here, I guess. I've never seen her grave until now. I was sick when they had the funeral and Pop didn't think it would be good for me to go. And after we left, he didn't want to come back."

"Did you want to come back?"

I nodded. "Maybe. Sometimes. But we lived in Helen and it was where I married your daddy and where you were born. It's home now."

Penn moved through the other stones, reading the names and dates aloud. As I watched her wandering through the crumbling stones, some of them so worn she couldn't make out the inscriptions, I realized Doris was right about selling and taking Penn away from Evertell. We would be the first to break a very long chain.

"Look at them all," Penn said. "Right here, together." She stepped carefully.

"They lived and they died," I said gently. "They were women just like us. And we can come here to respect that. Even be grateful for them." Penn frowned. "Evertell is a gift that will give you a future these women would want for you."

"What if I decided what I wanted was right here?" She stood with one hand atop a headstone, the other shielding her eyes against the sun as she looked up at the bell tower.

It wasn't unexpected that she would consider the option. If I felt alarm at the thought, it was a feeling I squelched, knowing she changed her mind a thousand times a day. "Well, I won't sell Bell Isle. It's the family chapel. I couldn't do that. So technically, if that's what you want, I guess you can come back one day when you're grown, same as we're doing now. When you're independent. Move into the Selectman's cottage and ring that bell day and night," I teased.

"But Evertell won't be here. Not like this."

"I don't know," I said carefully. "But we have a home. We have Imegine. This place, it's like a ghost for me, Penn. It was gone a long time ago."

Penn was quiet, and we looked over the headstones. The cicadas buzzed their sawing song and the water of the tidal creeks glistened between the island and the mainland. "I'm glad you won't sell Bell Isle. I can feel them all here."

I lifted my chin, my eyes stinging from the tears that came so easily here. "What do you mean, feel them?"

"I mean, it's like they're here. Or not here, exactly, but their feelings. It's like they're a cloud of all sorts of secrets and they're whispering to me but I can't hear them, really. It just makes me dizzy, buzzy. Tired. A good tired. Like when I was little and you'd put me in my bed for a nap with the fan running."

Comfort. That's what she was experiencing. The last thing I was feeling. The book grew heavy in my arms. Penn seemed to sense this too.

"I'll come back to see Doris while we're here, but I want to go back to the house now. I want to look at the book," she said, as if reading my thoughts. The tide was turning.

꙳

In the boat, Penn asked to take my place at the oars and I allowed it. I looked back to see the chapel, cast in a golden light. I kept my arms wrapped around the commonplace book. As Penn pulled hard on the oars, my thoughts settled into a rhythm, the distant memory that had arisen in the chapel. I heard myself whispering the nursery rhyme of descendants' names, the way I'd learned them, as my mama taught me. They sounded like an incantation. *"Eleanor Dare, Agnes Marquez, Catarina Abreu, Marguerite Abreu, Francoise Abreu, Esmé Laurens, Garnet Lee Rutledge . . ."*

Penn was listening, mesmerized. I went on, but stopped short of my own name or Penn's, and instead finished with the singsong chant.

"Look there, so fair, the Evertell heirs of Eleanor Dare."

"Oh my gosh," Penn gushed. She was soaking up every little detail. "Did you just make that up?"

"Grandmama Claire taught me that." There was more to it, thanks to Charlie Hawkes, who had added cruel lines, taunting words he'd used to tease me. But I didn't say those to Penn. This was where Eleanor's story met my own.

"Doris was right. You remember the homecomings, don't you? You remember when Pop stopped the bell ringing."

"I remember," I heard myself say. The history was long and murky in my memory, but I remembered that. "It was a home-coming. But that day, I was the reason they rang the bell. Me and Grandmama Claire." My heart slammed hard against my breast-bone and I took a long, careful pause to be sure my words were in order.

"Everybody was there, like they were every year. They all came after the harvest. But Grandmama Claire and I were missing. We'd spent two days in the forest behind the house. Everybody was in a panic to find us. We'd got separated and Grandmama Claire found her way back before I did. Sonder found me. He brought me home and they rang the bell. It was how they announced we were safe so all the other searchers could come in. After that, it never rang again."

"I thought you said Evertell heirs can't get lost?"

"We weren't lost. We knew the way there and back. She knew where she was taking me. She was looking for the stone. But it had been stolen."

In the weeks following my thirteenth birthday, Mama and I had recited the names of the descendants. "Just say them with me, Alice. Say them now," she'd pleaded. "Mother then daughter."

I'd spoken each name like a bead in a rosary, with passion and something else: hope. Sometime in the weeks before my birthday, I heard her whispering them as she walked past me in the hall, as if pleading on my behalf, and on occasion, even at the dinner table when we bowed our heads for grace. Later, when she took me deep into the forest, she talked of the Evertell vision that came to each of Eleanor's descendants, the secret I hoped would be revealed in the final pages of Eleanor's Tale, which she'd refused to finish telling me. She was playing a game. I was meant to guess, to somehow know how she meant for the tale to end. I would close my eyes and wait and watch to see when the vision would come to me, when I would finally know the secret to the Evertell, the silvery light that was supposed to be inside of me. I longed to write my name beneath the other heirs, those enlightened girls.

"You could just tell me how it ends," I would plead when no vision came. "What's the secret? Tell me and then I'll know. Then I'll see it."

But she never did. She believed in me. Even when time seemed short, she'd trusted I was an Evertell heir.

"Mama, are you okay?" Penn asked, watching me.

"I'm just out of breath," I lied. "That's all." I tried to shake myself out of the memory, even as I heard the names in my head. "And I'm hungry. Are you hungry? We can drop a crab trap off the dock and later we'll boil them for dinner. How does that sound?"

"You know how to catch crabs?" Penn laughed. "You're

different here. Everything's different here. We're the Evertell heirs of Eleanor Dare," she called over the water, then said, "Thank you for bringing me, Mama."

I knew as we pulled up on the far shore, as I always should have known, that I was no different from my mama or maybe any of the descendants who had come before us. All the mothers who had written their names in that book. Women who had only been doing everything they could to keep from disappearing, to keep from breaking the hearts of their daughters.

We dropped the crab trap and later we ate. I put Penn off from reading, sending her to replace the trap and catch fireflies, and then she waited for me in my mama's old bed long enough that she had fallen asleep after a day of discoveries and sun off the water. Finally, I took the book and sat at the writing desk. I would share the book with Penn in the morning. It was hers now, after all.

And just as I'd done for more than twenty years, I followed that well-known path in my mind as I began to tell myself the story of that night in the woods all over again.

))(

My mama walked ahead, always, holding my hand, leading me. I couldn't see where we were going, although I knew the feel of the lawn beneath my feet. I could tell when we stepped onto the rough path that led into the forest of white pine and underbrush, nettles and saw palmetto that scratched and stung. I didn't argue with her. She was excited, making a soft panting sound as we went. I knew she was completely out of her mind that day. She wouldn't stop coming after me with the plan to slip off on a quest for my Evertell vision. Mine was late, she said. So late. But she knew the secret. "You'll see."

She had a little gunnysack full of who knew what. I guessed herbs, maybe a few cigarettes, not the commonplace book. It was too big and heavy to fit. Whatever she carried with us, it was important that it worked, for her sake as much as mine. I was like any desperate daughter who knew she was not living up to her mother's expectations. I had a secret of my own, one that would change everything. I knew exactly what we would see when we came to the place where the stone once stood in the gloom. I'd given up my vision to save her. She would understand what it had cost me. She would throw her arms around me and know how much I loved her. Later, when people tried to figure out what made me follow her into the forest that day, I swore I would have followed her right out of this life.

"Come with me," she said. "I'll tell you. I'll tell you the secret to Evertell."

⋊⋉

In the cool quiet of that first room, I found the edge of the blue velvet ribbon and ran it through my fingertips, soft and smooth. My hands trembled as I opened to the page it marked at the heart of the book, the place where the story ended. But it was easy now. Whatever my mama's story had to say to me, I was a woman, not a girl. I was ready to hear it. I was ready to see.

But as my eyes drifted over the final page of Eleanor's Tale, I felt all my hopes dissolve. My mama's beautiful handwriting offered no conclusions. What I found instead, shockingly, was the beginning of another story, Eleanor's daughter's story. *Agnes.* And while it might have been a thrilling discovery for some, I could only stare at it. Only a few scant sentences, not even a paragraph. Incomplete. Mama's scrolling penmanship curling like the blue ribbon across the page.

Agnes

Agnes Lavat was a walking miracle, or at least that's what people said. She never believed it herself.

The sickness of 1607 came in the autumn with word that

I turned the page to find it blank, flipping carefully and then furiously through until I came to the list of the descendants, every page coming up empty. Unwritten. Silent. I hurried back to the blue ribbon, searching for signs of the rest of the story, of Agnes's fate, and stared at the smooth, unmarked paper until I realized I was already looking at the place where it should have been, a ragged edge at the book's heart. Pages had been removed. Ripped out in a hurry. I felt myself suspended in a kind of nightmare. For a long while I ran a fingertip over the uneven paper, whisper thin, like the edge of a feather, a broken promise. My mama's final words, stolen from me.

In my mind I heard the accusation of my conscience that I'd always heard when there was no end to the story: *What did you think you deserved? Who are you?*

There was no ending. There was no answer. There was no secret to Evertell to help me at the edge of the known world. Nothing here to pass on to my daughter to light her way, assure her of her place, teach her how to love even when it would cost everything.

I sat at the writing desk through the night in a kind of fugue state, so like the one I'd seen overtake Penn of late. I heard Sonder's steps as he left the house while Penn slept on upstairs. When morning came, she would have more questions about our family, the house, me. I would answer them best I could, as I'd always done. There would be work for us, plans to be made, a dinner to make. We could navigate all of that together. She would ask to open this book, search it for treasures, and what she would find in its poems and cures and prayers, its recipes for fish stew and how to grow roses and the names of all the women who came before us, would unfold in a glorious legacy before her. *"Look there, so fair, the Evertell heirs of Eleanor Dare."* That, I could give to her. A list of mysterious and magnificent names of women who had ventured forth into their own wilderness. That was the vision I'd hoped for her, wasn't it? What any mother would hope for her daughter.

But not this abandonment.

As the dawn broke, I followed the only example I had. I carefully tore out the remaining pages of Eleanor's Tale from the book, one by one. I tied them with the blue ribbon and locked the unfinished story away in my mother's desk.

Chapter Six

Penn

The book was theirs now. *The Book of Eleanor Dare*. The pages had opened straightaway to the entry marked by the blue ribbon and immediately, unbelievably, to a charm.

Charm for the Evertell
    Bitter tea
    Sweet balm
    Guide by your mother's light

"This is it, isn't it?" Penn asked, thrilled. These were the things the heirs needed for a vision. Girls just like her. Evertell heirs. "This is Grandmama Claire's charm?"

The words were written in the most beautiful looping, swirling penmanship in blue ink. But Penn couldn't imagine what they might mean. She looked to her mama.

"What?" Mama looked up at Penn and blinked blandly. Her

voice sounded hollow, as if she was barely aware she was speaking. She was touching the edge of the page where the ink had soaked deep, leaving an indigo stain where the charm had been hastily scrawled. "I missed this. I never saw it."

"You never saw the charm?"

Mama waved a hand to dismiss the book. "Oh, Penn. Don't think this is magic. That's not what this book is. This is just another recipe, like all the rest. A little game for children, that's what this charm is. Or was. We're both too old for that, don't you think? You see what we can use in there for our dinner. Plan something nice. Whatever makes you happy."

Penn liked the idea of using the charm for their dinner, something an Evertell heir would have done for her guests in this house. But she wasn't giving up on the idea that there was a secret message for her in the charm, one that would help her understand more about what it meant to be an Evertell heir, a Dare descendant, a girl who dreamed again. Since they'd come to Evertell, everything seemed like a piece to a puzzle that she was putting together, and she felt that she'd just found another. She'd dreamed about the bell. Penn said, "I'm going to ask Sonder to help me fix the bell. Maybe he has the part that fell off. And that man at the store would give you the piece he has if you asked, don't you think? If you were nice."

"If you want to ask, that's fine."

Mama looked as if all the air had been let out of her. That troubled Penn. Mama's hands shook as Penn watched her tenderly smooth the blue velvet ribbon. Even if Mama thought she was hiding her tears, Penn knew she was crying. She didn't want Penn to see. She'd never wanted Penn to see, and that made it seem like Mama's feelings were all Penn ever saw. When she closed the book and put it into Penn's arms, something about the way she did it felt so final, as if she was done with it. Maybe done with part of Penn.

She was giving up. Penn felt alarmed deep inside. Mama kissed the top of her head just like she used to do when putting her to bed.

"I'm going to have my bath," she said.

Penn knew better than to follow her. She felt a terrible loneliness in the empty room after Mama left. She settled herself on the bed and buried her nose in the musty pages of the book, reading aloud at times from weather reports, sappy sonnets, cures for colic. A fragile paper pasted into the book reported the hanging of a woman in 1702, on the island of Barbados, Sunbury Plantation. Penn shivered when she saw it and hurried to turn another page. When she worked her way backward, she found a scribbled entry noting only dates and names: *Catarina Marquez Abreu, Marguerite Abreu of St. Augustine. Stolen away by Robert Seale, pirate. Sold.*

Penn marveled at discovering such things. It hardly seemed any of it could be real.

But there was nothing else about the charm. She imagined all the Dare descendants before her, coming to the book for help and comfort, just as she was doing. When she arrived again at the page marked with the blue ribbon, Penn fingered the frayed edges where pages had been ripped out of the book, but her eyes wandered back to the scrolling penmanship: *Charm for the Evertell.*

Penn's heart leapt each time she read it. She felt her head swim with determination to figure out the riddle. *Tell me what to do*, she thought. *Show me what comes next.*

> Bitter tea
> Sweet balm
> Guide by your mother's light

She tried to imagine where she would get these ingredients and then what she would need to do with them. But there was no one to

THE LOST BOOK OF ELEANOR DARE

ask. Yesterday Mama had been hoping to see the book again, but something had changed. Penn couldn't understand what. She tried to think like a woman, because Mama had said this was a woman's book, full of women's wisdom and mysteries.

It was late morning by the time Mama came back and crawled beneath the blankets, something Penn had never seen her mother do. Penn tucked the book safely beneath the bed and headed back to the only other woman she knew nearby with any mysteries or wisdom, back to Bell Isle.

)(

The boat was heavy and hard to push down to the water. By the time she'd shoved it into the rising tide, she was sweating and tired and worried she wouldn't have the energy to paddle anywhere. She might have given up, but then she saw the red roof of the bell tower peeking through the trees.

Penn gathered her strength. "Eleanor, Agnes, Catarina, Marguerite, Francoise," she said as she pulled the oars through the water. "Esme, Garnet Lee, Sally, Angelique."

She stopped. Held her breath. All the world seemed strangely smothered, as if she'd put her head underwater. Occasionally she would descend into this kind of quiet, safe bubble, an airless space where everything stalled, and she had no control over when or why this happened.

She closed her eyes and told herself it was nothing more than light-headedness, probably from the effort of rowing. She opened her eyes and tried to focus on the bell tower as she mustered all her strength and pushed hard toward the other shore.

Penn suspected other girls didn't sit around feeling like they were disappearing while they brushed their hair or rode their bikes or whatever other girls liked to do. Penn was less clear on the details of an average young lady in Helen than she was on the exact steps to change a quart of oil.

An ordinary girl might have been frightened by such an experience, the possibility of madness or magic, or both. But Penn had never been ordinary, even before they came to Evertell. It was why she'd wanted to go away to Brenau, to learn to build things, to invent something, to see something, to become something more than the girls expected of themselves in Helen. She didn't know what or where it would be, but she wasn't afraid to find out. If she was a disappearing kind of girl, and an Evertell heir of Eleanor Dare, she wanted to know what that meant.

On the crossing, her arms began to shake and she ran out of breath before she ran out of names—fantastic-sounding names of daring girls—but she was smiling. Paddling, as it turned out, wasn't her biggest challenge, but the current pushing her inland. The entire twenty minutes it took to make it to Doris's dock was a fight against the water. By the time she'd reached Bell Isle, Penn was desperate to pull ashore. She'd slipped and collapsed on the muddy bank beside the boat, out of breath, but delighted with her adventure.

"Bernadette Telfair, Camille Parish, Delaney Beaufort, Flora Vaughn, Calista Clerestory. Claire Merely. Alice Young. *Me*." Penn took a deep breath. She believed if she spoke her mama's name and her own, they'd soon be written in the book where they belonged.

Finally, she bounded onto the porch and knocked at the door before she realized how filthy she looked. Doris answered the knock, shaking her head.

"What on earth have you been doing out there? Rolling in the mud?"

Penn laughed and nodded. Doris took her back down the steps and around the house to a spigot where she filled and dumped a bucket of water over Penn's back and shoulders. Then Penn sat on the porch in a swing to dry while Doris steeped a pot of tea before she came to sit beside her and gave a cup to Penn.

Penn couldn't imagine this woman could make the crossing alone as she'd just done. "How do you get back and forth?"

"Mostly I don't. When you've been living on a little spit out in the middle of a river long as I have, you get where you don't like to go much. Sonder hauls me now and again if I want. Mostly when I help with the farm stand over by the store. Bill brings me a sack of groceries, or his grandson. You met him yet? Did you have your breakfast?" Penn shook her head in answer to both questions. "Well, I don't have much. I don't eat much. See if you can drink some of this. It's not what you're used to. I made tea like this for your grandmother."

Penn thought of the bitter tea in the charm, the tea Doris had offered them yesterday, and couldn't help the smile that broke on her face. She'd come to the right place. "Really? You made her this exact tea?" Penn took a sip and couldn't help making a face at the taste. "And she drank it? What's in it?" she asked, resisting the urge to spit. Penn needed to know, but she didn't want Doris to be suspicious.

"Indigo." Doris drained her cup, then added, "You drank it fine yesterday. Feeling a little full of yourself today? Now you've got that big book?"

"I read it and I found out what to do."

"About what?" Doris listened, looking interested, so Penn pressed on.

"I think it's a riddle. Or a charm or something. It's called a charm, anyway. Some kind of advice Grandmama Claire put in the book about dreaming or visions and it's got a list of all the things you need to get one. Like a recipe. Mama says it's just a game for children." Doris made a soft grunt of understanding. "But I'm going to work it out. And I need a woman to help me know what it means because it's a woman's book of mysteries and wisdom. Mama said that too. Not a children's book. And you're a woman."

"That I am. And I guess that's what you want? To be a woman?"

Penn shrugged.

"But I am not an heir of Eleanor Dare. Do I still count?"

Penn nodded. "I think so. You live here on Bell Isle. You'll be buried here, like George and Jacob. You're a cousin, like you said, right? And you knew Grandmama Claire. Maybe you'll understand what she wrote."

"All right. Try me."

Doris seemed entertained. A bit more animated. Penn took advantage of that. "Well, first I have to find the things on the list." Penn looked hopefully at the empty cup in her hand. "It says I need bitter tea. What is this?"

"That's easy. It's midwives' tea. I used to give it to all the girls hereabouts who needed a little soothing now and then. Takes the charge out of you. Your grandmama called it Charged Water." Doris nodded. "Drink that. You're flighty."

"Flighty?"

"It's in your blood. The tea will help settle you down. That's what's needed. Settling down."

Penn tried to slurp the last of her tea in one gulp, to make quick work of it, and burned her throat and wished for something to take the taste out of her mouth, a roll or a piece of cake. Even from the porch, Penn could smell the scent of cinnamon so strong it made her stomach grumble.

"Too bad you don't have any of that cinnamon cake. Why don't you make it anymore?"

Doris scowled. "I don't know I'd remember how. Good chance

that oven doesn't even work anymore. Likely it would blow us to kingdom come if I tried to light it."

"Are you afraid of it? Because of what happened to Jacob?" Penn said.

The old woman made a terrible face, her lips pulling back from her long white teeth. "Why would you say such a thing?"

"Because if it was me, I might be. I'd be afraid of being alone out here too."

"You're a little smart aleck."

This hurt Penn's feelings. "No, I'm not." But Doris's mood had turned sour.

"What's the use being afraid of any of that? We all die. It's just going to happen and you might as well get over it."

"What about being alone?"

"Who in their right mind could think they're alone? Look around you. Are you alone?"

Penn smiled. "No. Not now."

"Not ever. You wish you could be alone in this world is what I say. People who think they're alone are just too wrapped up in themselves, that's what."

Penn knew what was wrong with Doris. She was embarrassed. "You don't wish you were alone either. You invited me here."

"You talk a lot when your mama's not around." With that, the old woman picked up their empty cups and went in the house. Penn followed her and held her tongue while Doris worked on scrubbing down the kitchen countertops, until she finally asked, "What else do you need from me for your little project?"

"It says sweet balm, but I don't know what that is. And then it says to follow my mama's light. I think that's Grandmama Claire's candle."

"Oh. So you want my candle back, do you? That's the reason

you came to me?" Doris narrowed her eyes. There was something she knew, something she wasn't saying. "When you get all these ingredients together, what are you supposed to do with them?"

"It doesn't say. But maybe we'll have the charm for our Sunday dinner. You'll come, won't you? Or if I fix the bell for after the harvest, for a homecoming. A new season, like they used to say."

An expression came over Doris's face; an understanding bloomed. "Give it your best shot. But I'll tell you, you can work all the little charms you've got in that book, and even if you fix that old bell and ring it till the cows come home, there's just some people I'd rather not share a table with, if you want the honest truth. And I'm not the only one who'll say that. New times aren't going to look like old times around here. And Lord, I hope not."

"I don't know what they looked like. I just want to see what they're going to be now. I want to do what an Evertell heir is supposed to do. I'm the last one."

Doris sighed. "Well."

Penn stood there waiting, not going anywhere without the help she sought.

"Seems to me, if it was Claire's charm, she'd have gone to Bridie Quillian for that sweet balm."

Penn had heard the woman's name before. "The same woman who the lawyer said took everything out of the house?"

"The lawyer? Again? That man said a lot, didn't he?" Doris had no use for him, Penn could tell. "I wouldn't listen to him. But everybody knows Bridie Quillian has a resale shop down on River Street in town. In Savannah. *I know* it was her grandmama who planted those herb gardens at your house a long time ago, and then Bridie's mama took care of them for a while and used to make her tinctures and balms and whatnot. Bridie always kept some at the shop, kept me stocked up for the little mothers around here. You go see her about it. Tell her I sent you. She'll know what you're talking about."

Doris seemed to be tired of talking. "That's about all the wisdom I have for today. Make of it what you will."

"Thank you." Penn wanted to hug Doris, but she held back. She didn't know her that well. "I hope you'll come to Sunday dinner. I can come get you. You can sit by me. And at least you won't be here by yourself."

Doris grunted.

Penn hesitated. "I don't know if Mama will let me go to Savannah though. How far is it?"

"Six, maybe seven miles. It's an easy little piece up the road."

"But I'm only thirteen."

"Why should that matter? What are you afraid of? Girls and boys your age go sneaking off to *wars*. You got a relative done it, in fact. Angelique Reece put a hat on her head and rode out of here to fight the English."

"That's true?"

"So far as I've heard. That's her piano sitting up at your house. She wouldn't let the English have it. She dragged it out into the marsh before she left, hid that piano and the workers from Evertell while she led the troops on a chase away from here. I've heard people say it still smells like pluff mud when it's played."

"You're making that up."

Doris shrugged.

"Mama won't like me going by myself."

"She let you come here? Anyway, how do you know? Did you ask her? Why wouldn't she take you herself?" Doris crossed her arms. "Are you fighting over that school? Or has it been this way since your daddy passed? Or just since your granddaddy?"

"No. She doesn't really talk about any of it. Not to me."

"And you're just tired out, is that it? The both of you?"

Penn nodded, suddenly feeling weepy, and turned her face. "I'm tired of feeling all her feelings."

"And you have your own feelings that are awful heavy without carrying around your mama's too."

Penn thought about that. It was true. "I have both. Like right now, I have mine and I have her sad ones. And I have yours a little."

"Is that so?" Doris seemed slightly taken aback. "What right do you have to my feelings? I didn't say you could have them. I'd like them back, please."

"I never thought about that."

"Well, maybe you ought to think on it. Smarten up. Stop taking the world on your shoulders." Doris nodded. "Deal with your own self and let that be enough."

For once, Penn did as she was told, but she surprised even herself when she sat on her knees at the woman's feet and confided in Doris. "I want to take care of myself. I'm not afraid. That's why I came to see you."

"Is that right? I think you need to tell your mama what you want."

Penn frowned. She didn't know exactly what she wanted. That was part of the problem. But she knew she wanted to do whatever it took to keep that little chime ringing inside her now that she'd heard it.

"Can I tell you something else?"

"I'm an old woman on an island, afraid her oven's going to blow her up, who talks to the dead. If you can't tell me, who will you tell?"

Penn smiled. "I heard something this morning, when I knew what to do. When I was coming across the water to see you."

"And what did you hear?"

"The bell. I heard it in here," Penn said, tapping her head. "After Daddy died, everything got really quiet in my head. Do you know what I mean? And not just in my head, inside me all over, all my feelings. Like I couldn't care about anything."

"Mm. That's a bad way to be."

"There's nothing left of him, you know. He's not even buried where we put his marker. They'll never find him, I don't guess." Penn sucked in her breath. "But this morning, when I found the charm and I came on the river, I heard something ringing, really quiet. Inside me."

"That church bell, you say?"

"You believe me? That I hear it?"

Doris tilted her head back. "Well, there's lots I don't know. Maybe you do hear a bell." Doris looked at her a long moment, deciding something. "I'm going to come to this dinner of yours, but you're going to tell your mama about your plans. I won't have her worrying and blaming me for your big ideas. I do believe if you ask her, your mama will take you into town to get whatever you need. But if you want to carry yourself, look in that barn of yours. My Jacob's old bicycle ought to be around there someplace. Sonder stored it over there for me."

Penn felt a flutter in her stomach at the idea of riding a bicycle down to Savannah.

"Thank you for the tea. For telling me everything. Can I have some of that tea to take home with me?"

"Well, sure. I don't see why not."

Doris stood and Penn followed her into the kitchen for the jelly jar full of Charged Water.

"Can I come back here? Will you tell me more stories, like about the herbs and about the piano?"

"I don't know why not. Maybe I'll put you to work, helping me clean up the gravestones."

Penn loped toward the boat. "Deal," she called back.

※

Pulling ashore in the shadow of the main house felt like waking from a dream. Penn stopped to catch her breath and glanced back at Bell Isle, just to be sure it was still there and not a trick out of her head. Her brain was swirling with everything she'd discovered as she approached the house. She hurried across the deep green lawn, beneath the low, curving branches of the oaks with their moss, through the hush of the thick, tropical leaves Penn couldn't name and the extravagant blossoms with their sugary, spicy scents. She felt small and warm and somehow cradled by this place and she was lost in thoughts of her plans, of Savannah, of the boy's bicycle in the barn and the charm for the Evertell.

But when she thought of saying goodbye to old times and ringing in the new, she thought of losing Evertell before she'd even gotten to know it. She thought of leaving Mama and Grandma Imegine and Merely's, of going to Brenau, a place she'd never been. Mama said Evertell's legacy was hers, but she meant the money when she sold it, and there was one choice she hadn't given to Penn: the choice to stay where she was.

Just then, Penn stumbled aimlessly over a fallen brick. It had come loose from one of the tall, thin chimneys on the house. She bent to pick it up, thinking maybe she could tuck it back into place, but the pattern of the bricks had shifted so they were alarmingly jumbled. When Penn looked up, she felt a deep sorrow for the precarious predicament of the structure, so close to collapsing. Like maybe it wanted to go on and fall. On impulse, Penn reached to slip another of the loose bricks away from the chimney and waited, breathless.

But the chimney didn't fall. The house seemed to say it had withstood worse than a little girl who didn't know what she wanted.

"If you fall, I'll tell Mama I don't want to go away," she said aloud to herself, to the house. "Maybe if she can't fix you, she won't sell you."

Moving quietly, Penn concealed the brick under her shirt, consumed with the guilt of her intentions. Her heart hammered in her ears. She was shocked by what she'd done, but already her mind was racing ahead. If she kept pulling down the bricks, one by one, they had to go someplace. She had to hide what she was doing. The cool of the shadowy edge of the forest, far behind the kitchen house, seemed right. She stepped through a tangle of high grasses, clumps of an unkept garden that sent up a sweet smell that filled her nose. When she stubbed her toe on a small fieldstone that seemed out of place in the thick grasses of blooming periwinkle, Penn thought for a silly moment that maybe she'd discovered another of Eleanor's stones. But when she glanced around, she saw there were half a dozen small fieldstones scattered nearby, none of them marked with anything other than moss and lichen. Surely nothing but time had passed this way.

As she carelessly dropped the brick, a hand clamped hard on her upper arm. She gasped, caught in the act, and looked up to see Sonder's stern face. He hauled her up on her toes a few steps out of the glen before speaking. "Come on out of there. You should be careful where you step. That's a resting place."

"I'm sorry," Penn said, feeling a shiver down her spine at the realization that she'd stumbled over another graveyard.

"What do you want back here?"

"Nothing."

He didn't like that she was here. She couldn't ask for his help with the bell when he was upset. She had to give him an answer to make him like her, but he'd asked the same question Doris had asked. The answer was complicated, and she didn't know what he'd like to hear. She wanted to know about this place, before it was too late. She wanted to fix the bell and hear it ring in the start of something new. She wanted to go home to Merely's, but she wanted to go everywhere else, too, and she wanted it all at the same time. Sonder wouldn't care about any of that. Maybe he cared about the bell, maybe he would understand why she wanted to fix it, but the only things she could be certain mattered to him were Evertell and the lonesome messages he listened for at night. As she looked at the forlorn fieldstones in the high grass, her answer came to her.

"I want to see where the Dare Stone used to be. Before it was stolen from here."

He let her go, took a few steps into the shadowy glen, and bent to retrieve the brick she'd dropped there. Penn could barely make out the tops of one or two of the stones.

"Who's buried there? Why aren't they on Bell Isle?"

"Nobody knows, I don't guess. These aren't family, they're workers. They're older than the cemetery on Bell Isle. They don't have names. Some of the stones have been moved, just knocked around over time. But we don't disturb them. You stay out of there."

She nodded, but she had to ask. "Older than Evertell?" Penn's eyes widened and she took a closer look.

"These people built it."

Chapter Seven

Alice

Eleanor, Agnes, Catarina.
Marguerite, Francoise, Esmé, Garnet Lee.
Sally, Angelique, Bernadette, Camille, Delaney.
Flora, Calista, Claire.

When I woke, I'd slept away the morning and it was coming up on noon. The names still marched through my head. I groaned, remembering I'd overlooked the page with the charm in the book. I wanted to believe it could do no harm, but I'd have felt better if Penn had never seen it at all. She wasn't in the house. I assumed Sonder had taken her on the boat or perhaps she'd gone to the loft to see his pigeons. My thoughts were cloudy and my mouth was dry. My muscles felt stiff, as if I'd been working too hard, and that's what I wanted most now. To work hard.

The afternoon sun slanted over the lawn. I stood over a large washtub and wringer. I was running our traveling clothes through so the water dripped out into the tub and enjoying a light breeze off the river.

There were posts for an old clothesline in the side yard, but the wire between them had long since rusted away. Instead, for the next half hour, I made use of the low, gnarly branches of a peach tree at the edge of the small orchard so our clothes dangled in the breeze. I was hanging one of Penn's shirts when I heard the harsh screech of the peacock. It was just behind me.

"Not you!" I startled and cursed the mean thing, dodging and hurrying away as he darted toward me with his black beak. "I don't have anything for you. Shoo!" His shiny ebony eyes seemed to accuse me and I kicked dust from the yard in his direction. He lowered his head and hopped to the side before stretching his neck long and making a worse noise of displeasure.

"I don't like you either!" I shouted. "How on earth are you still here? Why don't you . . . migrate!"

I hurried back to the house and watched from the porch as he strutted away toward the garden. My heart slowed and everything quieted. As I came around the side of the house, I saw Sonder's boat, still on the shore. I looked to see the farm truck was parked by the mill.

"Penn?" I called, but got no answer. The same in the loft. "Penn!" I called inside the house to nothing but an echo.

At once, I was aware of how irresponsible I'd been, leaving her to her own devices after only three days here, how vast the estate was and how small a thirteen-year-old girl could be out on a marsh deep in that forest. I hadn't issued warnings or set boundaries or had any time to teach her the first thing. I'd neglected these things because I'd always been right there, watching, advising. I'd given her so little independence. I should have known she'd jump at the chance for any freedom.

I tried to talk sense to myself. I thought back on our conversation, hoping for an idea of what she might have gotten up to. She'd talked about writing in the book, but when I found it tucked safely beneath our bed, and no sign of her, I began to truly worry.

Most likely Penn was getting my goat, sitting in a tree close by. But as minutes passed, I still couldn't find her. I called for her until I grew hoarse, stomped over fields, followed fence lines, and finally made my way down to the curve in the river where the water ran deepest. For a moment I was queasy, but the tide was out. She could've easily walked across to a little sandbar if she'd wanted without the least bit of danger, and there was no sign she'd been on the muddy banks. No sign of her inside or near my mama's chandlery either.

But as I stood on the oyster shell path, another possibility took hold in my mind. I saw where the shell petered out, becoming a sandy footpath leading into the wood. I knew it would take me back to the place where the stone once stood.

A thin layer of pine straw cushioned the forest floor beneath my feet and I stepped over and around fallen branches, calling for her. The path had been there when I was young, but it was obvious someone had continued to walk this way many times since then.

I called Penn's name and ignored the clawing anxiety in my chest as the tall oaks and moss and saw palmetto closed around me. It was irrational to be so upset. But everything looked the same as it had that summer, long ago. I was sweating and nauseous, slapping at mosquitos when I reached the deepest part of the forest and stopped to collect my wits.

"I am not lost," I said out loud. Then said it again. The sound of my voice was muffled by the towering trees and thick vegetation and I felt claustrophobic, taken back to the terrible morning when I woke there, alone.

Then I heard Penn's high-pitched chatter.

"Pennilyn Young! Pennilyn, you answer me!" I screeched. I took off in the direction of the sound, farther ahead on the trail, out of breath and almost out of my mind. I looked up to see Penn coming toward me, followed by Sonder. My chest seized. When she was beside me, I grabbed her by the arms so hard she slapped me away.

"What is wrong with you?" she demanded.

Sonder walked toward me with his distinct limp. His face was stern and worried. I'd seen the look before. I pulled myself up to my full height and glared in his direction.

"What are you two doing all the way out here? I couldn't find her."

It was Penn who answered. "Mama, stop it." Her eyes were big. I knew then what I must look like. She hurried to calm me. "It's not Sonder's fault. I wanted to see the place where the stone used to be. I asked Sonder if he'd show me. That's all."

Sonder spoke softly in the face of my fury. "I figured better that I take her, rather than let her wander around by herself."

"Fine. It's fine. I mean, but you should have asked," I snapped, trying to get a handle on the twitching inside me. "Somebody should have asked me."

"She's just mad," Penn grumbled. "I told you she would be."

"I think she's scared," Sonder said. He had gentle eyes and his voice was low, as if he were speaking to an animal that might bite. He'd aged just as he should with some gray coming in, weathered round the edges in a way that only softened him. Penn was safe with him. He took a deep breath. I took one as well. I felt my panic dissolving.

"Yes, I am," I agreed, fixing him with a cool stare. "Which is why he should know better. And so should you," I said to Penn.

I didn't want to stand in this place and remember my mama or

Charlie Hawkes or how Sonder had seen me that day. All I really wanted was to get Penn home, slam back a cup of coffee, and rip up the rotten porch. "I just want to get out of here. Sonder should have told you, there's nothing to see."

Sonder took me by the elbow and I let him, surprised to appreciate the small effort to steady my steps. I swallowed hard, aware that Penn had her eye on all of this.

Ж

"What I don't understand is what on earth you were thinking, going into those woods?" She sat at the dining room table, unapologetic, while I put a lunch of boiled eggs in front of her.

"Something is wrong with you. I'm sick of eggs. Why didn't you get something else at the store?"

"You can't take off like that. You don't know the lay of the land."

"The lay of the land? When did you start talking like that?" Penn took a big bite of an egg and said, "Why not? You used to walk in these woods all the time. You always found your way home. Why can't I? I just want to know things. I want to see things here. You were asleep. What was I supposed to do all day?"

She didn't sulk. I liked that about my daughter. She gave it right back to me. She was right. I'd gone to sleep without talking to her.

"I'm sorry. I thought you would spend the morning with the book. Isn't that what you wanted? Or maybe ask Sonder to help make plans for that bell?"

"I was going to ask him, but then you came, screaming. And I did read the book. Some of it. I already know the names. Listen." Penn recited the list of heirs, then complained, "But your name's not there. Why isn't it on the list, under Grandmama Claire's?"

I avoided looking at her.

"Don't try to distract me from what we're really talking about. You've never lived anywhere like this and I know you want to explore. That's fine. But what you don't know can hurt you here. The creeks change with the tide, and if you get far enough out, it all looks the same. You can lose your sense of direction and end up out toward open water. Believe me, that's no place for a girl who's never been on this river. It's the same with the forest. It's deep and murky in places. You might find your way home, but I promise you won't enjoy wandering around out there getting eaten alive by the mosquitos and gnats. There are alligators here. There are hogs. If you want to go out there, I'll take you. I know the way."

Penn's eyes flashed. "That's the real problem, isn't it? That's what you think about me, that I'm too little to do anything without you. You won't let me grow up."

"I want to let you do *everything*! Why do you think we're here? And all that time you're wandering around out there, even if you're just fine and dandy, what do you think it's going to do to me if I wake up and can't find you? If I don't know where you are?"

Penn sighed. Thirteen was coming on strong with her. "I was with Sonder. I wasn't by myself. And I was with Doris. Nothing happened. I'm not doing anything bad." Penn dug her heels in further. "She knew Grandmama Claire. She made tea to help settle her nerves and she made it for me too. It's called Charged Water. It's bitter tea, Mama. *Bitter tea.* She helped me and I know everything I need for the charm now."

I reacted before I could stop myself. "And you drank it? We don't even know what's in it, Penn. Do you feel okay? Is your head swimmy?"

"Stop it, Mama! She didn't hurt me. Nobody's going to hurt me!"

Again, I felt she was looking too closely at me. Sniffing out my half-truths. I was shaking as the tension built between us. I could have told her then that the charm had already failed us.

"You don't listen to me," Penn cried. "You don't trust me. You think something's wrong with me because I've been sad." She stalled, breathing hard through her nose. "Doris says I'm old enough to go to Savannah by myself, and she only just met me! She trusts me! Why don't you?"

My thoughts lurched to a halt at the accusation. I felt everything between us unraveling, and I thought of the stone, the curse, the pages of Eleanor's Tale I'd torn away and pushed to the back of the drawer in the writing desk. "What are you talking about?"

"All you do is keep your account books, and that's how you treat me too. Like you're keeping me in line, adding everything up, but I'm not math, Mama. You never really talk to me. Grandma Imagine does. She talks to me when she makes biscuits. I know you're afraid of me, since Daddy died. I see how you look at me. You think I'm broken."

"I don't. I don't think that. I think your heart is broken. That's not the same. I talk to you," I argued weakly. But I knew she was right. I'd buried my feelings, buried myself in the books at the service station. I didn't want to see what was happening to her, and when I did, I had no idea how to stop it or how to help her. And really, even before that, what had I ever had to talk about with her when I wouldn't talk about my own years as a girl her age? As much as I'd hoped she hadn't noticed, Penn knew it too.

"Daddy talked to me about stuff all the time. And he taught me how to fix things. He thought I was strong and smart, and he would let me do things and go places. If he was here, everything would be different."

The passage of time went unaccounted for as we stared at one another, as she waited to see what I would do with her challenge.

"I'm sorry," I said. "I'm not afraid of you. I've been afraid for you. But I'm sorry." I saw the brightness of her eyes cool and soften and she nodded. "I'm afraid a lot lately. But this is why we came here. It's why I brought you. Now, what do you want to talk about?" I finally said, lowering my voice. "You could have asked me about the stone. You can ask me anything. You don't have to go sneaking off."

Penn considered this. Then she went straight for the prize. "You never told me about Evertell. You never told me about any of this, or the homecoming. You never told me what happened to *you*." Her words scorched a trail right to the heart of me.

Who are you?

I felt the jagged loss of my mama as if her death had only just happened. It felt to me that anything I told Penn of that time would only confuse and hurt her more. I thought of the missing pages someone had ripped from the book, hidden from me. Maybe my mama had protected me in the end. I took comfort in the thought of the pages of Eleanor's Tale, locked safely away in the writing desk. At least this I had in common with my mama. At least this I understood. It had to be the right thing for us all, separating my mama's final ramblings from a story that was already complicated enough. I took a deep breath.

"You've only been here three days. I grew up here. I know Evertell, the people here. They may disappoint you and I hate telling you that. But really, we had good reasons for leaving after Grandmama Claire died. People weren't always so nice to us. I'll tell you something, just a little thing I remember. That rhyme you thought was so fun yesterday? The one I told you about the heirs? Well, it was something Grandmama Claire really loved, but when I remember it, it's something else. And I blame it for losing her, I guess." My confidence began to waver as I watched Penn's face, but she'd asked and I owed her an answer to satisfy her curiosity. And a boundary around all her questions about Evertell that she could respect.

"Grandmama Claire was beautiful. She was loved. She made people think this place was magic. But in the end, my mama was absolutely out of her mind and we all knew it, Penn. Because of that, people started to make fun of her, make fun of me, make a joke out of our legacy here, starting with that stone, the book, the things she said about Eleanor. It was way too important to her; it was an obsession and it killed her. She was trying everything she could think of to break that curse, like the stone was our problem, hers and mine."

"Everything like the Evertell charm?"

I nodded. "And it drove her over some kind of edge when the charm didn't work. Because people don't die from curses, Penn. The truth is, they die of consequences. The stone was gone, but she was still just as sick. Worse. Nothing in that commonplace book was going to save her."

Penn's cheeks were red, as if I had slapped her. She was trying to understand.

"Look there, so fair, the Evertell heirs of Eleanor Dare." I sang the rhyme in a quiet, singsong voice. "It sounds good to you, doesn't it? Well, it doesn't sound so good to me. I know where it led us."

"It's just a stupid song." I heard the doubt in her voice.

"Well, it wasn't stupid," I said, keeping my voice calm. "Not the way she sang it. But you know how people tease. They changed it and the things they said hurt me, so that hurt her. I promise, it won't hurt you now. It's just a silly rhyme, only words."

Penn nodded. Maybe she really didn't want to hear the rest and I knew I didn't want to sing it for her, but I had slept through the morning and look where it had gotten us. I couldn't sleep through

Penn's thirteenth year. I took a breath and spoke the rhyme quietly, gently.

"Little Alice, better beware
When your mother says her prayer.
Crazy Claire will serve you tea.
Oh no! Not tea! She'll poison me!"

My voice hitched on the last words.

Penn looked stricken. "She tried to hurt you? She gave you the bitter tea to poison you?"

"No. I don't think so. People just say things. They didn't understand she believed she could protect us. It seemed like a game to them, a silly woman singing silly songs, charms and stones and tall tales about descending from mysterious women with a name like Dare. But Pop and I, we were living a nightmare, Penn," I said, blinking back tears. "We were losing her and they were making play out of it. I think they were jealous. I think they wished they were half as special as my mama."

She wiped her nose on the back of her hand, glaring at me through tears. "Who said this about you?"

"It doesn't matter. I'm not telling you this because you need to defend me or Grandmama Claire or because I want you to think badly of Sonder or Doris. They had nothing to do with this. And the fact is, it was a long time ago and I was a kid. It's got nothing to do with us now. The reason I'm telling you is so you'll understand. The history here, it's not just about Eleanor Dare. I lost a family here too," I said, softening my tone. "Now, we're staying three weeks. We're selling Evertell. And then we're going home. To our real home, with Imegine. Where we have lives and things to look forward to, not back on." I reached to smooth her hair from her forehead. "Deal?" I said.

"I still want to make dinner. Is that okay?"

I nodded. "And the bell. If you can fix it, maybe that would be a nice gesture. To leave something better than we found it."

She smiled then and the warmth of it eased the tightness behind my eyes, convincing me I was doing the right thing, giving her the story she needed. "And I want to take the bike to Savannah to get sweet balm from Bridie Quillian. I know it's not magic," she hurried to say. "It's just what a Dare girl would do, I think. Even if we're leaving Evertell. That's still who we are, right?"

I was touched she would think of it that way.

"Bridie Quillian?" I asked. "That's where Doris told you to get sweet balm? Well, we'll talk about it. We'll talk about lots of things, okay?"

I watched her turn, satisfied, and run up the stairs. It was a fragile truce, but for a moment I felt we were on more solid ground than we'd stood on since we'd come back here.

X

It was true. Things would have been different if Finch had still been with us. On that much, Penn and I agreed. Finch had known how to love in a way I never had been able to manage, even with our daughter. He'd known how to be affectionate. I was the opposite, my daddy's creature, remote and often harshly practical. I had never known how to completely be myself with Penn, or how to let her come to me in the same way. She wanted me to share my memories, but even long after leaving Evertell, my own life was an example of the pitfalls of growing up a motherless girl. Not a curse, but absolutely a consequence. But the last hour gave me some hope.

I thought of Imegine and missed her terribly, a woman who stood on her own without a list of strangers' names to prop her up.

She knew who she was and what it was to want to be in charge of her own destiny. We were the same, in that way.

"I want to get out of here," I'd said to her once. "I want to have my own life."

"Nothing wrong with that," Imegine told me then. I was still young and trying to make a mother out of her. "You know what you want, a home and family of your own."

I'd pondered what she must have meant. I'd looked to the example of women around us, what they had, what I thought I wanted. Homes of their own. Families. It looked like independence to me. I'd stupidly counted the days of my cycle and marked them on a calendar I kept under my mattress. Two months later, when I announced to Finch that I was pregnant, his wide-set blue eyes never looked panicked or dismayed. He simply said, "You should marry me."

It wasn't a suggestion. Or a proposal. It was a statement. That's what Finch did, he made statements.

I hadn't answered him. I'd married him. I'd believed we were both getting what we wanted. It seemed a fair deal until Finch moved into the little room with me at Merely's, happy to take his place beside my daddy in the garage each day while my life stayed the same. I'd expected we would have a little house of our own, and I could play at being a wife and mother. I realized too late that I had sealed my fate in a way I hadn't foreseen. Ten years went by and my daddy and Finch filled the space in our home. Imegine and I faded, became background noise. She was happy having us close. It was the home she wanted. The family she wanted. Nothing had really changed except after that I had no way to leave. Like the wardrobe, my traveling days were over.

But I had one thing Imegine did not, and it made all the difference. I had Penn.

When she was born, I was unprepared for the onslaught of an infant. I was overwhelmed with the fragility of her. I'd anticipated that she would cling to me and that I would revel in that kind of bond. Instead, Penn was independent from the start. She rarely cried. She was quiet even when she was awake, her round eyes calmly taking in the world. When she slept, hours could pass without the first whimper or grunt, and I would sneak close to her cradle in the night to press my hand to her warm back and check to make sure she was breathing. And even then, I knew she didn't need me to live. Every day this truth had become clearer as I watched her grow fearless and happy. The only thing Penn needed from me was her freedom. I'd promised it but never freely given it. But now, I was trying. I refused to think about how, in this strange turn of events that I never could have predicted, when she'd asked for the truth in her thirteenth year, I'd brought her back to Evertell. And given her a nursery rhyme while I locked away the parts that mattered.

Just like my mama.

Chapter Eight

I'd put Eleanor's Tale away where it belonged, where it had started, where it would stay. Where it sprang from my mama's imagination. There seemed some sanity in that. What I would do with it from here was still in question.

And I knew Penn was, for the time being, safe; that was the important thing. She could sit upstairs with her book of harmless poems and recipes and gardening advice and listen to me rip this house apart. I looked down at the rotten floorboards of the front porch. At least this would be simple. Ripping out the soft, rotten places required a shrewd stubbornness, something I had in abundance. After that, I'd be less in my element, starting fresh with something solid. I'd never driven a nail in my life, but it was a skill that was as straightforward as it gets. Surely I'd be able to manage it. No charms or secrets or dreams required. "I'm doing this for your own good," I said.

Over the next few hours, I poured all the emotions that arose from those memories into wrenching the boards loose. I worked my way from the front to the side, leaving great holes behind me.

Blisters formed on my palms and fingers. Sweat poured down my back and between my breasts. I wiped it away from my forehead and upper lip. I should have been paying more attention before the last, desperate yank when big chunks of dusty debris flew up into my face and my mouth. I choked and sat down hard. Tears streamed as I rubbed the back of my hand over my stinging eyes.

I didn't hear Sonder's approach and jumped sideways when he cleared his throat to get my attention.

"Oh! Don't sneak up on me like that!" I yelped. "Sonder. You scared me."

"Sorry," he said. "Didn't mean to interrupt."

"No, don't be silly. I'm not crying. I just got something in my eye." I squinted up at him.

"Aiming to tear the whole house down?" he asked. He surveyed the damage I'd done.

"I was thinking about it."

I stood on the first step, which brought us closer to the same height. I knew I looked horrible. I could barely open my eyes to see him, sniffing a runny nose, and I felt silly for having made such a scene earlier in the woods.

He offered me a handkerchief. I wished it had been a smoke, like the first night. "You wouldn't have a cigarette?" I asked.

He shook his head. "I'm not desperate enough yet. I told you, I save them up for when I need them."

I sighed.

"Looks like hard work. Want some help?"

"Actually, this seems like a good time to take a break." I wiped my face and tucked the handkerchief in my pocket. "That peacock still hates me," I said.

Sonder put up his hands in surrender. "If you want the birds to like you, take them corn."

"Corn? You mean bribery. I should've thought of that." I pulled out the handkerchief to blow my nose. "Think it'll work for me?" The amused look in his eyes made my face warm.

"I did keep your daughter out of trouble today."

"We could argue about that." He had me curious. "What do you want?"

"Reckon you're going to leave me a place to live?"

I sighed, feeling ridiculous for teasing him when he was here with a serious concern. "I guess we ought to talk about that." I tried to pretend I thought he was funny, but it made my throat tighten. "I could use some water."

We walked to the pump together and he worked the handle while I bent to drink. The evening song of crickets had begun, a high, thin trill. I felt my blood race under my skin and I knew it wasn't from the work I'd been doing but the man beside me. "I have thought about what happens when I sell, what it means for you. If you want to stay, I want you to have the mill and thirty acres, the land you farm. But would you really want that? Maybe you're ready to go."

"Where would I go?" he asked as if there were no question what his answer would be. He ducked to have his own drink, then said, "This is my home. Has been for over twenty years."

I nodded my understanding. I cared deeply about what would happen to Sonder. "I'm talking to my daddy's lawyer again in a few days and I expect he'll help me draw things up."

"Surprised you'd sell at all."

"Well, I might as well tell you it's for Penn. I wasn't going to say anything until it had all gone through, but the money will go to school for her. A place she's talked about for years. I was trying to surprise her, but she overheard me discussing it with Mr. Lewallen when he was at the house."

"She's happy with that?" Sonder asked.

"I think so. She's happy to see this place. But she's got her eye on bigger things, I think."

I cast about in my mind for a way to change the subject. "Somebody finally found our missing stone, you know," I said, looking toward the forest, thinking about the years he'd spent here. "You saw it made the news? All the way back up in North Carolina. Surprised me they ever found it. I guess it's famous now. I noticed there's still a trail through the woods here, though. Somebody still goes out there."

"Oh, that'd be me. I've walked that way the same as I knock around most of this place."

"Well, you can stop looking."

"Looking?"

"You found me a long time ago. No need to return to the scene of the crime," I teased, trying to make light of things, as if that day hadn't changed all our lives. He gave me a look from the corner of his eye, not buying what I was selling.

"A lot of regrets from those days."

"I guess I owe you an overdue thanks."

"I didn't find you," he said. "You always knew right where you were headed and people with any sense knew to get out of your way."

I laughed. "That's not how I remember it."

I liked listening to his slow drawl, his round, low voice. It rolled over me softly and I relaxed. "Did you always know how to do it? Divine things?" When he hesitated, I said, "I don't have anything to bribe you with except my charming personality."

He sighed and scratched the back of his neck before saying, "Not things. Not people. Divining's only for water."

"Too bad. Gold? Pirate's loot?"

He shook his head, grinning at me. "Sorry, just the water."

"Shame."

"Isn't it? When I was a kid, I thought everybody could do it. You don't know you're different until other people tell you, do you?"

I shook my head, surprised at the idea that he thought we had this in common. He thought I was unique.

"Told my mom about it on my tenth birthday and you'd have thought I told her I wanted to join the circus." He grinned. "Might have done better if I had."

"You'd have been great in the circus. Such a clown," I teased, imagining a ten-year-old Sonder amazing his mother. "You never told me about your family. You know all about my childhood, but I don't know much about yours."

"Talking's never been high on my list."

"Funny, Penn just said the same about me."

"You already had some big ideas back then. I figured it was probably better if I didn't encourage you."

"I'd have been just as impressed with the divining as the big top. Actually, I was just as impressed when you taught me to fish."

"You were a quiet kid. Makes a good fisherman," he said and I smiled. I knew it was a compliment.

It was strange, reminiscing about that time and feeling like this, able to be happy with Sonder. I knew if I looked to either side of the image in my mind of a boy teaching a little girl to cast a net over the water, I would see my family coming apart at the seams.

I glanced up at the cupola. Sonder understood. Penn was there.

"She doing okay?" he asked.

"Oh, she's fine. Thirteen. Not quiet," I said. He smiled. I was glad to talk to him. Through his eyes, things were simple. In that way, he reminded me of Finch. But Sonder had always settled me. "I've got a crab trap out. I need to go pull it in, if you want to walk with me."

We ambled across the lawn in silence, getting comfortable with one another, the palm leaves sawing around us in the breeze off the water. I thought there was something about the hour that lent itself to whispering confidences. If he'd asked me then, I might have told him any secret: how I'd married a man who was a shade of him, how I'd had a daughter thinking it would set me free and instead I'd been locking myself away every day since, how I was selling Evertell to prove I'd give her everything I had, but I couldn't tell her who I was because I was still a stranger to myself.

We stood at the end of the dock, the water moving past us, and I took my chance.

"Did you ever have kids?" I asked.

"Me? No. Never did. Never seemed to have it in me to commit."

I thought that must not be entirely true since he'd stayed at Evertell all this time. "You don't have someone?"

"Oh, a lot of someones," he said dryly.

"Really?" The thought of Sonder carrying on with countless women made my skin heat up. I couldn't tell if he was joking with me.

He laughed. "Never seems to stick for me." At least he seemed to dismiss these women without sentiment. But then, that made me sad for him too.

"Better than being with the wrong person for the right reason." I hadn't intended to share such a thing, but there it was. The honest truth. "I loved him. Love him," I said. "But it wasn't what it should have been. Penn, though. We had Penn together. Sometimes I think he's the best part of her."

He bent and caught the rope to pull the trap from beneath the water and I watched the muscles in his forearms tense. "I never figured I was cut out for marriage, fatherhood. Besides, the world doesn't need another one like me."

I scoffed at that. "I don't know. You were good to me when I was little. I know I was a lot of trouble. A kid underfoot. You never made me feel that way though. What are you, ten years older than me? I never really knew."

Now the years between us didn't seem so important.

"Not so much as that. Four years older. I'd have been seventeen that summer," he said.

"Is that all?" A lifetime ago. "We were babies." Twenty-three years later, he stood here a consummate bachelor at forty and I was a widow of thirty-six. "You seemed so grown up to me. You'd been places."

He grinned. "Too many places. I was lucky to come here, lucky your family gave me work when they did." He set the trap on the dock and I could see two crabs clambering over one another, neither really big enough for a meal. He opened the little door and looked to me to see what I thought. I wrinkled my nose and shook my head.

"Looks like Vienna sausages tonight," I said. He tossed both of the animals back in the water to live another day, then dropped the trap beneath the water again, to settle on the sandy bottom. I looked to the house, to the windows of the cupola, for any sign of Penn. I shouldn't go too far. "She wants to go everywhere, or she used to. She'll follow you around and ask you a million questions if you're not careful."

"Ready to head back?" he asked. He could see I was anxious about her.

I nodded. "You're patient with Penn," I said. "I didn't appreciate it before, in the woods, but I should have." He wiped his hands on his pants and we walked back toward the house. "She's maybe too used to men, growing up at a service station. Don't let her get in your way."

"She's just curious about this place."

"Maybe. She's got the book now. We found it in the chapel. Thank you for that. And she's definitely got plans. She's found a fish stew recipe. God knows what else." If Penn wanted to drink tea by perfumed candlelight, they'd humor a little girl. "She wants a Sunday dinner. I'm afraid that's my stepmother's influence—a table full of food will fix anything. You'll be coming." I sighed.

He smiled.

"But the trouble with Penn," I continued, "has nothing to do with Evertell. Not really. It's been hard since my husband died. They never recovered his body. And since my daddy died, it's been worse. She was slipping," I said, struggling for a way to explain what I'd seen in Penn.

"You saw your mama," he said. Of course he knew.

I nodded. "But it's not the same, not really. She's just exhausted, hurt, looking for answers. She's afraid. If she wasn't all of those things, then I should be worried, right? She's lost a lot and she's too young. I've seen her change, though, being here. She's interested in things again, she's brighter."

"That's good."

"It is. It's why we came back instead of handling the sale through correspondence."

"Not for you?"

"Mostly for Penn. And I thought it would be a good distraction from all the losses." I looked at him but had to look away. I had feelings for him that I didn't understand. There were things between us that were very old, but they were childhood ghosts, and what I was feeling now was none of that. "She's got an idea that being here's going to make everything make sense. But death doesn't ever make sense. I don't know what to tell her."

"If she's like you, you can't tell her anything."

"You always said that. How I know my own mind. But I don't.

Not really. Most days I don't think I know anything at all." But I was glad when he didn't offer hollow condolences.

We'd reached the porch and I was sorry the conversation would end. Instead, he sat on the step and said, "You know, my mom wasn't amazed by me. She was scared."

"That's why you told Penn I was scared today? Because you think I'm the same?"

"You are, aren't you?"

"Not of you."

"Of yourself. What she'll think of you. I've seen men like that, the way you were today. Something takes them back."

"You think I have shell shock?" I tried to laugh at the suggestion, but my throat was raw.

"You know what I'm saying."

"No, you're right. It's called motherhood. Believe me, it can feel like war. Like shell shock. They don't have a name for what we have, the people left behind, do they?"

"I'd think anybody who's in charge of another human being must be scared. Anyway, my mama said to me once, 'You just can't tell other people some things. They'll be afraid of you. They won't see you like your mother does.'"

I swallowed hard. They were so like the words I'd said to Penn only a few hours before. I sat beside him. "About the divining, you mean?"

He nodded. "I figured it wasn't worth taking the chance of passing something such as that down to a child. That's what you're worried about here, ain't it? Not about your mama. That Penn will be like you?"

"What?"

"Afraid."

I might have argued that was a ridiculous thing to say. But I understood exactly what his mother meant then and what he meant now. And so I said nothing. Sonder spoke.

"I was fourteen when she sent me away," Sonder said. "She seemed like an old woman to me, a recluse, if you want to know. She had a little money saved and it all went to Mr. Asch, a Jewish man, a neighbor she trusted. She'd arranged he would take me on as a ward," he said.

The idea of Sonder's mother sending him away as a boy, of him living a life as the ward of a neighbor, a Jewish man, and not with his own family, intrigued me. I felt desperate to keep him talking. I hadn't created him out of my imagination after all. There was someone to know here. "Where were you born? Where was your dad?"

"West Virginia," he said simply. "Never knew my dad."

All I'd had to do was ask. What if I'd asked so many things, years ago? "West Virginia?"

"Mr. Asch and his wife had no children. He had connections who promised work in the coal mines. I'd go to make a place there, send for my mama later. She seemed determined it was a good plan. It never occurred to me that I was leaving her, or that she'd get sick. Spanish flu. She was gone before I even heard about it."

"That's terrible. I'm sorry." I thought of the miner's lantern he kept in the cupola. I searched for other words, better words that would connect us in this shared loss. "No mother wants to send her child away, but she knew she'd taken care of you. That's what she wanted."

He nodded.

"But I know how it feels, for you, I mean," I added, "thinking you could have done something differently and everything might have changed. My mama cried all afternoon after the stone was stolen. Looked me straight in the face and swore she would be dead by morning, that she was going to drown in her own tears.

She actually said that to me. I couldn't stop thinking about that. I thought it was up to me to do something to make her happy and when I didn't, well . . ." Absently, I reached to pick up the crowbar I'd been using to pry up the porch and held it on my lap, running my hands over the smooth iron surface.

"It wasn't your fault, how she died."

"Oh no. I know it was an accidental overdose. Just an ordinary accident. I know it in my head, but that doesn't change how it feels. I can tell you all the details, but none of that matters when I think about what happened with her in those woods. She was asking me to save her, Sonder, and I couldn't. And I can't talk about that. Not to Penn. So I say the treatment at the hospital, that's what killed her." I recited the facts just as I'd read them on the report. "I saw the death certificate. Bromide sleep, they called it. One sentence to sum up her life: 'Cause of Death: Owing to misunderstanding of directions in this case, an extraordinary amount of bromide was given within the first few days, wherein an old nephritis developed into an acute one and the patient finally died of uremia.'"

"John told me."

"Did he?" I wondered how much he'd told Sonder. "We never talked about it."

"Maybe you should have."

"I always thought at least Mama would have liked the extraordinary part. But it wasn't fair for any of us, how it ended. Not for you either." I was on the verge of crying again, too tired from being up all night the night before, too close to him. I made a stupid joke. It sounded hateful, even to me. "I mean, you lost your fishing buddy. Must have been awful for you."

The crack in my voice revealed my emotion. The peacock wandered around the porch and stopped a few yards from us to preen his feathers. I kept an anxious eye on him, but he came no closer.

"Come out to the Cox place with me," Sonder said. "They're looking to dig a new well and I'll show you how I divine."

"Is that a dare?"

I thought he might have blushed. This Sonder, the real Sonder, was becoming flesh and bone to me. He was looking at me the way he looked out over the water for the shadow of a fish. I felt as if something was coming, a kind of anticipation I hadn't experienced since before Finch died, maybe ever.

"I'll have to see," I said, feeling self-conscious for my flirting. "I need to get some paint slapped on this place. Lipstick on a pig."

"It's your house now, Alice. You do what you like with it. I appreciate the offer for the mill and I'll think on it. Whatever you decide you want, just remember, you can ask for help."

The peacock pecked aimlessly at the ground, near enough to appear he was eavesdropping. He settled an interested eye on Sonder and took a few steps in his direction. I kept hold of the crowbar, ready to scare the horrible bird away.

Sonder bent and closed his large, heavy hand over mine for a moment, startling me. I tried to draw away, but he held firm. I felt the terrible stinging of the wounds on my palm. It had been a long time since any man had touched me. He didn't look at me, but at the bird. I had the urge to raise my other hand to touch the curve of his jaw.

"Do you think you could let go?" he said.

For a moment I was confused, then I understood he meant the crowbar I was holding tight. I released it to him with a nervous laugh.

As he walked away, I sorted through what had just happened between us and the feelings his touch had raised in me. I knew I'd spent too much time behind the desk at Merely's, detached, running the station, taking inventories, ordering parts, working out payment plans with men who only needed brake pads or mufflers or work on their transmissions. Sonder was asking for something else.

I watched the bird follow him at a safe distance, inexplicably docile, nothing like the way they charged me. I thought of all the women he must have disappointed, a man who could feel secret streams running beneath the ground. I felt the pull of him. No wonder even the horrible peacock adored him. Then I saw him drop something from his pocket, a scattering of seed, and I jumped to my feet.

"Cheater!" I cried. I heard the low rumble of his laughter as he walked away, and found I was smiling too.

Chapter Nine

Penn

Penn didn't believe in things like magic, she told herself. But she liked following steps. She liked having a set of directions. And she liked the feeling she got when she thought of working the charm like other Dare girls had done before her. Maybe Evertell heirs could always find their way home, like Mama said, because they knew what to do. They'd been here five days and she'd been reading the entries in the commonplace book like a manual for being an Evertell heir, like Daddy would have done. It made each day make sense in a way that kept Penn calm and awake. She hadn't felt either of those things in a long time.

She found the bicycle leaning against the wall of the barn, just like Doris said, covered in dust, a peacock feather stuck in the spokes, and missing the chain. It would take some work, but work was what Penn craved. Action. Purpose.

She dug through several shelves and boxes in a feed closet in search of the chain, but there was no sign of it. She dragged the bike outside where she could wipe it down with a rag and inspect it further in the light. The seat was worn but still functioned. The frame was rusted but solid. The tires were in poor shape, the rubber was dry and unforgiving, but she might make it as far as Savannah and back again, if she was lucky.

She kicked at the tires on the bike. She knew she couldn't replace them. Rubber was for the war effort, for other people's daddies who might come back home if people like her did their part. She'd just have to patch them and hope they held out. But she wasn't going anywhere without the chain.

She found Mama in the kitchen house making an inventory of the pantry. A suspicious business for a woman who called a can of Vienna sausages a meal.

"What are you doing?" Penn asked.

"Good morning to you too. Did you have breakfast in the garden again? There's nothing in here."

Penn's stomach growled. She missed Grandma Imegine's cooking; she missed home. She'd never been away this long. "I'm not really hungry. Can I go to the store or is that off-limits, too, since you're scared of Bill Hawkes?"

"I never said that." Penn saw Mama hesitate just before she wiped the back of her forearm across her lips where sweat was collecting. She really didn't like Bill Hawkes. But then she said, "Actually, I think that's not a bad idea. We need a few things today and I'd like to place a standing order for while we're here. You can do it. I'll make a list of what we need for dinner. And I think we can do a lot even with the sugar and meat rations. We have a garden full of vegetables and a river full of fish and oysters and shrimp. And we have that." Mama jerked her chin toward the commonplace book on one of the tabletops. Penn hadn't noticed it there.

Penn grabbed it up, dusting the cover gently. "You can't just leave it lying around like that."

"I'm not going to ruin your book."

Mama seemed almost excited, so Penn reluctantly placed the book back on the table. "Fine. But don't spill anything on it."

She watched her mama scribble a list on a notepad and hand it to her, along with ration cards. "Just a few things. And you can take the mailbag for Sonder. It's there by the door. What is it you want from the store?"

"A bike chain. And I'm going to ask him for the part for the bell."

"Hm. Good luck."

Penn reached to heft the heavy mailbag over her shoulder.

"But don't stay gone long. And don't talk about me," Mama said. "My advice is you talk about Pop. Say Pop would have wanted you to have things. Bill's a sucker. He'll give you what you want. And if his son is there, Charlie, don't talk to him at all. Deal with Bill. You understand?"

"Okay," Penn said slowly as she walked toward the door, unwilling to ask any questions that might cause Mama to change her mind.

"And call Grandma Imegine if you want," Mama called after her. "Tell her your harebrained ideas. Tell her I'm cooking; she'll love that. Tell her you know about Brenau. She'll be excited for you."

Thirty minutes later, list in hand, Penn cussed Sonder's heavy mailbag. It wasn't nearly as heavy as the huge bag of return mail they'd brought to him that first day, thank goodness. She thought about opening the bag to read through the postcards, but she didn't want to stop. Besides, part of her felt jealous of the families who would get these messages when she'd never hear from her own daddy again.

She thought about what she would say to Grandma Imegine about the Sunday dinner and the bell, maybe about the charm in the book. She didn't think she could tell Grandma Imegine what she hoped for, that by the time she worked the charm she would understand, like other Evertell heirs, who she would be, what she wanted, what she should do. In fact, when she thought about the book and all the names there, she thought about Grandma Imegine alone at Merely's. It seemed mean to call and bring up any good things happening here.

Mama was so excited about Brenau, and proud, too, of the thought of Penn there. Mama talked about Penn's dreams to go to the school like Penn had just asked to go yesterday, but the truth was, it was something Penn had wanted years ago, when she was only a little girl. Now she was thirteen. Her daddy was dead. She didn't know what to want anymore. She didn't know if she could dream that way again. She didn't know if she could dare.

It had seemed like a very fancy place where she would wear a uniform and all the girls would be smart, with stacks of books and tight braids and beds lined in a row. She'd heard of another girl, Brenda Sullivan, a girl she'd never even seen but was a cousin of one of her classmates in Helen, who had gone to Brenau. That was how it started. And from there, Penn had played at a fantasy of what that would be like, how she would live, what she would see and learn at such a school. It helped to think about something so far away, so different from Merely's and the mountains and the people she knew, something so much better than thinking of her daddy, who had gone to Italy. Easier than remembering him around every corner. Something to talk about that wasn't the war. But he'd died. And dreams had stopped.

Now she couldn't remember the last time she'd thought about Brenau, or any school at all. She'd just gone quiet, like the bell. In fact, it seemed to Penn that she could only think of things she couldn't imagine. She couldn't imagine going away to school and leaving Mama and Grandma Imegine. She couldn't imagine going back to Helen or seeing the friends she'd ignored and forgotten. The last thing she wanted to do today was call Grandma Imegine and have to tell her any of that.

By the time she reached the store, her shirt and shorts were sticking to her. She climbed the porch steps of the little A-frame building, walked inside to ring the bell at the counter, and dropped the mailbag with a soft thud.

"Who's that?" a man's voice called from a storeroom in the back. "Be right with you."

Penn didn't answer but waited for the man to appear. She assumed this was Bill. He was old as Pop, at least, short and round with grizzly gray hair that waved back off his high forehead, and his nose was too red for the rest of his face. She guessed he was a drunk. She'd heard Grandma Imegine say a man with a nose like that lived in a bottle. Penn couldn't help a smile when she thought of trying to fit Bill Hawkes into any kind of bottle. He squinted at her as he approached the other side of the counter.

"Well now. That's a heavy load for a child."

"I'm Penn Young," Penn said, watching the man. "I'm not a child. I'm thirteen."

From the back room, Penn spied a pair of eyes looking back at her. It was a boy, maybe a little older than her. A hank of dark hair fell over his forehead and he stared at her as if he already had a reason to dislike her.

"No? Then you're old enough to know people in these parts will say you're spreading enemy propaganda with these postcards and I reserve the right to deny service in my own store."

Penn couldn't tell if he was kidding. "But you won't." Penn said it with confidence enough that the boy in the back room shut the door. Well, fine by her, she thought.

"I have a list of things I'm supposed to get," she said. "We need a standing order for while we're here and it's supposed to go on our account." She slid the list and the ration coupons across the counter. "And I need a bike chain."

For the first time she saw Bill Hawkes's scowl start to loosen up. And his eyes smiled at her, even if his mouth did not. He went to work, filling the order while Penn watched. When he'd finished, he set a cloth feed sack with everything inside on the counter in front of her. He folded his arms across his wide chest and gave a sigh that whistled through his nose. The smell of corn feed and tractor grease filled Penn's head and another wave of homesickness for Merely's overcame her just as she caught sight of the piece of iron the size of a huge fist on the sales counter.

"My mama told me what happened, that she accused your son of sneaking around Evertell." Penn realized too late that she'd forgotten her mama's advice. She was supposed to talk about Pop. She wasn't supposed to talk to Charlie. But she didn't know if she could talk *about* him.

"Your mama ought to get her story straight. It's because of your mama that people got the idea my son stole that stone, but that's a lie that's been set straight."

Penn shrugged. "Who do you think took it?"

"Damned if I know. Seems like there wasn't any need to steal one when there was plenty to go around. People making those rocks left and right." He pounded the tip of his thick, hard finger on the top of the glass case between them so Penn looked, and what she saw made her head dizzy. It was a collection of newspaper reports with pictures of various inscribed stones, the largest of those, the Dare Stone. She put her face close to the glass to read that one.

"That's it? That's the stone that used to be at Evertell?"

"That's the one. The Dare Stone, they call it. Here, you want to have a better look?"

Bill Hawkes opened the back of his case and pulled out the

article. He placed it in front of Penn. "There, now. Take your time. No rush."

She read the brief report and the translation of the inscriptions on each side of the stone.

```
Ananias Dare &
Virginia went
to Heaven, 1591


Any Englishman show this rock to
John White, Governor of Virginia


Father, soon after you
left for England, we came
here. We've known only misery and war for
two years. Above half of us have died over these two
years, more from sickness, being twenty-four.
A Savage with a message telling of a ship came to us.
In a short time, they became frightened of revenge and
all ran away. We believe it was not you. Soon after,
the savages said spirits were angry. Suddenly
they murdered all of us, save seven. My child and
Ananias, too, were slain with much misery.
We buried all nearly four miles east of this river,
upon a small hill. All names were written there
on a rock. I put this there also. If a Savage
shows this to you here, we
promised you would give them great and
plenty presents.


EWD
```

Penn stared at the picture of the big, brown rock and marveled at the small, cramped letters in disbelief. Finally, she was able to look away from the photograph and back to the old shopkeeper. "I never thought I'd get to see it."

He kept right on scowling at her, but Penn didn't think it was personal. It just seemed to be the way his face was made, or maybe life had made it that way. "All those clippings there are about the other rocks they've found, just like that one of your grandma's. Upward of forty they've turned up, with about as many different versions of that poor girl's tale scratched on them."

"There's more of them? Which one is real?"

He said, "Could be any one of them's the real deal. Or maybe not. Either way, any life worth telling about is a life with a lot of different stories, that's what I say."

"But I mean how do you know which ones are true?" Penn asked.

"Depends on who's telling the story. That's history for you," Bill Hawkes said.

He leaned down behind the counter and shuffled around before coming up with a new bike chain in his hand. "Will this do you?"

She nodded. Bill Hawkes had been scrutinizing her ever since he'd laid eyes on her, but now he turned his attention to the sack of mail on the floor. He came around the counter to heave it over his shoulder. "Sonder's a lucky son of a gun. Didn't have to go off with the other boys on account of his leg."

"Maybe he doesn't think he's so lucky." Penn didn't like how Bill Hawkes was talking. But she saw his eyes then, soft and wet. "Do you think the broadcasts are lies? Is it wrong what he's doing?"

"Maybe. But I guess it's the best he can do, taking down what the radio says, sending those messages on. Letting people make up their own minds. A man has to fight his battles, even if he can't change what's gone wrong."

"You like Sonder." Penn smiled. "You're not what I thought."

"Most people ain't. That's a fact and don't forget it. You weird like your grandmother? Or stuck up like your mama?"

"I guess some of both," Penn answered honestly. Most people might have been put off by the old man, but Penn liked his straight talk. "I'm like my daddy some too. He's a mechanic. Like Pop. Well, he was. He could fix just about anything inside a car."

"Is that so?"

"I'm going to fix the bell at the Evertell chapel."

The old man acted like he wasn't listening to her, but Penn thought maybe the trouble was the bell had gone quiet inside Bill Hawkes too. He studied Penn for a moment and she watched his chest working hard to manage his emotions in front of her, the way a man will do. She'd seen the same in Pop. Penn waited longer for him to speak than she felt good about, but it didn't seem right to just leave with him standing there. Finally, she asked, "Are you waiting for somebody who's in the war?"

She reached a fingertip to trace the words scratched into the piece of iron on the counter, but while he watched her, for some reason, she couldn't bring herself to ask him straight out if she might have it.

"That there's nothing that's going to make the papers. That's between me and your mama," he said. Penn knew it was a refusal.

Bill Hawkes pulled open the sack for the bike chain and groceries and, without a word, carefully emptied his display of the dozens of news clippings. He tucked them inside the sack, folded the top, and handed it across the case. It wasn't everything she'd come for, but Penn couldn't say she didn't want his news reports, or that it wasn't more than she'd expected. She clutched the paper bag and stared at Bill Hawkes for a moment longer. She looked at the telephone closet and made her decision. Then bolted out the door.

Chapter Ten

Alice

Not long after Penn took off for Hawkes's store, it became clear to me I'd maybe been too optimistic about Sonder's faith that I could do anything I pleased around here and the power of the commonplace book to transform me into a happy cook. Nonetheless, I was resolved to help Penn with this dinner. I ran a finger down a list of mysterious recipes for breads and sweets, even as I saw they all seemed like too much trouble.

To Bake Apricots
To Make an Italian Pudding
To Rough-Candie Sprigs of Rosemary
Apple Cream
Herb Pye
Pear Preserves

My eyes wouldn't commit to the work. They searched the fields I could see from the kitchen house window for signs of Sonder. I hadn't stopped thinking about our conversation and the way it made me feel to be near him again, even if I knew the circumstances were temporary. Maybe that was why I found myself making a little effort, pinning my hair behind my ears and straightening my rumpled clothes. It couldn't last. Surely that meant the consequences of such an attraction would also be brief.

When I stepped outside, I found the wood planks from the barn had been freshly cut to match the length of those I'd pulled up and then stacked neatly near the front step. Another kindness from Sonder, even if he might call it a bribe. After a few hours of work, the porch was more of a hazard than it had been when I started. I surveyed it with disgust. The uneven boards bowed up and down, didn't meet flush, and nail heads sprang up at odd angles so they barely held the structure together. My hands weren't in much better shape. I'd wrapped them with torn flour sackcloth and I looked like a prizefighter, although maybe not the winner of this round.

The travesty was not only a testament to my lack of skill as a carpenter, it also seemed to me a stubborn example of a desperate woman trying to get away with being something she was not. I felt the crumbling foundation of the old house understood that I was as fake as all those Dare Stones.

"This is the best I can do, okay?" I muttered, speaking to the house or myself or maybe all those disapproving heirs looking on. "Unless you need me to balance your books. I can fix you up there. Otherwise, this is all I've got."

This was my guilty conscience at work, my true feelings about forsaking Eleanor's Tale. I wasn't balancing the book that mattered.

KIMBERLY BROCK

I moved around the yard, picking up discarded nails, dropping them into the can they'd come from. The sky had grown overcast, as it often did in the humid afternoons on the coast. A thunderhead was building to the east and a breeze was kicking up. Still, my eyes were drawn again and again to the forest. *Maybe Mama was right*, I thought. Maybe there truly was a great magnet there and I felt its pull. It wasn't long before I abandoned the nails on the porch steps, drawn back to the opening of that tangled path, faring forth.

What must it have been like, I wondered, to have been one of the women who came before me, so sure of what that stone meant to them, seemingly so certain of their way? They had been able to add their voices to the commonplace book, make their marks without shame, add their names to that long list. Did they have their doubts? I was jealous of every one of them.

)(

The myth made us special, if you believed it. But there was nothing extraordinary about the place where the path ended in the forest. Nothing I could ever see. The wound the stone's weight had once left in the earth was now washed away and grown over.

I wasn't looking for any stone anyway. The practical side of my brain understood. I was searching for assurances that I was making the right decisions for myself and for Penn. But like the stone, Mama had gone the way of all lost things and wasn't here to tell me how to be a mother to Penn. She wasn't here to help me teach Penn how to grow up. I was making this up as I went along, not really so different from that myth I'd heard at bedtime.

The air had grown cool with the approaching storm. The canopy of trees whipped around in the gusty wind. I hurried back, catching my toe in a tangle of vine and pitching forward onto the

158

ground. I tried to dust myself off, but the rain was coming down in sheets by then. I was a muddy mess when I came through a freshly mown hayfield and stomped the rest of the way to the house. I was mortified to see Sonder waiting there, out of the rain. My heart flipped over. It happened like that every time I saw him.

I stepped up onto the porch beside him, pretending not to notice as a nail head pressed against the sole of my shoe. "Storm caught me off guard," I said, knowing I looked ridiculous.

"They come up fast like that this time of year," he agreed. "Just stepped up here to cover my head and let this blow over."

"Right. Well. They move through fast. It's already clearing."

So we'd come to this, talk of the weather. Try as I might, desire wasn't easy to dodge. I felt the skin at my throat flush as he looked at me. That wasn't anything to do with a childhood crush. That was very real and right now. His eyes were the color I remembered, light brown, gold. The bridge of his nose was burned, a kiss from the sun. His hair was a rusty brown, cut close to his head, and the tips of his ears were burned pink, giving him the appropriate look of a summer farmer. I smelled the delicious aroma of freshly turned earth.

"I got your latest bribe," I said, kicking at the crooked floorboard. He flinched at the horrible repairs and I laughed. "Corn might have been a safer bet."

"Funny you bring it up. I wondered if we could talk about the corn," he said, nonplussed. "Harvest is coming up. I planted the two bottom fields for a cash crop."

"Oh, sure. I wanted to ask you. Mr. Lewallen says that's how to pay the taxes."

"The money's there in the crop for the tax bill," he assured me, all seriousness. "Once it comes in. I had to wait after a poor season last year, but it will be paid."

"It's early for corn, isn't it?" I wasn't sure at all when a corn harvest came in, but I tried to sound like I knew what I was talking about. Maybe there was something about it in the commonplace book. I'd have to look for it later. "Up where you are in the mountains, it would be later. Down here, we get the crop earlier. Sweet corn comes later in the fall. What we've got is feed corn, not the sort we mill for the table. And even at that, it is early, you're right. But only by a few weeks. For what we're growing, the season's allowed it. Lucky for us."

"Mm. Lucky for us." I liked how he was including me, but I knew that underneath all the talk of corn, we were really talking about dissolving a few hundred years of Evertell as it had always existed. His life would change more than mine. "Good news at last."

"In a little more than two weeks," he said, "I've got extra workers coming. May first."

"May Day. Will they dance too?" I said, trying to make light of things.

He ignored my joke this time and I felt uneasy, aware he was working up to something. "Same fellas I've used these past years. They get paid once the work's done and crop's sold."

"Workers? Are you worried paying them won't allow for covering the taxes?"

"No, that's not an issue."

"Except for you, the only man I've seen here is Bill Hawkes, who looks old as Methuselah. Where do you get them? They're not jailbirds?" I was mostly kidding. "Not that I have any objection to that, if you make a good deal and we come out in the black." I had no idea how to flirt, but I knew I was doing a bad job of it. I'd already fallen back on accounting.

"Prisoners of a sort. From the camp south of here."

"Camp?" I stared at him, working this out. When my mind

lit on the answer, I felt the implications rip through me. "God almighty, Sonder. Germans? We can't have them here with Penn."

"Italian. Since they switched sides, the program lets them work for the home front. They're allies."

"You're joking?" He shook his head. Clearly he was serious. The knot in my gut tightened. The reminder of Finch made me feel like I'd betrayed him just hearing such a suggestion. "No," I said flatly. "No, I won't have that."

The revulsion that snaked up my spine and squatted in my belly was unlike anything I'd ever felt, thinking of Italian men enjoying the sunshine on this lovely farm while Finch had died in an Italian field because of a war they helped to start. While his body wasted away and became part of the earth there, unknown, unsanctified. It hit me hard. What kind of rest would he find with a wife who'd abandoned his memorial to flirt with a farmer and employ his murderers?

"It's a good deal both ways," Sonder insisted calmly.

"No, there's no deal. I don't want them here."

"Come on, Alice. The corn won't harvest itself. They get the job done. You're not having them to tea. They're men to work."

Tea! I thought of Penn's dinner plans and how I'd thought the same, that she was playing house. I felt bad about it then, but I was infuriated that Sonder would suggest the same of me, a woman who couldn't see the practical side of things. "Penn and I can work," I said, chin out. Sonder only shook his head. I knew it was no kind of solution, as ridiculous as the two of us repairing the house. No one was in a good position, not us, not the prisoners. The corn had to be brought in. Did I really care if the sweat was Italian sweat on our behalf? I most certainly did.

"God, you really have no idea what you're asking me?"

"These men have never been a problem."

The remark was full of implications. For years he'd been doing what had to be done, without my permission or my comfort to consider. A reminder that this place had carried on without me and my misgivings. And it would continue on without me when we'd gone. The harvest was a necessity in his life. He wasn't just doing his job. Evertell was his home. I was just passing through. That was my choice. But he was misunderstanding my refusal now.

"I have good reason to disapprove of Italians. *Italians*, Sonder. They killed my husband."

The color in his face drained. Now he understood. I took a breath and lowered my voice.

"So tell me, how do I invite them here and explain that to my daughter? Do you want to have to do that?"

"I should have thought," he said. "I should have considered."

"Yes, you should have."

"But the men have been planning to be here since before. I know them." *Before us.* That was what he meant. He struggled to find some compromise. "Alice, can you think about it? You want to tell Penn something, tell her these boys just want a day out in a field to work and think about their own farms and families, a long way from here. When you meet them, you'll know that too. If they do that day's work in our field, all the better." Sonder settled his hands loosely on his hips. "Your mama would've—"

"What? Rolled out the red carpet? Thrown a homecoming party? Why would you even say that?"

"Shown people a fair shake."

I was shaking my head. Seeing my reaction, he let a stream of air hiss between his teeth. "I don't want a fight."

"Is that what this is?"

"In case there's been a misunderstanding, I'm nothing like my mama."

Before Sonder could say anything more, Penn came into the yard, back from the store and yelling my name.

"I got the bike chain!" she cried. She threw herself into my arms like she hadn't done since she was small. "And the reports on all the stones they found. There's so many. It's a whole other story, all about what happened to Eleanor Dare. Do you want to see?"

Sonder and I stood there, slung up in the moment like two ends of a low-hanging hammock. There was a real and dangerous world all around us, completely out of control. When neither of us responded to her, Penn pulled back and looked between the two of us.

"What happened?" she asked.

Sonder was watching me, the tenderness in his eyes so unguarded that my heart turned over.

"Sonder's telling me how we'll harvest our corn," I said.

"When?" Penn asked, looking confused by the tension. "Will we be here? Can we help?"

"There are workers coming."

From beneath his arm, he pulled out a ledger I hadn't noticed and offered it to me. "Great. Another book."

"Everything you'll want to look over, all the records for the estate. What this harvest means," he said in answer to his original reason for stopping in. "There must have been other ledgers, but this is the only book I ever saw. I took up where your mama left off."

"My mama?" I asked, disoriented. I knew the estate was in my mama's name, but I'd expected the finances and farm had been managed by my daddy.

He nodded. "Sure. It all belonged to her. Now it's yours. You say what we'll do. Who comes. Who goes."

I jerked the log from his hand. The self-loathing I felt must have been all over my burning face. My mama might have extended grace and generosity like a queen, but I was a girl from a grease pit.

I'd forfeited such luxuries long ago. Penn looked up at me, trying to work out what was happening.

We could leave a day early, avoid any argument with Sonder, avoid my own feelings about these men and how it would confuse Penn to see them here. We had no real reason to stay. But I couldn't bring myself to give up even one day, to be run off by Italians. "May Day, you said?"

Sonder nodded. I did not want this authority over him and so I threw it in his face. "It's not really my problem anyway, is it? All the decisions about this place were made a long time ago, without me. This one included. But if this is what it takes to sell the crop and that means Penn and I get free of this place, I guess it's like everything else these days: hold your nose and swallow. One man's as good as another. Won't matter to Penn and me. We don't need to have anything to do with them."

He looked at his boots and not me.

✕

"We don't have to stay, Penn," I said, even though I felt differently. I had to consider her feelings too. "We don't have to be here for this. There's no reason. The house can be sold as it is. We might not get an offer as quickly or for as much as I was hoping, but other than that, Mr. Lewallen can do everything he needs to do by correspondence. We can go home to Grandma Imegine and get Merely's opened up again. We got what we came for: we have the book; you've seen Evertell. We can have our Sunday dinner and pack it in, honey. I don't know. Do you think maybe it's time to go?"

Penn looked dejected. "But the harvest isn't for weeks and I haven't had time to fix the bell. And Bill Hawkes won't give me the part. He said that's to do with you and him. You have to go ask." I frowned at her. "We don't have to go so fast. When you sell Evertell, there won't be any more Evertell heirs of Eleanor Dare. And then it really will be like we disappeared, just like the stone. And even if we come back, it won't be the same place. It will change, like everything else does. So I want to stay a little longer."

The way she said it, I suspected there was more to it. Things she wanted to tell me but wouldn't.

"Are you worried about the money? Because you don't have to. I can show you the books. If we get even twenty-five an acre, we would clear more than enough profit to cover four years at Brenau, Penn. And Imegine and I have Merely's and your daddy's pension. We're just fine."

"It's not that."

"What, then?" I said, lifting her chin. "You just have to tell me what you want."

"I want to see the harvest. I don't care if they're Italians."

"You don't *care*?" I asked, finding that hard to believe.

"Well, I do care. But I want to see *them*," she said sheepishly. "I just want to see what they're like. If I see them, they'll be real. And then I'll know if maybe I can not hate them. Is that bad?"

"No, it's not bad." My chest ached at the thought. "No. You're a better person than me."

A smile broke slowly across her face. "And it's going to be May Day," she said, as if this should mean something to me. "It's a celebration of spring, I think. Or maybe the first day of summer? Girls dance around maypoles with flower crowns. I know this." Her enthusiasm caught me off guard.

"How do you know all this?" I had a vague memory of May Day in school but had long since forgotten any particulars.

"Because they do it every year at Brenau. It's a big reunion.

There's a pageant and everything. I always wanted to go. It's like homecoming." Penn beamed.

"Well, maybe," I said, doubtful it would be the scene she imagined here. "But I don't think there'd be corn and sweaty Italians, if that's what you're thinking." Still, this was the first she'd spoken of Brenau in a way that made me want to encourage her.

Penn pulled a face, but she got serious. "I know it's not exactly the same, but it's something, isn't it?"

"It could be," I said.

"And we shouldn't run away. We shouldn't be scared. Daddy wouldn't want us to." She waited to see what I would say to that. It wasn't really hard to guess. She'd shamed me and I deserved it, when there she stood trying to think better of her fellow man.

"No." I had to agree. I tried to smile at her. "He wouldn't."

)(

The remainder of the day slipped by like the river rolling past. At nightfall, Penn and I stayed inside, sitting in the cupola counting the stars and I watched as she paged through the commonplace book. She seemed to have set her mind on making something of her own of May Day, although she wasn't sharing everything with me. She surprised me further when she pulled out my mama's blue ink and her fountain pen. It startled me to see them, but if she'd found the pages I'd taken from the commonplace book, she would have said.

I didn't speak as she made her first marks in the margins of one of the pages, the same pattern of stars I'd pointed out, one of the constellations my grandmother had loved. I looked on as the careful details took shape and wondered at the ease with which she was establishing herself in this place.

"When did you start this?" I finally asked quietly. She lifted one shoulder and let it drop. "I like it. Have you done any others? Can you show me?"

"It's the first one," she said, concentrating. "Maybe I'll do more."

Perhaps I'd done something right. If she could face Bill Hawkes and Italian POWs and celebrate her family and her future in the face of wars and wakes while she doodled across generations of mystery, she was truly fearless. It had not happened as I'd expected, that in trading Evertell away, I would become the mother she deserved. Instead, she was making me so.

And yet, the only mark I'd made in the commonplace book were the torn places at its center, the same way I was tearing up the house. It didn't seem possible the love behind my actions couldn't count.

Sonder interrupted my thoughts when he came to monitor the radio. Only when he continued knocking softly and Penn's eyes grew round and sad did I go down to allow him inside, looking like a man compelled by a terrible fate beyond his control, but his expression changed upon seeing my own. I longed to make peace. He winked at me, a little sadly this time, and a quiet relief came over me as he followed me up the stairs and I watched him ascend to the cupola.

When I crawled into bed beside Penn, she smiled at me, then confessed, "I didn't call Grandma Imegine. I got upset when Mr. Hawkes gave me the news articles and I just left."

"You can go back to call her."

"But when can I go to that shop in Savannah?" Penn asked. She was watching me carefully. I thought she was learning well how to choose her moments.

"You got your bike chain. What do you need me for?" I asked.

"I want you to go with me." Then she added, "And I want you to make Bill Hawkes change his mind."

Her independence had been so important only a few hours ago. The tides of teenage girls shifted swiftly as creeks in the marsh.

"I want to know why you said his son stole Eleanor's stone," she said.

"Oh good grief, Penn. All the questions." I sighed. But I could see in her expression, she knew I was putting her off. "I think I'm the last person who can persuade that man to give anything to you. And I don't think there's a charm for an old man with a grudge in that book."

Penn thought a moment as she finished her drawing and blew softly over the ink so it would dry. "I think he kept it all for you. So if you came back, it would be there."

"What would be there?"

"All the stories. So people can decide what they believe happened to Eleanor and the stone. It's like Sonder's messages."

"I don't follow," I said.

"Bill said people who need to hear the messages probably can't listen because it would just be too hard, in case it's all lies. So Sonder listens for them."

"And you think that's what Bill's doing for me?" I said, waiting to see exactly what she'd worked out. Thinking how smart she'd gotten. Thinking about Eleanor's Tale, how I was keeping those pages from her because their unfinished story had disappointed me so, and I wanted to spare her that. Was it really all the same?

There was no time to dwell on the thought. Penn was growing annoyed with me. She groaned. "Just go ask him for the piece of the bell. Please. That's all."

"Fine," I promised reluctantly. "And if he doesn't hand it over, then I'll just steal it back."

Penn giggled.

Chapter Eleven

Penn

A bike for Savannah
  Bitter tea to remember
  Sweet balm to comfort
  Harvest on May Day
  A homecoming dinner
  A light to guide by
  A bell to ring in a new season

Penn felt calm, going through the list even before she was fully awake. Orderly, sensible, one step leading to another so that they fit together on that final day to accomplish a thing. She imagined it now. In the glow of her grandmother's candlelight, looking at the sad, sorry faces of those Italians, she would stand from the table, certain of herself, an heir of Evertell, a daughter of Eleanor Dare. A new girl.

She'd seen other girls play games, silly ones with folded papers that they wrote words inside so they could open flaps in random ways and exclaim over the answers they exposed. They were all writing down the same words: *house, babies, love.* But maybe the war had changed things. Maybe more girls like Penn were writing words like *travel, work, adventure.* What a young girl's heart always longed for. They yearned to grow up.

Penn had promised to help Mama today to get ready for the dinner, but she wanted to find Sonder and ask for his help with the bell and she needed to see the herb garden Doris had told her about, planted by Bridie Quillian's grandmother. She'd checked but didn't find anyone named Quillian in the commonplace book. That didn't mean her entries weren't there. Penn might have missed them. Even so, she knew where the plants would be and she wanted to touch them, smell them, think of how long they'd been growing up from that same ground. She pulled on her clothes and the black boots and went to stand on the bank of the river to watch the light turn the water to glass, her view so different here from the one she'd known from Merely's, the sad little curve in a crumbling two-lane highway going nowhere.

The whole world here felt like a mirror of the heavens in the morning light on the river. The beauty of the scene seemed at complete odds with what she was about to do before she went to look for the herb garden. It gnawed at her guts as she made her way purposefully around the east side of the house. There, she considered the chimney and the bargain she'd made with the house before she'd known about the charm. *If it falls, I tell Mama I don't want to go.*

This time she took a bigger chance, anxious to have the deed done. She slipped more than a dozen bricks free of the crumbling chimney. She dropped them at the base, just as if they had landed there of their own accord, in a way that wouldn't look like vandalism should Mama take notice. But even then, precarious as it seemed, the chimney did not fall. Penn let out the breath she had been holding. Partly relieved, partly disappointed.

The house had decided. Today she had more time.

She could have told Mama that she didn't know if she wanted to go to Brenau. But her courage failed her every time she thought of doing it. If the chimney fell, if Mama thought she might not get a good price for Evertell, then when Penn finally said the words to her, maybe they wouldn't seem so bad. By May Day, she would be ready to work the charm; what she wanted would come clear. Seeing the Italians, Penn thought, would be like seeing the last thing her daddy had seen. She couldn't leave here without doing that.

Seeking the assurance of hay and seed and nest, she made her way to the pigeon loft, early enough to meet Sonder for their breakfast. He hadn't told Mama about the brick she took from the chimney. He was on her side.

Penn loved the huge aviary where the birds could scratch around outside and fly up to the rafters. Sonder kept more than thirty birds. She'd learned they were all females. The hens were sweet and their bright, quick eyes filled Penn with something like hope. She was waiting at the door to the loft when Sonder arrived.

"Don't you think they get sad in here?" she asked as they tossed out feed. "They can see everything right up through those nets. Don't you think they know what they're supposed to do?"

"They scratch worms and eat mealy bugs and drop eggs. Nothing can get at them in here. They're fat and happy."

"But they're birds. Can't you train them? So they could just fly certain places or go in a circle right back to you? I thought pigeons did that, came home when you let them loose."

"Only if you teach them right after they hatch. It's too late for that. They were already grown-up birds when they came here.

These ones don't know the way. They'd just get lost. Or get eaten up by a hawk."

"But it's not fair, is it? I know you didn't make them this way. But it's still not right. They're trapped."

"Which is better? Fair or dead?" He only shrugged.

"You kept the birds, but you didn't keep any girlfriends?"

It was Sonder's turn to laugh. It was a quiet sort of laugh and Penn liked it. "Women don't like being trapped."

"But you didn't ever want to be married?" Penn asked, feeling nosy.

Sonder looked sideways at her, clearly deciding whether he ought to be talking to her about such things. "Mostly I like things just fine how they are. Sometimes I like to take a friend to have a Coca-Cola and a dinner. You? Ever want a boyfriend?"

"Not really. But I like Coca-Cola."

"Well, all right then. I think we understand each other."

"Mama likes Coca-Cola. But she's sad a lot since my daddy died."

Sonder considered this and Penn appreciated watching him think, as if he were really trying to understand her. Really listening to her. "Lot of sad women these days, don't you think?"

"Yes."

"Not as easy as being a little bird that just needs a warm place to light," Sonder said. "A little feed thrown out now and again, safe from the hawks."

"I have to ask you something." He waited and Penn announced her intentions. "I need to find a piece of the bell clapper, the part Bill Hawkes doesn't have."

"Why's that?"

"Doris said you would help me fix it. And if I can't find the old one, I'm going to make one."

"Really?" Sonder almost smiled. Like maybe he doubted she could do it. But he didn't know her yet.

"Yes. Don't laugh at me. Tell me if you know where it is."

His eyebrows edged up. Maybe she sounded rude, but Penn wanted to get to the point.

Sonder said, "What makes you think I'd know where it is?"

"You know everything about Evertell. And you could find anything, right? Doris said you find water. You found Mama. You found Jacob."

He shook his head and settled his hands on his hips. "That Doris," he said, annoyed. "First off, the divining part is only water. It's not kids. And it's not loose change or things that end up in a trash heap. Second, I know that bell weighs at least fifteen hundred pounds and the piece you're talking about, put together, maybe a few hundred all by itself. No way you could get it all hung up by yourself."

"Yes, I can. If you help me." When he didn't agree, Penn explained, "I already know how I'm going to do it. I can rig a pulley. I know about things like that. I'm good at it."

Sonder looked at her with a serious expression, more serious than usual. "Lastly, I guess your pop had good reasons for having it taken down in the first place. He didn't want that bell ringing anymore. Did you think about that? He had Bill Hawkes take a hacksaw up there and cut the clapper right out of it."

Penn had expected him to say this. "But Mama doesn't mind now. Doris doesn't mind. They both said if I want to ring it, I can. Maybe it had to stop ringing then, but things have changed. We've got good reasons too. As good as his." Penn pulled herself up straight. She didn't flinch. She didn't care about excuses.

"Only time people ever ring a bell is for a wedding, or to mark a day, or a baby's born, or to remember the dead."

"Yes! You know. Commemoration. We're going to ring it at dawn after the harvest, like the tradition. A new season." Penn smiled, a warm feeling of excitement creeping through her. Sonder was the first person she would tell. Maybe Sonder would understand. "Do you know about compound pulley systems?"

Sonder hesitated and shook his head, but Penn felt him relenting.

"I want to rig a block-and-tackle. There are big rafters holding the bell. We can anchor it easy. Don't you think? Bill Hawkes should have thought of that, instead of just letting those pieces fall. I saw the mark in the floor."

He said, "Speaking of falling, you're just going to keep at me like a little rat, like you're going at that chimney, until I give in."

"I'm not a rat." She decided how much she would confide in Sonder Holloway. "Besides, that chimney is about to fall anyway. Maybe it doesn't want to be sold. I thought maybe the house should decide."

"What will be, will be? Leaving it up to fate? If it falls in on itself, would it even be a house anymore?" Sonder easily came to the correct conclusion.

Penn nodded. She wanted him to know she understood things about him too. "You let fate decide things. Those messages, the broadcasts from Berlin," she said. "Do you believe they're really our soldiers, real American boys trying to talk to us?"

"I like to have faith that some of them might be."

"Then it's the same, isn't it, as letting the house decide? A message like that, coming over the radio so you can write it down and mail it to whoever needs to hear it, that's giving them the choice. I'm giving the house a choice."

He cocked his head and sniffed, looked out across the river. Seemingly to change the subject, he said, "Seems like I remember that piece you're talking about for your bell is still out back of the chapel. I'll look around the toolshed for what we'll need to haul it up. Maybe there's something in there. Likely a marine pulley or two. But you've got to put the clapper back together first. We'll need a welder to patch it up. Long as your mama's okay with it."

"She's okay. She's very okay." It was more than Penn had truly hoped for and she reached out to shake on it. When Sonder took her hand, she said, "I've watched Daddy and Pop use a soldering iron. I can maybe figure it out."

"No, we'd need more than that. This is more industrial-size work, a bell that size." He thought a moment. "I may know a girl."

"A girl?" Penn said, astonished. "You know a girl welder?"

"At the shipyard. They're making Liberty ships left and right out of Savannah. Girls get the job because their hands are small. They can get into tight places for the rivets."

"Would she come here?" Penn thrilled at the thought of meeting such a person. "Or could we go see her there?"

"Where? The shipyard? I guess so." He saw her excitement. "You'd like that? Well, I'll see when we can ride over."

"I have a bike now. I could go myself. If you're too busy, I mean. I'm going to see Bridie Quillian too." She wanted him to say she could go alone. She wanted to see the shipyard and the girl welders and she didn't want to do it like a baby, with a babysitter. Reluctantly, she added, "I'll ask before I go."

He nodded. "All right, I'll call down so Sammy knows to expect you, see when she's on the line. They'll let you through if you give her name at the gate. Sammy Hunt."

Penn didn't know how to thank him for treating her like a grown-up, except to offer some advice of her own. "You're coming to dinner tonight, aren't you? Mama's not a good cook. You'll have to hide it if it's bad or you'll hurt her feelings. Do you know where there are herbs? I'll bring her some and say they're from you. A lot of them."

He winked at her, something she'd noticed he did a lot at Mama. Penn thought if he'd let those birds fly, they would all come back to him. If she was a bird, she would. Maybe a diviner like Sonder didn't really find things at all. Maybe lost things couldn't help but come looking for him.

ᛉ

With the chain on the bike, it was an easy ride over to Hawkes's store and Penn flew over the sandy path. The tires held up and she imagined herself, all on her own, taking that bike into the city, riding between the tall buildings, down to a little shop full of everything that had been lost from Evertell. She imagined it would smell of the herbs from the garden. That it would glow with the candlelight from Grandma Imegine's candles.

Inside the store, there was no sign of Bill Hawkes. Penn hopped on the phone and asked the operator to connect her, watching for the old man. When Grandma Imegine answered, she thrilled to hear her voice. And then she was suddenly overcome with missing her. Penn's throat tightened and she hurried to tell everything she'd wanted to share about Evertell, the stones, the empty house, the pigeons, the dinner they were making. Grandma Imegine laughed and laughed, happy for them.

"I know about Brenau," Penn said. "She sent my stupid essay. I wrote it when I was ten. It will sound like I'm a baby."

"Oh good. She told you." Grandma Imegine's voice was soothing.

"Did anything come yet?"

"No, not a thing."

Penn didn't know what to say or how she felt about that. It was hard to explain feeling both relieved and disappointed at the same time. And then, without thinking, without even knowing she would do it, she asked, "If anything comes, will you bring it here? So we can open it together? We're staying for the corn harvest. On May Day. I'm going to make a homecoming like all the Evertell heirs used to do. Oh, Grandma Imegine, could you please come? I miss you."

Chapter Twelve

Alice

Pale light from the east poured in through the leaded glass window as I looked over the ledger. Here was a book I could understand. The most recent entries were all neatly penned in a small print that I knew to be Sonder's careful handwriting. I flipped back through the pages until the lettering changed and I found my mother's flowing signature. Aside from the fact that a female once managed the finances of this great estate, I saw nothing unusual or noteworthy. I felt a sharp disappointment, although I couldn't say why. I thought of what Penn had said to me. *"I'm not math, Mama."* I smiled. No indeed. She was not. We didn't add up so easily.

On one of the pages I discovered scribbles in the margin. I looked closer to see that the scratches were actually poorly formed drawings of tiny sunshines. I could only guess the artist must have been me. It was so much like what I'd seen Penn doing in the commonplace book the night before. There was something dear about the idea of my mama sitting as I sat now, while maybe I'd

THE LOST BOOK OF ELEANOR DARE

perched upon her lap or leaned on her shoulder, decorating her work. Maybe that's why I'd taken so naturally to the accounts at Merely's. Some part of my early memories must have held on to that precious moment with Mama. I wished I could call it up now. Another part of my story, missing.

Instead, I thought of Imegine, with her domesticity and practical outlook. She must have known she couldn't compare to the dream mother I'd left in the woods and yet she'd been there to comfort me, advise me. The savings Daddy had left to her and ownership of Merely's would keep her comfortable the rest of her days, but it seemed impersonal. We'd need to hire a new mechanic soon. Imegine would never mention that. She might not even think of it. She'd just keep things running as they were, pumping a little gas, making her plates of barbecue or fried chicken. Generally, she took things at face value. But I'd gotten the idea she might want an adventure too. Same as me. Same as Penn. She might feel restless. It seemed like we'd been living in a lull for years now, even before Daddy died, and I couldn't shake the feeling that now we'd come back to Evertell, when I sold this place, we'd all shoot out of a cannon in different directions, nothing to hold us in place. I didn't really know what the future had in store for us.

A knock on the door surprised me. It was barely after eleven in the morning. I wasn't expecting anyone until dinner. When I answered, I found Lewallen, hat in hand.

"Mr. Lewallen," I said, at a loss. He looked worse for wear. In fact, he seemed shocked to find himself here.

"I'm sorry. Did I get the time wrong?" He squinted at me, disheveled.

"For dinner?" I asked, not wanting to embarrass him, though it seemed a lost cause.

"Oh, Mrs. Young. No, no. Pardon me. I believe I've made a mistake and come for lunch."

I plastered on a smile. There was nothing else to do. "Well, then you're right on time. Come on in. Let me just take your hat for you."

He shuffled back into the dark room and I followed hesitantly. A fan was running loudly on a side table near the ratty sofa and he settled himself there. He looked as if he'd just awoken from a morning nap, or could use one.

I had nothing on hand to offer him to eat or drink and I settled on business instead. "Since I've got you here and we have some time, I wonder if we could discuss a thought I've had about parceling out the property."

I perched on the corner of the only other stick of furniture in the room, an upholstered chair. Mr. Lewallen smoothed his hair and attempted to straighten his suit jacket, seeming a little more aware of his surroundings, so I relaxed a little.

But then he said, "Make yourself at home," and flapped a hand. He then muttered some legal jargon I assumed in response to parceling the property, but it was unclear. I took a closer look at him as he seemed to sway a little in his seat and finally sank back and let his head rest against the back of the sofa. Clearly, he'd wandered in here on a bender.

"I see. And that would manage it?" I said absently, wondering what I would do with this man for the remainder of the day. I considered asking Mr. Lewallen for a nip of whatever he'd been drinking.

He nodded. "It's all very standard, I assure you."

"Okay, then. Thank you." There was an awkward pause as I hesitated. He seemed satisfied. There was no point continuing the ruse of a conversation when he was three sheets to the wind.

"You're still set on selling Evertell, I see." Lewallen leaned at a

THE LOST BOOK OF ELEANOR DARE

slight angle and I worried he might tip over and sprawl on the sofa any moment. He was a sad sight, maybe as alone as I felt. "John Merely was a good man. Never met a stranger. Gave his tithe regular. Honest John, that's what we called him. Hate to see you go, that's what. Just hate to see it."

I suddenly felt a deep need for any little memory Lewallen had of my daddy. It made me feel my daddy's loss all over again, and a sense of security slipping away.

"I'd love to talk to you more. I know my daughter would love to hear your stories."

In his pickled state, Mr. Lewallen's head bobbed and he wore a pleasant expression, if slightly bashful. "Oh sure, sure." Then I watched his head tip all the way back and come to rest on the sofa, his jaw agape. After only a second, I heard a soft snore. He'd passed out.

)(

Penn was lurking in the door, a bunch of herbs in her hand, roots still hanging from the plants. "I brought you these. I don't know what they are, but they smell good. What's he doing here?" she asked. "What's wrong with him?"

"He's drunk, I guess," I said bluntly. "And early. And asleep, thank God. Just leave him be. He won't hurt anybody. Let him sleep it off. Stay out of here. We'll be in the kitchen house anyway. He can have his privacy."

I took the herbs, the bright scent of them filling my nose, and sent her, wide-eyed, for a mess of collard greens, saving myself the walk along the path toward the garden where the peacock held court. When she came back, I was standing over an empty pot and the recipe for fish stew, trying hard not to feel like Oscar

Lewallen's unexpected arrival was a bad omen for the evening to come.

"Come on in here," I said to Penn. "We're going to do this together." I stabbed a finger at the commonplace book. "It looks simple enough. We've got to start somewhere, right? How hard can it be?"

Penn squirmed, looking like she'd rather be anywhere else. "I wish Grandma Imegine was here."

"No. No. We're doing this. Me and you. We don't need Imegine. Now, start chopping this stuff up." I gestured to the carrots, onions, tomatoes, and potatoes laid out across one of the worktables. "There's a knife right there."

When she looked doubtful, I pushed the book toward her. "It says right there, chopped vegetables. I'm going to start the broth. Herbs and water and fish." I picked up the herbs she'd brought from the garden. "Whatever this is. We'll make do with what we have. It'll be fine. I put a trap out last night. It ought to be full."

"Full of fish?"

"Well, crab, hopefully. And shrimp, maybe."

"We should have asked Sonder for fish."

"Penn, come on," I said, growing upset that she had so little faith in me. "We're not helpless. We don't have to go running to somebody else for everything we need. We're the Evertell heirs of Eleanor Dare," I said, prodding her with my elbow. "What happened to you this morning? I thought you were happy about this last night."

"I am. I was," she said, squirming away from my reach. "Sonder's going to help me with the bell. I asked him. He has the other piece too. He knows a girl at the shipyard who can help weld it back together. They have lots of girl welders, he said, because their hands are small and they can reach the rivets on the Liberty ships."

I asked, "That's good, right?" Penn nodded. "Then what is it?"

"I called Grandma Imegine."

I stopped what I was doing, put the knife down. "Is she okay? Is everything all right?"

"She's fine," Penn said. I relaxed. "I just miss her. I miss home. I wish we'd brought her. She would like this. It doesn't feel right she's not with us. She's getting left out of everything."

"I don't think she feels that way about it, Penn. But I miss her too. Did you tell her what you're doing tonight?"

Penn nodded. "And some other stuff. I told her about the harvest. But not about the Italians."

"Mm."

"And all the news articles, about the big stone that went missing, the one that used to be here. It was so close to us all this time. Did you know there were more of them? A lot more."

I shook my head, feeling unsettled, as if the old stone had been following us, which was ridiculous, of course. "I knew they found more rocks, but I really didn't keep up. Last I knew, the big stone was in Atlanta, then up in Gainesville at Brenau. After that first report, I didn't want to know more. It brought up all my sad memories, Penn. I didn't want to think about it at all." I went back to the vegetables, cutting them, adding them to the pot a few at a time. "But I don't mind talking about them now, if you want."

"I just don't know what they mean," Penn said.

"About what?"

"About Eleanor Dare. About us."

Penn rambled on then like she was giving a book report in school, perched on the edge of the worktable while I got on with the vegetables, reciting the facts from the reports. I tried to keep up as best I could make sense of it.

According to the newspapers, the old stone that had been at Evertell was only the first one they'd collected since 1937. Over forty more stones had turned up over the next few years, discovered by a bunch of farmers and moonshiners. They'd been found in rivers and gullies and fields throughout the southeastern United States. The messages carved into them were all attributed to Eleanor, detailing her time in captivity and, finally, her death. I'd been aware of all those other stones, but only vaguely. I'd avoided reading the reports when they ran in the papers and been glad when it had all been dismissed. Now I would have to pay attention.

"But they're mixed up. The stories don't all match," Penn said. "It's like lots of people wrote them and they got things wrong. Like when you play the rumor game and you're supposed to whisper the same thing from one person to the next, but it's so wrong by the last person that it's nothing like it was at the start."

Nor did they match Eleanor's Tale. Although Penn wouldn't know about that. She finally got down to what was eating at her.

"I guess somebody just made it all up," she said, perturbed. "What if we're not even who we think we are?"

"Who would we be?" I said.

"I don't know. But not the people Grandmama Claire thought we were."

"Then who's buried in those graves over on Bell Isle?"

"You know what I mean. It has to be *our* Agnes's story in these stones. Not just *some* Agnes, or a made-up Agnes. If Agnes isn't real, none of it is. There wouldn't be any heirs of Eleanor Dare."

"Seems to me, we inherit the legacy of Eleanor Dare either way."

Penn frowned. "What does that mean?"

"Well, it means somebody just like you scratched those stories into those rocks, all stories about Eleanor Dare. Just imagine. That's not an easy thing. That's a desperate soul, for sure. Needing to be heard so badly you have to dig your words into a stone. Those stories are important, whoever's stories they are."

"You just want to argue," Penn growled.

"Then why don't you throw the articles away? Throw this book away, too, while you're at it." I shut the cover on the commonplace book. "Why do they matter to you?"

Penn pushed on her temples with her fingers. "Because . . . I don't know," she admitted. "It's like the stones I stepped on under the trees, way down behind the house. Sonder said they're gravestones, but they're not marked. He said they're Evertell workers' graves, but how can you even tell? Do you know about them?"

"Hm." I nodded. "I do know. And Sonder's right, you should leave that place alone." I remembered the little plot that had been old and silent with its scattered stones, even when I was Penn's age. I'd not thought of that place or those stones since then and I didn't want to think about them now, much less give Penn something else to brood over. It seemed to me that since we'd arrived here, she'd started to show a preoccupation with the graves that marked Evertell, and I wasn't sure it was good to dwell on such things. I wanted her thinking of the living, of the life stretching out in front of her. I changed the subject. "I'll tell you what else I know—we're going to have a very nice fish stew."

She went on, a little teacher giving me a lesson. "I found music in the book. Look. She put it in here. But I don't know how to play it."

Penn carefully flipped to the page in the commonplace book where a piece of sheet music had been pasted. At the bottom, Angelique Reece had signed her name. "Look at that. That's real, eh?" I said.

"Sammy Hunt is real," Penn said. "She's not an Evertell heir, but if she helps me, maybe I'll draw a Liberty ship too. And a bell."

"Who?" I didn't follow or recognize the name.

"That's the girl Sonder knows at the shipyard. He said if you say it's okay, I could go talk to her and see if she'll help me repair the bell. I could take my bike."

"We'll see." I was surprised to find that it didn't upset me to remember Angelique's tale, to be making fish stew, to ponder this old book and the stories of the Dare descendants with Penn. Maybe I really was finding some perspective about this family. I felt hopeful that I had turned a corner over the last few days. And hopeful about the dinner, too, as the pot simmered and the smell of the herbs filled the kitchen house. It all seemed promising. But I wasn't so sure about Penn taking a bike to the shipyards in Savannah. That was another conversation and it could wait.

Penn followed me down to the dock to bring in the crab traps. She bent over the water, watching as I pulled them in. Six large crabs crouched in the wire cage, and I saw the delight on Penn's face as she looked from them to me while I pulled them out and tossed them in a deep bucket to carry back with us. I hadn't been out to fish yet, but I had a package of Vienna sausages in my pocket. I dumped a few of those into the trap as fresh bait, then gestured for Penn to grab the long, wet rope that lay coiled on the dock.

"All right. Now you lower it back down the way it was."

"I know," she said, eagerly repeating the way I'd drawn the trap in, only in reverse.

She looked at me then the way she looked at the commonplace book, as if there was something extraordinary about me. For a moment I glimpsed myself the way Penn must see me, a woman on a dock, pulling in crabs from a river, the same as her ancestors had done for time immemorial. The way I'd always wanted to see myself.

X

Something was different about Doris. Sonder had brought her across in our boat and one of us would carry her home later. Her hair shone, brushed back and pinned up neatly. And she wore a nice brown dress with a black pair of lady's shoes I imagined might have once been her church clothes. She sized me up, too, taking in my loose curls and the blouse and skirt I'd changed into. But neither of us felt the need to comment on the changes.

Doris asked, "What is Oscar Lewallen doing out there?"

I came around to peer out the kitchen house window beside her. "Taking a piss, looks like." It was true. Mr. Lewallen had finally come to after his nap and made it only several feet outside of the house before needing to relieve himself.

"Lord, Lord," Doris huffed.

"Makes you miss Mr. La Roche?" I teased. Doris made a growling sound and I laughed. "It's too bad we don't have coffee."

"That man's been liquored up so long, coffee wouldn't make a dent. I didn't know he'd be here."

"I don't know what Penn was thinking, asking him. But I hoped he might tell Penn something nice about my daddy. Now I just hope he can sit upright."

Doris made a grunt of obvious disgust. She didn't like him.

X

"But we followed the recipe straight from the book, except we used crab. Maybe it doesn't work with crab." Penn lamented the flavorless meal at the table.

Obviously, the commonplace book wasn't magic. It might have given us a list of ingredients, but the outcome was up to us and now our dinner guests suffered the consequences. Graciously they assured Penn that the meal was plenty satisfactory as they sipped politely at the soup. Mr. Lewallen, likely regretting accepting my invitation, looked exhausted, a little green, and slightly humiliated.

This was the part I couldn't pull off, the perky conversation of a gracious hostess. I avoided meeting Sonder's steady gaze.

Not surprisingly, I thought of the first dinners at Merely's when Imegine came to live with us, of her tidy kitchen, how she made it seem like we were eternally playing house. It was all she wanted in the world, a family around a dinner table, but she'd had to rig the whole thing. Somehow we'd never been at ease that way, she and my daddy, later me and Finch, and finally Penn. Yet it had been nice, too, those last months, just Imegine, Penn, and me. Now I was struck by an unexpected homesickness for the garage and for her, same as Penn. For all the heritage we were surrounded with at Evertell, aside from my daddy, she was the only family Penn and I had known in the world. But part of me was glad she wasn't there to see this dull outcome. Heaven knew, she would shake her head at me now.

Out of nowhere, Penn addressed Mr. Lewallen. "Did you have enough? Do you want more? I can take your bowl."

"Oh no. Thank you though. That's kind." Mr. Lewallen dabbed at the corners of his mouth with his napkin and looked to me. "I should get going."

"Please stay," I said. "Tell us some stories. Penn would love to hear. Earlier, you were saying you remembered my daddy." I addressed the table. "I talked with Mr. Lewallen today. He's helping me divide the property for the sale. I think Daddy would be happy to know you're all here and will have a part in the future of Evertell. My mama, too, of course."

I felt Penn's eyes on me. In fact, it seemed to be the theme for the evening in this room full of uncomfortable people. There was no getting this bunch to warm up to one another. I watched them refuse to look at me or each other until Mr. Lewallen sputtered more thanks and apologies, folded his napkin, and pushed his chair back to stand.

At least he seemed to have sobered up. "I have to admit you were right about trying to take this place on, just me and Penn. Try not to break your neck on the front porch steps. I'm no carpenter."

Mr. Lewallen made a low chuckle, accepting my ridiculous admission of defeat, although I doubted he'd noticed the steps or anything else in his previous condition. Sonder was oddly silent on the matter. Doris began to clear the table. I couldn't understand how things had gone so horribly.

"Tonight's just practice. I'm going to ring the homecoming bell when the sun comes up after the harvest, just like you said," Penn announced into the silence. "It will be May Day when the Italians come, did you know? People have reunions on May Day. You're Pop's friend so I'm inviting you, special," she said. "I'm inviting people from around here. Anybody who has anything to do with Evertell. We'll have better food, I swear."

"Well," Mr. Lewallen said, "I can't say I ever thought I'd live to see the day that bell would ring again. No more than I thought I'd be receiving such invitations as I have from you ladies." And then his tone took on a quietly vicious edge that was completely at odds with the broken man I'd seen all afternoon. "Old Hawkes'll like that, won't he?"

Sonder stood from his seat so quickly the scrape on the floor startled us all and I thought it would tumble over. I sat up in my chair.

"That's enough from you, Oscar Lewallen," Doris said firmly. "I believe that about does it for tonight."

I looked between the two men, unsure what to make of the moment.

"Thank you much, dear, for extending kindness to your neighbors," Doris said to Penn, then looked to me. "I believe we'll call it a night. You can carry me home, would you? Sonder will need to drive this fool."

Sonder looked at Mr. Lewallen with a grim expression that did more to sober him up than any pot of coffee might have done. Penn looked crestfallen.

"So early?" I said weakly, although I was honestly relieved to see them all go. They were such a glowering lot.

"Sorry about the stew," Penn said as they left, also at a loss. "It was supposed to be fish."

Chapter Thirteen

"That was not my finest hour, I have to say," Doris said as I rowed her over to Bell Isle in the last light. "I should thank you anyway." But she did not, in fact, thank me.

"Penn was sure glad you came. I know she thinks the world of you. She misses my stepmother. I hope she's not been too underfoot."

"Not under my feet, no. I think she's trying to light a fire under my rear end, if you want the truth."

"That's true for all of us," I said. "After the time she's had, it's good to see. Believe me."

Doris fell silent. The evening air had grown cooler.

I cleared my throat. "I think we must have stepped into something tonight unintentionally. Are you going to tell me what that business with Mr. Lewallen was about?"

"Oh, Oscar's a man living with his regrets, like any one of us," she said gruffly. "It's nothing to do with you. Penn just poked an old hurt, that's all. To tell you the truth, I was surprised to see him climb out of whatever hole he lives in these days, much less darken your door."

"Should I be apologizing here?" I asked, confused.

Seemingly out of the blue, Doris said, "Once, I saw a good man beat to death on my account, right here. The night Jacob died. I might have stopped every bit of it. Oscar Lewallen had his part in it. Bill Hawkes. Sonder. A place like Evertell has a long history, and some of it's not yours."

I stopped pulling the oars, horrified at the blunt revelation. My muscles burned and my ribs ached. But I stopped because I couldn't quite believe what she'd said. "Oh my God, Doris."

"Well, I should have told you, but I didn't want to talk in front of little ears. If Oscar hadn't turned up in the mix, there'd have been no reason to drag it all out. But if I'd known he was going to be at that table, I'd have said something. It's like you said, you and your daddy were gone awhile before this, so you wouldn't know."

"I think you'd better tell me now."

"Walter Kreischer was his name. He'd come out here to work at the turpentine still. But you know the Great War hadn't been over that long and people weren't friendly to them."

"Them?"

"Krauts. Germans. Walter was an immigrant, fought for the kaiser. People were looking for trouble from a man like that. When the still blew, people said Walt caused it. They wanted any reason to be rid of him. Sonder got here first, to tell me about Jacob. He was pitiful. But Bill showed up right behind him. He ran Sonder out. I shut my door on the both of them, but Bill stayed right out on my porch."

Doris had a faraway look on her face. I waited a moment before asking, "What does this have to do with Mr. Lewallen?"

"A mob went after Kreischer, people who'd been waiting for an excuse. They didn't wait on the police, I'll tell you that. They dragged that poor man over here to Bell Isle, out of vengeance. They thought I had a right to say what happened to him. But I never did open the door. I couldn't seem to do it. I was out of my mind. When I didn't come out, Bill sent them away. He said they ought to take it to the police and let justice run its course."

"That surprises me," I said sourly. "I wouldn't expect him to step up."

Doris ignored me. "They stood out there for so long. They made him sing the national anthem. I could hear it from my bedroom, right up there." She pointed to her house, only a few yards from where we floated. "They made him swear allegiances. Like it would prove he was loyal to this country. Like it would change anything they had in mind. And he did it, all of it. He asked to be buried in an American flag. He knew what was going to happen." She shrugged helplessly. "I didn't even try to stop it. Sonder tried."

"Doris—"

"Oh, they'd have killed him anyway. It's the way things were headed for Kreischer. They weren't going to listen to me or nobody. I stood at that window right there and watched them march him a long way down the riverbank. I swear, I thought they were just harassing him, wanted to humiliate him. I figured they were going to run him into the marsh, out of town. But we don't know when it's happening, do we? We can't imagine the people we know are capable of such things. It's only after that we can look back and know it for what it was."

"No, I know. You couldn't stop them, Doris," I said, breathless. She shook her head.

"Aside from seeing Bill out at the store and Sonder if he runs an errand for me or comes and goes from that chapel, the lot of us have rarely deigned to so much as share the air we breathe since that night, much less sit around a table together." She fell silent and I thought the story had come to its end. I couldn't think what else to say and so we sat there with the water lapping at the side of the boat. The evening was so quiet on the water, nothing like the night she was describing, and I struggled to reconcile the two realities.

Finally, Doris choked out, "They were charged with murder, the twelve of them. After some of the men were taken in, Bill was called to testify. They were men from what used to be a part of that American Protective League. Old friends. Neighbors we've known seems like our whole lives. Bill took it very seriously, told what he knew. He believed the courts would set things right. It cost him, aged him, bearing witness to such as that. Cost us all. No kind of justice in that mess. Patriots, they called themselves. Hid behind that word. That was Mr. Oscar Lewallen's idea for their defense. The judge agreed with him. But you can see the result. Oscar crawled in a bottle, and I can't say I blame him."

"Doris, I didn't know. I never would have dealt with him."

"Trial took only a day down in Savannah and then they were turned loose. There was a couple of Jewish men came for the body right after Kreischer died. I think Sonder had something to do with bringing them. He wanted to see the man buried proper, at least, and Kreischer didn't have a soul around here. Their people go in the ground right away and nobody was going to argue. Officials were happy to have him off their hands and mostly out of the news. Laid in Stranger's Ground—or whatever they call a pauper's grave—I never knew much about their ways, how they call things, the Jewish folk."

I felt the words settle deep in the pit of my stomach, cold and heavy.

"A synagogue, I believe it's called. I never knew much about their ways, the Jewish folk. But they sit up with their dead, same as we do, even for a man they don't know. Even a man they hate.

Sonder had told me this. That impressed me. I like to think some-body did that for the poor man. And put a little headstone out for him. Sonder told me that too. I made him keep up with how every bit of it was handled and asked him to let me know."

"You've been over there?" I was honestly surprised.

"Bill took me a time or two." Doris sighed. "Anyway, that was it. It was murder, but it was justifiable, the judge said, under 'unwritten law,' on account Kreischer had been a German soldier and fought against us. He was still the enemy. But I never blamed that man for a thing. Never even knew him. Plenty of folks felt that way then, likely still do, and I guess Oscar Lewallen did too. I think about him every day of my life. Every one of us does. That's what came to dinner with us tonight. He might as well have had a seat at that table, and I guess he should."

I suddenly remembered the first night we'd come to Evertell and what I'd said about Sonder's radio monitoring. "Oh no. I made a joke. I said Sonder was a German spy. I shouldn't have done that."

"People say things like that all the time. It doesn't mean any-thing," Doris said, dismissing my concern. "They only see things when they're looking for them, you know that. And they never found anything to prove Kreischer was nothing but what he said. A loyal American."

A chill moved through me even as I heard the words. Doris made no further explanation. Shaking, I picked up the oars again. I was exhausted from the work, but my heart was tired too.

"I wish you'd said something before. I could've driven Mr. Lewallen back. Saved Sonder that, at least."

Doris shifted to face me. "Oscar's no different from any of us. A man living with failures that are eating his guts. We live with what happened that night and after, and we've been living with it a long time before you got back here. And as I said, I might not have even brought it up, but now I think it does have to do with you and Penn."

I was alarmed. "How is any of this about us?"

"It's part of this place, same as you. I saw your face when Penn said you'll be here for the corn harvest. When she said the Italian men were coming to your farm. I know what you're feeling about that. It doesn't take a genius to figure that out. These are confusing times. Everybody's scared. Afraid of radio messages like they're mustard gas creeping over here after us. Afraid of U-boats out in this water that's our own home. And you have a girl who wants to ring a bell and set all of that right.

"She's looking for a miracle. I know. That's what Jacob wanted. The only reason my boy was caught up in what happened out at the still that day was his grief over his daddy. He'd heard all about a miracle man."

"Sonder."

"Sonder's days riding the rails, being a gypsy, his divining ways, that seemed like the answers he needed. I was just grieving and losing my way. It cost us all. Sonder was no magic man. Just like that stone of your mama's was just a stone. Like that bell in that chapel is just a bell. Penn can gather up all the pieces and have everybody in the world willing to help her do it. But what will she do when it rings and rings and the world looks the same?"

Doris folded her hands in her lap and settled a look on me.

"I don't know how to show her any different world than one that disappoints," I said. "All I know to do is be there when it does. And I don't think I should stop her trying."

She reached to touch my face, but I pulled back hard on the oars.

"No. And I don't think you could. Alice, do you know what I'd do if Jacob were here with me now?" she said, her voice taking on a dreamy tone. "I'd make sweet cakes all the day long, like we used to. I'd fill him full with them. I'd dress up in my best hat and take him to Savannah to see those ships. I'd send him out on that bike with a brand-new chain and tell him to stay out all day, don't come home until it's dark, until you've watched the moon rise and counted the stars. I'd let him go as fast as his legs would carry him. I'd let him go. And maybe I'd go with him. I never did do that. What do you think, that you have all the time in the world?"

My heart became a fist inside me and I remembered thinking almost the same thing only the night before when Penn had been up against me, reading from the commonplace book.

I said, "I don't know how to believe all's forgiven, like we're all just a big happy family. I can't do it, Doris. And I'm afraid, even with my best intentions, playing the gracious hostess for Italian POWs just feels like I'm being asked too much. Nobody took my husband on a nice ride into the country and let him work in a warm cornfield on a pretty day. Nobody fed him biscuits and gravy or gave him a loving cup to drink from."

The boat rocked softly as we pulled near the dock on Bell Isle and all I could hear was the lapping of the water against its wooden sides and my own labored breathing. If anyone could understand, it would be Doris, who had lost her son to a pointless death and been widowed by a man she clearly still adored.

"No, you're right about that. A lot has passed between the people here. And the two of you are going to grieve Penn's daddy a long time. But she's not looking to the bell to change the world. Penn knows that won't happen," Doris said, as if it were the most obvious conclusion. "She's trying to change the two of you, Alice. You remember what that's like, honey."

✕

I watched Doris walk back toward her cottage. She was a lonely figure on her spooky old island and I pitied her. God knew, I wished it was as simple as she wanted me to believe, that we could just throw our doors open to those who had done us harm and be one big family under the roof of Evertell. That I'd be a better mother and the world would somehow right itself for Penn.

Doris had been at my miserable dinner table earlier in the evening and look how that went. She'd had my sorry soup. If that wasn't proof enough she was wrong, I didn't know what was. But I thought of what she'd said about Jacob and it was true too. Coming here had been about giving Penn a chance at a dream, free of imagined dark curses and the deep regrets of a past for which she had no responsibility. I wanted her to be the girl flying fast on the bike toward great things. But could I fly with her? I didn't know if I had that kind of faith inside me. And again, I thought of the pages I'd locked away, the parts of Eleanor's Tale and myself that I hadn't been willing to face.

I cried hot, angry tears while I pulled the oars to move the boat back across the water and came up hard on the opposite dark shore. High above me, in the rafters of the house, a soft light burned just as it had the first night we'd come back to Evertell.

I looked in on Penn, already sleeping. I was relieved.

Sonder was high in the cupola, monitoring the heavens by the light of his miner's lantern and the radio dial, crouched over a stack of postcards, pencil in hand and headphones snugly in place, listening as if it were his own life that depended on those messages.

I climbed up and took a seat beside him in the window, reeling from everything Doris had said. "You sit up here and pluck their words right out of thin air, don't you? Any advice for me up there?"

He looked at me patiently. Maybe he couldn't even hear me. Then he frowned deeply. "It's radio waves, not prophecy."

"Is there a difference? Are any of them really coming home?" I said. He didn't respond, but I felt a hum beneath my skin, an electric connection between us. If he touched me then, I felt certain he'd have scorched a path with his fingertips. I could smell the water and the fields and something beneath that, a sweet, tangy smell that was only male.

I had to move away from him. The old guilt crept up like cold fingers that laced in my hair and settled on my skull. Doris La Roche's lecture had done a number on me. "I don't know if I could live with myself if I made that kind of deal, peddling fantasies to desperate people. You know, people probably get nervous you're a German sympathizer after that Walter Kreischer business," I said. "I know about it. Doris just told me."

Sonder pushed the headphones down so they hung around his neck and turned to me. I could hear the tinny sound of radio voices as the broadcast continued, although it wasn't loud enough for me to make out what they were saying, and I worried he would miss a message. "Is that why you're up here tonight? You think a mob's going to come after me? Warning me off for my own good?"

The question hung between us.

"No. I want to. But no."

Sonder bristled but didn't say anything.

"If I'd known about Mr. Lewallen before dinner, I wouldn't have asked him here. I sure wouldn't have let you drive him home." I sighed. I could only imagine the conversation that might have passed between them on that ride. But maybe it ended in Oscar Lewallen pulling himself up and out of squalor. I tried to appreciate how Sonder might have offered some sort of grace. "I know what you think of him," I said. "I suppose I don't have to work with him on the sale."

"What I think is Lewallen—whatever he thought he was doing,

his reasons for whatever he thought of Kreischer or those men he defended—he's suffered for it."

"All the same, that's a dinner party that never should've happened." I turned and looked out over the dark yard below.

"Penn didn't know."

"Yeah, but would it have stopped her?" I said. He sniffed at that. "I think Penn's adopted Doris for a long-lost grandmother. They're both so preoccupied with death. The woman practically lives in a cemetery. That can't be good for a person." Then I said, "I can't believe this thing happened at Evertell."

I looked back at him and Sonder lifted one of the headphones to his ear but never shifted his gaze from mine.

"Doris told Penn about the homecomings, made them sound like a fantastic thing," I said. "Now Penn's got the idea that's what she's going to make out of May Day. She's declaring herself an Evertell heir. She thinks the people around here, total strangers to her, will come strolling out of the woodwork and love her to death if she rings that bell. I'm worried she's going to be disappointed."

Sonder didn't shift in his seat. "Why?" He dropped the headphones to his shoulders again and put a hand on my arm. "Did you tell Penn that?"

"Of course not. But, Sonder, *nobody* is going to come here for a homecoming. Except a bunch of Italian prisoners. You know that. She's lost her daddy and then her pop in the last two years and that's more disappointment than a girl ought to have so young. She's already getting too attached to Doris. And you. I'm worried we've already been here for too long. We came here to leave it all behind us. So she can go off to school and when this war ends, we can have some kind of life. But Doris thinks I'm wrong, selling. Imagine thinks I'm wrong. You think I'm wrong, selling Evertell, don't you? Hell, even Oscar Lewallen thinks I'm wrong. But is that about me and Penn or about you? You can't say you don't have a stake in this too."

When I came to the end of my little speech, I felt breathless for his response.

"I think you've got a lot of reasons for what you're doing."

"Just not good ones. Damn it, can you not just once say what you think? The food was awful tonight and you choked it down. You never say what you think."

"You'll do what's right by everybody, you always do. I'd just like to see you do right by yourself, Alice."

He settled the headphones in place again and went back to his work, the absolute right thing to do, tuning out my temper tantrum. I felt mildly chastised. My decisions weren't his responsibility.

"Doris said you were the one who made sure someone came for Walter Kreischer's body. You knew he was a Jew. You took care to let the right people know so he was buried with respect. That was a lot to do for a stranger."

"He wasn't a stranger. He was a worker here. I was manager of this farm and he was an employee. It was easy enough to make a call to the rabbi."

"You knew to do that because of Mr. Asch, the man who fostered you when you worked in the mines. He was Jewish."

Sonder nodded. "Mr. Asch meant a lot to me. But I know men from the synagogue here. It's a big congregation, an old community. Old as Evertell."

I thought about that. About the people who had come to this riverbank to settle, the list of names in the commonplace book, women and men from places I could barely conceive of, trying to make a home here. In Helen, a Jew would have been something unheard of, a mystery, someone people wondered at, or worse, feared. There was no synagogue. But Savannah was a port city that had been here for centuries. It made me reconsider what I'd first assumed about the feelings toward Walter Kreischer. And I thought of my own feelings toward the Italian POWs, based solely on what side of this war they'd been fighting on when Finch was killed. I couldn't miss the similarities.

"Can you tell me what happened? How he was buried? I feel like I ought to pay my respects some way, from my family. Like you said, he was an employee, he was part of Evertell. I want to do something. So he's not been forgotten."

Sonder nodded but spoke slowly. I could see this was a difficult memory, and I wouldn't have asked if I hadn't believed it was important. "They weren't going to let that murdered man be forgotten."

As Sonder explained the details of Walter Kreischer's interment at Bonaventure Cemetery just outside the city, in a quiet corner of the Jewish section in a pauper's grave, and the customs that assured that poor soul would be remembered, I sat there staring out at the stars, listening so that I could tell it all to Penn. Occasionally Sonder returned to the radio monitoring, squinted at some faraway point in the night sky, and scribbled down notes on the legal pad he kept within reach. He didn't even look at the paper as he wrote down names of soldiers, their ranks and official numbers, their addresses, and then the messages. He didn't miss a single detail.

> Mom and Pop,
>   I am somewhere in Germany. Doing fine. In good health and they are treating me real good. Do not worry and I hope you can help end this war before long. Take care of Betty. I'll try to write soon.
>   All my love,
>   Tom

Observing his earnest expression, I believed if there were lies in those messages, Sonder Holloway was divining some kind of truth from them.

"What is it that makes you believe what you hear?" I asked.

Sonder looked at me then as though I'd finally hit on the point he'd been trying to make. "It doesn't matter what I believe. Just that somebody's listening."

It was that simple. I reached for a pencil and asked for the headphones.

"Let me try."

)(

When the broadcasts ended and Sonder left, I took the miner's lantern with me and climbed down from the cupola. I went to the front room, tracing the seashell patterns in the walls as I passed them and coming to my mama's writing desk as I had the night we'd first found the commonplace book. Doris's words crowded my head, images of that terrible night on Bell Isle. Mixed with them was the face of Oscar Lewallen today, passed out on my settee. And Daddy, fallen out of the wardrobe at Merely's.

I thought of Sonder, desperately listening to the broadcasts for messages from boys he couldn't bear to fail, and even Bill Hawkes, with his news clippings in their strange display. I sat in the dim light from the miner's lantern, reckoning with my own ghosts, and unlocked the drawer to take the pages from where I'd hidden them. I worked the blue ribbon free and let my eyes fall on the first words, only the first page. The beginning. It was a start. To read a story written by a mother for a child. For me.

ELEANOR'S TALE

London
Spring 1585

They say there are no real mysteries left in the world; no silver-scaled dragons of the air; no fantastic lurking monsters in the deep, nor invisible people of the wood. But Eleanor White could have told you with certainty that these things were real. She'd seen them in her father's sketches and watercolor paintings, an artist who traveled beyond the map and came home to tell all of London of the beasts of the sea and native people, the painted men and women he'd lived among. Her father kept her away from his work when she was young. She lived alone with him in the house on Fleet Street, and was without him when he left for months on his travels. The house was divided in half; half they lived in, while the opposite side was a studio that housed the wonders he'd witnessed. He had added these rooms the year her mother died, and in this way, he never had to leave his work. He curated an exquisite gallery where he entertained important guests, dignitaries of state, and lords and ladies who would pay to see his most unusual collection of sights unseen and fund further expeditions to the world he was discovering.

Known for his former work as a limner, Eleanor's father had once made a fine living painting the most lifelike miniatures. But a man can get lost in such detail. And when the sudden deaths of his beloved wife and young son shocked him and left him faithless, and he might have drawn comfort in his remaining only daughter, instead he locked himself away and soon found himself standing at the great precipice of his grief. Unable to continue the work of portraiture, he set out on voyages to the New World, for he could no longer live in the one he had known. The work was dangerous, but necessary, and it was then he fell in love with shorelines and mountain ranges and star charts that could always be depended upon to guide a man's next step. He was charting a sure and certain future, so no man would ever have to know the kind of uncertainty he'd known.

But secretly, it was Eleanor who wandered through her father's forbidden gallery. She barely noticed his maps. Her curiosity led her to her father's paintings; for what Eleanor longed for most was not the destination, but to catch a thrilling glimpse of the unknown.

Chapter Fourteen

Penn

Another dozen bricks on the ground. After the first, she realized she didn't need to hide them and instead left them as if they'd fallen of their own accord. Mama hadn't seemed to notice. The chimney would not fall. Penn had stared up at it and fought the urge to give it a kick. Instead, she'd wound her way back to the spot where Sonder had shown her the herb bed, near the shady glen where she'd dropped the first brick among the silent fieldstones of the Evertell workers.

In a handkerchief, she bundled several different leaves she pulled from the plants in the herb bed. Their sweet, pungent smells covered her fingertips and she liked having the leaves folded into her pocket. Today she was going to tidy the Evertell cemetery and she was taking the herbs to Doris to learn their names. If Doris didn't know, then she'd take them to Bridie Quillian when she went to her shop. Something tugged at Penn when she thought of the woman in the shop who had sold all the furnishings from the house, whose grandmother had planted here, and Penn couldn't work out the feeling. She was learning one thing though: Evertell was an old place with many stories she did not know, some of them buried deep, and not all of them were happy. Not all of them found their way into a pretty book. Some of them were secrets in the soil and the sand and the stone.

✕

Mama was hard at work with a gallon of white paint, doing her best to cover the soft, rotten wood around the edges of the porches and windowsills.

"A fresh perspective," Mama said. She looked brighter, too, in some way. Pleased with herself. "Nice and bright. At least it'll give a good first impression."

She'd stopped Penn before she could take the boat to help Doris clean the graves on Bell Isle. Now she talked quietly while she worked, explaining to Penn what she'd learned after the terrible dinner, about Oscar Lewallen and a night when a man mistakenly blamed for Jacob La Roche's death had died on Bell Isle. Mama was careful how she said things, but Penn understood enough to know why her dinner party had gone so wrong.

"It wasn't anything to do with us," Mama said gently. "But I wouldn't bring it up with Doris, or Sonder, or anybody, in fact. That's not any of our business. Best to just let it be."

"But the Italians are coming."

The new energy from Mama disappeared and immediately upon mention of the POWs she had the old frown on her face again. Everything about her tightened up, locked down, pushed Penn away. "What does that have to do with anything?"

"Because that's why Mr. Lewallen left, isn't it? Because it's the same? They killed that man just because he was German, and nobody could stop them, but everybody thinks Mr. Lewallen is bad because he didn't stop them either."

"He defended them."

"Sonder said it was his job. Maybe it wasn't his fault nobody went to jail. We're letting Italians come on the farm and giving them dinner, even though they killed Daddy just because he was an American. So won't everybody think we're the same as Mr. Lewallen?"

Mama sighed. "I don't know, Penn. A war is different. It just is. I can't explain it to myself most days. I don't have all the answers."

"Try."

"The people who killed Mr. Kreischer did it because they'd just seen a little boy die, so they used that as an excuse to do wrong things. But all of it was wrong. All of it. What happened to Daddy was because he tried to do what was right for the world, I think. What he thought was right for other people, not just him or us. He died because he wanted to make the world better, not because he hated anybody or wanted revenge for anything. And now things have changed. The Italians aren't enemies. They learned something and changed sides because they want the same things Daddy wanted. So, no, we're not like Oscar Lewallen. We're not defending them. And they're already in prison, aren't they? But while they're here, we're going to let them work on our farms and, I hope, treat them better than they treated your daddy. Because we believe that's what's right." Penn nodded, but her brows were knotted. "I can't make it make any more sense than that."

"Maybe I'm a sympathizer," Penn said.

"Where did you hear that? Did Bill Hawkes say that to you?" Mama slapped paint on the porch and Penn watched it splatter across the front of her shirt and pants. Frustrated, she chose to ignore it.

"I know the word. Bill Hawkes doesn't have to tell me everything. I know sympathizer." Penn watched her Mama's frown deepen at this. She took a breath. "I don't hate those Italians. I know I should, but I won't. Daddy would tell me not to hate them. And he would tell me to ring the bell. I just didn't mean to be ringing it for them too."

What she hated was the tremor in her voice.

"You're right." Mama put the paintbrush down and stepped back to look at her work, then back at Penn. She'd lost some of her steam. "But what's happening now, those POWs coming to work here, it won't be the same as Walter Kreischer and Oscar Lewallen. You don't have to be worried about that."

"I'm not." Penn chewed her nail and thought a long while about all of it, deciding a repeat of something so awful was hardly possible. What bothered her was that it happened at all, and here at Evertell.

Then Mama said, "What do you think? Looks brand new, right? Just right for new times. That's what we're after, isn't it?"

"It's kind of gloppy."

"It is gloppy," Mama admitted, tossing the paintbrush into the bucket. "And it's going to take me until kingdom come to finish it." She sighed.

Penn took a breath. Kingdom come. She didn't have that long to learn everything about Evertell.

"Do I look like Grandmama Claire?" Penn asked. "There weren't any pictures of her at Merely's and I can't find any here either."

"Why would you ask that now?" Mama swallowed hard. "You look like you."

"There's lots I don't know. I've decided to ask all the things I want answers to about our family, even if I don't like them. Do you miss him?" she asked. "Daddy? We never talk about him. I'm afraid I don't miss him as much as I used to at first. I thought that's what I wanted, that it would be good to not miss him. But it feels worse sometimes, when I forget to miss him. I think sometimes he didn't come back because he's really got some other family."

"Oh, honey. No. You don't have to think that. If he could be here, he would. He loved you." Mama was nervous. Questions about family and feelings always made her nervous.

"He loved us."

"Yes."

Mama painted some more and Penn waited to see if she had more to say or if it was okay for her to go take the boat across to Bell Isle.

"I'll be gone with Sonder for a while this afternoon," Mama said. "He's asked me to come with him to look for a spot for a new well nearby. We shouldn't be long. I expect I'll beat you back."

After a moment, Penn blurted, "It's okay if you love Sonder. I know you do. He loves you more, I think." This was something she knew.

"Why on earth would you think that?"

Penn rolled her eyes. Mama acted like she was really shocked. "I don't think it. I know it. Everybody knows it."

"Everybody?"

"Everybody who knows you and Sonder."

"Then you're listening to the wrong people. Things are more complicated than that. Sonder and I grew up together, sort of. We've known each other a long time. And he works for me now, so it's different. We're friends."

"Mama, really? He brings you things you need all the time. He ate your fish stew."

"He's just being nice. He's polite."

"Sonder's not polite. He'd tell you the truth."

"Then I guess I should thank him for having such bad taste."

Penn considered this a moment and it made her think of something she'd wondered about. "He doesn't want people to thank him. Did you know he never reads the thank-you cards? He doesn't even open the mailbags. Why wouldn't he read what they say? He puts them all out in the barn, just like his birds."

Mama shrugged. She scowled too. She didn't really like anything Penn was saying. "Maybe he just doesn't want the attention. Or maybe a lot of that mail is nothing to do with thanks and more to do with people attacking what he's doing and he'd rather not see that side of folks. Or could be he's afraid he's got it all wrong."

"You mean he might find out it wasn't really true, what he sent them. So he just doesn't look."

Penn felt her lip tremble. It came as a surprise, but what she wanted in that moment suddenly came to her so clearly that she gasped. No matter what she'd been saying, the truth was, part of her was just like Sonder, afraid to look. Regardless of her best intentions to stay and face down her fears, as the day grew closer, part of her wished Mama would stop all her beautiful plans. The realization shamed her. She was desperately disappointed in the miserable dinner and disappointed in the crooked chimney, still standing. Now, she imagined the Italians, their dark eyes and hateful mouths, and felt like an awful little coward.

But, she reminded herself, she'd asked Grandma Imegine to come. Sonder was helping her find ways to fix the bell and sending her to meet Sammy Hunt at the shipyard. Doris was helping her bring herbs to Bridie Quillian. Mama needed soothing from the bitter tea, the sweet balm, and the glow of Grandmama Claire's candles. And if she didn't go through with everything now, how would Penn ever have her own Evertell vision and know what she really wanted after they left Evertell behind?

Worst of all, she was starting to imagine things going wrong. What if she rang the bell and nothing changed? What if everything went back to the way it was before, when everything inside her was quiet? She didn't think she could stand it. She wasn't quiet anymore. She was full of very loud doubts.

Mama pulled Penn to her. Put her arms hard and tight around her so that she was pressed into her thin chest. It should have felt good. Penn should have wanted to stay there forever, like Sonder's birds tucked up in their loft. Instead, she felt trapped, like she might choke on all the words she could not say.

X

An hour later, after eating tomato sandwiches with Doris, Penn climbed up into the bell tower to see the silent dome hanging from a thick hewn beam in the rafters. It was a hulking, solitary thing, but when Penn pulled a rope, it moved smoothly, if silently, on its wheel. It looked like a massive headless figure with strong, sad shoulders. A dark, wingless angel. She'd trembled and hurried back to the safety of the chapel's sanctuary and joined Doris on a pew.

"I don't believe I'll make it," Doris said, "but thank you for the invite."

Penn frowned. "Make it? But you have to come. I'm planning for everybody to be there. Even Grandma Imegine. I called her and asked her to surprise Mama."

"Everybody is something I'm not interested in." Doris gave Penn a knowing smile but Penn ignored her and picked up a hymnal from beside her on the pew to thumb through its pages. "I think I'd like to make peace my own way. There's nothing wrong with what you're doing, but I believe I'll stay home with mine. Bill might drop by. You'll be glad to know I'm thinking maybe I'll make a cake."

"Cake?" Penn repeated.

"To remember Jacob. He loved a cinnamon cake."

Penn clamped her mouth shut, ashamed she'd been about to complain even further. She wanted to ask, to be sure she understood, but Doris's face told Penn everything. May Day was a day Doris wanted to remember her son; maybe it was close to when Jacob had died.

"People remember their dead in different ways. Your commemoration will be just fine for me from over here at Bell Isle."

Doris changed the subject and went on to tell Penn all she knew about the bell. "It's a bronze bell, made by the Revere Company. A gift to your family in 1803," Doris explained. "One of the last bells that Revere cast himself."

"Are you talking about *the* Paul Revere? The one who yelled his head off?"

"Yeah, well, I guess he made big bells to do the work for him after that. Or maybe he'd already made them." Doris flapped her hand in the way Penn had come to expect when the woman was having trouble getting her memories straight. "Revere was a silversmith before all of that though. Not just a soldier."

Penn imagined Paul Revere on his ride, the way she'd been taught, and then she imagined this bell ringing, a bell he'd made just for Evertell.

"Which heir was here then? Who was the bell for?"

"That was Camille Telfair Parish, that poor girl. It was a birthday gift when she was three years old. She's the one who disappeared later on, as a young woman. Nobody ever knew what became of her. Her husband claimed she took a lover and ran off. I don't think so. A mama doesn't leave her babies like that and she had Delaney, just a few years old." Doris took a breath and seemed to think better of whatever she was about to say. "I guess that's a good thing we can be thankful for, isn't it? Or you wouldn't be here, would you? Delaney—let's see here, she married a Beaufort, I believe. Had a whole passel of children, if I recall. But the first was a daughter. Always was so with the women in your family."

Penn was still thinking of Camille. "Evertell heirs always find their way home. That's what Grandmama Claire said."

"Then there you go. Another mystery in your book."

Doris didn't have to say what they were both thinking. Whatever happened to Camille, it was the reason her mother had believed the stone was cursed. This was the story Mama had told Penn when they'd walked down the drive to Evertell that first night. "Do you think the stone cursed us?" she asked Doris now.

"No. I think there's bad folk in this world. And good too. And Evertell's seen its share of both."

Penn's head was full of too many mysteries and discoveries to know what was real anymore. "Can we just stop talking and go clean the graves?"

They took a couple of spades Doris brought from the garden shed. Doris led the short distance to the cemetery, waiting in silence beneath the deep, green shade of the trees. Penn felt some of the anxiety she'd been carrying slip away as she exhaled and dropped to her knees near one of the headstones, barely visible beneath the thick palmetto fronds. She pulled at weeds and dug out others until the headstone was tidy again. Penn made a huffing sound and Doris straightened, stretching her lower back. She frowned at Penn. "You are a moody bird."

THE LOST BOOK OF ELEANOR DARE

"I wish I was a bird." Penn sighed. "I'm doing what Mama wants and pulling up traps and gagging on fish stew. But nothing's changing."

"You mean *she's* not changing." Doris chuckled. "What did you expect? She'd kiss Sonder and turn into a fairy princess?"

"Don't make fun," Penn pleaded. "It doesn't make me feel better. Did you know there aren't any pictures of my grandmama Claire or of Mama? Not one."

"You're jumping all over the place."

"I've looked," Penn insisted. "It's like she didn't even exist. These gravestones are all there is. And the commonplace book. But Mama won't put our names in it."

"Do you ask her about any of this?"

"It doesn't matter. When it's over, she's going to sell Evertell. She just is. Even if I ring the bell. Even if I do everything right. Something bad happened. I know Grandmama Claire died, but I think there's something else she's not telling me."

Doris said, "Listen to me. You can't control everything by marching around ringing old bells and working fairy charms." Penn raised her eyes to avoid Doris's gaze, instead looking at the stones. Doris went on, "Here's what we do: We trust. We love our people and whoever gets put in our way. We remember our dead. That's all. And life will send you what you need. Like it sent you to me, way out here."

"For what?"

"I don't know! I'm just an old woman, Penn. To live, I guess. To wonder what's coming next."

"I don't know what's coming next. Except more fish stew."

Doris chuckled again. She was doing that more lately. Penn liked the sound. She took a little hope from that.

Doris said, "I agree we ought to find your mama a new set of recipes." She shrugged, then stood and wiped at her knees and surveyed their work.

Penn moved back to the gravestone she'd exposed and remembered the small, misshapen fieldstones in the glen behind the house as she ran her hand over the surface of this ornately cut memorial. "Sonder told me to stay out of the glen behind the house." She hated to say what she was starting to suspect. "There are stones there, but they aren't marked. Sonder said those are Evertell workers, but you can't tell it to look at them. He said they built Evertell. That means they're older than the bell or anything here, except the book." Penn's feelings about those stones made her want to ask questions, but at the same time she didn't want the answers.

"Oh yes. Those people were brought here to work this place when Georgia was still British." Doris's tone was brittle, clipped, matter-of-fact. "They're unmarked because nobody knows their names, honey. By now nobody even knows which way they've been laid out. Those are slave graves, Penn."

Penn felt uneasy. She'd already guessed as much, but her unease came from thinking she'd had every right to that dark little cove, stepping all over stones she'd judged as no account, hiding her misdeeds among them. "I didn't know it. But I guessed it."

"There's a lot to this place, more than that old house and your grandmama's stories," Doris said. "George could've told you. The two of you would have been thick as thieves. Savannah and everything around here's built on top of one grave or another. Well, don't look surprised; this is an old place. Where do you think those people go? One group comes and lives on a bluff or a creek awhile and calls it home until another one comes along and wipes them out and plops down right on the same spot. Pretty soon, they forget anybody else was ever there before them, or they just don't want to remember it. They built a garden right on top of a Yamacraw Indian mound—or maybe it was Muscogee, one of those ones that's so old there's none around anymore—in the city and grew the first peach orchard in Georgia. Did you know that?" Penn shook her head. "Well, they did. Or that's what I've been told. There's not a tree to be found there now, but it's the story. Georgia peaches, grown right up from those bones.

"Then there's plenty of soldiers who had to be buried no matter what side they were fighting on, which war they were fighting. Droves were killed by yellow fever and they were put in the ground wherever there was a place to hold them, just out back of homes and what have you. A lot of streets run right over those people now, every kind of person you can think of, people who came here like those people in the glen behind your kitchen house—Irish, Jews, the poor, Negroes."

Penn could hear the implication that she was still only a child and there was plenty more she didn't know. She lowered her eyes and pulled the folded handkerchief from her pocket. The herbs were limp and wilted. She handed them gently to Doris.

"Is that why Bridie Quillian's name's not in our book? If her grandmama planted these, is she buried in that glen?" Penn had only seen six or seven stones and that didn't seem like a lot of workers to build all of Evertell, but she also knew some had been moved.

"Mm. I wouldn't have any way to tell you that. But they weren't all buried there, the ones who worked Evertell over the years." Doris picked at the herbs, carefully sniffing them and looking at their shapes. "I don't believe her people are here or she'd make the trip out from town now and again. I've never seen her do that."

"If I take her herbs from Evertell, will she like it? When we go get sweet balm from her store?"

"I think that'd be nice of you to offer. Sometimes the nicest thing we can do is take a little handful of herbs, try to think about somebody besides ourselves." Doris looked up. "Now, look around here at what we've done. Peace and quiet. This is a place I can rest. What about you?"

Penn nodded feebly, but she meant it. She spent the next hour alongside Doris in silence, tidying the graves of her own family in earnest, chastised. Quiet, but not at peace. They were not the same thing. She closed her eyes for a moment and let her mind settle. Deep inside she could see the faint silver light, pulsing, marking each breath. Her fingers still smelled of the crushed herbs. And Penn thought of the terrible things that had happened at Evertell, of the secrets those stones were keeping, of the streets of Savannah built over so many bones. It should have made her upset, but somehow she was not. Instead, she felt as if she'd discovered something about herself. And she thought of the peach orchard that now was only a story.

Chapter Fifteen

Alice

I'd done my best with the paint and Penn had taken off for Bell Isle, leaving me with her questions and fears. They combined with the voices from the Berlin broadcasts still warbling through my head and the hopefulness of the beginning of Eleanor's Tale. I hadn't been able to make myself read any further. I wanted to remain suspended in the optimism of that young girl, daring to peek at her father's paintings to see what the wide world might hold for her.

I found more of Penn's ink drawings when I flipped through the pages of the commonplace book: a sharp-featured fish with shining scales beside Angelique's recipe for fish stew. There were delicate moons shown in all their phases beside Flora Beaufort Vaughn's planting calendars for the garden that fed her family in the years following the War Between the States, and a perfect sketch of the iron gate at the end of the drive to Evertell beside an entry detailing its commission by Delaney Parish Beaufort. Beneath it, I read the newspaper bulletin regarding her mother's disappearance, Camille

Telfair Parish, in 1822. There was no death date for her, no indication she'd ever been found. But her daughter, Delaney, grew up to have eleven children of her own. I imagined that gate had been a way she'd hoped to keep them safe.

I'd never read some of these entries until now, certainly never passed any stories on to Penn, and I found that like my daughter, I wished there was more in the book about each of these Evertell women. There was so much I didn't know. "*Stranger's Ground*," I remembered Doris saying. In many ways, that was what Evertell felt like to me, but we belonged among these women, didn't we? For good or bad.

)(

If anyone ever needed a lesson in divining, it was surely me. I needed to find the courage to look for my mama once again. Luckily, I had an invitation from an authority.

The ride with Sonder out to the Cox farm was a peaceful thirty-minute trip. Sonder brought us to a beautiful meadow, but divining, as it turned out, was little more than a slow amble over the ground. With not much else to distract me, I spent the time running an apology through my mind. I didn't hear Sonder's quiet explanations for his methods until he said my name.

"I'm sorry," I said, embarrassed and suddenly ridiculously inarticulate. "I don't know what you were saying. I was trying to think of a way to tell you something."

He chuckled and I appreciated his good nature in spite of everything. "Doesn't say much for my chances of success with the circus."

"No, I mean I'm sorry for the way I've been acting. I need to apologize for what I said to you after you came to me about the Italians coming for the harvest."

He stopped and turned to listen to me. "You don't owe me an apology for that, Alice."

"Well, I'm not saying I don't have reasons for my feelings, like you said, but they aren't your fault. So I want you to tell me what I can do. Can we just forget what I said?"

"What changed your mind?"

"Honestly, Doris had a lot to say last night. And then Penn let me have it this morning. But I don't know if I would have listened to either one of them."

"Doesn't surprise me."

I deserved that.

"It was the broadcast last night, hearing the soldiers. I thought about my husband, but I also thought about the mailbags full of the responses from the families you reach. And then the men you want to bring here. Who's the enemy? I don't know anymore. Even if I did, do I think I could march them out on a roadside and murder them like they murdered Finch? No." A warm breeze passed softly over the open field and over my skin, but I felt chilled and wrapped my arms tight around myself. "But then, what? All I can think is, what am I going to do? What's the right thing? And I really don't think storming off, dragging Penn kicking and screaming, leaving here the same—"

He spoke then to stop me. "Alice."

"No, I need to do better than that for Penn." I took a breath and wiped the back of my hand across my mouth to stop my lips from trembling. "Do you know I can't even look at myself in the mirror? Remember that old wardrobe, the one my mama wanted me to have?"

He remembered. "I took it apart to load it for the trip when you left."

"Of course you did." I owed him so many thanks. He smiled

at my expression and waved a hand to dismiss my remorse. "It has that big mirror on the door, remember? I loved it when I was little. It smelled like evergreen, like her. My mama. The inside was lined with cedar. But after we left, I couldn't stand it. I swear I do everything I can to keep from even seeing it out of the corner of my eye. It gives me nightmares. If I look, what am I going to see? I don't know anymore. But what really scares me," I said, choking on my words, "is that if I never have the courage to look, how will I teach Penn? I want to stay here and learn how to do that, look myself in the eye again. I want to face those Italian POWs and see men, just men. And show Penn some humanity in all of this nightmare. I'm not sure I want to sell. At least not everything."

I saw the surprise leap into his eyes, even if they were still and quiet as a pond. I added, "If we go, Penn has to see it's our choice to go, instead of feeling like we're running away. I want her to feel like she's launching on a new adventure. That she's free to fly. Because as beautiful as Evertell may be, it's still a cage unless she's free to leave it. See there, I've learned something from your pigeons. Maybe the damn peacock too."

I could see my words had hit him squarely. He shifted his weight and listened more intently but didn't interrupt me.

"I've been thinking about the expectations I had when I came back here and the secret my mama promised me. When we opened that book, Penn and I, I thought I was going to find the one thing I needed from my mama, a neat ending to a story she was telling me. I thought it was about us. Maybe about me. I thought it was some kind of secret way to help me grow up or forgive her. I don't know. But it wasn't there." I shrugged. "She didn't finish it. Or she hid it from me. Somebody tore the last pages out." I didn't mention I had finished the job and taken the rest, keeping them from Penn. "Anyway, it felt like another betrayal. But I've had a few days to think about it, and maybe it wasn't my mama's secret to tell. I'm starting to think maybe the end was never the point."

Finally, he spoke. Sonder knew the value of words. He didn't waste them. "What is?"

I shrugged, feeling better for having admitted I had no answer. "I really don't know. I may never know. But last night when you said that to me, about doing something for myself, I decided to read that story again. It's all I have of her. She gave it to me, maybe the best thing she had to give, and I want it to mean something. Even if it's just like the bell for Penn, a way to remember, a way to say goodbye. I need to figure that out. She wants me to let people into our life and she wants to start with POWs," I said wryly.

Sonder considered everything for only a moment before saying glibly, "Well, if you're going to make another dinner, maybe just stick with sandwiches."

"What?" I gulped down a laugh. "Is that a joke? You know what you're asking for."

"Just feed them, Alice. They'll be hungry after the work. It'd be nice to give them a meal before sending them back to the camp."

I couldn't argue with that. I nodded, my throat scraping with emotion. Sonder gave me a slow smile and I felt the hard cold that had lodged inside me warm and ease into the empty places around my heart like the wax in my mama's molds. I searched for the word to describe the feeling until my mind finally caught on it: *forgiveness.*

I thought of what Penn had said about the return mail for Sonder and his refusal to read the thank-you letters from the families. It was a terrible thing, penance.

"Penn tells me you know girls who weld on the Liberty ships. You know a lot of girls, then?" He smirked but didn't defend his friendships. I felt a twinge of something like jealousy and it embarrassed me. I looked away as I said, "She asked if she could go down to the yard and meet one who might help with the bell. Is that really someplace I want to send a thirteen-year-old girl by herself? I'm not sure I like the idea."

"Sammy Hunt," he said. "She's seventeen, a Girl Scout."

Now I felt ridiculous.

"I didn't say I was worried about the girl. I'm worried about sending Penn down to a wharf full of sailors and who knows what else."

"I know what you're worried about. I talked to Sammy about Penn. She'll take care of her while she's there. And I figured I might need to take a drive that day, stay nearby. Keep an eye on things. Penn won't know I'm around."

"I like that better," I agreed, relaxing. I couldn't help thinking of the pigeons with their netted aviary and my own little bird trying to take wing.

We walked on. Sonder knew how to let the silence sit on the day and I appreciated that, listening to my blood run until it had slowed to match the calm of the afternoon and the steady man at my side.

"So how does this work?" I asked after some time. "Don't you need those divining rods? I've heard about them."

"I don't use the rods. Never have." He shrugged. "Like I was saying to Penn, you learn what to look for."

He simply walked, his palms brushing the tops of the tall grass. The sun was bright, and I held up one hand to shield my eyes so I could see him better. He was attuned to everything around us, the land beneath his feet. Me. But I was skeptical, thinking of the post-cards, the stones. His mother was right. This did put me in mind of circus acts. I didn't know how to believe such a thing.

"It's a skill, not a trick," he said, as if he'd read my thoughts, making me blush. "It's about seeing something you don't even know you're seeing. You check for signs like the direction of the breeze, the way the tree line runs along the hillside, the slope of the meadow, the smell of the earth, and the kind of minerals that turn up in the rocks around a certain place. Water shows itself a thousand ways. Most things do."

I grasped hold of what he was saying. "It's not magic. It's science."

"It takes both, the mind and the heart, to know what you're standing on."

I watched him register each of these things with his senses and I tried to read any meaning in them.

"I wish I could see the way you do." I met his steady gaze. "People are like water that way, aren't they?"

He nodded, although I thought he looked a little grim around the mouth. He didn't want to talk about it. "Run through with memories."

"Especially the people in a place like Evertell."

Over the next several hours, we talked very little. Sonder occasionally warned me about low spots or stopped to explain how he surmised the minerals hidden in a certain area or asked me to note how the flora changed the scent of a place where water might be hiding far underground. I felt like a blind person, stumbling, unknowing. I had no sense for the secrets that were leading him, but I felt safe to follow. I felt an irresistible urge to touch him, to reassure myself that he was flesh and bone and not a ghost of the past, like Penn had first guessed. Without a word, I reached out and took his hand. He gave my hand a squeeze in return and I felt inexplicably happy. Safe enough to venture an intimate question.

With my free hand, I gestured toward his prosthetic. "Tell me how you lost your leg. I was always afraid to ask when we were younger. I used to imagine you were a soldier, but you were too young to have been in the trenches. Did this happen in the mines?"

"Lots over there were just kids," he said. "But not me, no. You're right. Never been to war. I had no idea what on God's earth the fighting was about. Not really. I was in a cave-in. Lot of men didn't come out that day. It only got part of me." He spared me the details and I thought maybe it wasn't a memory he wanted to revisit. But I still felt the horror of what he was telling me.

"Dear God."

He nodded. "That's what I said. That's what I call this fellow." He tapped the prosthetic with his knuckles.

"No," I said, trying not to smile. "You do not."

He grinned. "Better than some of the other names I've used for it. The doctors fit me with this thing. I learned to hobble along well enough. People sometimes don't notice. I figure I'm as close as any man ever gets to walking one foot in this world, one in the other."

He stood there in the soporific glow of the sun, still holding my hand, and kept talking. I wanted it to go on forever. I stayed very still as he explained that after the shaft caved in, he was alone. He had no relative to go to. He took the only work available to a young man who wasn't whole, the dangerous kind, signing on with the railroad.

"I remember that you rode trains. So how did you come here?"

"Fate. That's what I always thought, anyway. Seemed like I was always coming here, when I look back on it. I worked first as a brakeman, coupling and uncoupling train cars in the yard, and eventually took on duties as a switchman. They control the track switches."

"What happened to make you leave?"

"I felt trapped. Like part of me was going to always be back in that mine. Then one day I was standing on the platform for a smoke break when the urge hit me to leap on one of the open train cars."

"But how could you do it?" I asked in disbelief. Clearly it would have taken a great effort in his condition to jump on a moving train car. "I mean, with Dear God and all?"

"I just done it. The train was pulling out, picking up speed. There was only the one open car. If I'd waited, this lost leg wouldn't have allowed me to make it. I grabbed hold of some handle on the car door so I scraped the hide off my knuckles and just heaved myself up. It was the best feeling, I'll tell you that. Like I could finally breathe. I didn't know where I was going and I sure didn't give a damn. You know?"

I leaned in close, listening.

The unknown turned out to be a cold ride in an empty car on the line south through Georgia. He rode all the way to Columbus, thrilled with his adventure, thinking once he reached the end, he'd jump another car headed back to where he'd started. And this was how he filled his days for the next few months. While some men had addictions to liquor or women or cards, Sonder had been obsessed with risk and rush and movement and the company of strange men who huddled in box cars in threadbare clothing. They nodded to one another, a brotherhood not unlike the one he'd known in the mine. Sonder had looked into their hollow faces and fishy eyes and felt certain he was riding with ghosts; he felt himself to be one.

Time didn't exist in the railcars. They might have been riding for minutes or centuries; they were separate from such margins. But more powerful to transform Sonder and his league of bums were the stories they told.

"It sounds wonderful. And awful. I've still never really been anywhere," I said, feeling strangely envious.

Sonder scowled. "Nothing but lies, men reinventing the past, reinventing themselves. Every day they were reborn princes, kings, heroes. But we were just bums. I'd meant to take a joy ride one afternoon," he said, "and instead, I discovered the ability to completely forget myself."

Each time he had successfully hopped another train, each time he'd deceived someone with a well-told invention about his acts of heroism or concocted a more harrowing story of survival, he felt he was wiping out the past.

"My daddy was like that, when we left here. Not the inventing part, but the blending in part. He sort of became nobody, anybody. The John Merely you all talk about, he disappeared." *I did too*, I thought.

"You miss him."

I thought for a moment. "I missed him a long time, I think. I missed the way he was when we were here. I think a part of him was always waiting to get back to my mama. Maybe that's just my way of trying to resolve everything with a happy ending. It's morbid, I know."

Sonder didn't judge, only finished what he'd been saying about his own journey to Evertell. In the end, it was his leg, not his nerve, that failed him.

"I was here, at the Savannah railyard, when I fell. After all that, just tripped and fell. I guess I'd outrun myself. Knocked my head hard enough on the rails they sent me to the hospital."

When the doctors questioned him about his home, he revealed he had nowhere to go. Until one day, someone came for him.

"Who was it? My daddy?" I asked, thinking it was poetic, how they'd met. Like me, I imagined how my daddy must have come across Sonder Holloway and discovered something he'd always wanted in a boy: someone he could make into anything. But Sonder shook his head.

"Nah. It was your mama. She'd come out to the hospital to see old George La Roche."

"Doris's George?"

"One and the same. He'd died that afternoon. And when Claire left there, she brought me home."

Within the next few minutes, Sonder seemed to find what he was looking for, a certain color to the ground, the vegetation he knew to look for, the smell in the air, perhaps. I couldn't have told one spot from another, but he seemed satisfied he'd seen what he'd been hoping to and we made our way back to the truck to carry the news to an eager farmer.

I thought of the afternoon I'd first seen him, how I'd spied on him. "When I saw you that first day in her chandlery, I believed I'd dreamed you up. I thought you were mine, like I thought everything here was mine. But I couldn't imagine where you'd come from. The next morning, when you weren't in the chandlery, I thought you'd gone and I would be alone again. It was the first time I felt like this place wasn't the whole world. Why did you stay?"

"You already asked me that. It's the wrong question."

"What should I ask you, then?" I was trying to divine a man.

"Ask me, did I find what I was looking for?"

That's when I knew I was in love with him. "Did you?"

"I knew when we got here."

London
Summer 1586

Long ago, her mother's people were fishwives from the Nordic countries. Her mother, a tall woman named Tomasyn Cooper, had borne Eleanor and an infant son gone to heaven too soon. She'd sworn that generations after her ancestors left their homes in the frozen fjords for the comfortable fires of their English hearths, their daughters still carried the cold in their bones and their hair always smelled of evergreen. Every woman in Eleanor's mother's line waited for the day when her heart would be ready and she would have a vision, her Evertell, a sign she'd come of age and with it the gift of guidance from her forebears. Eleanor knew little more of her mother's people except for a few inscriptions in a commonplace book, its pages filled with prayers and contemplations on Scripture. This was what passed from mother to daughter—a book of women's wisdom and mysteries.

At first, Eleanor hadn't seen there were hidden messages in the pages, but as she became a better reader, she found advice in the recipes, hope in the secret charms and cures, dreams of things her father knew nothing of. And in this way, Eleanor felt she finally had a secret of her own. She'd inherited her mother's stories.

People said Eleanor had too much freedom to wander alone about Fleet Street. It made her an odd girl, to be on her own so often. She despised the pity of her neighbors, women who pretended concern for her loneliness but enjoyed speculating about what she did with her time. To spite them, she polished her mother's red boots and wore her gray cloak so she always seemed to be about something important. Rather than spending time at the hearth or spinning cloth or diligently at her prayers, she most often loitered outside the print shop, watching the printer set the blocks. She was interested in words.

People might have guessed she wore her finery and haunted this door because she was in love with the man, but they'd have been wrong. What Eleanor loved was the smell of ink and turpentine. In some ways, it reminded her of the smells of her father's paints, but it was more than that. She was enamored of the process and the power of each stark symbol to make sense of an otherwise, in her opinion, senseless world. There was magic in the making of a book.

And so, when her father's pictures of dancing natives and painted warriors were to be used in pamphlets to convince the queen of the value of the explorations, Eleanor longed to play a part. The artwork had to be copied and made into printing plates. The work would be done by an expert printer, a man the queen brought from Frankfurt. It was on the day that this man visited with Eleanor's father that Eleanor was invited into the gallery. She was nervous, hiding her sweating palms in the folds of her skirt, as they walked through the rooms that had been forbidden to her for years. She stole glances at the watercolor canvases and sketches on easels and the maps he'd displayed on his drafting table. She'd seen them all before, but never with his permission.

She felt protective of her father's paintings, for they'd been her only means to travel through their beauty, in her imagination. The stranger had come to persuade her father that the copies he would produce would be true to the vision of the original art. But it was plain enough that the Dutchman was uneasy and awkward, lacking confidence. And Eleanor watched her father grow doubtful. Eleanor offered them tea, hoping to give the Dutchman a chance.

The man set out to explain his craft, in hopes of persuading Eleanor's father of his skill. He exposed the set of tools he'd brought from his print shop, something Eleanor had longed to hold in her own hands. At sight of them, Eleanor drew in her breath too sharply. Seeing her interest and that perhaps he might further his cause by charming his host, the Dutchman offered the graver's tools as a gift to her. He would make her his apprentice. Her father hesitated only long enough to nod. She understood that she'd been invited to be part of this work, the thing she'd wanted most. It was common for wives to work as printers, the men said as they discussed a plan. Female names did not appear on the pages they made, only the names of their husbands. But it was a respectable trade and one that might serve Eleanor well.

The men came to an agreement. John White would trust his daughter alone with the reincarnations of his images, and as apprentice to the Dutchman. Of course, only the Dutchman's name would go on the engravings. Eleanor would be an invisible artist, something that didn't trouble her in the least. Invisibility was something at which she was already skilled.

From the moment Eleanor felt the tools in her hand, she could think of little else. This was something powerful, more permanent than the fragile state of ink or paint or paper, something as divine as the scripture her father recited. Her father brought copper plates from the very print shop up the street where Eleanor had dreamed of making a book of her own. When he spread the smooth, rectangular plates before her, they looked like the shining scales of the dragons of the air and the monsters of the sea. She thought of the fishwives from the north, the women who had written their secrets in the commonplace book. And Eleanor knew that the magic of her mother and the faith of her father met inside her in this way.

With the graver's tools, Eleanor cut into the soft metal, creating depressions, intricate etchings, making space so that an image appeared in the empty places where her tools had cut and the ink would fill the wounds she'd left and the press would leave a print, the mirror image of Eleanor's work. She engraved her favorite images from her father's paintings—the plants and the sea creatures, and her technique became more and more detailed and delicate. While he was away, her lamp burned all night. She worked to surprise him with a fine collection. She imagined the pride he would take in her skill. And she put her heart into her final plate, her own original work, an image of a wide shore, a sky that stretched high and bright, a sea full of motion and mystery, a world shining with possibility so that any way she turned the copper plate, it caught the light. She'd seen it in a dream. This plate she marked with her own initials. She prayed that the engraving flashed so brightly that her father's eyes would be blinded by wonder. When he wiped away the tears, he would again see his daughter, the wild girl with hands as cold as ice and hair that smelled of evergreen, who had always been there, waiting for his return.

When she was younger, Eleanor's father had gone against convention and secretly taught her to read, as he would have a son. Transformation was the theme of her education. But it had taken Eleanor a painfully long time to comprehend the scripture from his Bible, and he'd seen soon enough that he could not replace what had been lost. Still, she had dutifully read the entirety of his book three times by her seventeenth year. And she grew to understand her father's past was one of want; his God was fierce and his moral instruction was focused on the reality of sin and the judgment of man. But the parables were Eleanor's favorite, so these were the lines she copied into the commonplace book to help her commit their wisdom to memory. Although, to Eleanor, even parables seemed out of place in her mother's book. Scripture was written by men. The commonplace book was full of the language of women. And while her father believed in the supernatural, in visions and sacred rites as they were laid out by the prophets and saints, as though God were a distant star or a ghost, he would have disapproved of the notion that the divine existed within the ordinary world of creation, much less that a woman had any claim to it.

And so upon his return, just as he had overlooked the value of the commonplace book, he overlooked the divine in his daughter's work. Eleanor's father never noticed the perfect flash of her engravings. The Dutchman enjoyed his favor and credit for the prints. She never saw a copy of the pamphlet for herself. If her father even saw Eleanor anymore, she wasn't sure. Instead, he credited the book, not Eleanor, for his latest commission and talked feverishly of another voyage, this time under Sir Walter Raleigh, which he called the most important of his life. Again, he locked the door to his studio, leaving Eleanor on the outside.

She watched from her window when an emissary arrived, accompanied by a native man like the ones she'd seen in her father's paintings. He wore the clothes of an Englishman, but they were ill-fitting. Eleanor felt pity for the fear she saw in his eyes. He was surely a long way from home, and as beautiful as her father had ever claimed. Proof his paintings of the New World were true.

She listened at the door to hear if her father was offered this new commission. Whatever the details, she could not tell, but she wanted to go with him. She knew he could invite her as easily as he'd led her into his gallery and accepted the Dutchman's apprenticeship, or he could leave her behind as thoughtlessly as he had locked her out.

Chapter Sixteen

Penn

The ride to Savannah to finally meet Bridie Quillian was only eight miles, over so quickly that Penn barely had time to know what to think. But she was delighted Mama had come along.

"I see what you're trying to do," Mama said. "The least I can do is drive."

"You're just trying to keep an eye on me."

"Like I said, I see what you're doing. I like watching."

For now, Penn didn't argue. She liked having Mama with her today. She carried the commonplace book—she wanted to charm Bridie Quillian—a basket full of cut herbs, and a thousand hopes in her head.

She'd never seen a city this size, except in pictures. They'd never driven down to Atlanta. She'd only heard people talk of towns like this. When they drove from Helen, Mama had taken all the back roads, avoiding traffic, and Penn had been sleeping when they skirted the city and took the road out to Evertell. Now she was so excited she was sweating through her dress even with the windows down and the warm breeze blowing. She knew she'd look wild by the time they reached the shop but she hadn't thought about tying a scarf around her head until it was too late.

"How do you know where the shop is?" Penn asked. Penn had never heard of a Negro woman owning a business in a city. She'd never even thought about such things before. Certainly they'd never walked into such a place.

"Sonder's done business with Bridie Quillian for years. You should pay attention. We'll drive past the road that takes you over the shipyard, so you'll know your way when you come out here tomorrow on your own."

Penn thought she must have misheard. "Do you mean it?"

"I thought about it. I talked to Sonder. He called ahead and got everything set up. You'll go straight to the gate so they can send you to see the girl. Nowhere else. There and back."

Penn squealed and Mama laughed.

Suddenly, they rode up on the first few buildings—a service station that reminded Penn of Merely's and a furniture store. In this way, Savannah was not what Penn had expected, not some golden city rising up in front of her like Oz. Instead, the road looked like any other stretch of highway until they took a turn and all at once they were inside Savannah's squares.

Doris had described the city as a gracious lady with a dirty face, and as soon as they drove into town, Penn understood the expression. Great churches made Penn squint to peer up at their spires. She thought of Europe and wondered if her daddy had done the same. Everywhere she looked, Savannah seemed to be a watercolor painting. The historic homes were beautiful and ornate, but there was an element of neglect that hung over the city. People ambled along the sidewalks, past colonial buildings and military monuments, horse-drawn carriages and modern shipyards. Penn loved it on sight.

They turned onto a main road that led deeper into the historic buildings, beneath a thicker canopy of oaks, past the famous Cotton Exchange, a fine redbrick building flanked by a row of other brick warehouses backed up to the riverfront, busy with cars and working people. Her heart raced, and Mama smiled. "You like it?" she asked. "Just hold on," Mama said. "The roads get bumpy down here. Cobblestone down by the water where we're going. Look out that way." She pointed. "You go down that way for the shipyard. You'll cross that bridge and see where you are."

Penn was taking everything in, nodding, trying to remember. There was nothing to it, really. It was almost a straight shot. But she'd never been any such place and there was so much to see. The shop wasn't facing the riverfront but tucked behind those buildings, off an alleyway, beneath a footbridge, and she was glad now to be carried along and think only of the grand houses that lined the streets, graced by gnarled oaks with sprawling branches draped in moss.

When they came to a stop, she leapt from the truck's cab and followed Mama down a stone staircase where they stood before the water on River Street. Men in workman's clothes and some in military uniform hurried in every direction. Boys not much younger than Penn ran in groups, laughing. Women with baskets of vegetables or flowers chatted and laughed, and Penn was pleased she carried a basket of her own. There was every sort of person to see, including the soldiers and sailors, and Penn smiled to hear their baritone voices rumbling. The uneven streets were built of discarded ballast stones and she had to concentrate to keep her footing. The air was filled with the smells and sounds of a bustling waterfront. The river was busy with boats, and in the distance she could hear the construction across the river at Southeastern where crews worked on the great Liberty ships. Savannah felt to Penn like a fevered heart, like her own heart in her chest, pounding out life. As they ducked down the alley and approached a small turquoise door, the kind Penn imagined she would find on the house of a dwarf or a fairy, Mama stopped short of knocking and turned to Penn with a serious expression.

She seemed nervous and Penn thought it must be because she was about to come face-to-face with things from her childhood. Penn wished she had thought of that before. "If it's a strange place and you want to leave, just say so," Mama whispered.

"You too," Penn said. She reached her arms around Mama to give her a squeeze and Mama returned the hug briefly. Penn wished she'd hold on.

The doorknob was brass, intricately carved and large, with an enormous matching door knocker. But the door stood ajar, and Mama ducked to avoid banging her head on the low frame. Penn followed her inside and heard someone shuffling in what appeared to be a back room of the dim shop.

"Hello?" Mama called.

"Here. I'm here," a thin, high voice answered.

As Penn's eyes adjusted, she could begin to make out the bizarre space. Shelves of glass jars were lined up behind a long countertop. A collection of long, curling peacock feathers jutted out of a large jar near a mortar and pestle filled with some unknown substance. Penn wondered if the feathers had come from Gustave. Dangling from a wood beam ceiling were bunches of dried herbs, wax tapers, and a large scale, presumably for measuring wares. The space was barely a closet, and Penn and her mama huddled with their backs almost pressed to an exposed brick wall, the aroma of spices so thick Penn felt a bit smothered.

A woman who had to be Bridie Quillian emerged, a tiny black woman no bigger than a child, shocking Penn, who'd expected someone like Doris, not this wild-looking elf with gray hair springing out from her head so she seemed a strange moon approaching them through the darkness. But when she smiled to welcome them, Penn was delighted by her.

At sight of Mama, the woman sucked in her breath and said in a way that sounded like a song, "That's not Claire Merely's girl? It is! Look here!"

"Yes," Mama said in the tone she used when speaking with strangers, uncomfortable and a little arrogant. "I'm Alice Merely."

"Alice. Yes, you are. You are. Doris told me you were coming, now look at you."

Bridie Quillian made Penn smile as she stood before them, coming no higher than Mama's breastbone. "Where've you two come from? I forget."

"Helen," Mama said. "Up in the mountains, actually."

"Helen," she said, as if she were tasting the word.

Bridie hadn't taken one look at Penn yet. But she motioned for Mama to follow and led her toward the counter. She rustled through the lower shelves and brought something out to place before her. "There. What do you see? The last one. I never sold it to nobody, that one."

The candle was dusty, but the impressions left by the candle mold were clear. Mama traced a finger over the lines. Bridie shrugged. "Supposed to be indigo brings clarity, reveals truth." Bridie cocked her head. "I should say, there's talk about goings-on out your way. You've heard it? Some man out there ruffling feathers."

"No," Mama said stiffly. "What kind of talk?"

"They say a sympathizer's taking food out to U-boats. They've seen him on the river."

It was Mama who seemed ruffled by what Bridie was saying. "We're too far inland for anything to do with U-boats. It's a rumor. You shouldn't pass it on." Penn's heart thumped in her chest. Mama stepped closer to Penn. She tried to sweeten the comment. "But if they want to come watch for anything else, I'll serve them tea on the porch."

Bridie nodded, seeming to file Mama's words away. "People talk, that's all. I'll put the word out I heard straight from you that there's nothing to it." She added, "Now, what did you come by for today?"

"Actually, we came by today for Penn, my daughter," Mama said. Penn swallowed hard and tried to ignore the dark corners in the store and the low ceiling that seemed to press on their heads. For the first time, Bridie flicked a glance at Penn. Penn felt a charge run through her and folded her arms tight over her chest.

"What is it you want? You tell me. It's a pawn shop, baby. It's likely there's something here, someplace."

Penn looked around the cramped little store.

"Doris told her you might have things from Evertell," Mama said.

"Oh yeah," Bridie confirmed. "We had all kinds of things in the store. But that's been awhile ago now." She scanned the little room as if she were looking for anything she might have forgotten. "Nothing too impressive came here that I can recall. Just knickknacks, really. You're not hoping for the family silver?" She chuckled.

"No," Penn said, finally bringing herself to speak up. "Doris said you might have sweet balm?" Penn clutched the basket over her elbow and the commonplace book close to her chest. She felt her voice go high and nervous. Bridie turned to Mama.

"Here, tell me what you think of this," she said. Penn watched the shopkeeper grab Mama's hand and smooth something over the skin. Mama withdrew, but Penn could smell the honeyed aroma thick in the air. "My own mama's herbal balm for whatever ails you," Bridie explained.

"Mm, smells good," Mama said politely. Penn couldn't have been more shocked when she added, "If you really want to know what I want, could she stay a moment while I run a quick errand? I could be back in less than twenty minutes, if that would be all right?"

Bridie smiled. "I think that'd be fine. Me and Miss Penn can get to know one another."

Penn wanted to talk to Bridie, but she also feared her a little. She felt strange about her mama going off on unknown business, leaving her with this Negro woman she did not know. She had to work to contain the emotion that rose up when the shopkeeper agreed she could stay. But it was all settled so quickly. Mama slipped out through the tiny door and suddenly Penn stood in the shadows, alone with Bridie Quillian. Penn tried to imagine she was swallowing the bitter indigo tea and forced her limbs to grow languid, her pulse to slow.

Bridie smiled. "Did you know my people been at Evertell three generations? Doris told me you might want to know about that." There was something in her voice that slipped up the back of Penn's neck. She held Penn's gaze. Penn thought of the unmarked stones, a little constellation of white shapes in the tall grass. Penn nodded.

"I was born at Evertell, but born free," Bridie said. "On account of my daddy. And my mama was free when she died. Your great-great-granny, Flora, made that happen as soon as her husband and both worthless boys got killed off in the War of the States."

Penn's curiosity ran ahead of her manners. She set the basket and the commonplace book on the counter. "That's true? Could she really do that?" She wondered how old Bridie was, to be talking of the Civil War as if it were only yesterday. But the graves in the glen were much older than that, Penn reminded herself.

"Oh yes. The day she did it, nobody'd yet heard Flora's oldest boy was dead. But I imagine Flora and my mama were scared when my mama took a pair of garden shears and chopped off Flora's long, black braid and put a pair of trousers on her. When they were done dressing her up, Flora looked just like her boy. Like that, my mama trotted right alongside Flora down to Savannah, giving her courage." Bridie was a good storyteller. Penn had forgotten her nerves already. "Mama could make you do anything. Flora signed those papers—zip, zip—with her son's name and nobody was the wiser. If anybody'd ever bothered to check when Anselm died, they'd have known a dead man gave my mama her freedom. Mama always said they did it together, her and Flora."

Penn held her breath, caught up in Bridie's story.

"We stayed at Evertell all my mama's life, till she died. They grew that garden, stuck there together, Mama and Flora, something sweet like sisters. Bickered like sisters too. Women can do both, you know."

Penn thought of Mama and Imagine. "Why?"

"Usually because of a man." She furrowed her brow, seeing she was going to have to explain. "My daddy wasn't the man my mama married. He was the man that owned her. Thomas Vaughn. Your great-great—"

"Oh." Penn didn't know what to do with adult secrets like these. Evertell secrets that made it hard for Penn to know how to feel or what to say. Like she didn't know how to feel about the dinner with Oscar Lewallen or the POWs who were coming to the farm. None of it was her fault, but if she had a place at Evertell, it was all a part of her story now.

Bridie must have seen it all on her face and Penn knew she was kind because she took pity. Bridie lowered her voice conspiratorially when she said, "Mama reckoned Flora belonged to that man the same as she did and when he died, it was no sense acting like either one of them was too tore up about it."

Penn sorted through all Bridie was saying. Bridie's grandmother was not a daughter of Eleanor Dare, but she was an Evertell heir all the same. Her name would not go on the list in the commonplace book, but her mark was in the earth at Evertell, in the herbs, in the very charm Penn was counting on now. They were family.

"Now, I know you came here wondering about those graves out back of your kitchen house. I can't tell you one soul's name that's back there. I doubt anybody ever could. They're not my people. My people are right under here, holding Savannah up. Under your feet," she said, and gave her small foot a tap. Penn looked at the floor and back to Bridie, eager to understand.

"Calhoun Square. You can't tell it now, but the Negro burial grounds got some of those pretty squares built right over the top of them. Some folks were exhumed and moved over to the new ground. I've been told that's where my grandma is now, near my mama, but there's no kind of record. So I don't know for sure, do I? Either way, I remember my family every step I take."

Penn's throat was tight. She was glad when Bridie didn't expect her to say anything to that.

"Now, those folk at Evertell, they came with the first of your kin. They built the oldest part of your house. And that's about the only thing I know, except what the house can tell you."

"How can the house tell me anything?"

"You've seen those stones in the shade? How they sit, not too many of them? When I was a girl, my mama said it was two families that died early days of building Evertell. She showed me how to look at those stones and then go inside your house and find a map in your wall." Penn was astonished and Bridie nodded. "When slaves were buried, they didn't mark their stones with names. Slaves weren't supposed to read or write. But sometimes, if people wanted to leave a little something on a grave, they might leave a bone or a seashell, like it had just found its way there. Whoever built those first walls at Evertell, they put their seashells *in the wall*, one for every one of those gravestones, laid out in just the same order. Nobody could carry that off, could they? As long as that old house was standing, there they'd be. You go look and see if I'm not right when you get home. They're still there."

"I will." An apology seemed wrong. But Bridie had earned Penn's admiration. "Would you come and see them again, with me, if I ring the bell like old times?"

Bridie's expression changed, her eyes clouding, and Penn felt she'd stepped inside that glen again, a sacred place where she was trespassing.

"Oh, now. I think that's a fine idea you have," Bridie said, but she was only being polite. And even though Penn heard no anger in her words, the invitation had not been accepted.

But Penn had not come empty-handed.

"I wanted to give you this," Penn said, remembering the herbs. "It's not a May basket, but almost. Doris told me your grandmama planted the herb garden. I pulled the weeds. I'm taking care of it and brought you these bunches. I hoped you'd tell me what they are."

Bridie considered the basket before she turned her eyes back to Penn. It seemed she could see right down inside her. Penn stood very still. "Honey, that's the nicest thing to think of me like that. Did you know, people come and go from here and come asking for this or that. Girls come for the sweet balm and they thank me, bringing me pies and blankets and all sorts. Show me their babies. It's sweet, it is. And I love them all. But this." She ran her fingers through the

THE LOST BOOK OF ELEANOR DARE

herbs and put her nose down into them to inhale. "Comfrey, mug-wort, rosemary, thyme," she said, showing each one to Penn. "You brought me what I love most. Everything good from her garden's in here, everything she taught me."

Before they could speak any further, the door swung open and Mama swept inside, bringing with her the smells of the docks on her warm skin and windblown hair. She smiled brightly at them, stirring a curiosity in Penn.

"You had enough of her?" Mama called, teasing.

"This sweet thing," Bridie said breezily. The shadow that had settled over them moments before had lifted with the aroma of the herbs as Bridie gently turned the bundles over.

"Well, say thank you to Mrs. Quillian. It was nice of her to let you stay."

"Oh, we had a good time, didn't we?" Bridie said. "I'll make you a list of these herbs and what they need to grow and send it in the mail. You watch for it."

"Thank you."

She reached her small hand out and drew Penn's long ponytail around so the hair draped softly over her shoulder, then smiled at her. "I just happened to think . . . This one was asking after any-thing that came out of the house, and y'all might want to run by the Telfair Academy, take a look at the art on display. I can't promise it's still there, but I know that used to, they had a portrait of your grandma, Alice. A big old picture hanging in the front room, over the mantel, looking like a queen with those big old peacock feathers in her hair."

"That ended up in a museum?" Mama said.

"She supported the place for years, first museum in these United States founded by a woman. When y'all closed the house, that painting went to them. You might be able to see it."

Penn beamed at Bridie, who then pushed the jar of sweet balm across the countertop and said, "Now, don't forget this, baby. It's a gift."

Penn thanked her, delighted as she swiped the balm and the commonplace book from the countertop, clutching both tightly as she hurried out the door.

"Do you know where it is? The museum?" she asked Mama as soon as they'd stepped outside. "It has to be right here, close. We could just run by, like Bridie said."

They stood at the truck and Mama sighed. "I think I know where she's talking about."

"We have to see it. We can't just let it hang there and pretend we don't know. Not now. Mama, please."

Mama nodded and Penn gave a little leap as she came around the truck. They walked up a set of stone stairs set into the sea wall that bordered River Street, leading up to the squares of Savannah. Mama asked a man on a park bench and he pointed them in the direction of the museum. The beautiful old home with its creamy peach walls and stately columns sat on the corner of Telfair Square. Walking past the gate with its tall urns overflowing with green fern fronds, they climbed the steps to the imposing, polished wooden doors, only to find them locked.

"No," Penn groaned. She couldn't have been more disappointed. "How can they be closed?"

The hours for the museum were clearly posted on a bronze plaque beside the door. They'd missed them by only an hour.

"I guess we'll have to come back." Penn caught the reference to future plans, as if Mama meant to be here in Savannah. Or to return. Both ideas sent a zing through Penn.

"Maybe somebody's here. We could knock and tell them who we are and they would let us come inside to see your grandmother, wouldn't they?" Penn didn't wait. She knocked loudly on the door. But there was no response. She pressed her nose against the glass pane, trying to see into the dark entry. There was no sign of movement. But as her eyes adjusted, she gasped. "Mama, look! Come see!"

Mama's disinterest fell away as she hurried to stand next to Penn so they peered through the door like two naughty children. On tiptoe, necks craned, they could just make out the mantel over the fireplace in the parlor at the front of the house. There, as Bridie had described it, hung the enormous portrait of Calista. She wore a deep green dress that complemented her pale blue eyes, with a white fur stole over her left, bare shoulder. Her lips crooked up on one side so like Mama's that Penn's hand flew to her own mouth. Her dark hair was piled high on her head, embellished with a pair of peacock feathers, just as Bridie had told them.

"There she is, all right," Mama said.

Penn couldn't take her eyes off the painting. "She's the one they built the cupola for? She loved the stars?"

"Yes. She had consumption. She slept up there for the air."

"You remember her, don't you?"

"Barely. I was too little when she died. But I remember this portrait."

"Doris was right. You do look like her now you're wearing your hair loose."

"Maybe I do. A little."

Penn saw Mama soften while they looked at the face behind glass, their own features reflected back at them, a strange mirror that seemed to open to both past and present.

The bitter. The sweet.

London
Winter 1586

Over the days that followed, Eleanor's father drew a new map, much as he'd done before. But she worried at the pall of his visage and the long stretches when he went without food. He labored endlessly over his drafting desk, never allowing her near and only sipping at the cider she kept in a mug near his elbow. He grew thin and hawkish and snapped at her. He glared with a confused expression. This man seemed mad. Just to look upon Tomasyn Cooper had brought him joy, he'd said. But when he looked upon Eleanor now, she was fairly certain he was seeing nothing but a reminder of the love he'd lost.

Perhaps she looked nothing like her mother; she couldn't know. He'd burned the miniatures he'd painted of Tomasyn Cooper long ago. Her mother might have soothed him with a song or a story or a fine meal. Eleanor didn't dare sing, for she had no talent for it. And the only stories she knew were the ones her father had taught her. Finally, Eleanor turned to the page in the commonplace book with the most ancient cures. Had Eleanor's father ever taken the time to decipher the domestic writings contained in the book—pages filled with instructions for how to brew a tea for good luck and how to make a charm for warding off bad dreams, the best phases of the moon to plant by, and when the fruit of a tree or the wall of a woman's womb would ripen—he'd likely have declared it witchcraft and burnt the book to ashes.

But when Eleanor read the entries in the book, she saw only love, heard only her mother's voice. And now she prepared a tincture from one of the recipes, an unpleasant tea made from bitter woad leaves. Charged Water, the receipt read, scribbled by an unknown hand. For clarity.

Eleanor let the tea steep for longer than called for, until it turned dark, the color of ink, then she offered it to her father. "To inspire you," she said.

To her dismay, her father took only the smallest sip before making a mewing sound of distaste and refusing to drink more. In that moment it was clear to Eleanor, her father was a man who would not be helped.

When he'd finally taken himself off to bed, Eleanor crept into the studio and peered with astonishment at his mysterious drawing. It was only another map, like so many he'd drawn before. But at the bottom he had signed his work with a flourish and a single word that told Eleanor the difference in this expedition. It was not the destination, but that her father didn't mean to return. *Governor.*

The sight of it filled her with despair. Eleanor couldn't remain where she was or bear to be abandoned again. There was no one to advise her or change her fate. She would have to find a way to do it herself. In her father's cup the tea had gone cold. On impulse, she drank it down. The bitter taste made her teeth ache. Its sharp scent burned her nose like a terrible regret. Then just as she wiped her sleeve over her burning lips, an experience overcame her.

Before her eyes, a waking dream played out, the same fight and flash she'd engraved on the copper plate, a vision of splendor that shifted and breathed, both shadow and light, a new world come to life. Eleanor strained her eyes and held out her hands, but the silvery scene slipped through her fingers. She was ravaged by a longing she could not name. It was a feeling of both joy and wretchedness, her heart's desire dancing just out of her grasp. Her whole life she'd been waiting for this vision to come to her, as it came to all the women in her mother's line. The entire experience lasted no longer than a moment but left her prostrate on the floor, and for what seemed a long time she lay there until she heard the sound of laughter like the pealing of bells, and it was a revelation to realize the sound came from her own mouth. Her waiting time was over. To take hold of her Evertell, there was a choice to be made about what kind of girl she would be, and it was an easy one. She would not be abandoned. She would not be afraid of the unknown. She was her mother's daughter, the daughter of women who had traveled from the north, fishwives whose bones carried the cold and whose hair always smelled of evergreen.

Come morning, when her father found her asleep on the floor, he helped her to her feet. He worried at her pale face and shaking hands, but they were not signs of illness but the result of exhilaration. Without hesitation, she revealed that she knew of his commission and his plan to leave her behind, and when he appeared most guilty, she told him what she had seen the night before. She knew what she wanted. She knew who she was. It would take a miracle for her father to agree to take her with him, and so a miracle was what she intended to be. She pushed the copper plate into his hands so that this time, he could not look away. She called her vision a blessing, a visitation, and a sure sign that she was meant to stand alongside him in the New World. She was called, she said—called to be his guide.

He looked at her then as Mary's father might have looked upon his girl: a daughter who had gained the favor of God. She'd absolved him of the burden of a motherless child and transformed herself into a daughter who conversed with angels. She knew her father, who had taught her all she knew about faith, feared magic and mystery and all the ways her mother's book taught her to glimpse the divine. If she'd told him that her vision came from the leaves of a plant, the water of their own well, and the fire she'd laid in their hearth, he surely would have feared her. But Eleanor was smart. She kept her secret.

She ignored the lingering bitterness of the tea, closed her eyes to dream of the wilderness that awaited her, comforted by the sharp scent of evergreen on her pillow. She knew well that she had not become a saint. She had not even become a sorceress. She'd simply become a woman.

Chapter Seventeen

Alice

The house smelled of herbs from Penn's work in the garden. There were bunches drying on tables and windowsills everywhere, although we couldn't name them yet. But the aroma was sweet and earthy and my head was full of Eleanor's Tale, the idea of a girl who could conjure such a vision for herself, she'd transformed before the eyes of those who should have loved her best and changed her fate.

Maybe I could do the same. Since divining the well with Sonder, I'd begun to think we could stay at Evertell. I was no longer angry about a story without an ending or a secret wisdom my mama had taken to the grave. I was yearning for a future for Penn and for me and it had nothing to do with a mythical vision. We would forget the sorrows of the Dare Stone, something that was never meant to be here from the start. I would walk alongside Sonder as I'd done as a child. I would help with the farm, keep the books, plant and harvest more bountifully so that we lived off the work of our hands. I would save Finch's checks for Penn's future and Imegine would have Merely's, or she could come here to us. I wanted to believe that after all this time, I could simply live with my part in the loss of my mama and protect my daughter from the harder truths of Evertell. Surely it would be enough that I had saved the dreams of those I loved.

"See, it's a map in the wall," Penn explained, running her fingertips over the constellation of seashells embedded in the walls of the front room, overlooking the writing desk. She told me all Bridie had said about the streets of Savannah, the peach orchard growing from the bones of the first people to live on that land, and the story about the first builders of Evertell. Finally, Penn led me to stand outside the glen behind the kitchen house to count the fieldstones. They matched the pattern in the wall almost exactly.

I was in my late thirties and only now learning to see that the secrets of this place ran deeper than my own. They were hidden in every stone and bone and shell, marking every path. We were not the first to come this way.

)(

I should have used the morning to walk to the store and deal with Bill Hawkes, demand the piece of the bell that he had denied Penn. But I still didn't know what I could say to him to change his mind, and I wasn't ready to run into Charlie, the reason I'd been avoiding the store since that first visit.

I stood outside, looking at the house, but I couldn't stand the thought of spending another day covered in paint, and my hands and arms were aching from holding the brush. I'd begun to think about what I'd said to Oscar Lewallen about the money being in the land, that I could parcel off land as I was doing with Bell Isle and the mill and simply leave the old house to stand here as it had done all these years since we'd gone. What did it matter anymore? It did not haunt me as before. Or maybe I was just avoiding that responsibility too. There seemed to be so much about Evertell and the past here that I couldn't repair.

By afternoon, Penn would be heading for the shipyard, and unknown to her, Sonder would follow to watch over her. This morning she'd bounced out of bed early, asking a million questions about Savannah, about what to do if the bike failed her, what she should wear, telling me everything she knew about the bell, about the way she wanted to use the pulleys, about the girl welders and Liberty ships and what else she might see there. I'd barely gotten a word in edgewise and she hadn't noticed when I did. This was the Penn I'd missed, the girl I'd wanted to see again, and I couldn't help being aware that she'd shown none of this enthusiasm since she'd learned of the possibility of attending Brenau in the fall. In fact, she had not asked once if there'd been any response from them, any request for an interview. I told myself this was because she didn't want to get her hopes up, the same reason I'd kept the plan from her in the beginning. After all, seeing the girls working on the ships should excite her. This was the fire I wanted to see in Penn, and the one that would carry her forward to whatever future Evertell made possible.

I made my way down to the grist mill, walking the banks of Bell Creek as it tumbled over its sandy bed, running fast and clear. When I stepped through the opening in the thick underbrush next to the mill pond, a flash of movement caught my eye. Sonder knelt on the large, smooth rocks there in a patch of sunlight, maybe in prayer or watching a fish, I mused; he was a beautiful man. Only when he straightened to drop his pant leg did I glimpse that he'd been working to adjust the strap of his prosthetic.

I felt bad for invading his privacy and turned to climb the rest of the path to the millhouse where I found the side door open. Sonder had invited me to see the workings of the mill before running the corn in a few days and the rooms were open with their high ceilings. The sweet smell of grain filled my nose as I wound through the equipment and stepped onto a back porch overlooking the pond. When I felt him step up beside me, I said, "Morning."

He said the same and the single word felt like an intimacy. Every day it was stronger, the urge to place my palm along the side of his jaw where a soft stubble shone in the sunlight.

He asked, "You want to help me with something? I have to dress the millstones."

"Anything but the mess I'm making of the house." He chuckled and my face warmed at the sound. "Show me what to do."

He was watching me as he approached the enormous stones. "These are called burrstones. Fifteen hundred pounds of quartz, give or take. I cut a pattern that allows them to grind the grain. It wears down over time, gets dull and shallow with the work. So you have to sharpen it occasionally."

"And how do you do that?"

He picked up a dangerous-looking tool.

"Lobotomy?"

"Mill pick. It's tedious work."

I ran my hand over the surface of the enormous cool stone.

"A miller has to listen to his wheel to know it's set just right, and he can smell if it's too close. It will spark and you'll get a burnt smell from the stone's striking. You have to know from the meal as well. Is it too coarse to the touch, or too fine? That's where the saying comes from, having a miller's touch. The top stone, that's called the runner. The bottom stone is called the bed stone," he said. I blushed like an idiot and stared hard at the stone. "The bed stone is convex and stationary. The runner, she's concave and she's pushed by the power coming up from the water there, you see?"

I nodded.

"What I do is I balance them so they're only so far apart." He demonstrated with his fingers, showing me only a sliver of space. "So close, you can barely slide a piece of tissue paper between them. Eight harps on each of these wheels, the pattern they call it, going against one another so they scissor when they turn. Balance and a good dressing, that's the key."

He was confident as he talked.

"How did you learn all of this? You weren't born with it, like the divining."

"Your dad taught me. After I came here. He loved the mill. Loved this farm."

I hesitated. "You remember things I don't. Or remember them differently. How do you remember my parents?"

"They worked," he said. "There was a balance."

"Until there wasn't." I looked away. "He lost a lot. I know he missed the farm, but maybe it was too connected to her. I think he did love Merely's."

"This farm was as much his as hers. John taught me everything about this place. I envied John. I wanted to be such a man. He knew who he was." Sonder cleared his throat, choked up. "How did he die?" he asked.

Immediately I was mortified that it hadn't occurred to me that Sonder might not have any of the details, but of course I should have realized sooner. Another reminder that I had been thinking only of Penn and myself. Now I felt a pit in my stomach at my selfishness, seeing that Sonder was grieving too.

"It was a stroke," I said gently. "Imegine was with him. It was quiet. He was peaceful, I think." Sonder listened solemnly. He took

THE LOST BOOK OF ELEANOR DARE

a moment to accept the information, seeming to form a picture in his mind. "Of course, John Merely never asked for anything, you know that. So we buried him in Helen figuring he'd want to be close to Imegine. The life he'd made for us there. I hope it was the right thing."

"That's the best any of us can do," he said. "What we hope's right." We exchanged a look and then he said, "Step back. I'll run her for you. So you can see what she does."

We moved away from the burrstones. He threw a switch and the whole place came alive, noisy and dusty, churning and spitting out bits of meal that smelled warm and rich. He explained how the wheels turned opposite of one another, forcing the grain from the grooves cut into the stone called furrows, up onto the flat, high places called lands, in order that the grain was cut and then pushed out to the edges, emerging as meal or flour.

I let myself follow him, expecting some magical transference to pass between us while I listened to him explain the way the mill operated, peered at a simple system of gears and pulleys underneath the floor, and watched the cheerful waters of little Bell Creek run fast over a dam and then underneath the mill where a turbine turned in dark depths below us. He pointed out the stone pile foundation from the 1800s and the dangers of the current beneath the benign waters. Overhead, the mill ran in a noisy cacophony.

"Now, come on. You need to see something else."

He led me over the uneven ground beneath the mill, taking my hand so I wouldn't lose my footing. "Watch your head. It's just here."

I saw it then, on the other side of one of the stone pilings, like a great heart churning. In the dark beneath the building, my eyes adjusted. I blinked as Sonder flipped on a battery-operated camping lantern and I could make out the workings of the massive metal turbine. "I'd forgotten all this."

Hoisting up the miner's lantern, we moved into the recesses of the space. It was deeper than I recalled, damp and unsettling. Finally, we came to the source of the mill's power. Bell Creek rushed all around us.

"This," he said. "This is what it's like. Can you feel that? It's as close as you can get."

I tried to feel the things he was talking about, the runner stone and the bed stone fitted perfectly, the power of the water moving them, but I was no diviner. It didn't come naturally to me from some ancient memory, transferred through a mystic power. What I felt were my own yearnings, aching beneath my breastbone, behind my heart.

Then I saw a small door just on the other side of one of the stone pilings. My heart hammered in my chest as I followed him into the underground room. It was narrow and low, and clear that some-one had worked hard to dig out the space. We could barely stand up straight. It was cold and almost completely silent and smelled of earth and mineral water. I wrapped my arms around myself, not because the air was cool, but because my body knew something my mind was still trying to recall.

"This place was a secret," I said, certain of that much. "I remember now. I'd forgotten about this."

I had the sense that water rushed above and beneath us. Before us was a wall where there were stacks of crates. I recognized them, too, the same as I'd seen in the chandlery.

"It was John's stash," Sonder said. "His way of protecting your mama, keeping her occupied near the end when things got bad. These are all your mama's candles, what's left."

"I don't understand. Why was he taking the candles down here? What was she supposed to think?"

THE LOST BOOK OF ELEANOR DARE

"He was just trying to slow her down." He looked pale in the strange light of the dank little room and it gave me a shiver.

"I remember she was in the chandlery all the time," I said. "She was at these candles day and night, wearing herself out. I just don't know why this was her obsession. Why was she making so many? God, I wish I could ask her."

Sonder shook his head, clearly as mystified as I was. "Maybe it was just a thing to do, when she couldn't do anything else. She'd sell them to Bridie. John made a deal so he bought them all over again and brought them down here where Claire wouldn't know."

"Ever the businessman, making his bargains. I guess I know where I get that."

"It was a good bargain. He'd melt everything down so your mama never knew the difference and she'd start all over again. I guess he never got around to melting this last haul."

Tears fell without warning and I was surprised by the emotion, conflicted too.

"You asked how I remember them," Sonder said. "That's why I'm showing you. A lot of things didn't make sense around that time, but Claire knew what he was doing. They had an understanding, right up to the end. I believe they worked it out together, knowing how things were going."

"What?"

"She's the one who showed me. I remember, she looked at all this"—he gestured to the crates—"and she said this was how she knew John loved her. He kept her secrets, even from her if she needed it. I didn't know what she was talking about. Not then. But later, I understood, it was their way. When her mind went, John did what needed doing. I guess you know that. Bed stone and runner."

Certainly it was a picture of how we'd lived our lives after leaving Evertell, hiding away the things about this place that we believed would hurt one another. But it was also a way I wanted to remember my parents, like those two strong stones, fitted to their purpose, fashioned for what the other needed.

Sonder was close. Huddled in the cramped space, buried beneath earth, surrounded by water and mistakes, I could smell the sweat of the work he'd done on the mill stone. I reached my hand up to the back of his neck and pulled his mouth down on mine. He tasted of mineral salt.

⚔

Sonder asked if I wanted to go with him to follow Penn, but I stayed behind. She might forgive Sonder, but a mother hovering when she wanted so much to grow up would have hurt her. I trusted Sonder to keep her safe.

Instead, I went inside to the writing desk where I pulled out the pages of Eleanor's Tale. The story was taking a turn. I dreaded where it would go next. Even as I read, I couldn't help feeling she must've imagined how wrong everything could go. I read until my eyes failed me in the evening and awoke before dawn to take Sonder's miner's lantern to the desk before Penn could wake. I wanted to rush through this part of the story. I didn't want to think of Eleanor's dream slipping away. I didn't want the tide to turn. And so I read the pages in haste, carelessly, dismissively. I believed I knew the important part: Eleanor survived, otherwise we would not be here, Penn and I. That's what I wanted to read. I wanted to skip the rest.

And still, that night when I dreamed, I was the river; I was a current. In my sleep, I couldn't stop my yearning. I stood in the forest, my bare feet planted in the raw marks in the earth where the stone once stood. And I watched the tall, thin spire of a shape that became Sonder.

London
Spring 1587

To Eleanor's astonishment, her father immediately announced she would take a husband. The man, a stranger to her, was Ananias Dare, a brick-mason, and he would act as her father's partner in the new colony. Together, they would build a church. And to her despair, the copper plate she'd engraved for her father would be her dowry, for they owned nothing else of worth. Eleanor's position as the colony's new governor's daughter made her desirable as a spouse. She would provide Ananias with a wife. But when presented to her new husband, she could see there was no love for her, nor appreciation for her engraving in his eyes, only an expression of resignation to match her own. It was understood they made a convenient match. Still, she couldn't help wishing the giant man would turn and walk away to find a woman who would love him, instead of selling himself to her father, who stood there jolly and full of righteous purpose once more, praising her for it all.

"Tell me again of this vision," her father said to her almost every evening, so that Ananias began to resent that he sought her opinion over his own. Eleanor searched for the words that would end her father's questioning. Each time she recounted the blessing, the doubts that plagued her father about their coming venture seemed to lift for a time. He looked to her husband then with the assurance that his plans had been sanctified, while Ananias stood behind her, a husband who knew her as a wife, not a messenger of God, and Eleanor felt his disapproval growing. In only one regard was her husband truly pleased with her: he believed she would soon give him a son.

And so, Eleanor was always grateful to leave them to make the plans of men while she spent time in her mother's garden. She had a future of her own to protect as she took clippings, adding to her growing collection of herbs and seeds for various vegetables and flowering plants from the commonplace book. When her father asked what she was doing, she would only say, "When we're far from here, the sweet scent of the blossoms and herbs will bring us the comforts of home."

But Eleanor wasn't merely concerned with comforts. She'd witnessed the power of the natural cures in her mother's book, balms and teas that helped a woman through childbirth. And by the time they set sail on the queen's errand to make a new world, following her father's map, although she feared the dangers all women face when delivering a child, she prayed her mother's wisdom and her spirit would help protect the babe now five months in her womb, safe beneath the folds of her finest dress.

When the day came, alongside 115 other hopeful or desperate souls, Eleanor followed her father's footsteps, led by her husband's hand, on a mission from God and the queen. No purpose had ever been more ordained. Her father carried the commonplace book locked inside an iron box built to protect their most precious belongings, along with his folded maps and sketches and Eleanor's graving tools. He'd had the box made for this purpose, fashioned from iron rather than oak to withstand the elements. The casket was not very large, but it was heavy, and obviously precious for the effort it took to haul it. For weeks she'd calmed his nerves with the Charged Water. Unwilling to drink it at first, he'd developed a taste for the bitter liquid and now called for it more often than she'd like. He'd been having nightmares filled with images of starvation and torture. He developed a dry mouth and nothing could slake his thirst. Eleanor worried he knew more about what awaited them than he had shared. She feared what he had not seen fit to show the queen in his paintings.

For three months their small boats were at sea, bearing out all the gruesome and treacherous warnings of those who had endured such crossings before. But for all the ailments she had anticipated, the worst Eleanor suffered was one she had not anticipated, nor did she have the means to work a cure: loneliness. Somewhere along their voyage, while Eleanor remained the map at the heart of her father's quest, Ananias had become the star. It was this new son who helped her father guide by the heavens, who stood alongside him to read the way by the night sky and the astrolabe, a tool that was kept from Eleanor and that she came to despise as some wives hate mistresses. Eleanor, blessed daughter of the new governor, mother of the New World, was tucked away from the other colonists. And things unseen soon become things feared. She could hear them begin to whisper, fearing hers would be a precarious pregnancy, that she was fragile, that she was frightened. They'd pinned their superstitious hopes on this first child as a sign, led to the idea by her proud father. He'd told anyone willing to listen about her vision, hoping it would quell the doubts of the people in his care as it had quelled his own. But in fact, it only served to make them wonder if the man had lost his mind. Worse, it made them wonder about Eleanor.

When the crossing grew rough, Eleanor lay still through the nights, her anxious husband no longer sharing her bed. He had heard the suspicious and superstitious rumors. He worried the colony would turn on him too. But Eleanor clung to the belief that a well-born babe would set things right, and to the bright vision that had set her on this path. She focused her thoughts on the rolling, tumbling movements of the growing child within her. She'd become as much a vessel as the boat that carried the colony, and her ribs creaked and her heart beat strong enough for two.

By day, when she wasn't sick from the swells, she passed the time talking to herself and her unborn babe, this new love of her life, imagining what awaited them at the end of this crossing. She pored over her father's journals, full of watercolor landscapes and detailed sketches of plants that grew in the New World. Some were early drafts of the same images she had engraved on her copper plates. She pulled out the commonplace book and read the parables. While the boat rocked the mother and child, she began to tell a story of her own, how she'd come to this journey. But she did not write it down. She whispered it, memorizing the words. This was the sort of story that was dangerous for a woman to tell, of independent thought and skill and cunning.

But she could not control the hand of fate. When a wasting sickness took hold, the people searched for someone or something to blame. A rumor began that it was the babe inside Eleanor's womb, robbing all the strength of the people, and they grew to hate her.

Then one day, an unexpected offering slid beneath her door: her own engraving, solid and bright, even in the confined shadows. She was astonished to find the copper plate returned to her. It was Ananias who spoke from the other side of the door. She didn't have to see him to recognize his voice. For a moment she believed he had come to show his love. But this was not a gift of love, any more than it had been when her father passed it to Ananias. It was the price for his protection. Where she'd convinced her father that her wisdom came from God, Ananias believed her a blasphemer.

He started, not with threats of punishment, but by appealing to her

THE LOST BOOK OF ELEANOR DARE

better nature. He reminded her of the good graces of her father, who might have easily left her in an orphanage after her mother's passing or on the docks while he set out for the New World. Then he implored her, as her husband, to revoke the curse on their passage for the sake of the English child she carried, the future of the colony. He believed, as the other colonists did, that she had the power to set their course. Eleanor knew then she had not escaped her fate at home but had brought it with her. She was as alone as she'd ever been. And if the colony failed, the vision she'd given her father, the dream that had inspired them all, would be the end of her.

Chapter Eighteen

Penn

Only because Mama insisted, Penn had choked down a bologna sandwich and then gotten out of the kitchen house, all her promises made to be careful, be smart, be straight to the shipyard and back. Now there was a cool breeze at her back and it seemed to be pushing her along the way. She remembered the way easily enough, having just made the trip with Mama, but the eight miles certainly hadn't seemed so far while riding in the cab of the truck. Her legs burned like fire as she pumped and Penn gritted her teeth at the screeching sound that started from the contraption beneath her about halfway to the city.

The smells of Savannah reached her long before she could see the spires of the churches rising above the grand oaks. Sweet smells of baking dough and the fishy smells of the river, salt and sea. She thought of what Bridie had told her about the city being built on bones, holding everything up as Penn made her way through the squares and finally to the bridge that brought her directly to the shipyard.

She was amazed at the size of things, but she didn't let it put her off. She ditched the bike near a tree before walking up to the guardhouse at the entrance. A pimply faced boy, not much older than Penn herself, sat there with a clipboard, sweating through his shirt. Penn thought it must have been a thousand degrees in that wooden box.

"What do you want?" he asked. He sat up straighter.

"I'm here to see Sammy Hunt. She welds on the ships."

"What do you think this is, some kind of kindergarten?"

Penn pulled her shoulders back. "She knows I'm coming. My name's on the list."

The boy in the booth shook his head but sighed and, without arguing further, repositioned his hat and pushed a button that lifted the gate to allow Penn to enter. There was a loud buzz and she waited while it opened.

"Go on and head over to Dock G. Let somebody over there straighten you out."

Penn walked through the gate with no intention of being straightened out as she followed the signs to Dock G, never looking back. Her heart raced so hard that she thought the blood pounding in her head would leave her deaf. Winding around dirt pathways between buildings and along a dock where an enormous hull was covered in men, Penn tried not to look too impressed.

The sign on the building told her she was in the right place, and Penn took a moment to catch her breath before she stepped inside. She had to calm down and look absolutely capable. She was relieved to see a young woman sitting at a desk, who glanced up when Penn shut the door behind her. The room was very small, really nothing more than a closet with a couple of chairs along the wall.

"Can I help you, doll?"

"The fellow at the guard shack said to come here and you'd

help me. I want to see Sammy Hunt. My name is on the list. I'm Pennilyn Young."

"Oh, well, sure," the girl said, sounding the way adults sound when they aren't sure at all. She did take out a clipboard and scan it; maybe Penn's name was there after all. "Just sit down there and let me call down for Sammy."

Penn did as she was told, taking deep breaths until the woman replaced the receiver and went back to her work, head down, scribbling away until the door at the back of the room opened up. A short, stout girl stepped inside. She was wearing the same gray coveralls she'd seen the others wearing, but Penn's attention was squarely focused on her heavy welding apron. This girl was older than Penn, but not so old as Mama. She smiled widely.

"Sammy?" Penn said.

"Hey now, that's me, all right. And who are you? You think you want to weld on the ships, huh?"

Penn reached to scratch the long hair she'd tied up to try to look older, but it had mostly come loose and begun to itch along her neck. Sammy had a short bob that was neat and out of her face and Penn felt like a little girl in pigtails next to her. "Pennilyn Rebecca Young," she said. "No, I came to ask for your help. Sonder Holloway said you might could help me fix something."

"How old are you?"

"Fifteen." Penn tried to look taller. She wished she had breasts like Sammy. It would have helped. "Thirteen," she admitted.

"Oh, I'm just kidding. I know all about you. Sonder called me and told me about your bell. Well, let's have a chat." Sammy held the back door open so they slipped out without another word to the receptionist. Penn cast a glance around at the looming hull of a ship under construction and the towering scaffolding, feeling minuscule beneath such man-made structures.

"You really weld on the ships?" Penn asked.

"I do. My brothers are both overseas. Every day I work on the ships, I think I'm building the boat that'll bring them home. Bring lots of boys home. They like girls because we get the work done better than the boys. But you could have told them that, right?" she said.

"Yeah, sure," Penn agreed, liking her. "All the girls in my family are like that." These were not the words she'd practiced, but they were the only ones she could find to say. She wasn't sure she wanted to build ships, but it excited her to think maybe she could.

Sammy smiled at her. "Why on earth do you want to fix a bell? You could be doing farm aid, work a victory garden, or be a hospital aid. That sort of thing's what all the Girl Scouts are doing."

"I'm not a Girl Scout," Penn said. She'd never even thought about it. There'd been a troop in Helen, always selling cookies, but Penn had never paid much attention. With the little she knew of the group, she found them rather pointless and couldn't help feeling a little offended that Sammy Hunt would suggest she was that sort.

"Well, why not? Maybe you should be."

"Why?" Penn asked, doubtful. She was doing more important things. "We have a victory garden already. When our corn comes in, there's going to be POWs coming to harvest it. I'm going to help make them dinner. That's how it used to be at Evertell. That's why I want to ring the bell for everybody, like old times. But it will be new times. And when the war ends, maybe things will go back like they were here."

"I don't know about going back, but I like you're already on top of things. That's international friendship and even recreation aid. That's service to your community, your family. Even homemaking." Penn wrinkled her nose. Sammy saw this and said, "All right, well, all that's leadership. You could get merit badges for that in the Scouts."

"I've seen them." This conversation had taken a strange turn from anything Penn had expected. She thought of the sashes she'd seen the girls wearing in Helen. She thought they just liked collecting the little patches of embroidered cloth, something to brag about, something that made them part of a club, like girls were always doing. "Why would I want badges? What's merit?"

"To show what you know. A merit is a virtue. That's what leads to a real job someday."

"Really?" Penn's ears perked up. Now she had a reason to be interested. "Like what?"

"What do you want to do?"

"I'm not exactly sure. Just something that matters. Are you a Girl Scout?" Penn asked, still skeptical.

"Sure. I'm what's called a Senior Scout now. I'm going into the Wing Scout Program in a few weeks. It's two years of aviation training."

Penn couldn't believe her. "Girl Scouts teaches you to build ships and fly planes?" She thought then that this was all a prank. None of those girls in Helen looked like girls who could or would do such things.

"Not everybody in Girl Scouts does the same thing. You can choose. And I won't be flying, not yet. They don't have female pilots, you know. But I'll be ground crew. Planes are going to change everything. And I'll be ready."

Sammy Hunt was changing things, Penn thought. She was like Sonder's pigeons, trapped beneath their protective netting. But she hoped Sammy would get to fly one day.

Sammy was saying, "All of it's going to be important when this is over. We're going to need a lot of girls to be ready for anything.

Be prepared. That's the Girl Scout motto. They started here, you know."

"Savannah?"

"Yeah. Juliette Gordon Low. You don't know about her? They just christened one of the Liberty ships some of us worked on after her." Penn could see Sammy Hunt was extra pleased with this. "Lots of girls from Pape were Scouts. That's how I got started."

"What's Pape?"

Sammy looked surprised by the question. "It's a school here. The Pape School. You should ask your folks. You could maybe go there, if you stay. If you need a reference, I'm happy to write something for you."

Penn nodded her head to be polite. She couldn't seem to choke out the words to say she wouldn't be staying. "Thanks." There was a lot she hadn't heard about Savannah, about Evertell, about the world. But on this one thing, she heard Sammy Hunt loud and clear. There was a place for her here, if she wanted it.

Suddenly she longed for Grandma Imegine, the comfort of the kitchen at Merely's where there was nothing to be decided, nowhere she had to go. But the world had gotten bigger since coming here. Bigger even than Brenau. And she knew that if she said it out loud, that she wanted to stay at Evertell, she would be saying she wanted to leave Merely's. Leave her home, as if it wasn't good enough. Leave her daddy and Pop. How could she want that?

"Listen, tell me about your bell. What's wrong with it? I've got to get back. My break's almost over."

Sammy settled her hands on her hips while she listened to Penn talk about the bell. But she was looking at Sammy in her coveralls, with her welder's shield hooked over her elbow, with her heavy boots, with her neat, short hair hanging at her chin. Penn found herself telling the girl far more than she'd intended.

"My daddy disappeared in Italy. They shot him on the road there, but nobody knows where they buried him. They won't ever find him. He won't come home. When they told us, inside me, I stopped working. But when I saw the bell, I thought if I could hear it ring . . . It would feel good to fix something. Can you come? Can you bring your tools? I have everything to do it, except a torch."

So that was that.

"You want me to steal welding equipment from the United States government to fix a church bell? It's not my equipment. You understand that, don't you?"

"Just borrow. It wouldn't take long, right?" Penn felt her courage slipping away. She'd never meant for anyone to steal anything. Sonder hadn't told her that. Maybe he hadn't known.

"You've got nerve, kid. I like a rule-breaker, but maybe I need to think about this. Sonder didn't say I'd have to take equipment off the yard. If I get in trouble, I could lose the Wings program, you know? I'm sorry about your dad, but—"

"I'm not a kid. I'm a girl, just like you." Penn gulped emotion that threatened to turn to tears. She didn't want to cry in front of Sammy. She thought of Flora, scared to death, and Bridie's mama, marching into town beside her, giving her courage. "I'll just keep coming back here until you help me. Ask Sonder. He'll tell you. Girls in my family are like that."

"Yeah, you said that. Some family." Sammy seemed amused but then whispered, "Damn." Her eyes danced in the same way as Mama's, when Mama was laughing. Finally, she shrugged. "What the hell. When do you want to do it?"

"I have to do it by April thirtieth, the day before May Day," Penn said quickly, feeling a rush of excitement. "May Day's harvest. I want to ring it the next day at dawn. It's tradition."

Sammy agreed she'd be in touch with Sonder, even though Penn could see she hardly believed she was doing it.

"All right, then. See you, bell girl."

If there was anything Penn wanted to be, it was something like Sammy Hunt. Here was somebody who could give her answers. And Penn had two new, burning questions. "Wait," Penn said. "Can you tell me something else?"

"Make it quick."

"How do I get to be a Girl Scout? And where's the Pape School?"

Sammy Hunt grinned and came to put an arm across Penn's shoulders. "Well, let me tell you."

$$\rtimes$$

"I know who I am. I know who I am," Penn said to herself with the names of the descendants on her lips. In her pocket she carried a badge. It was small and embroidered, with red thread that formed a circle around a green clover, and in gold letters atop the red circle it said *Be Prepared*. Sammy Hunt had given it to her, her favorite badge she'd earned from the Girl Scouts. She said she kept it with her since she came to the shipyards to do what all badges do: tell her what she knows. Confidence she could do anything she set out to do. And giving it to Penn was part of passing on that confidence.

Penn made it home without even noticing how tired her legs had gotten and they almost folded under her when she stepped off the bike. But she hurried to the barn to find the garden shears. She pulled the sloppy braid she'd made of her hair across her shoulder, and just like Great-Great-Grandmother Flora, like Sammy Hunt, she cut hard and deep until it came free. The braid hung limp and heavy in her hand and Penn stared at it a long moment. The cool air on the back of her naked neck felt strange and vulnerable and incontrovertible. "I'm Pennilyn Young. I'm the seventeenth heir of Eleanor Dare," she whispered. "I'm prepared. That's my virtue. I'm that kind of girl."

There would be no way to hide what she'd done, cutting her hair like this. She'd imagined that it would hang nicely at her chin, neat and crisp, like Sammy's. Instead, when she reached around to feel the ends of her hair, it was a crooked, curling mess, with pieces hanging inches longer than others and the entire thing seeming to sit askew atop her head like a ridiculous hat.

But Penn only laughed. She didn't care. She'd done something that mattered. She'd made a change. She didn't even stop by the chimney to remove more of the bricks. Whatever the house wanted, it would have to stand or fall on its own time. Penn went straight to the dock to pull in the traps before dinner, to surprise Mama, and so they could celebrate tonight. Penn knew what she wanted, or at least a way to find out. Maybe just setting out to work the charm for her Evertell, just putting the pieces together, had already started to change her. Now all she had to do was decide how to tell Mama.

Her thoughts were swirling with all Sammy told her about the Pape School and the Girl Scouts. On her knees at the dock, Penn pulled hard on the wet rope to lift the traps out of the river, seeing the clawed, armored sea creatures that were caught there. She dropped the trap on the dock and stared at the water until the disturbance settled and she could see herself reflected there, imperfectly, in constant motion with the current. That was how she felt inside. She was shifting and moving and there were things beneath the surface in ways she hadn't guessed.

"If you wanted a haircut, you could have just said so."

Mama. Penn felt dizzy from staring into the water and gripped the boards of the dock for a moment to steady herself before standing.

"You wouldn't have let me do it." Penn tried to sound like her usual argumentative self. "But it's my hair."

Mama didn't look angry. "Maybe not," she agreed. "But maybe I would. Now we'll never know, and you look like you ran into a buzz saw. I wonder what you're going to do next."

"Nothing." Penn reached up to tug at the ends of her hair and try to smooth it down, her heart racing. She suddenly could have listed a million things.

"Leave it. We'll go and see if you can be straightened out."

"Go where?" Penn asked, her heart stuttering. Surely Mama didn't mean they were leaving already.

"Stop it. Calm down. I just meant we'll ride into town for a beauty shop. Did you get what you wanted? Will this Sammy Hunt help fix your bell?"

Mama didn't seem worried at all. She didn't seem to mind Penn's hair. She was looking at the crabs in the trap and seemed pleased with the catch.

"She's going to do it," Penn said. "She'll bring her torch. I told her by April thirtieth."

"Good. Then we have some time to do just what we want. I think we need a day out."

Mama sat down with Penn to hang her legs off the dock. "Are you still glad we came here? We have to see the ocean, too, don't forget."

She didn't say *before we go*. Still, this felt like Mama was ticking off her own list. Penn's fingers tingled, remembering the feeling of pulling the bricks free, regretting now that she hadn't removed a few more, just in case.

Mama interrupted her thoughts, saying, "Don't be nervous. It suits you." She reached up to brush at the ragged ends and tucked one side behind Penn's ear.

"My hair? You like it?" Penn felt herself blush, surprised.

"I like you."

"Did you know Flora cut her braid?" Penn said quickly. "After her husband and sons died in the Civil War, she went into town to free Bridie's mama. She was a slave here at Evertell." Penn watched the largest crab in the trap. "Bridie told me when we went to see her."

"I didn't know that."

It wasn't what Penn really wanted to talk about. They got to their feet. Penn was holding so much inside she thought she would explode.

"Well, it's true," she said, trying to work up to the things she needed to say. She walked alongside Mama back to the house to clean and boil their dinner like wild women, feeling herself transformed by the day, the haircut. "Do you know about Girl Scouts?" Penn asked.

"Sure. That something you're thinking about when we get home?" Mama asked.

"Yeah. I'm thinking about it."

It was as much as Penn could say. But that night they picked their teeth with the claws of the crab and, after the day she'd had, Penn was happier than she could remember being since before the war. She hardly knew what she might do next. And instead of feeling like a terrible thing, it felt like something better than certainty. Like the breeze at her back on the bicycle today. Like it might carry her anywhere.

Roanoke Island
Summer 1587

Eleanor could smell the change in the air from salt to fresh, the promise of trees and soil, long before her father came to tell her they'd be taking the ship's boats and going ashore. This wasn't their destination, he explained, which was farther north and much more promising. This island, called Roanoke, was only a place to rest, where they would meet a band of men from an earlier voyage. But from the first glimpse of the shoreline, she knew the place for what it was: a mistake. A crow flying from her left to right caused her to shiver even in the oppressive heat, a sure sign to take care.

Her heart grieved, for this was not the vision she had dreamed. Eleanor didn't dare raise her misgivings with her father or her husband, or any other colonist. She kept silent, overwhelmed by the extreme beauty of the desolate place. She whispered to herself the story of the daring girl that she had been, the tale she would one day tell this child. Over the coming hours, it fortified her when her father discovered no sign of the band of men they'd meant to meet, no one left to greet them, nothing but signs of violence and death. She whispered it to herself when, in the weeks to follow, they were faced with the certainty of a difficult winter ahead. But at night, Eleanor wished she were the naïve girl in her father's studio again, when nothing had been certain and the world was full of beautiful mysteries that shimmered and danced in her head.

Eleanor knew the others suspected she'd lost her wits, or feared she was speaking with a familiar spirit. She held the copper plate beneath her dress, against her breast, keeping it close to remind her of all her hopes. She looked at the engraving for hours, tracing it with her fingertips until they were sore, memorizing the dream. Was it the guiding vision of her forebears as her mother had promised? Was it only the dream of a forsaken daughter? She could no longer tell.

Nothing went as her father had planned. Everything the colonists planted rotted in the ground. Every fruit withered on the vine. The men who had come before had not been so heroic as he had painted them, and their careless legacy of plundering and killing prepared the way for this new colony's suffering. For every native friend they made, they also had a vengeful enemy. The English fought with one another and then fought with their native friends, mistaking them for enemies and, in doing so, creating such. Eleanor saw mistake after mistake being made, sometimes in fear, sometimes in wrath, all in the name of God. But the beautiful people her father had once called gentle savages, now his men secretly buried. Eleanor's faith in the pious appointment her family had so eagerly accepted began to wane as she witnessed the truth: their pride had made them thieves.

With the anticipation of a ship's return, it was decided her father, a man with the queen's favor, would travel back to England for supplies. Even Eleanor signed the petition to send him on the colony's behalf. Desperate from hunger, sickness, and growing unrest, they made plans for what sign they might leave to warn or signal one another, should they need to abandon their pitiful new home and find themselves separated in a wilderness. Eleanor's father suggested they mark trees and fence posts with the sign of the cross to be his guide to find them upon his return. If sanctuary was needed, they would travel south, to an island where the natives might still extend help. The people who once had bravely proclaimed this land was predetermined to be their new home now talked as refugees in secretive groups. Eleanor feared at least part of this was her fault, that it had all been a terrible farce, that her vision had truly been a curse. Her father could not meet her eye, so ashamed he was of himself. Only when she felt the first pangs of labor would he even speak with her.

"Do not let this child die," he begged. "A new life will bring us hope."

"Tell me of my mama." She'd often longed to know the details of how her mother had died, but it hurt her father to remember them. She knew enough to understand a broken heart, and her father's heart had been broken twice over. She knew Tomasyn Cooper had refused the doctor's care and that's what changed her father forever. "How did she die? Why would she not see the doctor?"

"The doctor told her she should not carry another child, but she went against his advice and it brought her end. She took the risk."

"Then she died for you," Eleanor said, "as she lived for you." Seeing it plain, Eleanor recognized love. She understood that Tomasyn Cooper had tried to replace the son they'd lost to assuage her father's grief. She'd tried to give him a child, as Eleanor had tried to give him a dream. "I'm sorry, this baby will not save us," she said. "If I could stop it coming to this awful place, I would."

But in fact, Eleanor could only do what every woman before her had done: bear down and pray. Her words were shocking to her father then, not a familiar catechism or a dying woman's desperate promises to Jehovah. They were an incantation, some said. A conjuring. From dawn until dusk, when her daughter's first cries at last pierced the air, she told herself the story of a girl who always took a dare, a girl who went to sleep and awoke someone else, a girl who could always find her way home.

The little girl, Virginia, was christened by John White, her name predetermined even before they'd left England, to honor their quest and queen. But he could not celebrate the birth of a grandchild when that dream was failing. He seemed a defeated man already, before he even sailed for London, even as he promised his return. Eleanor could see he did not even believe the words himself. She wished someone else might make the trip. She wished there was a ship that might return them all to safer shores. But wishing accomplished nothing. She'd learned that before she'd ever set foot on this journey, years ago when her father had first begun to leave her behind. She might have mourned herself to death over his departure now, had she not watched him go so many times in her youth. She'd learned then to be independent of him, to shut out any loneliness with business. To take care of herself. And now she had a daughter, someone who needed her more than her father.

Before leaving, John White had done her a final unkindness. He'd taken Ananias, not Eleanor, and two other men from the colony, and together they'd buried his treasured belongings, believing this would protect them until his return—his paints and brushes, his pen and ink, his maps, his collection of herbs and seeds sleeping inside their glass bottles. And the iron box with the commonplace book. A grave for all he'd loved. Eleanor felt he might as well have buried her too. He'd locked her out again, as he'd always done, frightened by the unknown, by all he might lose, of the daughter who had visions, of the wilderness of his own heart.

Eleanor did not watch when the boat disappeared from the horizon, but looked instead at her daughter's face. She felt sorry to think her father might never see Virginia grow, but she would tell her daughter he'd been a painter, a mapmaker, a dreamer. He'd given her a name. Then Eleanor let her hair loose from its tight knot to hang down her back and Ananias did not admonish her. He had eyes now only for his daughter, the first English child born in the New World. The light of his hope. Late in the night, Eleanor secured a shawl to her chest like the native women from her father's paintings. She went to reclaim the iron box, all of her father's brushes and paints, the collection of her mother's seeds, and the commonplace book and all the mysteries and wisdoms it could offer. She no longer needed permission to take her future into her own hands.

※

Within weeks of John White's departure, the gnawing in their bellies would not let the colonists sleep. They were suspicious and jealous of one another to the point of madness. Eleanor sprinkled the dried leaves of a black hellebore plant around her bed. Her mother's notes in the commonplace book had shown her to use the plant for protection. But if the colony feared her strange ways, at least they did them no harm. Neither was she cast out by her superstitious husband. Rather, she'd simply become unseen. When she closed her eyes, Eleanor could still see her vision. But she preferred her eyes to be open, for then she saw Virginia growing. Eleanor's heart belonged to Virginia.

It was for Virginia that Eleanor worked in secret to turn the fortune of the colony. She went to the commonplace book for the best times to plant, the way to bury a seed, and what it would need to make it grow. She burned sage, a tradition from the fishwives who believed in honoring the Creator by the natural magic of the created, and poured a tea of waste on the roots of the plants in the fields, feeding them as the colonists slept.

On the occasion that a desperate or exceptionally brave woman came to her door to plead that she work a charm on a quarrelsome neighbor or offer a cure for a stinging rash, Eleanor gave advice on herbs and whispered prayers in equal measure, for they were all the same to her, and made a trade for firewood or eggs. When the Irishwoman delivered her child, Eleanor was there to catch the baby and wrap her in Tomasyn Cooper's gray cloak and offer a blessing, for they were equals in motherhood as they should have been in life.

If the colonists had asked Eleanor if any of these things were magic, she'd have only laughed, because of course they were. But the one charm she'd never learned to work was the one to help them see they were also divine.

Then one day, one of the young Englishmen, barely old enough to have whiskers on his lip, stood next to her in the tidal pool where she'd come to collect mollusks. She knew his name was Griffin Jones and he made an awkward bow. "I've seen you with your book. I want to learn to read and write. Would you teach me?"

"Why would I do that? What will you trade?"

"Tomorrow we move upriver," he said. "I will carry your iron box."

Their journey would be a difficult one and Eleanor considered the offer. The colony had given up on her father's return, and Eleanor had to think of the future here. She turned to watch Virginia playing on the shore. She looked out at the horizon, a long flat line. The edge of the map. And she turned and shook the boy's hand.

Chapter Nineteen

Alice

A card from Oscar Lewallen came in the post. His sure, dark pen strokes were evidence of a steady hand and, I hoped, a sign our dinner of misanthropes hadn't been for naught.

> Dear Mrs. Young,
>
> I hope this letter finds you well. I am writing to inform you that I have decided to officially declare my retirement from the law, but will be happy to recommend a local solicitor for your future needs. I will be staying with my sister's family in Macon for an indeterminate amount of time and mail can be forwarded to me there, should you need anything from me. I do continue to hope you will reconsider your stewardship of Evertell, as the estate and your family have long played an important role at the heart of our community. I wish you all well and thank you again for your gracious invitation. I cherish the evening with friends and neighbors.
>
> Sincerely,
>
> Oscar Lewallen

I tucked the card away inside the writing desk but considered his message well into the day, especially his choice of the word *steward*. I had never regarded myself as such, nor my role at Evertell as of any consequence to a community.

I couldn't deny I felt some relief at being released from working with the man. The trouble was in having to arrange to work with someone new who might not know the property. But I thought of the pages I'd read the night before, of Eleanor digging up her father's iron box, retrieving the commonplace book and all of his tools, taking the future into her own hands.

I took a swim in the early pink light, and when I returned Penn was inside, cross-legged on the floor, bent over the commonplace book, hard at work adding more drawings to its margins. I'd peeked over her shoulder to catch a glimpse of her sketch, a small, neatly detailed pattern of seashells, ones I recognized from the tabby wall in the front room. But she'd shooed me away, wanting to finish her work without observation. Beside her, on the floor, was a small scrap of cloth no bigger than a half-dollar. It was embroidered with a small green clover, encircled with red, and in gold letters it read *Be Prepared*.

"What's this?" I asked.

Before I could reach to have a closer look, Penn swiped it up. "It's a merit badge. Sammy gave it to me."

"Oh. Girl Scouts? That was nice. What's it mean?"

"It shows what you know. Well, what Sammy knows. She thinks I'd make a good Scout. I already have a lot of virtues. She says I'm already doing all the right things and one day, if I can show I know a lot of things, I can get a real job. Like she has," she said matter-of-factly. "Sammy's going to fly planes someday."

"Really?" I asked, impressed if surprised by her interest.

"When they let girls fly. And they will. And she'll be ready."

I marveled at Penn's certainty in the girl's plans and at the marks she was steadily making in the commonplace book. Such a little thing, but I looked at the merit badge beside Penn and saw an interest that had nothing to do with a grave or a memorial or any death custom. I jumped on it. "When we get home, we'll see about the Scouts. I think it's a good idea. You can sell all the cookies your heart desires."

"It's not about cookies, Mama," she said, then ignored me. She was concentrating on the ink drawing, intent and quiet again. I left her to it, happy to see her so engaged.

The results of my own work were not so pleasing to the eye. Penn and I had covered most everything that stood still with white paint. The whole house appeared just as sadly in need of repairs as ever, only now shining ridiculously bright in the blinding sun, like an overzealously frosted cake.

When I brought a ladder around from the barn to get a better look at some of the holes in the roof, I should have known better than to be so careless as to lean it against the chimney. I should have noticed the scattered bricks near the foundation. I should have asked for Sonder's help, as suggested. But I'd been thinking only to assess the damage, not intending to patch it. I leaned as far as I could on tiptoe, standing on a top rung to inspect the missing shingles. Without warning, the precarious balance shifted beneath me as the chimney gave way. The ground came at me hard and fast and I let out a loud yelp as I fell.

Luckily, the structure collapsed in a slow, rumbling cascade. Within a few seconds, I lay in a pile of brick and shale, the breath knocked out of me, but otherwise unharmed. The noise brought Penn screaming like a banshee from inside and Sonder running from the mill to witness my beaten repose.

"Mama!" Penn reached me first. "Mama! Don't be dead! Please don't be dead!"

"My God, Penn," I wheezed. "Calm down. Look. I'm fine."

"No! No!" she shouted, pushing my hair out of my face, her hands racing over me, checking every limb as if she expected to find me in pieces, like the chimney.

"Penn, stop," I urged, trying to calm her panic while gulping for air. She threw her arms around me, down on her knees, holding too tightly as she burst into tears. "Honey, I'm okay," I croaked.

She was frantic with apologies, mumbling words into my neck that I couldn't understand. I could feel her trembling and I held her more tightly, starting to cry, too, upset because she was.

"It's not your fault," I said. "Penn, look. Look at me." I pried her off of me so I could see her face. "It was just a little fall. Nothing's broken. That old chimney was coming down any day and I knew it. It was stupid of me, leaning the ladder in the wrong place." We both looked up to where the chimney had ripped away from the house, leaving the wood siding exposed all the way to the roof, where a great portion of the eaves and part of the wall gaped open to the attic. "It was a hole before and now it's a bigger hole. It doesn't matter."

Sonder approached, finding us messy and tearstained. "Making more repairs?"

"Obviously," I said. "Do you like it?"

"Lets in the light." He reached a hand to help Penn to her feet first, looked her in the eye, then surprised me by wiping her face with his shirttail. If I'd been crying before, now the tears ran hot down my face. When he turned to reach a hand to me, I took it gratefully. But I was shocked by the difficulty I had in getting to my feet, already feeling my muscles and bones ache from landing atop the wooden ladder and bricks. He didn't hesitate or ask permission before scooping me up into his arms and hauling me into the house. When he started for the stairs, I protested.

"No, wait. I'm not going to bed like some invalid. Put me down."

"You're going to rest," Penn announced, rushing ahead up the stairs. "Just like you say to me."

"Enough. Now, stop this, both of you," I said, shoving at Sonder and scrambling out of his grasp so I landed on my feet, unbalanced but standing. "Listen to me," I insisted. "Nobody is carrying me off again. I fell a few feet, that's all." I dusted the seat of my pants and glared at the two of them. Sonder stepped back and held up his hands, palms facing me, in a sign of surrender. Penn rolled her eyes and made a small snorting noise of annoyance.

"Don't you need to go help Doris with something? Aren't you two supposed to be working on pulleys and bell business?" I asked them. I could see both hesitate. Sonder especially gave Penn a look, and whatever meaning passed between them, I knew they had a secret.

"I'm supposed to make herb bunches for the farm stand, but I'm not taking them to Doris yet," Penn said begrudgingly. "And we already found the pulleys in the shed. We don't have anything to do until Sammy comes and fixes the piece for the clapper before we hook it up. You have to get Bill to give us the Hawkes stone." She stayed put, but her voice had gone soft, as if she might cry.

All the color was gone from her face. It made me think of the way she'd looked for months before we'd come back to Evertell. A dazed expression filled her eyes. I reached a hand to check her forehead for fever, but her skin was cool to the touch. She took hold of my hand and held it, something I found unsettling. Sonder saw this too.

"You're welcome, by the way," Sonder said. "I can bring a tarp. At least keep the rain out."

"Thank you. I'm fine, I swear," I insisted. "We're going to be fine." I pulled Penn closer and Sonder took this as a sign we needed a moment. He nodded and left us, presumably to return to some pressing work at the mill. I finally said, "Penn, what's wrong? You tell me right now."

When she didn't answer, I gave her hand a little shake. Her head snapped up and she looked at me, present again, and her eyes filled with tears.

"It's my fault. I pulled the bricks down from the chimney. I've been taking some of them out almost every day since we got here. Just one sometimes. Then more. I made this happen."

"But why?" I asked, incredulous, caught between relief that she was reanimated with the confession and disbelief that she would have done such a thing.

"I guess I made a deal with the house, like you make deals with me. I said, if it fell and you couldn't fix it, then you wouldn't be able to get anybody to buy the house and you'd give up. You'd stop trying to sell it. I thought the house could decide. But it's stupid, I know. When I say it to you, I know. I just didn't want to be the one."

"The one what?"

"The reason we lost Evertell."

If the fall from the ladder had knocked the breath from me, Penn's logic now did far worse. I couldn't speak for a long, still moment. I felt all the memories of my own childhood colliding and my mouth went dry, my vision dim. I had to sit down. Penn folded her legs and sat on the ground beside me. Finally, I gathered my senses enough to say the only thing I'd wished someone had asked me before I'd followed Mama into those woods.

"Penn, you're running around here doing a million things, trying to make something happen. You just have to tell me, what do you want?"

"I don't know." She sounded miserable.

"But you wanted something. You must know." I tried supplying the options. "Do you hate it here?"

"No, I love Evertell," she said in a rush.

"Then what? Why would you destroy all the work I've been doing?" As I asked the question, I also came to a quick conclusion and I asked her all the same questions I'd only just been asking myself. "Did you think if I didn't sell that we'd stay here? How can we do that, Penn? What about Merely's? Grandma Imagine? What about Brenau Academy?"

"We don't have to stay. But you don't have to sell it either," she suggested.

She did not mention school plans. I wouldn't let her give that up, thinking she was saving something for me. Frustrated, I said, "Well, I've been thinking about that this morning. If you'd asked, I could have told you. I'm thinking of only putting up a few acres, just at first. I haven't decided, but it might be smart to see if we get any interest before we go. If we do, that would be enough to cover the first fees for school. I could figure out the rest after we're home. Now, does that sound like what you want?"

"I thought you'd be mad." Penn stared at me, conflicted.

I rubbed my forehead, a bad headache coming on. Maybe the fall had been more jarring than I first thought. "Well, I'm knocked silly," I admitted. "Upset. But that's not the same as mad. And I can't blame you for not wanting to lose Evertell. I understand how you feel. Anyway, nobody's hurt. A pile of bricks can be rebuilt. No use feeling bad about any of it." I stared up at the hole in the roof.

"I'm sorry."

"I know. Just no more trying to kill me."

"I wasn't—"

"Sure you were," I teased, actually beginning to feel relieved. I was fine. Penn was fine. I tried to ease her conscience with a joke. "Look at all you stand to inherit with me out of the way. Maybe Sonder's birds can roost in the rafters." For some reason this struck me as much funnier than it should have and I laughed. Penn's expression was incredulous, then stormy.

"That's not funny." She looked desolate, gazing up at the damage she'd done.

"Oh, come on, Penn. I'm not serious. Laugh a little. But the house doesn't decide. We do." She frowned, but the color was back in her cheeks. If anything, Penn was the one who was angry. "Imegine needs us back. You know that, right? The corn will come in soon. We'll stay until then, like we said. That was always our deal. We are going to bring in this harvest, ring that big bell, and then we'll see what can be done from home."

She nodded and rubbed her nose, seemingly resigned. But then she said, "There's something I want before we go. For May Day."

"Oh God, Penn. I don't know if I can do one more thing."

"No. It's not more. It's something we already have. I just don't want to take anything else from Doris." Penn shook her head and I frowned. "Can I have the candle that Bridie gave you? It's for the Evertell charm."

"Sure." I forced a smile, even though my teeth had begun to ache. But, as it turned out, I could do better than that. "Ask Sonder to take you under the mill. There are piles, stacks, boxes of them. All yours. Light up the night. But, Penn," I added carefully, pausing to be sure she was listening, "you know when you do this, nothing's really going to happen, right? It's just a sweet idea, a thing Grandmama Claire and the Dare heirs passed down. Like singing 'Auld Lang Syne' on New Year's Eve or blowing out candles on your birthday. It's not magic."

She hurried to kiss me. I gave her a squeeze. She seemed satisfied as she took off for the mill.

When I stood in the yard alone, I stared up at the place where the sky shone blue through the gaping hole in the roof. That chimney had stood for centuries before my determined little girl came along and gave it a choice. What she'd really done was give me a choice. I knew Penn. She didn't want Brenau, but she couldn't bring herself to tell me. It was clear she wanted to stay at Evertell. I couldn't see a way to give her that, but I hoped we'd found a compromise. The house had decided, just as she'd intended. I had to smile at that. Now light filtered down through the exposed eaves of the attic where only shadows had gathered for so long.

X

Stove up from the fall, I was crabby and thinking how Penn's idea about the house deciding for us was so like me at that age, looking for a way to put the responsibility of Evertell onto the shoulders of something or someone else. I hadn't realized I'd saddled her with that same pressure or that she would see it that way, and now I felt bad. I should have realized how it would seem to her, as if I were trading away something precious to me for her happiness, our family legacy for her dream. In some ways, that was exactly true, but it was also true that I had believed it was the best gift Evertell had to offer us. I had believed it was the right thing, that my mama and even Eleanor would approve.

And yet, I felt I was still searching. Searching Eleanor's Tale for the answers, searching my own memories, and I couldn't have told anyone what I was hoping to find. Faced with our very real departure, leaving behind Bill Hawkes, Doris and Bell Isle, Sonder, and even the peacock, I understood that it wasn't the disappearance of the stone that had left me without an identity. It was so much more.

On my way back inside the house, I let the memory of the day I took Charlie Hawkes into the forest flood back to me. I was sifting it, looking for something.

"Look there!" he'd called out.

I'd stopped in the road when I heard him approach instead of scurrying off to escape the rhyme. This time was different.

I turned to face him before he could go any farther. His eyes widened beneath a fringe of straw-like hair, but he didn't say anything else. Barefoot, Charlie wore a pair of worn overalls with holes in the knees, the only thing I'd ever seen him wear, in fact, while I stood stiffly in my yellow sundress and brown buckle shoes. Neither of us moved and he took it as a challenge and let out a low whistle. When I didn't budge, it was Charlie who came closer, a stupid grin on his wide mouth, so close I could see the freckles across his nose. They made him look sweet to me, and my heart lurched in my chest in a different sort of way. I knew then that I wanted more than to convince Charlie to stop the teasing or to stop drawing attention to everything that was going wrong with my mama. I was a shy, odd girl without many friends. I spent most of my time in a lonely old house or on the water with a kind boy who worked for my daddy and felt a little sorry for me. I wanted Charlie Hawkes to like me.

"I can show you the biggest secret you ever imagined," I said, not blinking. "If you're not as chicken as you look."

I couldn't remember ever actually speaking to Charlie before that, not at school or the store. From the look on his face, he was as startled by the sound of my voice as I was, but he didn't hesitate for a second before he rose to the challenge.

"You're lying. You don't have any big secret, except your mama's crazy as a bat."

He laughed at his own joke. Somehow I felt brave. Maybe because I knew the stone was real. I knew I was right, that Charlie would never imagine such a thing right behind my house, but he'd want to all the same.

"All right, then show me," he said, bouncing on the balls of his feet beside me as I walked away from him.

"I don't know if I should. I'm not supposed to tell anybody." He was keeping up with me. "It's a very old secret in my family."

"What are you? A werewolf?"

I rolled my eyes, but the sound of his giggles and the excitement of having taken control of the situation made me chew the inside of my cheek. "Wouldn't you like to know."

"Ah, come on, Alice. Just tell me."

I stopped and considered the choice as if I were having to make a very hard decision, then looked up to find Charlie watching with as much interest as anyone had ever shown me. "It's something you have to see. But you have to promise you'll keep the secret. And you have to stop teasing because this is serious. This is real. That's the deal."

He held out his hand to shake on it. In that instant, I could have changed my mind. I could have kept the secret of the stone, the poison of the curse. Instead, I took his hand, his sweaty palm pressed against my own. I could smell the sharp scent of the marsh on him and knew he'd spent the morning fishing, like me. I saw his nails were bitten to the quick, like my own. I felt my pulse jump when he grinned at me. "Deal," he said.

We went dashing along the trail into the forest behind Evertell. We arrived at the place where the stone stood in the gloom, out of breath and full of expectation. As we gasped for air and let our eyes adjust to the shadows, I said, "There," gesturing toward the stone. "That's it. The Evertell stone."

"What is it?" Charlie asked, hands on knees, bent at the waist, gulping air that smelled strongly of the marsh at low tide. "A big rock? What's so great about that?"

I told him like you'd tell a ghost story to a child. "They put it here when they built Evertell, but it's old. Really old. They had to hide it because they stole it off a grave."

"They did not," he said, already so excited I could see it wasn't going to be hard to convince him. He squinted at the stone. "It's got stuff written on it."

"It says the names of the dead, a daddy and a baby, the very first English baby to be born in the very first colony. A little girl. Some people think this rock is all that's left of them, and my family stole it to say we were their descendants. They were part of the Lost Colony of Roanoke."

"You're making that up."

"You can read about it in history books and everything."

"Nuh-uh."

"It's true. I swear it," I said with my most serious voice. "I'm the last living heir of Eleanor Dare."

"The one in the rhyme your mama told? That stuff's true? You're kidding me."

I nodded.

Charlie squinted at me and then at the stone. He moved to investigate the inscription, kneeling beside it, and I helped him read it. But he balked. Probably he was scared, I thought. Good. "That's the big secret? So what?" he finally said.

This was a question I'd prepared for. I stared at the stone for a long moment. I felt a trickle of sweat run down my spine as I looked at him, waiting. I suddenly feared he would walk away. That he wouldn't take the awful thing with him. I knew that my Evertell vision would go with it, but I believed it was killing my mama. I'd already weighed the cost.

In desperation, I said, "We're cursed. When you steal off a grave, you're cursed."

I saw the meaning of what I was trying to convey dawn across Charlie's face. His long eyelashes fluttered over his sweet eyes as he uttered, "It's an actual curse."

"It is," I said as he looked at the stone and then at me with the same awestruck expression. "But we can break the curse. I showed you so you can take it away from here."

"But then I'll be the cursed one."

"Are you scared?" I saw the challenge strike at his heart. He didn't want to admit it to me. "You don't have to keep it. That way it can't touch you. Just roll it off someplace. I don't care what happens to it. I dare you. I dare you, Charlie Hawkes." Still, I saw him hesitate. I thought I knew what he wanted, what all boys want. He wanted to be the hero in this story and I knew how to make him into one. A dare. A sacrifice. That's the way the stories always went. Before he could say no, I added the words I believed he truly wanted to hear, beneath all his teasing. "If you do it, you'll save my life."

Just like that, he gave me that lopsided grin. I thought it had worked. But I felt defeat when he said, "Why would I do that?"

Then I knew. Not even for all the glory in the world would Charlie Hawkes change his feathers. He was a bully and he believed he had me where he wanted me. He wasn't interested in admiration. He wanted power. And so, instead of a fairy tale, like I had hoped would transform him, I told him the story he wanted to hear. I told him he'd already beat me. I couldn't get rid of the stone. I had to do something worse. "I guess you're right. I shouldn't have shown you. If you took it and showed it off, everybody would see it's just some old rock. There's nothing to it. They'd think we've been hiding it in our woods to make everybody think we're something we're not, better than you."

"A stupid rock doesn't make you better than me," he agreed.

"You're right. I guess anybody could make a rock like that. You could carve your own name right in it. It doesn't mean anything."

"Maybe I will." He grinned at that. "And people will know your mama really is crazy. Crazy Claire."

Even then I worried it was a mistake. I could feel it.

I wasn't sure I believed everything I'd told Charlie that day. But I believed that to sacrifice the stone and make it a joke, make my family and Eleanor a joke, didn't seem like such a loss if changing our story would save my mama. My family. And if I lost who I was, at least it meant she'd be free of a curse in those woods, or in her own mind. I believed that until the night she brought me to the empty place where the stone once rested and keened like a high wind that tore through our lives so quick and fierce that nothing could stop how things happened next.

⋊

We should have seen it coming, Eleanor and I. She, crouched over the commonplace book reading parables with a boy, me whispering myths to Charlie Hawkes. But really, you never could, could you? For all the talk of visions in this family, from what I was learning from Eleanor's Tale and the commonplace book, and even my own day-to-day, we all seemed to make our way on blind faith.

As promised, Sonder had thrown a tarp over the hole in the roof and I went up to the attic to get a look at the damage caused by the fallen chimney.

A small set of back stairs from the second-floor landing led upward. The air grew warmer as I approached the third floor and then reached a set of double doors. The same iron key that opened all the doors and closets of Evertell fit this lock. I used it to let myself into the dusty room in the rafters. Before me was a space that had once been a low-ceilinged room, now open where the roof had been torn away, leaving a jagged edge against the pale blue sky. I stepped farther inside, ignoring the sweltering heat.

I could see that there must have been an alcove or closet tucked next to the exposed chimney. Amazingly, a small trunk still sat there in what might have been a hiding place, overlooked when the rest of the house had been emptied. Astonished, I stepped carefully around the rubble of the stone chimney and torn pieces of wood. Only the size of a shoebox, the box wasn't heavy and I knelt to open it, unfastening a small buckle so the lid flipped open with no trouble. As though I'd released a captive—a ghost that had been waiting for its escape—something soft and unexpected flew up and brushed my cheek. Spooked, I let out a sharp scream and scrambled away, throwing my hands in front of my face. I didn't want to see what it was, but I looked anyway and my breath burst from my body in a raw laugh of relief. A feather hung in the air, gliding on its spine and gently landing near me. A stupid peacock's feather. But it was the remaining contents of the trunk that set me reeling.

Maybe a half dozen photographs were stuck together, moldering, fading, crumbling. I peeled the only remaining clear image apart from the ruin and stared at a print featuring my young mother. Along with a group of unknown women, she stood outside a great stone structure that looked to me like a castle by its scale, with the many chimneys and turrets and endless rows of windows. The long wall stretched to the edge of the frame, but the line of women stood out starkly in their dark dresses and stout lace-up shoes. Their faces were bright and smiling, all lifted toward the camera.

Alongside many of the women were small children clinging to their legs. The faces of the children seemed uncertain and dour. Their eyes stared at the camera in defiance or fear, or maybe something else entirely. I looked more closely at them. They wore identical, drab little smocks, both the girls and the boys. On their feet, they wore identical pairs of shoes. They looked like tiny prisoners. And perhaps that was what I saw on their faces: the look of innocents who were present in body but absent in spirit. The whole scene made me horribly sad. And it made me curious, too, because in contrast, all of the women appeared almost blissful. Especially my mama. This must have been the orphanage she'd funded, I realized. This was France after the First World War. I knew Mama had helped support this place, but this was the first I'd ever seen of it for myself.

It was as if I'd opened a window into the unknown past to see a person who had disappeared into thin air, obliterated from my memory by the tragic last scenes of her life, and now I couldn't look at her enough. I scoured the photograph for the smallest details, my vision blurring from straining over the image of my mama up close, holding an infant in her arms. She seemed so happy, at ease, well. This was the woman Doris remembered, my young mother in her prime.

I flipped the photo over but was disappointed to see nothing written there beyond a date in pencil so faded I could barely make it out: 1917.

A few years after my grandmother Calista's death. I would have been eight when the photograph was taken, yet I barely remembered Mama this way. But here she was in black-and-white, proof she had been whole and happy and looking into a future filled with something like hope. Enough of it to pass along to these little wanderers.

I told myself it was only the unbearable heat and the strangeness of the great, open hole in the roof that made me feel light-headed. I could feel the sweat coating my back, my arms, my legs, pooling behind my knees. I needed to get out of the attic so I could think straight. I took the photos with me to the writing desk.

I'd come to the part in Eleanor's Tale when the worst happened—she lost everything she loved. This was where she'd carved the first stone, the grave of her daughter, her husband, her dream. And I knew what came next, but as a girl, I had barely listened to the rest. How could anything going forward in her life matter or compare after such loss? As a grown woman and a mother, this was what I wanted most to know. I barely remembered the details.

But even before I could open the pages to where I'd marked them with the blue ribbon, my own story was playing out in my mind, taking me back to those woods, when hope had been lost. When the stone was gone.

X

I'd been thirteen for three months when my mama chose the day to take me into the forest with the hopes of inspiring my vision, the day before the Evertell homecoming. One week since I'd taken Charlie to see the stone. I knew it would be gone.

In the days leading up to my birthday, I'd asked, "When you had your vision, what was it like?" The question was like poking at a bad bruise I knew would never heal. I was desperate for the moment she would discover the stone was gone, when she would know what I had done for her.

"Well, it isn't what you'd expect," she said. "It's a feeling, with a sense you never knew you had. It's a memory, maybe, of a dream. Did you know we can pass a memory down, one to another? If it's special enough, powerful enough? It's a memory we're born with. There's water all around, or maybe it's air, and all these little silver

flashes, moving so smooth and pretty. It's the breath of wings. It will feel so easy, Alice. So easy. That's what I want for you."

I could have asked a thousand times more and still I wouldn't have understood. I'd listened as she read Eleanor's Tale, leading right up to the end, but never finishing the story for me. That part was up to me, she'd said.

"Everybody thinks they were lost, but that's not the secret." She would wink at me and I would pretend to share her delight. "Don't worry. Watch and see. It will come to you."

But it did not.

She would close the commonplace book slowly, smiling at me as we recited the names of all the descendants together. It was our game and it made me feel that even at her worst, we had a connection.

We went stomping through the mud on that last day, on a quest. "Come on, come on," she sang like a little girl. "Before they catch us! Shh!"

No one knew that we'd gone off into the forest. She'd made sure it was a secret between us.

"How much farther?" I'd asked. We were going in circles, but surely she knew it. My mama knew this forest better than some of the old men who hunted it every day. She'd taught me the same. We'd walked on for what seemed like an hour, much farther than we should have gone to reach the place where the stone had stood. But it was all part of her game, I assumed.

"Oh, we'll have to see."

We giggled and sang her favorite song. "I'll see you in my dreams . . ."

But I grew tired and a little alarm started going off in my head. "Did you bring something to eat in that bag?" I asked. "Can we stop awhile, have a snack?"

"Not yet, no. We're not here to eat dinner," she snapped. "Just pick your feet up. You're dragging your feet, Alice."

But it was my mama who had slowed. I could hear her sniffle. She'd begun to cry.

If we'd wandered astray, I needed to take us back the right way. But my mama continued muttering to herself, and I knew what was about to happen. Her face, so alight with energy and joy when we'd started out, had screwed down tightly so her light brows were bunched over her blue eyes and her mouth was pursed like an old woman's. Her panic was growing. I could feel it.

I touched her arm lightly so she looked at me. I meant to reveal the thing I had done. I meant to say, "I've done it! I've rid us of the curse! I gave up my vision for our freedom, but the stone is gone forever. Look! See what a daughter I am!"

She didn't notice me. Instead, she began to whistle. Not a song anymore, but more like she was sending out a call. Suddenly she stopped and jerked my arm hard so I stopped too. "Listen," she wheezed. "Somebody's out here. They follow us, you know. They want to see what we do."

"I don't think so," I said, feeling the familiar clench of my teeth when my mama's tone changed in this way, became a sullen croak. "People won't come for the homecoming until tomorrow."

I had no words for what I felt. It was a barometric change. It was the magnet of my mama, the pole of her soul sliding off its true line. It would drag us right off course.

She crouched then, refusing to be moved as she strained her swollen eyes, casting her gaze forward and back across the ground. Her expression had gone slack and her mouth chewed.

"I hear them!" she screeched. "You know who I mean. They're scratching like little ferrets. Slick and skinny and beady-eyed. That's what they are. They want to see what we do."

"Nothing's scratching. Let's rest," I yelped. She heard that. She wrapped her arms around herself and rocked softly. I joined her near the ground.

I looked around for landmarks, familiar trees, the low-lying ponds to assure myself it was the right place. I checked with my fingers, pushing fallen pine straw and dried palmetto leaves aside until I could see the wound in the earth where the rock had left its mark. It was gone. We were squatting where the stone should have been.

"Mama," I said. My voice seemed nothing but a vapor, barely audible. "Don't you see where we are? You don't have to be scared now."

"Scared? What are you talking about?"

Her chest was heaving with her erratic breath. Her eyes were dull when she turned them on me. I saw the idea of what I was saying worm its way through her mind, but it did not take hold. Instead, she began to recite the terrible dirge of accusations and grievances that had become her constant refrain. I wanted to wail and thrash at the first words, sick to death of hearing them, knowing once she began there would be no end to it. Round and round she'd go until she was inconsolable.

"It was never supposed to be here," she insisted.

"I know."

"It's only made us miserable. Look at us and you can see. Anybody can see. Look at me, Alice. Look at me. Can you even see me anymore?"

"I see you, Mama." I couldn't help trying again. "You're right here. The stone's gone now. Look, I'm showing you. I sent it back to the grave."

Her hands grasped at the air. I tried to move so she could get hold of me, but I was not what she wanted. I hated to look at her lumpen shape. I hated the moldering smell of the damp forest floor. She could not believe she would not find the stone there. She would not stop scrabbling and crawling.

"I told your grandmother," she said. She spat the words out hard. "I was just talking to her and I told her, but she won't listen."

My grandmother was lost to her a long time ago. It alarmed me that she believed she'd been speaking to her.

"It doesn't matter how I've tried," she moaned. "She won't listen. Your daddy won't listen. And now here you are, not listening either."

In my horror, I only said, "Mama, we're all listening to you, I promise. You are all we hear."

My guts boiled. I would have said anything to stop her. The tortured echo of her unending lament. She raged on, unable to resolve some real or imagined betrayal, the confused anguish of love that had turned to hate, loathing for her family, for the legacy she'd treasured, all trapped inside the twisting of her mind.

The stone was gone, and the only vision left to me now was this broken creature. Something I wished I'd never seen.

Finally, I gave it up.

"We'll lie down," I said. "We can do everything the way you want. Tell me what to see. Tell me how. I'll do it."

"Fine," she said.

She was displeased. As if I were the one who had brought us here. I tried to think what to do next, but it turned out that was easy.

She hummed a short melody and drew a thermos from her sack. "I have tea, did you know? I need a drink of my medicine. Tea for two."

I'd almost forgotten the sack. I wondered fleetingly what else it might hold, but I knew the tea she was always sipping, a bitter *herbal to calm her nerves. She was never without it anymore. It left her addled and unsteady. I didn't care what might be in it, even as I remembered Charlie's horrible, childish rhyme. I wanted to tell him then that like me, there were things he'd been wrong about.*

It was me who poured that tea. We swallowed it by the cupful.

Roanoke Colony Inland Fort
Late Summer 1590

On the dawn of Virginia's third birthday, the sun shone on a colony no longer of a southern island, but a new settlement, a refuge of Eleanor's husband's making. Ananias had refused to abandon his purpose. He was a brickmason and he meant to build, not hide. He knew a secret some of the others had not heard. Ananias followed a map her father had made years before. And Eleanor had followed her husband, carrying Virginia. Griffin Jones had carried the iron box. She'd found respect for her husband for the first time. They had taken boats upriver, faithfully leaving signs along the way, daring to move into the wilderness rather than cling to the shore and the faith that John White would return.

They settled on a bluff where the river turned, a vantage point, and one the old governor had once marked on his map, then covered with a patch, should the map fall into the hands of an English enemy. Perhaps he'd feared it too dangerous to recommend this place to the colonists before he left. Perhaps he'd believed he would return to lead them there himself. Eleanor did not believe she would ever know, nor did she care any longer. They led themselves. And in some ways, as the years had passed, their small number had made a home. Although she'd told no one, Eleanor was again with child. And there was something of her old dream still alive.

Whether they knew it or not, their good fortune was often achieved with the help of one of Eleanor's cures or charms. They survived long winters and brutal summers because of the bounty of their gardens and the medicines she made. But she could do little about the precarious relations with the natives. She could not transform herself or any Englishman from what they were: a sign of what was to come. The colonists were living, breathing bad omens to the Indians. And now, on the very day when they celebrated the birth of Virginia, rumors reached them of the ship.

Nearby, native priests had their worst fears realized, more thieves come to steal their homes. The news had stirred their tribe to fresh fear and vengeance. There was nothing in the commonplace book to protect Eleanor and her family from their fate.

A hush fell over the day as they waited. Eleanor bent to harvest a patch of black hellebore while Griffin Jones read aloud a parable to bring comfort. She listened for the wisdom she needed, surprised to be reminded of her father's voice. But then there came a desperate cry. It was not salvation that came that day, not a celebration of life, but a native attack to end the lost Roanoke Colony, and Eleanor's dream.

Encumbered by the unborn life within her belly, she crouched there, a helpless witness to the slaughter of her kinsmen at the hands of the beautiful men of the wood, just as they'd looked in her father's paintings years ago. When she struggled to get to her family, Griffin Jones pulled Eleanor into a thicket where they wouldn't be seen. He was only a young man of fourteen, with life yet to live. He had no mother but Eleanor. The impossible choice was made. She saw Ananias fall first, and so many others around him.

Then came the terrible wailing of Virginia, her searching eyes, desperate for Eleanor, and the instant she knew her mother could do nothing to save her. Virginia. The name went to dust in Eleanor's throat. The terrible weight of a stone brought down on the soft curls, the tender head Eleanor had cradled at her breast and kissed only an hour ago. And the silence that followed, a murky feeling as though Eleanor were drowning. She shivered and closed her eyes and thought of the beasts in the deep and the dragons of the air and waited for the vision to transform her nightmare. But inside, her blood felt fiercely hot. It was not a fever, but the purest hatred of the violence men visit upon the earth.

Whatever faith Eleanor had known in the world that she could see and the one she could imagine, she lost sight of all of it then. She closed her eyes and felt herself sink to a place of darkness deep inside, where she finally abandoned the shore, the river, herself. There was something she had learned in that moment of a magic she'd dared not dream. Eleanor Dare learned to disappear.

Griffin Jones hid alongside Eleanor. She'd been so sure of her daughter's future that she'd been teaching him to read. She'd planned it so her daughter would have a literate English husband. Now they crouched in brambles and white blossoms, amazed to have been overlooked, horrified by the aftermath. And when, at last, they dared move, their legs were stiff and their hands shook and words failed them. The boy stumbled forth in search of survivors; there were seven in all, men and boys who wept over their wives, children, brothers, and sisters.

For days, Griffin and the few others who remained buried the dead, including Virginia and Ananias. Eleanor did not stand over the open graves. Instead, she pulled out her graver's tools from long ago and worked on a stone, carving words of the dead for the dead, for that was the only language she seemed to speak now. She forged letters small and cramped, cutting so deeply Griffin believed her words might never be erased, a declaration that would reach her father over the sea, through the ages.

In her quiet mind, Eleanor drifted. This was what it meant to become a curse. She imagined the sound of her graver would haunt her father. He would fear to lay his head each night for the constant scraping that would come in his dreams. Her fingers blistered and bled, but she refused to leave the stone until it was finished, ignoring the anxious pleas and rude demands of the others who were desperate to flee. Stupid in her grief, she gladly would have lain down alongside the stone and died, for she felt nothing. She was a grave. The forsaken men left standing in the forest begged her for a charm. They raged at her, too, when she failed to comfort their terrified hearts. But Eleanor barely heard them, so deeply had she sunk.

When they finally deserted her, and only Griffin Jones remained, the boy brought out the iron box. It held the commonplace book alongside her father's paints and the small cloth sacks she'd filled with seeds. And he brought out the pouch, unwrapping the copper plate. But Eleanor had no use for these tools now. And she had no idea what the vision meant any more than she knew if her father or anyone else would ever stumble over the stone she'd carved. She watched the light flash from the engraving and wished Ananias had melted the copper down and sold it long ago. It told her nothing of the kind of woman she would become or the life she would lead, only that she'd been a fool.

"None of it was true," she told the boy. "It can't have been." She knew nothing of the mother that her father remembered. For all she knew, he might have invented her, and the commonplace book, too, with its signs and secrets. Exactly as she'd invented the vision. "It was all only ever a story in a book."

Had she been alone, Eleanor would have remained with the stone she'd carved until she was bones. But the boy refused to listen when she denounced her story or the commonplace book or any of the thousand cures and charms she'd worked for the colonists who'd hated her. He feared setting out alone and wouldn't leave her, so near her time to deliver the baby. He talked incessantly of the place where he was born, a port in a land across a far, wide sea, where ships with tall white sails could carry a man from one world to another. She knew the chances he'd ever see that place again, but she couldn't reason with him and she feared what it would be to watch him lose his faith. And so they followed the river, moving south along its winding path again, because it was the way they knew. He was looking for the ocean, for a way home.

Eleanor wasn't looking for anything.

⚭

For weeks they walked, following the river with no way to know where their journey might end. They'd become the savages, truly desperate and hopeless people. Not the natives her father had first romanticized, then feared, and never understood, but very near to animals. Somewhere in the darkest corners of her mind, Eleanor remembered a phrase from her father's Scripture: they were strangers in a strange land. And not for the first time, she understood the land was not hers. It belonged to the stones and rivers and the secrets running deep within them.

The boy fished and foraged, but Eleanor would not eat. At times the trail almost disappeared, steep and rocky. The canopy of hemlock and pine towered above their heads. These names, and the names of plants she recognized from her father's sketches and paintings, were the only words she could form. The young man tried to talk to Eleanor of her life before, of her father and London, of happier times. Eleanor could no longer remember those days.

The leaves were turning scarlet and gold and soon enough winter would be upon them. At night she listened to owls calling through the dark. She thought they said, *"Who are you? Who are you?"* That was when Eleanor wept, when she thought of the names in the common-place book and the woman she might have been.

X

The boy hoped Eleanor might find strength in her unborn child, a remnant of those she'd loved. She knew there was no way to make him understand her indifference. Always in her mind, she could hear Virginia's voice, chiming, laughing, and whispering. He could not know that each step she took felt as though she would run screaming, farther and farther from the small grave where she'd left her daughter, abandoned to a wilderness that would wind round and through her fragile bones and hide her forever. It would horrify him to know that she fantasized every minute of turning back, of exhuming that grave so she could lie down in the cool earth, the only peace she could imagine. But when her time grew near to deliver her baby, she was surprised at how fiercely afraid she was to die.

Her pains came quickly. There was no time to prepare. Even if there had been, they had no means to make the birth an easy one. Eleanor spread her mother's cloak on the ground. But as hours passed, she grew exhausted, realizing how weak she'd become. The muscles in her body twisted and compressed. She thought of Virginia's birth and slipped into the heated memory, happy to be back there with the baby at her breast, then watching Virginia, older, toddling around the yard and on the shore. But the recollections soon twisted into a horror, her own screams mixing with the slaughter she'd witnessed as her kinsmen and daughter were cut down. That same gripping and tearing seemed to come from the inside. She couldn't escape, couldn't stop what she knew was coming. The blow came down upon Virginia's sweet head; it would end the same.

Late in the day, Eleanor cried out, not caring who might hear, but the nightmare held tight to her mind and the babe inside her was stuck, surely as dead as Virginia if she could not force it into the world. She remembered her words to her father long ago, about keeping her child from this place if she could, but life did not give us that choice. Griffin knelt by her side, smoothing her hair, helpless but to pray over her. Eleanor felt the words were worthless, but she hadn't the strength to tell him. She might have died then but for the strangers passing on the trail. Forgetting to hide, Griffin ran out from the place where Eleanor lay to beg their help.

When they came upon Eleanor, she had fainted, but woke in the grip of the next birthing pain to see the group of men standing over her. She didn't care who they might be, though she was relieved to see they were not natives. "Virginia," she said over and over again.

One of the men put his hands on her swollen belly and said softly, "Virginia, you must allow me, madam. My name is Gabriel Lavat. I am a surgeon. I will bring this child."

She screamed as he pressed hard on her belly. Between contractions, he reached his hand inside her to turn the child. In a flash of pain, again the world went black except for a tiny silver light that she struggled to see in the darkness. It moved so fast, darting just past the edges of her vision, forcing her to pay attention, to recognize what was at stake—a soul. It glided toward her, coming into focus as light must come to one who has been blind and then, miraculously, can see. Eleanor gasped and then cried, the first hot tears she'd shed in all the long months since Virginia's death, her consciousness returning and with it all the grief and joy she'd smothered for months. She bore down with all her strength, and her daughter tore into the world and into the waiting hands of Gabriel Lavat.

Chapter Twenty

Penn

Penn's nose filled with the smell of the river and the earthen walls of the room beneath the mill. Sonder hung the lantern high from a hook so they could see the stacks of crates that lined the walls, packed carefully with Grandmama Claire's candles.

"How many do you want?" he asked.

"All of them," Penn said. He raised his brows. "If we're going to leave, what are we saving them for? How many are there?"

"Looks to be about a dozen in each of these crates. About fifteen crates."

"She made a lot of light," Penn said.

"That she did," he agreed.

They carried the crates, going back and forth from the mill to the house, until they were all stacked neatly on the side porch.

"I guess you know what you're doing from here?"

Penn nodded. "Thanks."

"And you're ready to fix that bell?"

"I know what to do."

"I don't doubt it." Head to one side, he changed the subject. "I guess the house decided like you'd hoped? Lucky nobody got hurt. Did you talk to your mama about school?"

Penn sighed. "That was the deal. If the chimney fell, I had to tell Mama I don't want to go away." It was the first she'd said it aloud. But it was easy with Sonder.

"Is that all?" he said.

Penn wrapped her arms around herself. He had no idea. "She's going to think it's like before, when I quit everything, when I just wanted to be at home with Grandma Imegine. She's afraid of that." Penn hesitated. "She should be. Something was wrong with me. Maybe it's still wrong with me. I couldn't feel anything. I stopped caring. I just stopped." Penn swiped the back of her hand at her eyes. She didn't want to cry in front of Sonder. "I think she was afraid I'd be like Grandmama Claire. She says I'm not, but I don't know. Maybe that's what it is, being an Evertell heir."

"She told me a little," Sonder said. "And I knew your grandmama Claire, remember? You are like her." Penn looked up at him. "Seems to me you care more than most folks. That's like Claire. You've got the kind of courage I always wished I had."

Penn's breath came like a sob, feeling that kindness right at her center. She wanted to believe what Sonder was saying. She wanted to trust that it was the truth, that she was a courageous girl. She sat up straighter and finally said, "She's not selling the house. Just a parcel, so I can go to school someplace else if I want." Penn didn't let herself stop. She had to say it out loud while she could. "She won't leave Grandma Imegine. And Merely's is our home. It's Daddy's and Pop's place. I want to be an Evertell heir, and Dare girls always find their way home. I just thought I'd know what to do by now."

"Sounds like you do."

Penn nodded. "But it's too hard. I don't want to choose." It was as clear in her mind then as it had been since they'd left Helen. She could not be all or the other, Finch Young's girl on the side of the mountain road or the Evertell heir of Eleanor Dare, here. She was both. "I have to tell her that, don't I?" Penn said.

Sonder said calmly, "All you're asking for is a little time. Your mama's going to understand that," he said. "Maybe better than anybody. You know, just a few days ago she asked me about how this mill works. There are those two big stones and they have to work together to get anything done. Listening to you now makes me think of that. Because I told her that's how your grandparents loved each other. And look, here you are; you came from them."

Penn liked what he was saying. It made some kind of sense to her, but it also struck her as funny, comparing her to the product of the gristmill. She giggled, despite herself.

"What?" he said, grinning back at her.

"You think I'm courageous corn?"

Even saying it, she laughed. And it felt good. Sonder chuckled with her. She laughed harder and it was the relief of a deeper understanding, coming closer to what she'd hoped the charm would provide. Clarity.

"You said it, not me," Sonder said, walking away. She listened to him laugh on his way across the lawn and watched the party of peafowl come strutting from near the garden, trailing after him.

Ж

The day was mild and the clouds were high, but Mama was grouchy and nursing a headache that wouldn't let go. She'd been up to the attic and now her nose was stuffy and her eyes burned. Penn felt miserably responsible, although Mama refused to admit the fall had anything to do with it.

"I'm probably just allergic to all the dust," Mama said.

She was trying to find a way to explain everything Sonder seemed to understand so easily, but now it all felt jumbled in her head. She had found Grandmama Claire's fountain pen and indigo ink and drawn as many badges in the book as there were heirs, images to represent something she'd learned about each of them, to go along with other things about Evertell that she'd discovered since they'd come here. A peacock, a constellation of stars, a map made of seashells, a clarity candle, a fishing boat, a crab trap, the gate at the end of the drive, the leaves of an herb, a key, a book; the list went on. She was already planning more. And she'd spent the last hour pasting the news clippings from Bill Hawkes into the commonplace book. They seemed to belong there. They were part of the story. But she hated them too. They were something she still needed to talk about to know what she thought of them. She was conflicted when she turned each page, embarrassed, even, for her family. She thought maybe if they talked about the stones, it would eventually help her talk about herself.

"I don't know," she said slowly. "Maybe I shouldn't put these in the book."

"Why's that?"

"Because what if it's just lies?" Mama was listening and Penn took courage. "What if a long time from now, my great-great-great-granddaughter reads them and she can't tell if any of it's true? What if she won't believe any of it and nobody ever knows what happened to Eleanor? What will she think about us?"

"I'm not sure either of us will care at that point, Penn."

Penn sighed. "Some of the reports say Hammond was just a con man—he's the one who found the first stone in North Carolina.

Did you know he was already trying to run other hoaxes all the way back in 1931 because he needed money?" she mumbled. "He probably only came to Atlanta with the stone because of *Gone with the Wind*."

"What does *Gone with the Wind* have to do with Eleanor Dare?" Mama asked, mildly entertained. She was looking at the news clippings in the book with Penn. But she'd made a kind of joke of things and Penn wanted to be taken seriously.

"Well, there were lots of movie people and film agents in Atlanta then because of *Gone with the Wind*. He maybe thought the story about Eleanor would be made into a movie and make him rich. Plus, he really hated that Paul Greene had that play."

"Who's Greene again? I'm sorry, I can't remember all of this."

"Look. See," Penn said, pointing to an article about the outdoor drama in North Carolina. "Paul Greene wrote the Lost Colony play," Penn said in the voice she used to give reports in school. Clearly Mama didn't know about it. "They do a whole outdoor drama close to where they think the colony disappeared, with an amphitheater and costumes and all these actors pretending to pray to God and they're all starving and stuff. They make friends with the Indians, but some of them kill colonists because they don't want anybody coming to take over everything and claiming it's a whole new world. Then Eleanor has a baby everybody is excited about, but her daddy leaves to go get food and the queen of England's way across the ocean deciding there's a war. Then nobody can go back for Eleanor or her baby or anybody else because all the boats are being used to fight. The colony just gets left, hoping the Indians will help them. The end. So long, Eleanor. Say your prayers." Penn pointed to a photo of the actors in Elizabethan dress, lined up onstage, looking courageous.

Mama laughed. "Now who's being dramatic? What else do you

think she'd have done? She wouldn't have lived forever, even if the queen of England had gone back to find her herself. It's just a play, Penn. It's hopeful. People like a heroic ending. Eleanor might have liked that too. You don't like thinking she survived?"

"They don't really know." Penn liked knowing things. She liked having Mama listen to her. And wasn't she telling Eleanor's story her own way, too, when she really thought about it? Still, Penn frowned. "Hammond snuck in and filmed the play in secret on opening night. They caught him and threw him out. People said he wanted revenge or something. I think he just wanted attention. If he cared about Eleanor or the stone, why did he sell it in the first place?"

"Maybe he was desperate. People needed money, Penn. He probably had his own troubles."

She knew it wasn't so different from what they'd come here to do. "Yeah, but it still kind of makes me mad. Like Eleanor doesn't even get a say. It's wrong. Like everybody's looking at her through a window when she doesn't even know. When she never said they could. And then they say whatever they want about her."

"People do that about a lot of things."

"They're still fighting about it, but it's not about what really happened to Eleanor. It's about their stupid play. Everybody just wants to be the one who gets credit for solving a big mystery, but I don't think they care if they're right." Penn hurried along while she had Mama's interest. "I think the first stone—our stone, the one that was here at Evertell—was Eleanor's real, true stone. It even looks different from the other ones. You can tell from the pictures. You'd have to be stupid not to see that. Don't you think so?"

"I think Eleanor's probably laughing at every one of us, wherever she is. Somebody spent all that time scratching out a very clear headstone with a note to her dad on the back and we're still arguing over whether to believe it or not. But as long as we're arguing, we're still talking about her. Nobody forgot her, that's for sure." Then Mama quoted Professor Pearce from the *Saturday Evening Post*'s article, surprising Penn. "And 'if hoax it is, the hoax is more incredible, more fantastic than the story itself!'"

Penn was stunned. "You don't care if any of it's true? You don't want to know?"

Mama only shrugged. "They're stories. Stories matter not because they're true but because they've been told. The thing I'm sure is true is that a lot of *these* stories are being told by men. Me? I like our book here. Women's mysteries and wisdom. I think Eleanor's story is really right here with all these daughters." Mama pointed to the sketches Penn had made. "What did you call these? Virtues?" Penn nodded. "And here," Mama said, pointing to Penn. "Eleanor Dare had a lot more to say than she or anybody else ever wrote on those stones or in their plays or reports, don't you think?"

"I guess so," Penn admitted. "Okay, but what if we go see the stone anyway? Our stone. Back in Gainesville, at Brenau."

If they were leaving Evertell, at least there'd be something to look forward to.

"We could do that sometime." Mama cleared her throat. "Speaking of *Gone with the Wind*, I think we need to do something fun. Let's get out of here. I've had enough stones—let's see some stars. What do you say we take in a picture? The Lucas Theatre has refrigerated air."

"The Lucas? Really?" It was so unexpected Penn decided not to make a fuss about Gainesville.

"Really. This is a surprise from me to you. I got tickets when we were in town, the day you went to see Bridie Quillian."

"That was your errand? Movie tickets?"

"First we'll see about your hair, and then we'll take in a nice, cool show."

Penn narrowed her eyes, suspicious. "What do I have to do?"

"What do you mean, *do*?"

"You never do anything unless it's a good deal. What do you get?"

Mama almost laughed. "I see this as a very good deal for me, actually. And exactly the same one we always had about coming here. You wanted to see Evertell and where I grew up. Savannah is part of where I grew up. And it's not just junk shops and shipyards. There are things I want to see while we're here too. Did you ever think of that? I want to take in a picture and I hope you'll go with me. After that, maybe see a little more."

Penn beamed at her mama, glad to leave thoughts of the conflicting stories of the stones, the fallen chimney, and the hard things she needed to tell Mama about herself behind for now.

They dressed in their best clothes, Penn in a cotton dress that Imegine had made for her last spring and Mama in her only skirt and blouse. Penn's nice shoes felt tight after so many weeks in her boots around the estate. They rode with the windows down and the breeze felt good on the short jaunt, entirely different from having to pedal her bike the whole way. The surprises kept coming when Mama held the door open to a beauty shop on Whitaker Street so Penn could step inside the busy salon, the likes of which they'd never seen in Helen. With four large dryers running along a back wall of gleaming pink tile and five chairs in front of mirrors, all filled with clients, women of varying sizes and ages, the place was warm and powder-scented and abuzz with female conversation. They were greeted almost immediately by a wide-eyed reception-ist who tried very hard not to stare at Penn's chop job. Within minutes, Penn was in one of the chairs and a beautician scowled at the ragged line of her bangs, then glanced disapprovingly in Mama's direction.

"Don't look at me," she said. The beautician laughed.

Penn felt entirely out of place. The lady put her scissors to work to put a polish on the terrible bob and they were all relieved when it turned out better than expected, curling around Penn's face. Mama paid the woman and tipped her well enough that she complimented them. They stepped onto the street, both of them giggling their heads off.

"It's cute," Mama declared. But Penn noticed dark circles under her eyes from the headache, even if Mama was trying hard to be cheerful. "Very French. Very grown-up."

Music played on the radios of the shops they passed, drifting out to the busy sidewalk. They waited for the sign at the crosswalk to change and then rushed to the other side of the street. Penn felt very cosmopolitan and strangely out of time on the busy city street, just blocks away from the quaint charm of the quiet historic squares.

"I love it," Penn said, out of breath, speaking the words lodged in her heart as they rushed to make it to the theater on time.

The refrigerated air inside the Lucas Theatre hit them in the face and they both sighed. Overhead, elaborate light fixtures glowed and the light shone on marbled walls and floors all around. The extravagance was as breathtaking as the temperature. They passed plush velvet chairs and couches where girls paused to powder their noses. In the grand foyer they faced an astonishing staircase that led to the upper level.

"Not box seats, but we'll see everything fine from here," Mama said.

Penn couldn't remember ever being so excited. The lights dimmed and the crowd hushed.

Newsreels played before the film, reports of the goings-on in the war. They'd kept up with the latest on the radio. Now they witnessed American boys handing out cigarettes to Italians, smiling from boats like they were off on an adventure, bombers flying overhead in formation. Penn felt strangely removed from the images, as if they were only another piece of cinema and not the reality that played out in her nightmares of Daddy. She was glad when the reels finished and the screen was filled with bright colors and the thrilling music of the movie swept over them. For just a little while, she wanted to forget the ache in her heart. And soon she was lost in the story of a girl in love, caught up in the song and dance of a technicolor fantasy.

The time flew by. She could barely believe it when the lights came up in the theater. When the crowd applauded, Penn felt almost completely happy, almost completely safe. Almost as she had before the war, when she'd only been a girl full of expectations.

Penn tried to stay in that moment. They walked the same busy streets and quaint squares on the way back to the truck, but Penn's thoughts were wheeling and flying. The colors and sounds having changed to those of evening as if by magic, Savannah was awash in romance. The rush all around only seemed to lift Penn off her feet. They sang or hummed little bits of remembered tunes. Penn could feel her cheeks aching from smiling.

"Aren't you in love with Tom Drake?" Penn asked. "Do you think I'll meet a boy just like that? I wonder if I'll ever go to a World's Fair? Or St. Louis? We could go someday."

"Now you're talking."

Mama's steps slowed as they crossed a different square than Penn remembered before and soon they came to stand in front of a beautiful old building that Penn first thought was a church. Its spires rose high above the street and at the top of the building was an enormous belfry.

"Wow," Penn said. "I wish I could hear that ring."

"That's for sure," Mama said. "It's a synagogue. I wanted to see this."

Mama was quieter then, solemn enough about it that Penn kept quiet too. They stayed for a long moment and Penn marveled at the old building. She understood this must be about Walter Kreischer, the only Jewish person Penn had ever known about who was connected to them in any way. She waited for Mama to explain what they were doing. Instead, she took Penn's hand and they made their way back in silence. Finally, when they reached their truck, they took the streets through town and then a road leading them farther away by a few miles, following a river. "Where are we going?" Penn finally said.

"There's some remembering I think we should do."

She watched as they pulled up to a large cemetery.

"I think this is it," Mama said. A sign read *Bonaventure Cemetery*. "There's a gate we go in and a gate where we leave. You don't walk through the same one. It's Jewish tradition. Come with me."

Penn followed as they passed through a gate with two large stars carved into its pillars and stepped down the shadowy path, moss overhanging from the limbs of oaks. Ornate marble headstones glowed white in the speckled light, and there were sculptures so real they startled her at times. Among these graves were other stone structures, vaults where entire families were buried together. And a pretty brick chapel with large glass windows.

"They sat with him all night there," Mama said, her voice barely above a whisper and still it seemed an interruption. "He was a stranger to them, but it's their custom. Doris told me that."

"Walter Kreischer?" Penn asked.

"Yes. I thought you might want to know what happened to him."

Penn's breath caught. She looked around, feeling a sudden rush of emotion. "They brought him here? It's beautiful."

"They did."

It mattered. Penn couldn't understand why it mattered so much, but she felt relieved. And so sad at the same time.

"Do you want to know?" Mama asked. Penn nodded. "They would have washed his body and stayed with him so he wasn't alone. And in the morning, they buried him with respect, in a pauper's grave."

"What is that?"

"He had no family, no money. So it was just a simple burial. Nothing fancy like you see around here. But they followed his customs. And they didn't leave the grave unmarked. The congregation from the synagogue made sure there was a small headstone."

"How do you know all this?"

"Doris told me some. Sonder told me more. I asked him. I needed to know. Somebody reminded me of something recently, that we don't just own Evertell. We're stewards. That means all the stories here are ours to take care of, not just our own. I wanted to pay my respects to Walter Kreischer. I wanted to know he was taken care of, at least somehow. Remembered, always. And I thought it might be important to you."

Penn could only nod her head.

"Can we see where it is?"

Mama led the way and Penn followed a few steps behind. And then they stood before a grave like so many others, only a small, plain piece of marble to show Walter Kreischer's name and death date. But atop the stone, there were small pebbles, all shapes and colors lined up, at least a dozen. Below, at the base of the stone, the pebbles were piled up, reaching almost to the engraved name. Before Penn could remark, Mama offered her such a pebble.

"You'll like this. It's a Jewish custom to leave a stone, not flowers. Because stones last forever. A long time ago, shepherds took their sheep out and sometimes they had ten or sometimes they had twenty. So to help them remember how many they had with them each day, they carried just that many pebbles in their sling. When you leave a stone like this, even for a person you never knew, you're asking God to add this name to His sling, so they'll count. They'll never be forgotten. And He will watch over this soul, always."

Penn felt hot tears slide down her cheeks. She took the small brown pebble and closed her hand around it. She let it warm there in her palm a long while.

"Look how many people asked God to remember him," Penn finally said. "Do you think—"

"A thousand ways, yes," Mama said, before she could even finish. "God remembers your daddy. He hears us asking and naming your daddy a thousand ways, Penn. And I know He's watching over him."

Mama wiped Penn's face with her fingers and kissed her head. She wiped her own tears before stepping forward and adding her pebble to the ones that already rested atop Walter Kreischer's headstone. Penn did the same. And she thought of the map in the wall at Evertell, a constellation of seashells. She thought of that peach orchard. She thought of the bell. And she didn't have to close her eyes to know the silver light danced inside her.

Chapter Twenty-One

Alice

When Sonder opened the door, Penn grabbed him round the waist in a hug, then flew past him on her way up the stairs.

"What's this?" he asked, baffled.

"I took her to the movies," I explained. This was a different entrance from the first night we'd arrived at Evertell. I thought of the two gates at the cemetery, a tradition we could maybe learn something from.

"Good for you."

"And we stopped to pay our respects to Mr. Kreischer. I told her about the tradition of leaving stones. She appreciated that. Thank you."

Sonder listened, but he was stalwart while I was smiling. He stood with his shoulders hunched, his hands deep in his pockets. I stepped away from him.

"What is it?" I said, barely loud enough for him to hear me. I didn't want to ruin Penn's good evening. But there was more to the fear that leapt inside my chest. Everything seemed precarious, this good place, this balance I was barely managing. It could so easily come crashing down just like that chimney. I didn't feel well. I felt myself sway a little.

"Something's got at the birds," he answered quietly. "They're gone. Every one."

I couldn't help that I exhaled in a rush of relief, or that I smiled. "The peafowl? Oh God, that's fine by me. What was it? A fox?" But even as I said this, I felt a terrible pang of grief at the thought of losing the two stately old birds. Something was definitely wrong. I realized I was shivering in the hot night. The headache had gotten worse as the evening went on, not better. I could feel it behind my eyes.

"Not the peafowl. My birds," Sonder said. "The pigeons."

I stared at him. It seemed to take a long time to make sense of what he was saying. He raised a hand to my forehead, but I brushed it away, annoyed.

"Are you sick?"

"Maybe. But we were having such a good time, and I felt like I finally got something right at the cemetery. It's like whiplash. Tell me what's happened."

He looked less than convinced, but he left me alone. "Seems like the loft was left open."

I understood then that this had been more than a common fox. I followed Sonder outside and toward the barn, where I peered into its dark, silent recesses.

"I don't want Penn to know. Not now. It's too much for one night. Can we wait to tell her? Wait till morning?"

He agreed. "Just an accident anyway."

Something in his tone made my skin prickle. He wasn't saying what he meant. An awful possibility struck me. "You think it was

Penn, the way she took the bricks and made the chimney fall to get her way? You think she did this because she's always talking about letting your birds fly? No. She wouldn't."

"I didn't say that." He shook his head.

"Right. I hope not. And anyway, it could have been you," I said.

Clearly he didn't think so. I could see the strain on his face. My nerves were snapping and twitching when the real trouble dawned on me. "If it's not Penn or you, then it's not an accident, is it? Maybe somebody upset about the POW cards?"

"Alice, that's not what this is," he said. My thoughts were veering off in strange directions, panicked. I'd just stood at the grave of a man who hadn't deserved the judgment that came for him. I'd laid a stone on his grave and asked God to remember him and so help me, I'd been thinking of Finch too. This felt dangerous, like a warning. Someone had come onto our property, right near the house, and shown us how little they valued innocence. I thought of Charlie Hawkes and his hateful, relentless teasing and wondered what kind of man he'd grown to be.

"We don't know what people might do, Sonder, if they think the radio monitoring is a threat. If they think you're a sympathizer. Bridie told me there's talk. People in town are saying things. Did you know there could be U-boats off the coast? Our coast! Right now. Bridie told us they've seen somebody on the river at night who might be running supplies out to Germans. If people think that's you, they'll come here."

"If anybody's worried I'm doing such as that, they won't come to set my birds loose, Alice. I can tell you that. I shouldn't have said anything to you tonight. Look at you. Nothing about this has a thing to do with U-boats or the public opinion of my monitoring. I was only worried Penn's going to be upset."

"Well, sure she'll be upset. Aren't you?"

"To tell you the truth, I was already thinking she was right about letting them loose. Likely a few will find their way back. Things like that shouldn't be kept locked up because a man's lonely. Birds, Alice," he finally said quietly. "That's all this is."

"This time," I said. We stood there a few seconds, Sonder breathing hard and me fighting furious tears. I wanted to lie down. What had seemed like a little dust allergy before now felt like a fever. I wanted to sleep and forget everything. But I was terrified and it had nothing to do with the damn birds or Sonder's self-pity.

"I know what people do to each other, Sonder. I know. When they think nobody will stop them. You are not hearing me. I'm not afraid for the birds; I'm afraid of somebody coming on my property just to cause trouble. I'm afraid of what they could do next time. What if Penn had been in the loft?"

Sonder came to stand close. He took hold of my hand, brought it to his mouth to kiss my palm, then pressed it to his cheek before leading me from the loft.

"Nobody's going to hurt either of you," he said. "Get in the truck a minute. We'll talk."

I balked. I only wanted to go curl up beside Penn in the big bed and sleep until morning. "It's nighttime. I'm not leaving Penn."

"There's nobody out there, Alice."

"How do you know? You don't."

"I know," he said calmly. "I wouldn't leave here if I didn't. Penn's the happiest I've ever seen her. She's not going to worry. No reason to tell her until morning. You just need to get in. We won't be gone more than a few minutes. I promise it'll make you feel better."

All the fight drained out of me. I climbed into the cab and let my head fall back against the seat, exhausted, turning myself over to him.

"Rest," he said. "It's just a short piece."

I was surprised when I jerked awake, the motor of the truck silent and Sonder's hand on my shoulder, gently shaking me. He stood at my door, now open, waiting for me. I stepped out to stand beside him in the dark, feeling bruised. My skin was slick with a cold sweat.

"Where are we?" We'd come to some flat beach, but I couldn't make out much else, only a thick maritime forest to the north and the soothing sound of the surf in the dark. He took my hand and I let him lead me, silently. Closer to the shore I thought of Penn with a stab of panic that I'd left her alone, even for a short time. "I need to get back," I said.

Sonder shushed me. And then I heard a low roar, a mechanical roar, something I couldn't identify. I moved closer to him. The sound grew louder, such a strange thing in the quiet blackout of a coastal wartime night that I had the urge to run back to the truck to hide, but almost as soon as I had that thought it was followed by recognition. I saw the source of the sound, confirming my hunch.

"The blimps." My words were drowned out as the great airships passed over the waters. Their massive shapes seemed impossible and strange and wondrous too. Sonder squeezed my hand.

I knew about them, of course. Everyone did. But I'd never seen one before. They hung like giants over the horizon, a squadron of four silver orbs, otherworldly and enormous. I held my breath as they passed. They were patrolling the coast for U-boats. I felt the most overwhelming sense of awe and gratitude and, for the first time in months, a sense of safety, as though these monstrous ships were some benevolent group of celestial beings sent to watch over us all.

"They're here. They've come." I wasn't even sure what I was saying.

Sonder paid no attention, or didn't hear me. He had to raise his voice to be heard as he explained.

"Thousands of ships were lost in '41," he said, "when the Germans ran down the East Coast of the US with their U-boats. Every year since, it's been a little less than that. We started patrolling with the blimps out of Glynco up in Brunswick. If you're on the beach, you'll see them during the day, too, when they make their runs. They escort our ships, patrol the waters. Do you know how many ships were lost to U-boat attacks this year off the entire East Coast?"

"No."

"Guess."

I shook my head. My ears were buzzing. No, maybe it was a strong wind, a beating that might be my own heart. I turned my face up to the breeze.

"Three. Only three, Alice."

I heard Sonder's words, but he seemed far from me. I felt that if I closed my eyes, I might rise off my feet.

We watched until the blimps were out of sight and the sound of their engines became a quiet hum, and then there was only the sound of the surf again as we stood there.

"There are no secret U-boats in our waters, Alice. Just old Bill hauling groceries out to Doris now and again. No mobs with pitchforks and fire in our woods. You and Penn, you're safe. You're safe with me."

Sonder took my hand and moved close, his warm breath on my face. He wasn't afraid.

"I'm an idiot," I whispered. "And the truth is, I think my battery's gone flat."

"What? Alice?" he said, confused. I heard my name as if it came from far away.

Ghosts blew through the night air. Perhaps they'd followed me from Bonaventure Cemetery. I was frayed and so tender on the inside. I was hovering just as the blimps did, losing my grip.

"Alice, you're burning up," he said.

I drifted, carried along on words, sentences that made pictures and finally a whole world around me until I landed on my feet in a garden. Eleanor's garden. And it was mine.

Chapter Twenty-Two

I'd wandered into a beautiful garden. I'd slept in a very deep wood. When I woke, I didn't know what day or time it was. Doris was there. She held a cup to my lips. I drank the bitter liquid and slept, my head full of anxious questions. *Who put me to bed? Where is Penn? Is she okay after the night we had? Does she know about the poor pigeons?*

The next time I woke, Penn was at my bedside, book in hand. She was reading aloud. Hearing me move, she looked up from the commonplace book and I came back to myself.

"You had a high fever. I've been reading to you," she said. "Did you hear me?"

It was her voice I'd been hearing in my fever dream.

"You've been talking in your sleep. You said your mama was right, you saw them. Did you see something?"

I swallowed, but my mouth was too dry. "Blimps," I croaked. "Are you okay?"

Penn shut the book. "Mama, why do you always do that? I'm

not the one who's been in the bed for two days. Let me take care of you for once. Did you dream anything?"

"Two days? You're lying."

"Ask Doris if you don't believe me. She's been here looking after you too. And Sonder came, but you were asleep."

I was groggy and having a hard time following. "I told him you didn't let the birds out."

"He knows I wouldn't do that," she said as if I were being silly. She thought I was talking out of my head and I was grateful.

There were meals of broth spooned into my mouth by Doris, who cooed over me and put her cool hand to my forehead often. Penn brushed my hair and my teeth and insisted on rubbing the sweet balm on my hands and feet. "What's in this stuff?" I asked, grouchy.

"Comfrey," Penn said. "It's good for tender spots. Doris told me."

I felt like I was being mummified.

But by morning I was in no pain and the chills had passed. I got up, feeling frail and unsteady on my feet. I pulled the heavy velvet curtains away from the window so that light flooded the room, clear and warm. The corn was tall in the field, brown tassels waving. Only a few days and we'd have the harvest. It began to come back to me how badly I had overreacted to the news of Sonder's birds.

Before breakfast I went outdoors. Slowly, I stepped around the front yard beneath the oaks. Doris found me back on the porch in a metal glider rocker.

"There she is," she said. She looked like an entirely different woman from the one I'd met that first day at Hawkes's store, now in a navy dress with nice buttons down the front and less gaunt. I thought the improvement was a result of Penn's friendship and I was grateful for our lonely tenant. The benefits went both ways. "The early bird," she said in greeting. "Feeling better?"

"Some. I think by this evening I'll be back to myself. I'm sorry for putting you out. It was good of you to take care of me like this. I don't know how I'll pay you back."

Doris made a sound with her lips to dismiss the offer. "I'm already making a list," she joked.

I reached for her hand. "You've been good to us, Doris. A good neighbor."

"Speaking of neighbors, I believe you ought to come help me and Penn haul some vegetables over to the farm stand tomorrow. It'll get you some sunshine."

"I don't know," I said. "That may be a step too far for me."

"Give you somebody to talk to other than yourself. Something I have some experience with, honey. You were having some big conversations in your sleep." She gave my hand a squeeze and let go. "I guess I'd better confess. My invitation's not really all about the help at the market. I want to give Sonder a little privacy."

"Why? What for?"

"Sonder told me that you're scared after those birds got out, that you think people might have the wrong idea about those POW messages."

"Well, you told me that the first day I was here. And Bill Hawkes sure didn't like the idea," I said.

She shook her head. "It's not got to do with Bill. Not in the way you're thinking," she said. "It's me and Bill, both. When people first got wind about this radio monitoring business, there was a dustup. The government's telling people to close their ears and pocketbooks to those broadcasts, telling us they're phony and how people are being shilled just trying to get any little word about their missing boys. Sonder had to defend himself, but people had already decided to be suspicious. People who didn't have hope of any word because their own boys were dead. People who're just scared of their own shadows right now.

"So Bill and I agreed to keep an eye on things, real regular, and let everybody know we were monitoring the monitoring, so to speak. We looked over the messages going out and what was coming back this way. Sonder had no quarrel with this. It kept everybody off his back. Anybody who had questions or concerns, Bill and me handled that. But the more I read the letters coming back to Sonder, what the families had to say, seeing how much it means to them what he's doing. Well . . . it didn't seem like enough to go making excuses to people who doubt there's any value to it or, worse, feel like all he's doing is helping the enemy spread propaganda or false hope. Hope is hope. There's nothing false about it. And Bill and I felt like Sonder ought to get some recognition."

I relaxed somewhat. "All right, how's that?"

"There's a man with *Popular Mechanics* magazine coming out here tomorrow to talk to Sonder. Bill got the idea and I made the call from the store. They want an interview and a couple of photographs. It's about that particular ham radio he uses too. Something of an advertisement, I guess. But it'll get the job done, get the story straight about what he's done."

I gave her a doubtful look. "I can hardly believe Sonder's going to give any kind of interview, much less agree to advertise a radio. He doesn't even read the return mail."

"He loves that radio. You could talk him into it, Mama," Penn said, running around from the front porch where she'd been listening. She took up beside Doris.

Sonder was not going to appreciate a bunch of women co-ordinating anything that would cast him as some sort of hero over what he clearly felt was his duty. "No. This is Sonder's decision.

You shouldn't ambush him. His monitoring is personal to him. He wouldn't want the attention. He'll resent this, Doris."

Doris said, "No. I've already talked to him. He understands."

"Understands what?"

"That this is bigger than him now. This article is about honoring the people all over this earth who have done what he's doing, even with so many doubts, taking that risk, facing the criticism of their neighbors and their government, but believing what they're doing is too important to give up. And the people around here could stand to think about that. He's spent every night going on nearly three years sitting up in the sky, listening to a mess of lies, and he knows it. Making sure he doesn't miss a single American name, any word that might be the truth about one of those boys. That's how he's fought this war. And somehow the man hasn't lost his faith in this world."

Doris's vehemence surprised me. I knew she had defended Sonder's monitoring, but even I was moved to hear it described this way. No wonder Sonder had agreed to the interview.

"And I realize, too, this has to do with how he feels about my Jacob. He wasn't there for one boy, and it's in his mind that he's got to make up for that in some way. For Jacob and Walter Kreischer and maybe even you, Alice. It's a lot he's been carrying around and time he laid it down and had some peace, same as the rest of us. Don't you think?"

I glanced at Penn. I understood what Doris meant about Jacob and Mr. Kreischer, but I couldn't make sense of what Sonder had to feel guilty about when it came to me. He'd carried me home that day in the forest. He'd stayed here and cared for Evertell all these years. In any case, I couldn't argue with the importance of the interview anymore.

"Fine. I'll come to the farm stand."

"Now that's settled," Doris said, "I'm tired and going home, if Miss Penn will take me over the water. And I'll see you tomorrow."

I'd only made a few scant trips to that store and every time I'd held my breath, afraid it would be the time I would run across Charlie Hawkes. Even after all this time, I still didn't know how I would face him.

"I can't promise to be nice," I said. "Especially after what's happened with the birds. Who would do it, do you think, Doris?"

"Sonder says it was an accident. I believe I'll take his word for it. Seems most likely to me. Anyway, don't you think it'd be an awful silly thing for a grown man to do if he's taken issue? Whether Sonder took the wrong girl for a fish dinner or somebody's seriously questioning his patriotism, either one, they'd have shown up with a shotgun or fists, but this? Not likely."

Doris's logic made sense and with a clearer head, I began to see it her way.

"I'm bringing herbs," Penn said. She'd been looking forward to the farm stand, and I could see she was glad I would be coming along.

"I promised some of the women," Doris explained. "They'll be proud to meet the little lady who's keeping that garden these days." She turned to Penn and spoke as a conspirator. "I'll expect you over on my side this evening to load everything and haul it over here, but I want a nap first. Sonder usually helps, but I've told him it will be just us ladies this weekend. We'll get it all on the truck tonight. Tomorrow morning we can make it over to the market and get our stand set up by 7:00 a.m. so we're ready when folks start to show up. The car traffic on the highway picks up around nine and won't let up till we're done with business around four in the evening."

With the details settled, Doris swiveled her rheumy, blue-eyed gaze back to me. "It's a long day, honey. But it will do you good. Likely you'll see some faces you remember. Wear something comfortable."

X

Gerry Lynn Burgess was the last person I expected to be handing me a sweaty dollar bill for a bundle of sage at the farm stand, but I would've recognized her snub nose anywhere, even with thirty or forty extra pounds on her frame since I'd seen her. Her hair had gone white in streaks at her temples, the rest a tired rust color, yanked back hard in a knot at the nape of her neck. It made her look old. She wasn't old, not in years. She was about the age Mama would have been now. It made me wonder what Mama would have looked like today. The thought surprised me. I'd never let myself imagine such a thing.

I perched on a three-legged stool behind a long wooden table under a shed where five other farmers had their own displays of vegetables and assorted jellies and jams and mason jars of canned soups and sundries. Doris was taking a break, having a slice of watermelon across an open field beneath a stand of trees with Penn and several others I didn't recognize. Bugs buzzed in the grass and the heat pressed down on all of us, but I liked the earthy smell of exposed roots and crushed greens.

"I never figured I'd see you here with us again," Gerry Lynn said. She sounded like she smoked two packs a day. Life hadn't been easy on Gerry Lynn, I guessed, but how would I know? "Who'd have thought we'd turn out so good looking?" she said. I smiled, but I knew my lips looked thin because it was hard to make them stretch up at the corners.

"Did you want anything else? Just the sage?" I asked.

"Well, I'd take a little of everything you've got, if I could afford it. What the rations leave us with makes everything taste the same, don't it? I wish I'd learned to keep the herbs the way your granny did. Doris said your girl's about got that garden shaped up again. Every woman out this way will be trying to sneak over that wall like a bunch of raccoons to snatch a handful of this or that to throw in her dinner pots."

"Well, you're welcome to it," I said halfheartedly.

She leaned down so her full bosom threatened to spill over the top of her housedress. "I heard you already had prowlers a couple of nights ago. Word travels fast here, I know you remember. I'm sorry that's the welcome home you get, Alice Merely. But that's how it always is with boys, isn't it? Excuse me, it's Young now?"

"Thank you, yes," I said, uncomfortable with her sympathy. "What do you mean, *boys*?"

"He's got a sore ankle, is all, Nelson does. Twisted it when he was hightailing it out of there. A good lesson, if you ask me. Of course, you know a fourteen-year-old won't slow down long enough to feel such as that." She chortled. "But Julie's got him by the ear, going to drag him over here to apologize to you today."

"Julie?" I couldn't help scanning the crowd, even though I didn't know anyone named Julie, or Nelson, for that matter. I didn't know what to look for, except a pissed-off mama and a kid with his tail between his legs. Gerry Lynn interrupted my thoughts.

"Julie Hawkes. You know her. Charlie got killed in France about a year ago."

Charlie. I felt the blood drain from my head. "Charlie Hawkes? Bill's son, Charlie?"

Gerry Lynn nodded. "Oh, that's right. You'd remember him, wouldn't you? I didn't think of that. You poor little thing."

I was stunned. Of course I remembered. Everyone near Evertell should know why: that day of the last homecoming they'd witnessed my return from the forest to stand before my confused mother, and I'd accused Charlie of stealing the stone. The rest of my life had turned on that one miserable moment. For this woman to suggest that she'd forgotten such a scene, or would pity me for it, was unimaginable.

"Yes, another crying shame, losing Charlie," she was saying. "There's not going to be a man left to us before this is over. That boy of theirs has been wild ever since and it's all Julie can do to keep from losing her mind with him going on about fighting as soon as he's old enough. She had Sonder come try to talk sense to him, seeing as how Sonder can't fight." She said this last part in a loud whisper and I felt my stomach curdle, knowing how it must have humiliated Sonder. A wave of tenderness and also an impulse to defend him rose in me, but Gerry Lynn went on.

"Nelson, that's the boy. Poor Sonder took him out to see the blimps and what all, showed him those little birds of his. But now you see where that got him. Nelson's twisted up inside. He'd fight anything that draws breath so long as he thinks it'll make that ache for his daddy stop, don't you know? Julie worries he's going to run off, and then what will she have left? A dead man, a dead boy. Why don't they ever think of us, back here?"

Charlie Hawkes was dead. In the weeks since we'd been back, I'd avoided the store and hadn't asked about him, embarrassed for anyone to know how much I still feared facing him after the way things had been left. I'd been so focused on what I imagined that would be like, I'd assumed he was living a life much like his father's, going gray, letting out his belt, cutting his fields like the other farmers. I felt a wash of shame for never considering the obvious reason I hadn't run into him at the store. From there, it didn't take a genius to jump to the conclusion that this was why Sonder had no cause to go raging into town after the man who'd let his pigeons go. It hadn't been a man. It had been a grieving boy. Another child of war.

"You lost your husband, I heard."

The words jerked me back to attention. "Yes. Two years ago."

"Sorry to hear it. Just sorry, sorry, sorry." She shook her head and the genuine expression of sympathy made my throat close up. "Listen, I would love to see that garden of yours if you ever have a mind to open it for a few ladies, maybe an afternoon?"

"I hadn't thought of it."

"Nothing official with the garden club, mind you. Maybe we could just have a glass of tea and a little stroll, take our minds off things? I can tell you what I remember about your granny, and your mama too. Claire was just the sweetest thing. Liked to have killed me, what happened to y'all. We were like sisters growing up. Honey, I thought Claire hung the damn moon. I guess just about all of us did."

"That's so nice of you to say." This was not how I'd believed my mama would be remembered here. I listened, stunned.

"She was something else, that one. She made everything ordinary about our lives seem like it was shining from the inside out. People nowadays would have called her a philanthropist, but I don't know if many people knew what she did with her money. Your daddy would've known, of course."

"You mean the orphanage she funded?"

"Well, she was always supporting this or that, wasn't she? She was good like that. But your mama did more than throw money at them. She worked hard to help those babies, I know that. Doris could tell you stories."

The image in the photograph from the attic filled my mind, the stately building, the women standing out front, each with a baby in her arms or a couple of stark-faced children round her legs, my mama among them.

"You know your mama told me once that my hair was the color of a little red fox," Gerry Lynn said, pulling me back to the moment. "It was a little thing, but I always kind of liked to think of that. Can you imagine?"

I must have looked as though I was as charmed by the thought as Gerry Lynn, because she crinkled her eyes at me and patted my hand. "Don't be a stranger," she said, then took a deep sniff of the sage as she walked away.

I stared after her as others milled around and picked up this or that bundle. The rest of the afternoon passed uneventfully, but while Doris and I packed things in for the evening, I found myself wanting to ask more about the orphanage, each little piece of information like seeing my mama anew.

I saw Penn had made a friend. They were sitting on the back of a flatbed truck, a girl and a boy trying not to smile at one another. Penn had a daisy chain in her hair. Such an ordinary moment full of grace and innocence that it almost seemed impossible after the last few years. I didn't see any sign of Julie Hawkes, but I saw the stick-straight sandy blond hair hanging in her son's eyes, the freckles across his nose. I recognized the boy, so like his father.

⋊

"Can I go? You have to say yes. Nelson wants to take me, special," Penn pleaded.

"When I said we'd go to the ocean, I meant me and you. It will be the first time you see it. I wanted to be with you." She looked disconsolate. I had no real reason to say no. "Nelson, huh?" Even his name set my teeth on edge.

"Nelson Hawkes. And other kids too. It won't be just us, so you don't have to be like that."

Penn was invited to join the Hawkes boy and some other local kids for an afternoon at the beach on Tybee Island.

"Fine," I said, my throat a little raw with emotion, watching the smile bloom on her face, watching her grow up. "How old is he?"

"Fourteen. Almost the same as me."

"You make him keep an eye on you. You've never been swimming in the ocean."

Penn didn't even roll her eyes. She'd have agreed to just about anything to go.

"I know why you don't like him. You think he's like his father. I know what he did to the birds," she said boldly. She was going to defend him. "He told me. But he never meant to hurt them, just to set them loose so Sonder would be aggravated. He's angry because his daddy died and he felt like Sonder was trying to take his place." I could see the flame of empathy in her eyes. "Nelson thought the pigeons would just fly home. He's been watching for them, hoping they'll return."

"That's what he said?" I felt a twinge of sympathy for the kid. "Some of them have come back. Sonder expects a few more may show up, given a little time."

Penn nodded. "Nelson's sorry about it. He's so sorry. That's why he's taking me to the beach, because when I said I'd never been he thought that was how he'd make it up to me. But I didn't say it was okay. It wasn't. It isn't."

"No. That's just a bribe," I said, but I had to admit it was a pretty good one. And if anybody needed to be making reparations around here, it was me, not Nelson. Nevertheless, I couldn't help adding, "He shouldn't have been at Evertell to begin with."

"But you can understand. Everybody does." Penn shook her head. "I know you don't think so, but Nelson is nice. Mr. Hawkes at the store too," she said.

We stopped at the landing on the stairs. I could see where this was going.

"He has to give me the piece of the bell clapper or I can't fix the bell."

"I know and I'll go ask. I'll tell him whatever he wants to hear. But I can't promise he's going to give it to me, Penn. He's lost his son and maybe I can't make what's between us right."

"I know." Penn sighed. "I already told Sonder we might not get both parts. But we have the arm—that's the most important part. If we have to, we can make a replacement for the piece that's missing. The torch is hot enough. We'll just melt some things together in a lump good enough to get the job done. It doesn't have to be perfect, just solid. And maybe later, I was thinking, I could do a money drive to get the real part. People would help, I think."

I was impressed. "*Some things*, you say? Sonder's going to let you melt down his tractor?" I teased.

"No." Penn took a breath. "I can use some of Daddy's tools that I brought from Helen."

I felt my heart swell. I wasn't going to stop her. The tools were hers to use and they were meant to make repairs. It seemed to me that Finch would have been pleased. "Your daddy would be proud of you. I'm proud of you." I'd been waiting to say those words, knowing how important they were. We stared hard at one another. Tears collected in her eyes, but she blinked them back. She sniffed and looked away. I reached for her hand, but it didn't feel like enough. I'd never felt like enough and now look what it was costing her. I took a deep breath and said, as steadily as I could, "I'll make Mr. Hawkes understand. I don't know how, but Dare girls always find the way, right?"

⋊

We weren't poisoned; we were drunk. Or something like it.

I always believed my mama was leading me. In truth, she was wandering. I saw that in the forest. And I was born to be her constant so that when she ventured far, she might find her way back again. But when the tea was finished and I could feel the sunlight sliding low and the withering heat was hanging in the air like a wet dishcloth, smothering us, I knew I was failing her. It must have been close to dinnertime and my daddy would start to call for us. He'd be angry we'd been gone so long. I was out of time.

My eyes stung and my throat felt raw from the bitter tea. I reached a hand out and, as if in ecstasy, said, "Mama, wait. I can see something. It's exactly as you said."

I'd lied to her before. This was not the first time I'd playacted my way out of one of her delusions. But when she caught her breath and listened hard, when her vacant eyes lit up as she accepted the fantasy for reality, something was different. She'd forgotten her search for the stone. She saw me.

"I knew it! I knew you would have the heart for it, Alice!" my mama declared. She let go of me to use both hands and began to lay out a blood-red silk cloth from her bag, lining it with a collection of small objects along the border. Stones, seashells, bones. "Take off your shoes. You must take off your shoes."

I was eager. I slung my shoes in different directions. "Will you tell me the secret now? Tell me the end of the tale?"

I went along with the ideas she had then, just the two of us in the whole world. She loved me. It was the most intimate moment of my life. If I believed generations of mothers were swimming in a silver circle around my soul, it seemed right that we'd come to this place to offer ourselves like goddesses. The truth was, it thrilled me, the feeling of the breeze on my skin and the way we stood together on the red silk scarf, the soaring trees above us. Maybe the tea had done something to me. I was waiting for my vision. I was believing hard enough for the two of us.

I lay down while she massaged sweet-scented balm over my hands and feet and combed my hair with her fingers. She fed me dried apples and honey, or maybe I dreamed that. My mind wandered to stories from the Bible. I know she lit a candle and we stared into the dancing flame.

I tried to see through the trees, see the sky turn from azure to a velvet purple, to see something in the first dim stars. "Tell me what you see," Mama said.

My gaze was always drawn back to her. I wanted to be sure she was there. And so I told her the only thing I knew to keep her from disappearing from my life. "It's beautiful. It's everything. I see what you want, Mama. A silver light, dancing. It's all around us, isn't it?"

She laughed and we stretched ourselves out on the silk scarf. Later, she named the stars for me as they began to glimmer in the indigo sky. But she never told me the end of Eleanor's Tale.

I couldn't bring myself to remind her of the stone again. I knew Mama had broken from reality and it was dangerous to follow her. But there was something so fine about being chosen, that she would weave her fingers through mine and tug me along to this secret place. I coveted her madness, the bottomless wonder to which she'd abandoned me.

"It's late," I said after some time had passed. I couldn't say how long. No vision had come, but Mama believed that it had. The stone was gone. I'd protected us. I thought it was enough. It was everything I had.

I didn't want to go back. I wanted to stay with her. She was brilliant and beautiful. In those last strains of her sanity, I could feel her singing of the Evertell heirs, her song slipping past me, over

*me, around me. I wondered absently what was in the bitter tea. I
closed my eyes, drowsy and untroubled, and sank into the silk. I
imagined that I'd become the red scarf, spreading and spreading
until I'd covered the path all the way back to Evertell so that it
glowed, leading us back where they would see us and ring the bell
and say, "See, that's the only truth that matters. You can't deny
that kind of love."*

Ж

I missed my mother. The ache never dulled. Going back to the
memory of the night in the forest only made me raw and desperate.
Returning there again and again would never change anything for
us. There was no balm there. And that night as I read the next
pages of Eleanor's Tale through tears, I remembered the story well
and I didn't expect it to have changed. I knew Eleanor would leave
that stone. She didn't stay in that forest. I was trying to sort out
this single question that had crystalized in my mind, the one truth
I needed to understand. If Eleanor Dare had carved her heart into
that sad old rock, how had she ever walked away?

Spanish Colonial Trading Trail
Autumn 1591

For a week or maybe less, until Eleanor could walk a distance again, Griffin and the other men took turns setting snares and fishing. A fire smoldered all day and all night, and Eleanor ate everything they brought to her. She'd feared her milk might not come in and the baby would starve, but the surgeon gave her an herb that tasted of licorice and in those cold, quiet days, Eleanor, wrapped in her mother's cloak, nursed her little girl and gazed into her soft gray eyes. The darkness she had known so completely now hovered at her edges, and when Eleanor slept, she dreamed of that small silver light.

She came to realize that the doctor, Gabriel, was a Frenchman by his accent. Gabriel had saved her life and that of her child. She could not dismiss the irony of his namesake. Whether her faith had truly been restored was in question, but it was hard to ignore he seemed sent by some divine hand. From then on, she could think of nothing but survival. And because of this, she was careful to keep her name secret, allowing the doctor's mistake to stand while claiming Griffin Jones as her brother for fear they would know her as the British governor John White's daughter and make a prize of her and her child. Virginia Jones, however, was a name for any woman, anywhere. She gave her daughter the name Agnes, Tomasyn Cooper's middle name, not her father's light of hope or a tribute to any queen, but a name for a girl who would find her own purpose.

The older man, a Portuguese spice trader, was traveling from a Spanish colony, the port city of St. Augustine, far to the south. Gabriel had come with him, in his service, with some expertise in healing herbs, it seemed. Eleanor and her baby and Griffin Jones would be a feather in the trader's cap. He had added new captives to his company and declared they would return with him to the coast. In the month to follow, Griffin took up alongside the old man, sharing his dreams of sailing, hoping their captor would hear his plea. Eleanor couldn't blame him when she heard him trying to learn the language from the spice trader, but she suspected the old man meant to sell them as soon as he could. If Griffin could make a better way for himself, she wouldn't stop him. He was not her brother, after all. Or her son. Eleanor found she wanted him to find his way, as she wanted it for herself and Agnes. He'd saved her life in the deepest part of the wood and she would not forget it. He'd carried the iron box, and he'd carried Eleanor too.

When Eleanor had finally recovered well enough to ride, they began the journey south, a way the Portuguese knew well. Captive or not, it was a relief to have a certain destination. The Frenchman was ordered to lead her on horseback and made his journey on foot. One day Gabriel pulled something from his pack that looked to Eleanor like a curled bone, larger than her hand. He gestured for her to hold the opening in the hollow bone to her ear, which, by then, she could plainly see was not a bone at all. When she did, she could hear the emptiness inside. It sounded like a sigh. He smiled and told her it was a conch shell, a gift from the sea, and she thought he was like the shell, a mystery she might understand if she were patient and quiet.

He sang while they walked and it caused Eleanor's heart to burn. She was surprised to hear it, the beauty of his fine, deep voice. Sometimes he caught her watching him and he laughed. The lilting tune transformed him so that in her imagination, he took many forms. She began to dream of him, and in her dreams, he revealed a pair of wings. She woke listening for his voice, anticipating his songs. The melodies took her thoughts soaring—high above the forest, looking down, looking beyond to great seas and mountains. It seemed to Eleanor that they were both out of place.

Sometimes his song seemed full of joy, skipping along and driving their steps forward. At other times, often in the evening after their meal and before they went to sleep, the song became soft and mournful. He missed his home, she guessed. The herbs he gathered to use for medicine gave off a dizzying sweetness that reminded her of home, so she was never certain if it was their aroma or the man's kindness that drew her closer. He opened the small cloth bags so she could see the round nutmegs; the hard, dark cloves; and the sticks of cinnamon, teaching her both the French and Spanish names for each. He draped a purple silk scarf around her shoulders, and it was so smooth and light she asked if it was enchanted. She began to wonder about all the places he'd been and wanted to see them for herself. If ever she'd met a magician, it was this man.

)(

In the pale days of early winter, they felt the urgency to move faster toward the safety of the Spanish settlement. As they approached the

THE LOST BOOK OF ELEANOR DARE

coast, the bone-chilling cold of the forest became mild and humid as the woods changed from broad hardwoods to tall, thin pines and the soil that had been red clay turned to a sandy loam. Agnes was a little more than two months old and getting heavier in her sling. Eleanor walked at the doctor's side, shared his food, and one day noticed that he, rather than Griffin Jones, carried the iron box.

She'd supposed what she felt for Gabriel Lavat was gratitude for his company or his aid, for they worked together along the way. But soon she began to realize it was more than she'd felt even for her husband. When they stopped at night and she nursed the baby, Gabriel sat with her and told stories of the port with Spanish ships, soldiers and sailors, and a sparkling sea. He described the busy market with fishermen at work, who lived in small cottages where their wives tended gardens and flower beds and their children played in the yards. There were dangers—pirates and disease, but the life he knew there was not the terrible starving wilderness she had known. St. Augustine, he said, was a true and civilized town, with a blacksmith and a chandlery, and it awaited her and her child. Her heart lifted at the thought. Gabriel assured her that she would find work and make a life, as he had done. He'd been taken two years earlier, when the Spanish sacked the French ship he was aboard, Gabriel explained, and the Spanish governor had valued his skill as a surgeon and, lately, as a friend. Pressed into service, he lived and moved within the settlement at the governor's pleasure, working as their physician. He'd been sent on this journey to forage and to aid in the spice trade that would help him build stores for his own apothecary.

At once, Eleanor saw her opportunity, a way to make a life for herself and Agnes. She had a skill. She asked him to open the iron box and told him of her part in engraving the beautiful copper plate. She asked if St. Augustine had a printshop where she might make a wage. She saw the delight in his eyes, even as he put the plate away, out of the greedy sight of the Portuguese, who snored like a dog and paid them no mind. Eleanor knew the worth of the copper. She told him it had been her dowry. Now it was their secret. And again, in a way she never could have foreseen, it was her future.

She closed her eyes at night and tried to prepare herself for the city Gabriel described and to find courage in the memory of the sign that had come to her as Agnes was born. But Eleanor had lost everything she'd loved twice now, and she grew anxious about the Portuguese trader's plans for her, for Agnes, for the copper plate. She began to search the wisdom of the commonplace book again, looking to the cures and charms of the fishwives. The answer to her troubles came in the form of a tincture not unlike the one she'd brewed for her father. She offered the old Portuguese man a drink with her thanks for returning her family to civilization. He drank the warm tea in a single gulp and slept so deeply nothing could wake him. All the while, Gabriel Lavat looked on.

"I won't kill him," she said, looking to the old trader who farted in his sleep, startling the horse. "Only, he needs to believe that he's dying, so you can save him."

"Why would I do that?"

"Because it will earn you favor and influence."

"I have those things already."

Eleanor revealed her plan. "But then you can say I am your wife, and this child is yours. And I will help you with your work."

He shocked her by declaring he would marry her for love. He sat beside her under a rowan tree where Eleanor spread the pages of the commonplace book open in his lap.

"I have been a keeper of secrets," she said.

"Is there anything you have not been?" the doctor asked. She was surprised to hear the teasing in his question at such a moment.

"I'm not who you think."

"I knew who you were, Eleanor Dare, the moment you called for your lost daughter, Virginia."

It seemed a remarkable and unlikely thing to have come upon a stranger who could know anything of her in this wide wilderness. But he did know her, it seemed, and instead of being frightened, she felt safe for the first time since her father had sailed away.

"And then, who are you?" she asked, remembering the call of the owls.

When he asked if she wanted the truth, Eleanor was relieved to learn he was exactly what she believed: a Frenchman and a fine surgeon, yes. But he surprised her when he asked if she'd like to hear his story and challenged her to believe it. She could think of nothing she'd ever wanted more. She listened as he explained he was no accidental captive, but a French Protestant who'd escaped the Inquisition. The tale was long and winding, like the river they had followed, full of loss and adventure and impossibilities to rival her own. But the conclusion satisfied her heart, for she came from a long line of women who appreciated mystery. The newly named Mrs. Lavat was thrilled to learn her sly new husband, Gabriel Lavat, was a spy for the English crown.

Chapter Twenty-Three

Alice

Penn promised to bring home seashell treasures when I dropped her off to meet the other kids outside Hawkes's store. They were piling into the bus headed for Tybee, and Penn threw a giddy wave in my direction before she disappeared in a pair of my old shorts pulled over her swimsuit. It was a dream for her, a thirteen-year-old girl who had spent all her time with adults—a mother who hid in her broken-down house, a farmer who could find anything but hid in his corn, an old lady tending graves. I stepped inside to drop the mailbag and Bill leaned on the counter.

"How do?" he said.

"I do fine. You?"

I tried to remember what Doris had told me about the night Jacob died, how Bill had stayed on her porch, how he'd testified against friends and neighbors. For the first time since we'd come back, I took a closer look at the man, the store—quiet, dusty, no farmers leaning on the counter or standing on the porch for a long chat. There'd been consequences for hard choices. I noticed a framed photograph of a young soldier hanging behind the register and knew it must be Charlie. Bill saw me looking at it.

"I'm sorry for your loss," I said. "I just heard."

He ignored my condolences. "Got to apologize for my grandson. Want to assure you I've had a talk with him. You won't have no more trouble."

"Thank you," I said curtly. But I hoped he hadn't been rough on the kid. "My own daughter lost her father. I know what it's like." I could hardly believe I was saying the words, but I felt genuine sympathy when I saw grief pass over Bill Hawkes's face.

I looked at the chunk of iron on his countertop. I picked up a small pocket knife from a display, flipped it open, and scratched my own name into the metal while Bill watched. He didn't stop me. Or congratulate me.

"I want you to know," I said, "I told Charlie that stone was cursed. We were stupid kids and I told him that stone was what was wrong with my mama. I asked him to haul the damn thing off. He knew I was scared. He was trying to be my friend. The truth is, he was a lot braver than me."

Bill's mouth tightened. "Sounds like my boy."

Indeed. Perhaps I should have told him everything about how things had truly gone between myself and Charlie, how I'd laid down that mean dare and Charlie had only wanted to humiliate me, but I already carried the blame for the disappearance of the stone and rightfully so. And Charlie was dead in a war, not by some imagined curse. Any confession of a little girl's regret would have been silly and disrespectful of Bill's grief. Instead, I thanked him.

"It was good of you, letting Penn take the news clippings. You didn't have to do that."

"She's been in here quite a bit, that girl of yours." Bill cleared his throat. I might have thanked him for what he'd done for Sonder, too, but then he said, "There's another thing I ought to speak to you about."

"What's that?"

"Interest in your place. Seems serious."

This stopped me cold.

"My daughter-in-law, Julie, as it happens," Bill went on. "That land butts up against Charlie's acreage and it'd be good for Nelson."

I stared at him for longer than I should have without responding, but it took a moment to process what he was saying. "Charlie's wife wants Evertell?"

"That's what I said. Doris already told me you've planned to keep hold of Bell Isle and set aside the mill for Sonder, which is real fair of you. We're clear on that. Everybody knows the house is hardly fit for ghosts, but I don't guess she's looking to live there anyway. Julie figures you might like knowing that when you leave, at least the property wouldn't be broken up."

"Yes," I said. But I was shaking. "That's probably true. I just don't know that I'm interested."

"I ain't told you what she'll offer," he protested, taking a tone with me that made me move toward the door. "She'll give you a fair price. She's got some money from her own family and Charlie's pension, plus what I'm willing to put toward it. Best you're going to get."

"You know why I'm here, what it's going to take, Bill. If you even want to discuss Evertell with me, we start with what my daughter wants from you."

He reached atop the counter and picked up the heavy piece of iron. His expression was strained, matching mine. "I accept your apology. And in good faith," he said, offering the Hawkes stone to me.

But I did not take it. I looked at him a moment. "All right, deal. I'm not agreeing to anything, but we can talk. So long as you keep up your end. You take it to Penn yourself. Go see her bell. She'd like that."

X

I drove too fast back to the house with another of the heavy mail-bags full of return messages in the passenger seat, then headed to the garden to yank weeds. I threw out corn by the fistful until it was gone. For once, seeing the peafowl scratching in the yard was a comfort. They gobbled the corn and didn't harass me. And before the sun began to slant long shadows across the lawn, I found my way to the barn and the rest of the huge lumps of mailbags that sat in a dark corner, unopened. I struggled with the knot of one and finally pulled it free, spilling the postcards over the dusty ground, then sat down cross-legged to read. In the dim light that filtered through the barn, I searched each message. Surely one of these people had the wisdom I lacked, the words I needed, the secret to forgiving the ones we love for being human, being lost, leaving us. How do we keep going when the path is unclear?

But the postcards contained only the simplest words of gratitude.

Dear Mr. Holloway,
    I want to thank you for your kindness and consideration.

They described their boys, fair-haired young fellows, dark-eyed dreamers, rowdy or studious, young fathers or boys barely old enough to be called men. Here was a chance just to write their names again. I read for what must have been an hour, dozens of cards and letters. I could see these mothers and fathers in my mind's eye. I could imagine the boys they described, some of them returned safely by now and others still missing. Others who would never return at all. I thought of Finch and the horror of his disappearance, the hole that we'd filled with the worst imaginings, so much worse than the grave. I thought of Eleanor's stone, lost for centuries, bearing witness to a young woman at the heart of a mystery that seemed to sing in my own blood and might never be solved. And I felt bereft in the sudden, certain, and intimate knowledge that grief was nothing special at all. It was the most common thing, wholly unexceptional.

We were all heirs to that fate. These letters were proof of that.

Doris found me in the barn.

"Committing crimes, I see. You can relax, honey," she said. "The magazine men are gone. Sonder said to let you know he'd meet the bus and bring Penn home."

"I'll have to thank him." I shook my head, trying to clear my thoughts. "I'm not upset about the magazine men. It was a good idea you had."

"You want to tell me what's got you so wound up, if it's not the reporter?"

I hesitated. I had nothing to say about the postcards and I wasn't ready to talk about Julie Hawkes's offer on the estate. I worried I was an idiot not to jump on it. But there was one thing Doris might know. "Actually, I have some questions I want to ask, but it might be difficult. You don't have to answer."

"Oh? What about?"

"Well, first, I want to know what you remember about Mama's work with the orphanage. I want to try to remember her that way. I feel bad about it because I don't want to bring up Jacob, but is that where he came from? I know I don't have any right. Forget I asked if it's too hard for you."

"No, it's not hard." Doris didn't seem to mind the question at all. She answered easily. "And yes. Jacob came to us from a home in Lacaune les Bains, Tarn, France. You don't know this?"

I shook my head. "Not the details."

Doris settled her hands on her hips, took a breath, and continued. "It's shuttered now, but they opened it during the first world war to house the orphaned children who were pouring in from the occupation. They called them the Lost Generation. Of course, we had no idea what was coming.

"So many of the boys and girls were fatherless and their mothers couldn't keep them in their homes without support. We sent money for several years. People did. It was called 'adoption' to support a child and keep them with their own families, or in some cases the orphanages, until they could be reunited with their own folk. In the end, there were many who needed new parents, new homes. It turned out Jacob was one of those who hadn't any family when the orphanage closed. George and I never had any children of our own, so we took him. He was only three years old, but he had seen too much. He had forgotten how to play when they sent him here, to us."

"That's so sad. I can't imagine."

"No?" She gave me a look that made me feel she could see through me. "He got better after a while. But I know he always missed the poor mother he remembered, bless her little soul. We prayed for her at night when I'd put him to bed and I'd say she'd gone straight to heaven. Lord knows, if there's any justice, that's the truth. It was hard for him to understand she had died, and we couldn't tell him much more. That was 1918, when he came to us. We had him eight years."

"I'm sorry I don't really remember him."

"Jacob stayed close to the house those first years. And he didn't speak much English when he came. He was skittish of strangers. But your mother would come sometimes, on her good days, and bring him sweets. Jacob loved Claire. He called her *anielica*. Polish for 'angel.'"

My thoughts were swirling, energized, forming a picture of Mama I had never imagined before. "Jacob was Polish?" I asked, leaning toward Doris.

"Oh yes. The children at that place were from all over Europe, refugees. He had a love for the piano, of all things. I always wondered if maybe his mother played. Maybe he remembered that. I thought he'd die when he saw that little upright piano. Could've knocked me over when I saw your daddy left it and we were over at the house, closing things up. After that, I couldn't keep Jacob on the island. That's when he started tagging along after Sonder, just to get over here and play it. Sonder was kind. He didn't seem to mind. They both were orphans, I think. I'm just surprised you don't already know."

"Why would I?" I stuttered, trying to ask the question that burned behind my heart. "I know nothing about anything, really. Especially my mama. But since we came back there are other people's memories of her that I'm hearing and it's like a puzzle, putting her together, trying to get a clear picture. I feel like if I can just see her, finally see her, maybe I'll have some idea who I am." I hesitated before asking the other question, one I'd never wanted to ask before now. But one I needed to ask the most. "Doris, what do you remember about me?"

Her mouth hung open a moment. "Oh, honey. You are Claire's daughter through and through, born in that bedroom right up there." Doris reached to put her hand to my back. "I was here for it, I should know. I'm the one who caught you."

"Caught me? You mean you delivered me?"

"Oh Lord, yes. You and all the other babies around here for about thirty years. I tended the women in these counties. Until I just couldn't take bringing in one more child when I was so crazy over not being able to have one of my own. Can you imagine? A midwife who can't have her own babies? A sorry thing."

I cried then and Doris let me. I cried as if the river flowed from me. I missed my mama. Not the tragic idea of her I'd carried so long, some wailing woman, unreachable, obsessed, beyond my love. I missed her freely, truly, the mother who had held me, sang to me, told me stories by the light of fireflies. I missed the sweet mystery of her, and the soft certainty too. I'd left that mother here, deep in the forest, but she'd never been lost to me. And finally, I embraced her as both. The wisdom and the mystery.

When I could speak again, I dried my eyes and looked to Doris. It seemed in many ways I was seeing her for the first time. "You were a midwife?"

She smiled. "Just like my granny. She taught me." She must have thought the look on my face was funny because she snorted. "What? I had to be something, didn't I? You think you're the only one with a family that passes on what they know? You were the last Evertell baby for me. They rang the bell for an hour, Alice. How could anyone doubt who you are? How beloved?"

"I did." I felt wrung out.

I let Doris lead me outside, into the fresh air and light, to the garden. I could have lain down on the green grass. Instead, we leaned against the stone wall.

"Claire's work on the orphanage came after she lost her own mama. Did you know she was given an award for her work there?"

"Gerry Lynn was telling me. She said you know stories." I was ready to hear everything.

"Some French volunteers, several nuns from the Catholic order that was nearby, made it out of an old boarding school for girls, a big rambling thing of brownstone and those little attic windows and chimneys everywhere. Looked like a castle in the photos we saw. But it was your mother's money, what she donated and what she raised, that kept that orphanage running. She traveled there twice to oversee that the children were being treated well, had clothes, shoes, toys. That's why she was making all those candles. She made sure every one of them had one. A light to guide by, she said."

I recognized the charm. "That's why Jacob called her Angel? He knew her from that?"

"Oh yes. That's what they called all of the women who cared for them at the home. They officially recognized Claire for her part. The French gave her the Legion of Honor medal. And those peacocks. They knew she'd lost her own mother and the work was partly a tribute to Calista. Claire had talked about that portrait of her with the feathers in her hair. So they sent those birds over as a gift for her farm."

I gulped a laugh of astonishment. Even the awful birds were cast in a different light. "Well, now I know who to blame," I said. Then, "But when you say the French, you mean the government?"

"How could John not have told you any of this?"

I shook my head and Doris made a sound of irritation. "The certificate might be here still, somewhere in that house, but I thought John took that when you left. I know I packed up some photos your daddy asked me to save, but Lord knows what might have happened to them."

"I found them in the attic, after the chimney fell." It took Penn to show me that. She wasn't afraid to tear into things.

Doris laughed. "Isn't that always the way of it."

"Why didn't she talk to me about any of this? Why didn't she tell me these stories instead of asking me to believe in fantasies about stones and charms? I could have believed this. I could have known her."

"Known her? Do you think that's how it works? Do you think you could've forgiven Claire for dying so young because she did some nice things for some poor kids far away? No. You'd have resented her all the same. She wasn't a perfect human being. Do you think Penn loves you because she knows every little thing about your life? Lord, you and that girl of yours both have the same problem. You think mothers are some kind of magical founts of wisdom. Just because you push a human being out into this world doesn't mean you suddenly have all the answers. You have exactly the answers you had before, that's it. No more or less. And you filter through the little bit you know, all your mistakes, all you've seen and learned, good and bad, and do the best you can just to keep that baby alive. And heaven knows, they try to die on your left and right.

"You don't tell your children the awful truth about yourself, except the things they need to know to get them through. You take the rest to your grave. You know that, Alice. Otherwise, what else would we have when we leave here? The comfort we've done our best by our children, that's all."

She had me there. Doris was a woman who had watched mothers being made over and over again. But I thought of the secrets I'd kept. I thought of the stones and the POW messages and the value of being given the story, given the choice to hope. I thought of the pages locked in the writing desk.

Chapter Twenty-Four

Alice

I didn't want to go back to the empty house where I would only work myself into a lather, then clobber Penn with questions the minute she came back. Nor did I feel like heading out to the kitchen to do the responsible thing and sort through the pantry and make ready for the meal I'd be preparing for the Italians, just two days away. My feelings about those men remained complicated, and I didn't want to think too much about them. Instead, I went to the place that had been my comfort as a child, where Mama found her center when the unease in her mind raged, the place I'd feared most when we'd returned to Evertell, and where I'd often gone to commune with my own ghosts. I walked the quiet path to the chandlery in the hush of the forest's shade and my steps felt sure. I was ready to meet her there.

I pulled a stool close to the table, then lit one of her candles. Everything Doris had told me, including the story of my own birth and the ringing of the bell, settled to the bottom of my heart, to a tender place I'd been so afraid to touch. These were the stories I'd been longing for, a sweet balm that soothed the wound there.

I watched the small flame burn. Among the simple wooden molds, I reached for the metal one my mama had favored for her clarity candles and ran my fingertips over the etchings within the cylinder, some engraved so deeply that they pierced the sides. I lowered it over the candle I'd lit as she'd done when I was a child, when we'd watched the fireflies in my jar.

Who am I? Who am I? I needed to finish reading Eleanor's Tale. But even without the ending to my mother's version of a fairy tale, I realized I had my answer. I was the woman at the edge of the forest. I was the light-maker's daughter. I was the mother. A woman who used to dare, now searching for the courage to do so again.

✕

I fell asleep there, waking only when the candle guttered. The sun had slipped below the horizon. I hurried back toward the house and saw a light in the cupola; my heart sank a little that I'd missed Penn's triumphant return. But I needn't have rushed. Her sweet head was already dreaming in our bed. We'd each had a big day, I reflected, brushing her hair away from her forehead and leaning to kiss her above her ear. Then I went to find Sonder in the cupola transcribing postcards.

"Can I come sit with the Evertell phantom, or are you too famous for us now?" I asked playfully. "Did you sell a bunch of radios with your charm?" He grimaced and I laughed. "Thank you for bringing Penn back. I think she's drunk on the sun. She's out and I didn't even get to hear about her day."

"Drunk on something better than the sun," he said. I watched the corner of his mouth tilt up in a smile and I knew he was talking about Nelson. I started to tell him to stop it, but found that I was glad. She'd had a good day. A normal day. The kind of day I'd wanted at her age, and wanted still.

"That good? I've been worried about her infatuation with this place and now I have to worry about boys."

"She hasn't given up on her first love. She jabbered on about Dare descendants with the sea in their veins all the way back."

I hid my own smile. "Right. I guess that doesn't surprise me." It was strange to think of such things without the usual pit in my stomach that accompanied any mention of Evertell or Eleanor Dare. The shift was disorienting and heady. I found I was anxious to get back to the pages in the writing desk.

Sonder was concentrating on what came through his headphones. He scratched out another name, another message, another reason for someone to believe. There were reports being confirmed that Mussolini had been executed. The war was surely stuttering to its end. We were all holding our breath. I watched him there, a man in a tower, until the broadcast came to its end.

"A few of the birds are back," he said, not looking up from his work.

"Really? That's good," I said, hardly caring about the birds anymore. There were things I needed to tell him and it was long overdue. "I know why you didn't go after Nelson. I should have listened. 'Only birds,' you said. You were more worried about that boy. I should have trusted you. I was a mess." For a moment I faltered. I drew a breath before I could ask, "After we left, did Charlie Hawkes ever say anything about what happened to the stone? Did he ever say anything about how he got rid of it? I don't really know why it matters now. I just think Penn might like to know and I guess I'm putting off what I really want to say."

I thought of all those little birds and wondered, when did they decide to fly? The minute the door opened? Or did they sit there a long while, just looking at the sky?

"You want to know about Charlie and that stone?" he asked.

"Well, no. Actually, I want to tell you about it." I sighed. "I never told anyone what really happened that day," I said. "Not after the scene I made in the yard. But I want to tell you now. I want you to know."

Sonder wrinkled his brow, his full attention on me.

"A couple of days before the stone went missing, I took Charlie into the forest. Every day he was after me, teasing me because Mama had told the ladies at church about Eleanor's Tale and they all thought it was to raise herself up higher than all of them. Mama told them the stupid rhyme, the names of the heirs. Apparently they took offense. And Charlie heard all of that talk and decided to bring me down a notch."

The words tumbled out in a rush. I couldn't slow them. If I'd tried, I might have stopped for fear of the look in Sonder's eyes when he understood what I'd done. "Charlie didn't know how sick Mama was, how bad things were for us. I got so upset when he teased me and it only made him worse because he thought I was a brat. That's why I decided to show him the stone. I tricked him and we both paid the price."

Sonder reached to cover my hand with his and we sat there for a moment in silence. "You don't still blame yourself for that stone going missing? Nobody does, Alice. You don't have to say any of this."

"No, I do need to say it. You're good practice. I have to say it now so I can say it to Penn."

It was easier than I thought. He was a good listener.

"I didn't know if the stone's history was real the way my mama thought, but I knew it was hurting her because she'd grown to be afraid of it. It was the symbol of Eleanor's strength, her perseverance. Eleanor, who disappeared from the very face of the earth, but left her name, Sonder. Carved her story right there to last forever. One of us, a woman like that, a woman who had visions and took chances and passed that on to her daughter, in spite of everything. And do you know, I think that was what really terrified my mama. That she couldn't do that. She was losing everything and she knew it. And in the end, she believed she was paying a price for our family's disrespect to Eleanor's grief. That's what she blamed. Eleanor's message was for those she'd loved and lost, never about us. We'd stolen it. As long as it was there, my mother believed she was cursed. And I would be too. She wanted me to have the good things of Evertell, to inherit that kind of vision and courage and hope that Eleanor had. I just wanted to be that daughter for her, Sonder. Then everything got so twisted up in her head.

"And Charlie was after me all the time, teasing me, trying to humiliate me. One day I thought, Here's my chance. I can be rid of the stone, and him too." I drew my hand away from Sonder's. "I told Charlie Hawkes to take the stone. I didn't care what he did with it. I thought that curse could be somebody else's problem and I would get my mama back. I told him he'd be rescuing us, but really, I thought I'd be the hero. Mama would be proud of me. I could solve all my problems at once. But I didn't solve anything. I just made it worse. It got so much worse when she saw that the stone was gone and I watched her come apart in those woods. Whatever she thought was going to happen out there, after that, it didn't matter what I said or did." I choked on the last words. "And then she died, Sonder."

Sonder put an arm out and gathered me close to him. It felt as though we were apart from the world so high up in the cupola. I didn't push away although I felt like he must have misunderstood. "You were trying to protect Claire."

"But I was the reason she was in the hospital that day. If the stone had never gone missing, maybe we would have had more time. Maybe she never would have had that treatment, or even if she did, it would have gone right. Nobody would have made a mistake. I never stop thinking about that. And all this time, Charlie Hawkes knew that. He knew the truth about me, that I didn't care if I hurt him. That what I did killed my mama and I lied about him because I was so ashamed of myself. And then there was nothing I could do. I couldn't change it. I couldn't make anything right. That's why I didn't want to come back here. I never wanted Penn to hear what I'd done."

Sonder pulled me up by my shoulders so I would face him and insisted, "But your daddy wouldn't have seen things that way. He wouldn't have let you think this."

"I don't know. We didn't talk about it. I remember a few years ago, when it hit the papers that somebody had found the stone, I almost told him all of it. But we acted like neither one of us had even seen those reports. And it seemed far away from us, that news, down in Atlanta. Even when those men at Brenau took it over, we didn't have to be a part of that story. Evertell and every-thing that happened here was gone as far as we were concerned, except for Mama's old wardrobe, and it hadn't moved an inch since we got to Merely's. Eleanor's Tale ended right here, Sonder. Wherever that rock went, we both wanted to believe it wasn't about us anymore."

He drew a breath. "So you kept all this secret from Penn? And it's been eating at you all this time? John should have talked to you."

I was touched he would be critical of my daddy, that his concern was for me, even in light of what I'd just told him. It gave me a bit of courage. "Don't be upset with Daddy. Don't blame him. This was all me. He did the best he could to give me a home and a family, to help us get on with a life away from here. He was up against a lot, Sonder. Evertell was no small thing, centuries of history stacked up against a little garage on the side of the highway. He must've never felt like he could make up for what we left here."

Sonder shook his head.

"I'm going to tell Penn the whole story," I said. "After the harvest is done, but before we go. I want her to have her May Day. I already spoke with Bill Hawkes, and I hope it helped him just to hear me say Charlie wasn't ever to blame. It was my idea. And I think Penn can forgive a mistake, but not a mother who's a coward. If we leave here, at least this time it won't be because of that."

I saw no sign from Sonder that he'd heard me admit I was considering staying at Evertell. He was lost in his own thoughts about everything I'd just told him. *Ask me*, I wanted to say. Instead, I leaned toward him and let my head rest against his arm. He reached to lay a tender hand atop my head and we were quiet.

I wanted to tell him what I'd heard at the farm stand, about the orphanage and my mama, about the bell ringing for me. Instead, I said, "I think a lot about that night when I first saw you in the chandlery. How I believed I'd conjured you up for myself. I spied on you and watched every little thing you did. But you knew I was there, didn't you? The whole time. I thought I'd made you up and so I knew everything about you. I was just a girl. I didn't know anything, did I?"

"I was just a boy," he said into the darkness. His hand dropped and I could tell he was looking down at me.

I lifted my head so I could look into his face. I could feel his breath in rhythm with my own. I noticed his smile was somehow forced in the dim light of the radio, but the luster of his eyes was full and hot on mine. Perhaps, like me, he was thinking of all the time between now and then, when Evertell had been lost to me.

All at once, a wave of sadness washed over me. I could imagine a flicker of a life, just as I'd imagined him long ago, a full life beginning and ending with him. We'd missed that chance when we were young. I couldn't bear the idea of being an old woman, regretting I'd missed it a second time because I had been afraid I didn't deserve such a love. Sonder took my hand in his and kissed my palm. I could feel he was about to say something, move away from me, suggest we should get some sleep before another busy day. And he'd have been right. Staying here, together like this, complicated things when I'd made no promises to stay.

"I don't want to talk anymore," I said. We were both tired, but if I took my eyes from him now, I was afraid when I looked again, he might be gone. I heard my daughter's voice echo in my own when I asked, "Can we just stay here awhile?"

Spanish Colonial St. Augustine
Late Autumn 1591

It seemed she'd walked out of a dream on the day Eleanor finally heard the sounds of the Spanish settlement, a city called St. Augustine, long before they came upon the busy port. She felt the presence of other people with all her senses. As they stepped from beneath the shadow of the forest's canopy onto a flat and sandy road, she saw a great open sky. She heard the laughter of Spanish children and the voices of women calling them home. Walking past their small wooden cottages, she smelled their stew pots boiling and they stared at her from their porches and yards. Women. She noted their long black braids, which looked much like her own. She was filled with a longing to run to them, to be wrapped in their strong arms, her face pressed to their soft breasts, to be among their children.

The clang of iron striking iron startled her and the smoke from the blacksmith's shop burned her eyes. She recognized the pungent scent of ink and turpentine as the smell of her beloved commonplace book, and as they walked past the printer's shop, it gave her a thrill. Farther inside the city walls, she heard the shouts of tradesmen and sailors bustling about where a wide set of stairs led down to the water and she could see the tall white sails of ships, like great clouds. She witnessed the look of wonder on young Griffin Jones's face as he greeted the shipbuilders. She kissed his cheek, giving her blessing to the dream he held for himself.

Eleanor thought of the ways her own dream had transformed, of what she had seen the night she delivered Agnes, of the beautiful, shimmering light. She thought of the message she'd carved, a stone to speak for her long after she had gone. She realized she no longer cared if it was found, but one day she would tell Agnes about it. It marked the end of one life and the beginning of another. Eleanor believed she was destined for this New World, which turned out to be nothing new at all, only the edge of the map. And she believed that the commonplace book, the wisdom and mystery of its many curators, the fishwives from the north, had helped tell her who she was.

She wasn't afraid of the smell of salt in the air or the vast blue of the sea or the sighing sound of the waves that echoed in the curl of her ear, because she knew her story was not finished. She let Gabriel Lavat lead her out of exile, their rough hands fitted well to one another, the child they would call their own swaddled and bound to her chest. In her other hand, she carried her graver's tools, ready to make her mark. He had arranged to take her as his wife with the blessing of the governor, disappointing the greedy Portuguese trader, who had never found her copper plate. Gabriel had not traded away her treasures or betrayed her secrets. He had protected them all. In secret, they were married by one of the Franciscan priests. Then he had given her what she had wanted most, as if he had known her heart before it was broken: a home.

Eleanor found something then that she had not expected as she planted herbs near the entrance to their cottage so the sweet scent of her mother's garden would one day be as familiar to Agnes as it was to

Eleanor. She found work for her hands in the washing of towels for her husband's surgery, in the turning of earth, in the tending of her flower beds, and in the fish stew on her hearth. She found solid ground beneath her feet during the day and a quiet sense of safety when she laid down her head at night. She recorded the best times to plant and harvest, the secrets that meant the difference between starving and surviving in this land, but she also sketched images of the graver's tools and made notes on their use.

Gabriel asked her to show the copper plate she'd engraved with her vision to the governor, and he'd made a plan to send for a printing press from Spain. Eleanor had waited for months for the ship to arrive and then watched as the press was assembled. When at last she stood before it and lifted the first paper to the image of her engraving in ink, Agnes squealed with delight. No one looked twice at the symbols the doctor's wife hid within her beautiful engravings of plants or sea creatures, or suspected treason against the Spanish in the lines of maps. Gabriel's channels made sure the pamphlets and newspapers and maps found their way into the right hands, and Eleanor wondered if anyone would ever know whose hand had forged the marks. She found, after all, she did not care. What she loved most was knowing her part in the story.

Life in St. Augustine was not without hardships—the constant threat of a bad crop or a pirate attack or a wasting sickness—that befell the city often enough. But Eleanor had learned from her father how to see the beauty in the detail of a thing, and from her mother's recipes and grief, she'd learned how to hide in plain sight. And with her graver's tools she'd carved out a life for herself and her family. Eleanor had found herself.

When Agnes was almost five years old, the girl wrote her own name in the commonplace book, just beneath Eleanor's and that of the lost Virginia. Eleanor imagined the names that would follow, enough to fill the remaining pages. One day she would tell Agnes the truth of who they were. She hoped she was already telling her in all the ways that mattered. The early hours of her days were spent writing in the commonplace book. She made lists and sketches and receipts of all kinds for the plants and cures she'd learned from the Spanish women and imagined how pleased her mother would have been. It didn't matter that she couldn't recall her mother's features or know her favorite color or if she loved the sound of owls calling in the night. She knew she'd been loved because of what she felt for her daughters, and for Gabriel.

In the commonplace book she drew a map. Eleanor marked the lost place where she'd laid the stone to remember Virginia and the life she'd left behind. She dipped her brush again and again to show the long journey she'd made through the wilderness, beautiful and terrible, to the place of Agnes's birth, where her vision had returned in a silvery flash. Her marks were sure as she followed the long way along rivers and through a deep forest with Gabriel by her side until they'd come home.

Chapter Twenty-Five

Penn

Before she even opened her eyes, Penn knew she was in love. Not with a boy but with a place.

All night she had dreamed of the sea. Never before had she truly imagined the seashore would have stretched so long and wide. Or how the water would sparkle and crash in little white fits that felt like the reward for everything good she'd ever done, and forgiveness for all the rest.

Tybee Island had been a wonder, a miracle, and the true moment she knew where she belonged. As she stood on the sand, seashells were delivered at her bare feet like jewels. Salt had coated her skin, and even this morning as she woke, she ran her tongue over her lips and still tasted it. And when Nelson Hawkes had found her in the shade of a tree and kissed her, just a soft peck with his warm lips, she'd let him.

The kiss had been like another key and it had unlocked her

there by the water. She'd told Nelson everything. When she thought about it now, her pulse jumped.

"But if you don't have the Hawkes stone," Nelson had asked, "how are you going to make the bell work?"

"I've got everything I need," Penn had answered. She'd filled her lungs with a kind of expansive courage that came with the air off the waves, believing he would know what it was costing her. "I'm going to use a welder's torch to make a new part out of my daddy's tools."

She'd seen on his face that he'd understood her sacrifice and was thinking of his own father, like so many people would be doing when they heard the chiming. Seeing what could be made of the pieces left to them.

"There's a girl welder coming tomorrow from the shipyard to help," she'd confided. "She's coming on the three o'clock bus. Maybe you want to come too. Meet us at the chapel at four."

Nelson had agreed, nodding and smiling. "Yeah, yeah. I can do that. I can give her a ride from the bus, if you want. We'll come in my grandad's boat. He'll keep his word."

The sun had shone on them, on Nelson's golden head, on her golden plans. And everything had looked that way to Penn ever since: gilded.

She went through her morning with Mama like every morning since they'd come to Evertell, but the light bounced off Mama's face as she listened to the words from Penn's mouth, all the normal things about her adventure with her new friends at the ocean—sandcastles, the sunburn across her shoulders, how tired she'd been from wading in the surf for hours, how she couldn't wait to go back. She'd told Sonder and everything was set. If she kept the kiss a secret, wasn't that what girls her age were supposed to do?

Now, as the late sun fell across Bell Isle and Penn and Sonder pulled ashore, her heart hammered in her chest. Part of her wished Mama had come with them and that she was here instead of alone at the house, peeling potatoes and onions and whipping up whatever other disasters she planned on feeding the Italians. "Go on," she'd said, "this is yours to do on your own," just as easy as anything, as if she'd rather Penn were out of her hair, and Penn hadn't argued or looked back. But now things were in motion and Penn could feel herself being pulled along, alone, as if caught in a strong current.

She and Sonder were the first to arrive and Penn cast eager glances across the river, watching for the others even as she followed Sonder along the short path to the chapel.

A soft breeze whispered through the short pieces of her hair at her neck. She felt carried along by a sense of purpose and certainty, the heft of the toolbox like a counterbalance to the lift of her heart. She'd brought it with her in case Bill Hawkes went back on the deal. She couldn't be sure if Mama's apology had been enough. In the distance, she heard a ship's horn as it moved through the channel and she imagined the chime of the bell and how it would answer back. But Bill Hawkes might not want to hear Penn's bell ring.

When Sammy finally arrived, Penn was already in the rafters of the bell tower and she let out a whoop of welcome. Sammy climbed up to help Penn finish rigging the pulley and have a look at the bell, gauging the work that would need to be done. She admired Penn's hair and Penn's breath came fast.

"You look ready for anything," Sammy said.

Only a few minutes more and everything would be accomplished. It was happening so quickly. They climbed down to join the others outside where Sammy could don her welding gear and prepare her torch.

She saw Nelson then, his smile wide, and his granddaddy's white head beside him.

They stood together in the chapel and Penn watched Bill unwrap the thing he carried in a sling made from a flour sack. Penn stared at the coveted piece of iron she'd seen so many times on the sales counter at his store.

"Nelson here told me what you were planning on doing with your daddy's tools. I couldn't let you do that. You've made lots of friends around here that would agree those tools belong to you now.

"What your mama and Charlie got up to, they were just kids then. Nobody ever held a grudge about none of it," he insisted, a hitch in his voice.

"I believe you," Penn said quietly.

Bill shot a look at Sammy from under his wiry brows, a stranger to witness his confession, but he went on. "I'd like to hear that bell ring again. The way it ought. Not for me, but for Charlie, if you think he'll hear it. And for my grandson here."

He offered the heavy end of the clapper to Penn and she reached out to take it in both hands, surprised by the incredible weight. Sonder quickly put a hand underneath hers to help her hold it. The relief of what she held left her legs feeling like jelly. She looked at it, the names and dates and small artistic drawings that had been scratched into it over the years, not unlike the ink drawings she'd been adding to the commonplace book. It was perfect. She was surprised to see Mama's name there too.

"My mama signed this? When?"

"When last she came by the store."

A zing ran through Penn. "It's beautiful," she said. It meant something, what Mama had done. She just couldn't work out what.

They went to stand outside while Sammy worked. Sonder and Penn carried the ball to her, where she waited. It would take all of them to move it inside the bell tower before they could attach it to the block-and-tackle and hoist it high above.

"Will it work? Now you have both parts, can you put it back together?" Penn asked, anxious.

Sammy nodded. "Piece of cake."

In less than half an hour, Sammy's torch had done its job. The clapper had been repaired, with a strange, smooth scar to bear witness to Penn's pop's grief, and the inscriptions of the community, rusty and ragged, to remind them that this was their story too.

Sonder and Nelson helped position the clapper and secure it so when Penn cranked the winch, the whole thing lifted, seeming almost weightless. Sonder gave a low whistle when he saw the pulley work, even though he'd been the one to anchor the top. She loved him for giving her credit and swelled with pride that she'd impressed him.

Nelson cheered, "Hot damn!"

"All right," Sonder said to Penn. They all hesitated after the clapper was in place. "You gonna hook her up or you want me to do it?"

"No. I can do it. I know how," Penn said, grabbing Finch's heavy old wrench, filled with emotion to feel the familiar grip in her hand and grateful for it. All she had to do was tighten down the bolt. Nothing had ever been so simple. And nothing had ever felt so important. When it was finished, she was dizzy as she stood back.

"We put it back the way it ought to be," she said, as much to herself as anyone else in the bell tower. "All of us. We did that."

Sammy grinned at her. "I feel like we ought to salute or something."

Penn laughed. "Hoorah!"

They all shook hands and Penn gave each of them her firmest grip. The light was shifting, the sun low over the water, when

Bill Hawkes stepped off toward Doris's cottage. "Got to go see a woman about a cake."

For May Day. For Jacob. Penn knew Bill Hawkes would spend the evening with Doris, and tomorrow too. They would remember Jacob with a spice cake. It relieved her that Doris wouldn't be alone; everybody had their bell to mend. Then she remembered the Italians. They would show up for the harvest tomorrow and Penn took a deep breath, imagining everything the day might bring.

Sammy slipped out of her welding apron and gloves and got busy collecting her equipment so she could return it to the shipyard before anyone knew she'd borrowed it. Penn wondered if she'd really taken it without permission or if she and Sonder had just been pulling her leg.

Nelson offered Sammy a ride across and back to the bus stop in his grandaddy's boat. She took him up on it, but Sammy hung back as the group broke up and Penn looked at her, her gear slung over her shoulder.

Penn said, "Thanks for coming. I hope you don't get in trouble for it. What'll you do now?"

"I'm meeting some of the girls for a drink," Sammy said, a twinkle in her eye. "Maybe some trouble." She looked at Nelson, standing a few feet away at the water's edge. "Looks like you have your own trouble, sis."

"Shut up," Penn murmured. She felt her cheeks flame, but she couldn't stop the smile that broke out on her face. Sammy laughed. She knew it wasn't likely she'd ever see Sammy again, even if Penn attended Pape or became a Girl Scout, or if she went home to Helen and only returned to visit the people here. Things were changing for her, and for Sammy. The war would end, and soon, Penn hoped. People would be turned out again like pieces of a giant puzzle, and they'd have to find ways to fit a new picture.

"What'll you do when the war's over? Will you go for your aviation training?"

Sammy nodded. "Absolutely. They won't let us keep the jobs that ought to go back to the fellas who come home. Given the chance, they'll stick us all behind the desks again. I don't think I'm signing up for that. But you give me a call if you ever want to build something else, bell girl."

Bell girl. Penn nodded, feeling choked up for reasons she couldn't quite name. Was that who she was?

Penn reached in her pocket to pull out the badge Sammy had given her that day in the shipyard. "I keep it in my pocket, like you showed me. I've been drawing other badges for myself. About everything I know. To remind me I'm prepared," Penn said. "Maybe I'll be a Girl Scout. Maybe I'll get aviation training, too, sometime."

"See you in the sky," Sammy said, and turned to hurry toward Nelson's boat, where the boy was waving for her.

Penn took up her heavy toolbox and climbed in the boat with Sonder. She waved as Nelson and Sammy moved away down the river. From the corner of her eye, she saw the light spill over the water like a mirror, a flash like sparks, and when she turned her head, she thought she caught a glimpse of something, maybe a future she could almost imagine, just beyond the blue horizon.

Chapter Twenty-Six

Alice

Penn had come home victorious last night, ready to ring her bell when the work was done and dawn fell over freshly cut fields. She'd spent hours last night, setting up candles around the lawn, shooing me away. She wanted it to be a surprise. Neither of us had slept, from excitement or anxiety or both. This morning I'd left her drooling on her pillow and now I dragged myself to the kitchen house.

I'd finished Eleanor's Tale, or the pages that had been left to me. I'd told Sonder who I was and it had been such a relief. I was ready to give the pages to Penn. But before we left here, I would have to tell my own truth. I thought of the charm for the Evertell. Something to calm, something to soothe, a light to guide the way forward. Not back.

I knew the girl I'd been. The girl who failed. But whatever Penn would draw in the book about me now, she would know her mother. This was what I'd learned from Eleanor.

"May Day. Of course," I said to myself, before sending out my own distress signal as I sat at the table and lowered my head to rest it on my arms. "Mayday. Mayday."

But I was interrupted by the sound of a car coming down the drive and I rose to my feet. My heart gonged against my chest. I hurried out to the front walk where I could see it was a taxicab, a strange thing so far from Savannah this early in the morning. The door swung open and a woman uncurled out of the back seat, one long, stockingless leg at a time. For a moment I thought my eyes were fooling me. But only one person in the world had legs like that.

"Alice!" she squealed as she crawled out of the car. "Did you hear the news? The war is almost over. Any day now, they're saying!"

It was like that moment when thunder claps, seeing Imegine standing at Evertell, as if she'd materialized from some other world altogether. She ran across the yard and up the steps to grab me up like it had been a hundred years since she'd seen me, rather than a few weeks. She'd goggled at the house, immense, even in the early dawn light. "You didn't say it was like *this*!"

I led her up the front steps and held the door to Evertell as wide as possible for Imegine.

)(

"You're up late," I said to Penn as she pushed through the door to the kitchen house. "I thought you might sleep through all our company today. Look who showed up this morning while you were sleeping."

"Grandma Imegine!" Penn said. Her voice sounded funny, all breathy and high-pitched like a little girl, much younger than thirteen. "You're here!" I thought I could guess how Penn was feeling to

384

see her grandma so unexpectedly because I felt the same. But then she said, "I knew you'd come."

They exchanged a look and Imegine saw my face and I laughed. "Oh, I see how it is. Well, you'll be sleeping on the couch."

"Oh, honey," Imegine said, "I just couldn't stand missing you two one more second." Imegine held out her arms and Penn let herself be embraced. "Lord, honey. Look at you, brown as a biscuit!"

"Penn went to the beach with some local kids. All the way out to Tybee," I explained.

"But heaven's sakes, what have you let her do to her hair, Alice?"

"I cut it," Penn said.

"Well. Hair grows right back, don't it?"

Penn gave her a tentative smile. "Mama said that she likes it. She says it looks French."

"Did she? Good thing it's summertime. By the time winter gets here, it'll be down to your shoulders again and your neck won't get cold." Imegine made a noise in her throat and then her eyes swiveled to me. "But who'd have thought this one would have her hair chopped off like a scarecrow while you finally took an interest in those pretty curls of yours?"

"I don't know what you're talking about," I said.

Imegine chuckled, then grabbed Penn's hands to rub warmth into them between her own. "Well, sit down by me, Miss Pennilyn, and we'll warm up and eat something."

I turned away, seeing to the bacon in a hot pan that was smoking and threatening a grease fire and pulling a pan of biscuits from the oven just before they burned up. I slammed the oven door too hard, then sighed. "I don't know what I was thinking, agreeing to dinner."

Penn pulled a chair close and Imegine wrapped her in her arms while she jabbered on about everything—about Sonder, about the candles, about the bell, and finally, about the harvest and the workers we were expecting any minute.

"You're cooking for them?" Imegine asked, clearly stunned.

"Fish stew." Penn sighed, echoing my own misgivings, unable to hide her feelings about it. "And they're Italians."

Imegine gave me an arch look.

"Yes, I'm cooking, and yes, they're Italians," I spat. "My plan is to give them all ptomaine poisoning, Imegine."

The biscuits were too flat and too brown, but Penn ate up two of them with the bacon, washing down the dry crumbs with a cup of watered-down coffee. There was no sugar. I had used up the rations on the peach cobblers, so it was a bitter cup, but she swallowed her breakfast whole. Imegine nibbled her scorched bacon and gave a side-eye to the biscuits.

Penn asked, "Will you make biscuits while you're here?"

I made an unladylike sound through my lips. Imegine choked on her coffee and it broke the tension so I laughed until tears ran from my eyes. It was contagious and we all laughed, too tired, each for our own reasons, to do different. But soon enough we were interrupted by the sound of Sonder's truck approaching, and Penn watched me reach for Imegine's hand.

"What about fried chicken? Can we manage that? And some vegetables, maybe? To go with your mama's stew? I'll help you," Imegine repeated, laying her cheek against our clasped hands. I grimaced but held on hard, so hard our fingers were colorless.

)(

The truck stopped a few feet from where Imegine, Penn, and I stood. Sonder stepped out and walked around to lower the tailgate.

THE LOST BOOK OF ELEANOR DARE

We waited to greet the men on the front steps of the house and didn't move except to wave the dust from our faces.

"I swear it's like Grand Central Station," I said, grumbling to hide my nerves. "We've not seen this much coming and going since we left Merely's."

Three people crawled from the back. If Imegine's arrival had surprised me, it was nothing compared to the feeling that overtook me then. The feeling of disgust that clawed up from my guts made me want to turn my back on all of it, leave the whole lot where they stood and close my door on them. I looked at anything but the men. I looked at the truck. I looked at the swaying moss in the trees. I looked at the light on the water, shining and sparking so brightly that my eyes teared. But in the end, there was no avoiding what was before me. It felt monumental, impossible simply to lift my gaze to take in the toes of their worn boots. But when I did, they were only boots.

"Mama," Penn whispered, and I felt her narrow hand slip into mine. I kissed her head quickly and with the same swift move faced the POWs.

"Hello," I said.

"Do you think they understand English?" Imagine asked softly. But a couple of the men nodded and mumbled their own greetings.

These men didn't look threatening, dressed in overalls the same as Sonder's. They didn't look like anybody's enemy or like men celebrating the deaths of dictators and madmen. They just looked like plain men in work clothes with solemn expressions to match our own. Barely men, in fact. They were boys except for one older fellow. Their hair was cut neatly, their faces shaven, their eyes clear. Imagine and I exchanged glances as I went down to meet them. I shook each of their hands, all business, until I came to the last man.

"I am Paolo Gabrielli," he introduced himself. "Foreman." He was the elder by at least a decade. His eyes were dark and lively. I liked him, despite myself. Gabrielli. *Gabriel.*

I tried a strained smile and addressed Paolo and the rest of the group. "Thank you for coming. This farm thanks you." I sounded ridiculous to my own ears, but I thought it was the kind of greeting I'd have liked to hear if I were in his shoes. Again, the men all mumbled thank you with thick accents. Each one of them met my eye.

Imegine had mason jars filled with water tied to strings, which the men slipped over their heads to hang around their necks. I noticed Paolo Gabrielli's eyes followed her everywhere. She was still a good-looking woman.

Sonder watched all of this. I put a string with a jar around his neck. He smiled as he held the jar of water and then let it settle against his chest. There was a charge between us that snapped and I didn't want that to show in front of all these people. I didn't want Imegine to see the feelings I had for this man. Having her here complicated things, and there'd been no time for me to talk with Sonder and explain her arrival yet.

Sonder gave each of the men a dangerous-looking sickle-shaped corn knife to cut down stalks and led them out into the field to get busy with the work. Imegine and I headed back and stood around the kitchen house like mutes for a good ten minutes, likely imagining the possibilities that went along with those blades.

It was Imegine who finally broke the silence, scrubbing a pot for all she was worth. She stopped long enough to say, "I never thought Italians would be so pretty. Did you see that one's teeth? About put my eyes out they were so bright."

Penn stared at me from where she sat at the table. I figured that both of us were worried about the same thing, but her expression only made me laugh outright. The sound bounced off the walls and filled the small kitchen house. Imegine turned and snapped a towel in my direction, and soon we were all three smiling and slapping each other with towels like girls. For a moment it felt like the little apartment above Merely's. But thinking of Merely's brought Finch to mind and I was immediately sick to my stomach at what we were doing.

Imegine stared out the window alongside me. "They're just pitiful. I've hated them so bad, but look at them. They look just like us."

"I don't know," I said. "But they're not what I thought."

Everything was so uncertain. I was distracted by the strangers in our fields.

Penn put her arms around Imegine's waist. "You smell like sweet balm," Penn said, pulling away. Her brow furrowed and her tone surprised us. "You've been in my room. You took the jar of cream on my dresser."

Imegine put up her hands. "Well, excuse me for living. I wanted to freshen up. I didn't think you'd mind. It's pretty, isn't it? I was just happy to see your mama must be making a little effort with herself, smelling sweet like a woman ought to, even out here in the boonies."

"We're supposed to use it when we dress for dinner. Like ladies," Penn insisted. "You should have asked me."

Just like that, I was reminded of the realities of three women living together in a house, even this one. The bickering and sniping on the heels of such delight in one another. The normalcy of the moment was a strangely welcome distraction from the heaviness of all I was feeling. I knew my role when Imegine and Penn were like this, the moderator of their little domestic fits and peacemaker when I could be, somehow mothering them both, as they often mothered me.

I looked to Imegine. Nobody had ever needed a little *sweet* more. "Surely there's enough to go around, right, Penn?"

X

All afternoon swing music filled the spaces between us and we moved around each other, preparing a dinner of fried chicken and every vegetable that had come out of the garden. Imegine was impressed with the bounty, so much more varied than anything we had on hand at Merely's. But when Penn left to refill water bottles, Imegine's mouth quivered. She sat down at the table. She slid an envelope toward me and I saw it was marked with a return address for Brenau Academy.

"Did she get invited for an interview?" I could see the letter had been opened. Imegine nodded. The breath rushed out of me.

"*You* wrote the essay, so I'd say it's you they've invited for an interview, Alice," Imegine said, her irritation plain.

I sighed. "You might be right," I admitted.

"Penn looks so good," she said. "You've got a little spring in your step. Neither one of you will be able to stand being back at Merely's after having all this drop in your lap, and I won't blame you a jot," she said.

A horrible culpability turned my stomach. Only hours before, I'd been considering what it would be to stay here, start a life with Sonder, leave her behind, but with what? An empty service station and the graves of my daddy and husband? Now she was before me it was so obvious I could never do that. I'd made my choices long ago.

"What are you talking about?" I said, flipping a hand to dismiss the idea. "We'll be home in a day or two. We'll get Merely's running again and Penn off to school, wherever she wants, and we'll make a grand time of things, you and me, now things are looking up. With the war ending, we've got to make some new plans, don't you think? It's time we hire on a new mechanic."

I smiled to encourage her, but Imegine only squared her shoulders.

"Oh, listen, Alice. The truth is, I lived a lot of years with John in the shadow of this place. I just wanted to run down here and have a good look at it, not rush you back up to Helen."

"It's no rush. We've stayed to do what we meant to do. And there's a neighbor interested in this place. I've decided to parcel off some of the property and leave the house for now." Imegine folded and unfolded her hands in her lap. If she had something to say, she was holding her tongue. "I thought you'd be happy," I said.

"I'm happy if you're happy," she answered.

I felt entirely turned around by the conversation. If what Imegine said about Penn and me having changed was true, she should have included herself in the observation. And I began to wonder what I'd missed. From the roof of the kitchen house, the peacock raised his voice in a quick succession of six or seven startling squawks. *Eee-ooo-ii! Here I am!*

"Holy hell!" Imegine yelped in response. "What the devil is that?"

"A peacock." She turned round eyes on me. I shrugged.

"Well, good Lord," she said, smoothing her hair as if the bird's call had blown through the room. I laughed at her and she chuckled too. "Now, you give me something to do to help," Imegine said, getting to her feet and turning her attention to the job in front of us. "Let me be useful. Tell me now, honey. Where's your saucepan?"

X

"Dinner is served," Penn said, a little bashful as the workers gathered in the dining room. Imegine and I stood alongside her, Imegine's arm around my waist. I couldn't stop myself from leaning on her just a bit and being thankful to have her there to shore me up. Penn had insisted we apply generous amounts of the sweet balm to ourselves and my skin felt strange and sticky. In our hair, she'd pinned sprigs of rosemary and lavender so Imegine looked like a wood sprite, smiling ear to ear. Sonder winked at me and my face flushed with heat.

The table looked like we were planning to feed the entire Italian armed forces rather than three scrawny POWs. The workers sat together on one side. Sonder and Imegine sat across from our guests, and my seat was open at the head of the table, with Penn to my right. When I reached my chair, all the men stood, which made me smile awkwardly. If the people in Helen could see me now, John Merely's quiet daughter from the back room of a service station, now the May Day Queen, the lady of the house serving up supper to a bunch of Italians, what would they say? How did I ever get to be head of such pageantry?

The answer was Penn, of course. And she took it all in with wide eyes, as if she were memorizing the details.

Dinner went off well, with Sonder murmuring grace and the huge bowls passed around until plates were piled high with fried cabbage and mashed potatoes and vegetables from the garden. We'd fried chicken and made pans of cornbread. The scent of spices and herbs from the garden had the men reminiscing about their own homes in Italy. All of the food disappeared in less time than anyone would expect. Thirty minutes later, the men pushed back from the table, licked their fingers, and stretched their legs out before them. I was reminded of the return mail, the descriptions of our boys, boys like these, boys someone loved. And I couldn't help thinking of the first dinner we'd hosted with Oscar Lewallen and what a failure it had been. In contrast, tonight we offered a bounty from our gardens, our river, and our hearts to our unlikely guests, knowing full well we'd all come to the table wounded in both known and unknown ways.

I had changed. The hard place in my chest that had only become colder and denser, first with Finch's loss and then with Daddy's, had softened into a hot, pulsing vulnerability that could only be the result of the love offered me here. I felt humbled and grateful and amazed that I could offer these men the same grace.

I apologized that we had no coffee to offer and they asked if we had music.

"There's a piano, but I don't know when it was touched last. Imagine might sing. We can't have May Day without music, can we?"

The men all smiled and made encouraging sounds. Imagine looked startled. She shook her head, furious with me for putting her on the spot.

"Ah, don't worry. Paolo plays," his comrade offered.

The one called Paolo held up his hands and wriggled his long fingers. Penn beamed at me. This was what she had in mind for Evertell. She'd ring the bell and throw open the doors. She'd throw off whatever pall had been cast by my mama's madness, my heartbreak, even world wars.

"You're rescuing me," Imagine said. He quietly followed her to the front room where the upright piano sat, dusty and silent. He pulled the wobbly seat out and flipped open the lid to expose the yellowed keys. The soft, musky scent of the marsh rose around us and Penn smiled at me knowingly. But none of us were prepared for the horrid sounds that Paolo produced from the neglected piano, and the group burst out laughing at the out-of-tune cacophony until Imagine begged him to stop.

As the hour grew late, Penn waited for dusk before disappearing outside to light her candles as the peacock began his nightly performance from a distance. She insisted I stay indoors until her surprise was ready. The workers wandered out for a smoke and Paolo and Imegine went missing. I found them upstairs in the cupola, where I heard scuffling sounds and soft laughter before music suddenly echoed from the radio propped in an open window. The two turned to smile at me with a conspiratorial air about them.

"Come see," Imegine said, reaching for my hand and pulling me to the open window for a view of the lawn below. "See what Penn's done."

I gasped at the sight.

Beneath the low-hanging branches of the moss-laden oaks, what must have been a hundred candles burned. Amid them, our guests—the prisoners, all of them holding the last of the pillars so the light caught their faces.

"She wanted to surprise you."

My breath caught in my throat and my vision blurred to a soft, teary impression of a future as Penn wanted me to see it. I searched for her upturned face, a light all its own. I hurried down to meet her. I could hear the music, the dulcet tones of Jimmie Noone crooning "Virginia Lee." I felt the cool evening breeze off the water.

I'd believed I didn't deserve an Evertell vision, even as I'd longed for it to come to me. Now, when Sonder and these strangers stood before me, brave enough to burn so brightly in such a dark hour, I couldn't deny the shimmering flashes of something divine in my daughter's dream. And inside myself.

I danced, twirling, laughing, embracing Penn, and then the water diviner whose heart beat sure and steady in my ear where I pressed against his solid chest. I forgot the transience of the candles, which transformed along with the rest of us, and thought only of the light.

"Where's Grandma Imegine?" Penn asked.

"She's looking at the stars," I said. I didn't mention Paolo. I could not judge Imegine. Perhaps she was finding her own little happiness on this night. And in the early morning hours, when those stars began to fade and the candles were nothing more than repurposed wax, ready again for the mold, I believed that was true for us all.

Only when the radio slipped from the ledge of the windowsill, sliding down the roof and crashing to the ground, did the screams of the frightened peacock split the air. Imegine called my name from the window in the cupola as Penn rushed through the front door onto the porch, the flashing white of the pages I'd torn from the commonplace book in hand. She looked to me and I knew the fragile trust I'd begun to build between us had been horribly damaged. I saw the listless expression I'd feared return to her face as she let the pages fall. They drifted across the lawn, some of their edges catching fire and curling up from the candle flames that still burned low.

Chapter Twenty-Seven

Penn

In the warm flickering light of the candles, Penn had believed the whole world was charmed. She'd witnessed her heart's desires so clearly. She saw her life for what it was, for all she already had. The beauty of the moment took her breath. The glowing faces of the Italians, who were nothing she'd imagined, tired and grateful and quietly smiling now. Mama and Sonder lost in one another, laughing. This was what came next. This was her family. This was her home. She could go anywhere from here and always find her way back.

Penn believed in the Evertell vision in that sparkling instant, sensed the presence of each of Eleanor's heirs. She thought of the ink drawings she'd put beside their entries in the commonplace book, the virtues of Evertell, all she'd learned from them. She understood that her daddy and Pop were looking on, too, that they'd played a role in her work on the bell, their tools and their love in her hands. That Doris would see the lights across the water and know Jacob was remembered with each small flame. Walter Kreischer was a part of this story of strangers in a strange land, and so was every unmarked stone in the shady glen behind the house where Bridie Quillian's mother and grandmother had planted the herbs that grew here still and made the night air sweet. It seemed to Penn that her own grandmama Claire, who had wandered so lost, had brought them all together. And Penn felt certain she'd made something right. In a few hours, with the harvest done, dawn would break and she would ring the bell.

But just now, she wanted her family around her, here. So she went to find Grandmama Imegine. She'd forgotten to ask if there'd been any word from Brenau. Now she wanted to know. If anything had come, she wanted them to open it together. She was ready to know, ready to decide what came next.

She left the others outside and went first to the kitchen house, but there was no sign of her grandmother. On the porch, she dodged the uneven boards and stepped inside the foyer, remembering the first night she and Mama had come to Evertell. Tonight there was light in the house again. She peered into the dining room. The table still held the dishes from their dinner and the chairs sat at angles, their guests having rushed to the piano earlier. To Penn, it looked like the house was having its own party. She hurried across the hall and called Grandma Imegine's name, but the front room was empty except for the writing desk and the lantern that burned low there, Sonder's miner's lantern. Mama must have forgotten it.

Grandmama Claire's ledger lay on top of the desk and beside it, a stack of papers. Penn hurried to glance at them, in case the letter from school was there. But there was no sign of it. Only a blue ribbon that stirred a memory of the first time she'd seen the commonplace book in the chapel on Bell Isle. She'd forgotten the ribbon and she picked it up now and ran it through her fingers. Her eyes landed on the delicate, swirling penmanship on the papers beneath it. Stacked neatly, one atop another, there must have been more than twenty handwritten pages. Penn read the words of the title page, the name of a story she'd never heard but had longed to know since they'd come back to Evertell and she'd learned of their family's myth.

Eleanor's Tale

By Claire Clerestory

A story that might have answered all the questions she had about the stones and her mother and herself, but she'd never known existed. The pages that were missing had been here all along. Now that she saw them, Penn knew they'd been hidden from her, not lost. All of Mama's promises soured in Penn's stomach. She thought of how she'd struggled to make sense of the stones. She thought of Bill Hawkes and the lie Mama had told about his son. And suddenly Penn didn't know what to believe anymore.

She grabbed the pages and rushed up the stairs, calling for Grandma Imegine. When she burst into the room at the top of the stairs, Penn found her and Paolo, startled and scrambling to their feet from where they sat in the cupola. Penn rushed toward her, trying to explain, holding the papers out for her to see.

"She tore it out, everything Grandmama Claire wrote about Eleanor. Mama tore it out of the book and hid it. She told me it was mine, but she stole this. She never told me she had it. She never said it was all right here, written down. Why did she lie?"

Grandma Imegine looked stricken. She was shaking her hand and patting at Penn's arms and face and saying things to calm her down. "Honey, I don't know. What is this? You need to take a breath and we'll just go ask her."

"None of it's real, is it? It was all made up. It's all a joke, like they said. None of it's real. She lied about everything."

Penn didn't know if that was true. But it felt true. She turned then, without care for where they stood. She didn't care the room was small or that they were surrounded by windows. She didn't care that Sonder's table had them cramped and up against the walls or that the whirlwind of her anger over her mother's betrayal sent Grandma Imegine off balance, Paolo's steadying hand unable to catch her before her weight came against the radio propped on the windowsill.

The crash of the wooden machine hitting the porch roof and then the ground, followed by the silence of the music that had played all night, stopped everything on the lawn. Only the peacock's startled cries rose in the night. Penn slammed through the house and down the steps until she stood on the front porch again.

She saw her mother's face then. Saw her understand what had happened as Penn let the pages fall from her hands, a waterfall of paper and indigo ink. Sonder and the Italians rushed forward to gather them up, hurrying to put out any paper that caught fire. But Penn no longer cared what the pages had to say.

"You wouldn't let me unlock the door!" Penn yelled at her mama.

"What?" Alice said. She looked confused. Small. Penn watched as she began to walk toward her, glancing at the pages and deciding not to go after them. But she knew what they were. Penn was sure. "Penn?"

"When we came here, I asked. I said I wanted to be the one. I wanted to unlock the door and let us in. But you took the key." It hadn't seemed important then, but in the moment, Penn remembered the key, having it in her hand, and her mama wrenching it away. Pushing her behind so that Penn couldn't see for herself. Now Penn felt that way about everything Mama had done.

"You said you didn't want to come here because it made you sad to remember Grandmama Claire and I felt sorry for you. But you lied about all of it, didn't you? You told me stories matter because they're told. But that's not true either, is it? Everything here is a story. You made it up. You tricked me. You wanted me to go back to how I was before, when I was little and dumb and didn't know any better. To forget everything that's happened, about Daddy and Pop, and pretend. But I'm not a baby. I know what's real. He's dead. Not rocks, not bells, not stupid magic books, none of it changes anything."

Her heart was still broken and Penn didn't know how to go on living with that. "He's dead," she said quietly.

She heard Mama say, "Oh, Penn. I'm sorry." They stood there, frozen. The others began to drift away, one man returning the pages they had collected to Mama. She thanked him quietly and Penn couldn't look at her. "I wasn't going to keep those pages from you," Mama said.

"But you did." Penn's anger waned and she felt her eyes fill. "None of it was real, was it? That's what you don't want me to figure out. Everything she said about Eleanor and all those heirs, it's like all those fake Dare Stones. She was just crazy and maybe that's what's wrong with me, you just don't want me to know it."

Mama stood there shaking her head. "No. You're wrong."

"Who are we?" Penn finally wailed, and it ended with a sob. When Mama only stared at her and started to cry herself, Penn left her standing there.

She went to find something that might make sense to her, something she could do something about, the radio that had fallen to the ground.

The Italians had gathered at the edge of the yard. Mama and Imegine argued over how it had all happened and what a careless idea it had been, coming back here. Only Sonder dared come near Penn. He sat on his heels next to her, surveying the broken machine, picking through the parts. Penn could tell it was hopeless. She wrapped her arms around herself. She felt herself drift to the place with the soft silver light, deep inside her mind, and when she surfaced again, it was only because she could hear Mama calling her name.

She blinked, sleepy, wishing she could disappear again. Imegine was following after the POWs, apologizing, inviting them back again as if they were visitors and not prisoners while they clambered into Sonder's truck. Sonder climbed behind the wheel and pulled away to return them to the camp. There'd be no way for him to hear messages sent out into the night, thanks to Penn. She felt a twinge of dismay over that.

"This is not how it was supposed to be," she said. She felt like the words came from somewhere else, some other girl. "It was my idea to put the radio in the window, not Imegine's. Don't let anybody blame her. It was stupid. Just like the chimney."

"Penn, everybody understands," Mama said. Mama had rolled the pages up like a scroll and she held them tightly. "Sonder will find a new radio."

Penn shook her head. "But not tonight. He can't listen to the broadcasts and he can't make the postcards and people will never get their messages. Real messages that matter. Because of us."

"Penn, Sonder is not the only person who listens." Mama pushed the short hair falling over Penn's eyes behind her ear like she'd done since Penn was little. Penn slapped her away.

"Okay, you're angry. You should be. But I haven't lied to you about Eleanor. Not about the heirs. Not about Grandmama Claire and what happened to her. Everything you know about the Dare Stone is real, even if it's confusing and maybe not true. And I promise you, I promise I would have given you these pages. I wanted to read them together, just like you said. I just wasn't ready. You were, but I wasn't."

Penn did not answer. She did not argue. She had nothing to say.

"You don't have to believe me, but you can ask Sonder. I told him that after the harvest, I was going to tell you all of it. I just wanted to let you have this day. One day. I wanted you to have a good memory after so many bad ones. And I knew if I gave you Eleanor's Tale before that, Penn, then I had to give you mine. And it might ruin this for you."

"Why?" Penn managed to whisper.

"Everything we lost was my fault, Penn. I lied about Charlie Hawkes. He never stole the stone. I made him take it. I thought it would make my mama well, or at least give me more time with her, but it broke her heart, Penn. I never could get over that. When we found the book again and I saw Eleanor's Tale, I thought I would finally get to read the end of the story, the part she never told me, and maybe—"

"It would tell you what to do," Penn said. Finally, something she understood. She rested her chin on her knees and looked at Mama. "You thought it would tell you the secret to the Evertell vision." Mama nodded. "It didn't?"

"Nope. Wasn't even there. Somebody took the pages."

"So you tore out the rest?" Penn asked, incredulous. "Then you know how it feels!"

"I just wanted to make some sense out of them. I've been reading them, trying to know what to say to you, what we should do with this place now we have it back. Trying to believe I could deserve anything like an Evertell vision, or you, Penn. I've done a lot wrong. Made a lot of mistakes. I don't want to make them again. I lost the stone, Evertell, Grandmama Claire. And I've been trying to figure out how to give all of that back to you, without losing you too."

"You can't lose me," Penn said quietly. "Evertell heirs always find their way home."

Mama laughed softly, sadly. "Now that is the truth. You are the very living proof anybody needs to know that, Pennilyn Young. You are my home. You are my Evertell."

Penn reached for her mother's hand. Their fingers intertwined, Penn's nails stained with the indigo ink and Mama's ragged from the work on the house.

Mama said, "I'm sorry. Will you read Eleanor's Tale with me? Will you help me fix the book? Put these pages back where they belong?"

Penn shrugged, but she scooted closer. It felt good. And she was tired. It wouldn't be long before dawn and she wanted to sleep. "I'm supposed to ring the bell in the morning."

"You should. Do you know you made a beautiful night for us? You lit everything up." Mama pushed Penn's hair out of her face again and lifted her chin. "I found something else. Pictures. They were in the attic. I went up there because you ripped a hole in the place." Mama made a face and Penn couldn't help smiling back. "They're pictures of Grandmama Claire. Do you want to see them?"

Penn nodded.

"She worked for an orphanage in France. Can you believe that?"

Penn looked at her mama, afraid she might be trying to make up a new story, something that sounded better than the truth. "Is that true?"

"I swear. She made those candles for all the children who were alone there during and after the Great War. I didn't know that part. Doris told me. And after, France gave her those stupid peafowl because she told them about the feathers in Grandma Calista's hair." Mama nodded. "Now we can never get rid of them."

Mama surprised Penn talking like this, maybe more surprised than she'd been to find the pages of Eleanor's Tale. She had never talked about Grandmama Claire this way. "If we hadn't come back here, if you hadn't done what you did, I never would have known that story, Penn. I wouldn't have recognized a lot of other things that were right in front of my eyes. Come with me."

Penn followed and Mama gathered up guttered candle wax as they made their way across the yard and down the path that led them to the chandlery. Inside, in the gloomy light, Mama turned a candle mold over and around in her hand, peering inside.

"This was my mama's special mold," she explained. "The one she used to make her clarity candles. One time when I was a little girl, she put this inside a jar with lightning bugs and we watched the pattern on my bedroom wall. I always tried to think of her that way when I remembered her, but after we left, I spent a lot of energy trying to forget all about the magic she tried to make for me. I didn't like to think about the good memories because then I would always think about the sad ones. But it didn't work. I thought about them every day anyway."

"Like I think about Daddy."

"Just like that. But I remembered the magic, too, every time I looked at you. If I'd been brave, like you, I'd have seen this a long time ago." Mama ran trembling fingers inside the mold, feeling round the bottom until she raised her gaze to meet Penn's. Penn felt overwhelmed. Her head was swimming. The mold was a blue-green metal and she felt her breath come faster. *Copper.*

"It's there. Feel. The engraver's initials. *EW*," Mama said. She put the mold into Penn's hand, solid and cool. She showed her how to feel inside the curve for the initials. "I think I know what this is. Before they ever left England, before she was ever lost, Eleanor had a vision of the world she wanted, a future for herself and the ones she loved. It was a gift to them, to inspire and guide them and give them faith. It was everything she hoped for. And she engraved it onto a copper printing plate."

For a long while they traced the letters and the intricate engraving, imagining the careful marks had been etched there so many ages ago by a girl with a dream.

"Eleanor was here," Penn said quietly. She stared at the copper plate. "Do you think it could be real?"

Mama's eyes shone. "What I think doesn't matter. Tell me what you see."

"I think," Penn said, breathless, "we divined her."

Chapter Twenty-Eight

Alice

After I settled Penn into bed with the photos of Mama and plans to ring the bell come morning, I made my way toward the mill. The wind was slanting over the marsh, bringing in a storm. They'd rung the bell for me that awful day of the last homecoming, just as they'd done when I was born. And I was realizing now that when I heard it again, I would understand our legacy was never written in stone.

)(

I closed my eyes for only a moment, or so I thought.

When I woke, the forest was still dark. I felt for my mama beside me, reaching my hands across the silk scarf, but I couldn't touch her.

"Mama, what's wrong? Mama, I'm right here."

I said my mama's name over and over until I was yelling it. I forgot my shoes as I stumbled in all directions and my mouth went

*dry from calling her name. I strained my eyes as the first light fil-
tered through the trees, but each time I thought I caught sight of
her, it was only ever a tree or a shrub. She was gone.*

*I hurried in the direction I knew would take me back to the
house and prayed no one would be out to look for us so early, that
no one would discover me naked and horrified at myself. But I
prayed at the same time that they were bringing my mama in just
now, that someone was washing her face with a soft cloth and
wrapping her in blankets and telling her not to worry. I should
have watched over her. I should have kept my eyes on her. But the
tea, I remembered.*

*The jar bugs were already chattering so loudly I wondered how
they made such a sound.* "Look there, so fair, the Evertell heirs of
Eleanor Dare!" *the jar bugs shouted. Crazy. Cursed.*

*Then Sonder's black coat was suddenly wrapping round me,
heavy and warm, and he pulled me hard against him. I didn't know
where he'd come from. He got me over his shoulder like a sack of
potatoes and I couldn't stop laughing. Something was wrong. The
world was upside down. Every step he took, my teeth clacked
together and I bit my tongue so hard it made me cry out. But I hung
there and let him haul me down the winding trail, until I heard
my name called. At the sound of my mama's voice, I bucked and
squirmed my way out of Sonder's grip.*

*"I'm sorry! I'm sorry!" I wailed and pleaded. Gripping the black
coat tight I ran to her, as hard and fast as my legs would carry me.
She was whimpering alongside my daddy at the edge of the lawn,
and I flung myself at her, grabbing around her waist. She smoothed
my hair and gazed at me. So full of love. She was the moon, even in
such harsh daylight. "I tried to do what you wanted." I was overcome with relief at the sight of her safe and sound. I was anguished
that I'd failed to have the vision. "I didn't mean to lose you."*

But she is not lost, *I thought. She is here. Where are you?*

She was untouched by my strident panic. Her hair was fresh. Her clothes were clean. She had been home a long while. She trembled oh so gently, so tenderly. "Baby girl, what have you done to yourself?" she said without comprehension. "Who are you, child? Tell me."

My mama's expression was serene, sweetly concerned. I stared at her, confused. Even then, the bell was chiming to announce I was home. I lifted my gaze to see the yard filled with neighbors and friends.

I heard my daddy say to me, "Your mother has made herself sick, worried all night. Sick to death."

The bitter taste of the tea was still there on my tongue, some recipe for disaster. I looked to her for help, tried to pity her, but the beloved mother I'd known beneath the stars had vanished.

"The stone is gone," I said. "I lifted the curse. She'll be fine. We'll be fine."

The crowd was silent. My daddy looked like a hollow version of himself. And that was when I knew my mistake. I sounded as unhinged as her. "You have to listen to me! It's gone! It's over!"

Watching from the crowd, I saw Charlie Hawkes. He must have seen the desperation on my face. "Tell them! Tell them what you did," I pleaded. It came out like a sob. For just that moment, I felt sorry for poor Charlie, that I'd dragged him into our nightmare.

"I never took it!" he yelled. "I never touched that stupid old stone. You're crazy as your mama!"

Mama began to sing, "Look there, so fair, the Evertell heirs of Eleanor Dare."

"What is wrong with her?" I screamed.

Quietly, Daddy took her hand and led her inside the house

and I stood alone on my naked feet, shivering inside Sonder's black coat.

I let out a sound like a wounded thing and it was Sonder who carried me inside and let me cry. It was Sonder who stayed with me in the cupola as the neighbors left. We could see the yard below grow empty and the daylight dim as the car pulled around to take my mama to the doctors at Central State Hospital.

X

I'd seen my mother fighting to hold on. And finally she'd clung to me, not with hands but with words. She'd whispered a story to see if I could finish it. What was it she hoped I would see?

I knew now; it was love. How wildly she'd fought for me.

I started to knock, but tried the door and found it unlocked. I climbed the stairs to the little room on the second floor where Sonder slept. He hadn't gone to bed, but sat up in a chair in the corner, his head lolled back.

"Sonder." I said his name softly and he looked up at me, groggy from the long day in the field and the late night after. I went to him and sat on his lap, winding my arms around his neck. I buried my face in his shirt, still stained with sweat.

"Nobody ever locks their doors around here," I said. "I'm supposed to make sure you're not upset with Imegine for knocking the radio out of the window. Penn's worried those messages will be missed and nobody will ever hear them."

"I'll go into town for parts in the morning."

He drew a cigarette from his pocket.

"Last one?" I asked.

"For now."

He lit it and we took turns taking long, slow drags until we'd reached the end and he ground the butt out in an ashtray on the floor. The smoke hung in the air and I felt easy in a way I could not remember, maybe ever.

"I told her everything," I finally said. "She knows what I did. I think she understands." I took a breath. "I'm going to sell part of this place to Bill Hawkes," I blurted. "Actually, it's Julie who wants it. For Nelson." Sonder went very still. "I won't sell the house. I've already promised Penn. But we'll get enough to cover any private school she chooses for the next four years. Or if she wants, it could pay for college later."

Sonder shifted beneath me. "Why are you here, Alice?"

"You know why."

"I mean, what are you doing over here with me?"

"I had to come because Penn—"

"Charlie Hawkes never did steal that stone."

I stared at him, trying to make out what he was saying. "I'm sorry? But I told you. I took Charlie into the forest. I told him to take it. I told you, it was me." I started to stand but he kept hold of my hips.

He was shaking his head and I felt an awful confusion. I could hear the rain start, heavy drops hitting the windows and roof. A low rumble of thunder echoed.

He cleared his throat. "I know what you asked him to do, but Charlie never did it. He tried. Twenty-plus pounds give or take, it wasn't an easy thing to haul out of there. He came to me. He said what he was doing, what you had told him to do, and he was scared. So I helped him haul it away."

"What did you do with it?" I blurted. My voice sounded too loud in the small room.

"I put it up under the mill with your mama's candles. But then, when y'all left, I didn't like much that it was down there with me sleeping up here. I called John and asked him what I ought to do. He told me it should go back where it came from—that's what Claire had wanted. They'd talked about it and decided awhile back. It was supposed to go with her."

"With her?"

"When she passed. She wanted it back where Eleanor left it, not sitting here for you to worry over. So I followed that map in her book and took it to North Carolina. We figured somebody would trip over it in a day or two. Something like that would hit the news and we'd hear and know everything had been made right. That's all any of us wanted, Alice. But then it didn't turn up. It sat out there and after a while, I just figured John would've told you what happened to it."

"I feel sick," I said.

"Then, of course, when they finally found it a few years back, I thought that was it. Everybody would put it behind them. We were all just trying to do right by your mama. But then you got back here and I started thinking something was off."

"Why didn't you say something?"

"I only realized you didn't know what happened to it when you told me about Charlie. If John let you go thinking that was the truth of it all these years, let you blame yourself for what happened to your mama, I knew it would hurt you if I told you what we did."

I rubbed my forehead, my eyes, trying to clear all my jumbled thoughts. "He wouldn't have said, because I gave him every reason not to. I told him everything he wanted to hear. I said I didn't want to talk about it. I didn't want to come back here. I said I didn't believe anything about Evertell heirs or that stone."

"When we were under the mill, I said it was how they were with each other. They'd worked it out between them. And I thought you knew."

My head was bursting, pounding. My heart was breaking. But I could see the self-loathing in his face and that hurt worse than what should have been an unforgivable betrayal. "It doesn't even matter, does it? All this time, she wanted it gone. She wanted it back where it should have been, where Eleanor put it. And that's what we did, I guess." Thunder crashed overhead. The storm was on top of us. The wind pushed against the walls of the mill so the wood popped and moaned.

Every few minutes the air crackled and flashed. The heavy rain had already calmed to a soft patter. The wind tapped at the shingles, as if to apologize for making such a fuss. Inside, there was only the sound of Sonder's breath. His skin was as familiar to me as the land I walked here. His musky scent was the marsh that met the forest.

Like a man waking from a long sleep, Sonder blinked at me, his eyes clear and tender. I felt his grip on my hips tighten. He was asking me a question. If I'd known how to listen, I'd have known he'd been asking it since I'd turned the key in the door that first night. "Will you stay?"

The heat of him made me shiver in the cold room, and the desire of him too. "You think because you ignore everything I say, you bring me chairs and tar paper and corn for the peafowl and carry a curse away, that I'll stay. Can't you do better than that?"

He smiled. "I love you."

Once we began, I found I couldn't stop. It surprised me when Sonder seemed shy. I urged him on, opening his shirt and pulling my blouse over my head so we were skin to skin. He groaned with the pleasure of having me in his arms and I smelled liquor on his breath and felt our mutual exhaustion. He kissed me more and more deeply until he pushed me off his lap, stood over me. I fell lightly across the small bed behind me. He had no idea the way

I'd been with Finch, far outside myself when he'd made love to me. With Sonder I didn't want to disappear. I wanted to watch his face. I wanted to see myself reflected in his eyes.

Later, when we were spent, we curled around one another. I said, "There's a charm in the commonplace book that's supposed to bring a vision to an Evertell heir, the way to see love when it's right in front of you. I don't know if it will ever work for me. This may all go wrong."

But we knew each other, Sonder and I.

"Alice, I already told you." He was a man who didn't need a map. He measured the earth by his own steps. He would wait, as he had always waited. He knew his steps matched mine. "That's the thing about divining. It's a skill, not a trick."

Chapter Twenty-Nine

Well before dawn I walked the wet banks of Bell Creek in the dark, through the tall grasses of the lawn, beneath the long-hanging moss and the arms of the oaks, in a world washed new from the rain. The air smelled of earth and brine. Somewhere high in the trees, the peacock and his hens slept. I carried the jar of sweet balm out to the kitchen house where a light burned. Seeing Imegine there, the breakfast table set, I felt my two worlds colliding.

"I wondered when you'd get back up here," Imegine said, apron tied round her waist, Betty Crocker smile glued in place. "Is Sonder coming in? There ought to be enough."

"Thank you, no. He usually manages his own." I kept my eyes down, ridiculously bashful that she obviously knew where I'd been. "It's just us." I saw she'd put the pages I'd torn from the commonplace book on the table. I took a deep breath.

"There's nothing to drink but this tea that's bitter as piss."

"It's Charged Water. Something Penn found in an old family recipe. A neighbor brought it when I was sick. Supposedly it clears your head."

"Mm. Better take our medicine then." She poured us both a cup, then drew a bottle from her apron pocket. She raised an eyebrow. "Too early for you?"

I shook my head, then settled back in my seat as she poured a generous amount of whiskey into each cup. She set the bottle on the table, half empty, and we sipped quietly. I felt the heat of the liquor giving me courage.

"Listen, I want to talk to you."

"You're upset about Mr. Gabrielli, I know. You don't need to be, I swear. He's a nice man. He's not just a musician, he's a piano tuner, a family man. He told me I smelled like his mama."

I wrinkled my nose.

"No, it's a good thing." She was already infatuated with the idea of the Italian piano player. "His mother grows roses."

One of Mama's candles, left over from the night before, sat on the table. A tin of matches was beside it. I picked up the candle, held it to my nose, inhaled the soft smell of the beeswax, then lit the wick. The air filled with the soft scent.

Imegine spoke again, her voice taking on a dreamy tone. "He told me I should come to Italy and see all her roses, Alice. What do you guess he means by that?"

"I think he's looking for a girl to take home to Mama."

She giggled. "Oh God. I couldn't ever do that."

"Of course you could. That's what I want to talk about. It's important."

"Don't be silly." She sounded like she'd just run into something hard. "I'm not going off to no Italy."

I didn't believe her for a minute. She had arranged for Paolo to tune the piano this afternoon and he'd promised Imegine a music lesson. She told me all of this while I noted she'd tricked herself out the same as she taught me when Finch came courting. Her nails were freshly painted and she reached for the balm on the table and slathered on too much.

"Oh, I should've asked about that stuff. Tell Penn I asked, would you?"

"It's okay. I want you to have it." She was nervous. She paced the front room, watching the drive for any sign of her suitor, while I kept my eyes on her. "Maybe you'll get married and bring Paolo back to the station and change Merely's to a piano shop."

She sighed, seeming more and more anxious. The liquor wasn't taking the edge off for either of us. "I mean, I was thinking about it. It's like you said. The war is almost over. They say it every day."

"Surrender. It's a good word."

"That's it. We'll win and people are going to be dying to hear music, play music, dance to music. There's going to be music everywhere. They'll need people like Paolo Gabrielli to make it," Imegine said, her voice tight with determination as she inspected a nail. She might as well have gone out to stand by the mailbox on the street with her suitcase. "Did you see his hands?" she asked. "Did you see his fingers, how long and delicate they are? He's an artist, Alice. Think of that. Think of that kind of man."

I reached for her hands. I pulled her to sit beside me and didn't release her hands right away. The flame between us flickered. "I have to talk to you."

"You're not coming back. I guessed right, didn't I? You never wanted to be there. You told me once. Remember that? I thought you'd be happy if you had a little girl of your own, somebody to love on, the way I got to love on you." Imegine pushed away from the table. "You ought to stay here. This is your mama's place and it's where you belong. John couldn't change that. He knew."

It was true in many ways, but there were other truths too. Words I wasn't going to let go unsaid anymore. "Imegine, just because

Daddy left me this house doesn't mean I'm going to choose it over you. How could you think that? You were my mama too."

My throat closed up and I had to take a sip of my tea to control my emotions. Imegine did the same, draining her cup to the dregs.

Finally, I said, "The truth is, I need your opinion. I can't decide what to do. You have to tell me. I am expecting an offer on Evertell," I admitted. "From a neighbor, a war widow, same as me. I've decided it's a good thing, keeping the farm with a family that's part of this community. I'm going to keep Bell Isle; the chapel and the cemetery are there. But I'm keeping the house, too, and a few acres. Sonder will have the mill and the fields he's worked all these years."

She looked a little shocked but not displeased. "Well, it sounds like you've got it all decided. What do you need me to say?"

"We'd move back with you, if you'd have us. But the money would mean Penn would never have to worry, she'd have security. She'd have independence. She could go to college, travel. The world would be open to her."

She stared at her empty cup for a long moment before she said, "She wouldn't be like us, you mean?" She sighed and gave me a tired smile. "Alice, for just this once, could you not be so hard on yourself? You don't have to lock yourself away like you've done to these pages."

When I looked at her, I saw myself in her eyes and I was no longer the desperate girl in need of her guidance and approval. She saw it too. But she gave me her advice anyway. After all, that's what a mother does.

"You don't owe me or your daddy or Finch, none of us, a thing. You've got to live your life and stop using the rest of us as your excuse not to."

"Then come live here with us. Just let me talk to Penn first."

For a moment I thought she might stay, that a miracle might happen under Evertell's strongest charms. But this was another woman's house and Imegine knew it. I wasn't really surprised when she swiped up the sweet balm and moved around for the door. She'd made her choice a long time ago. But then I saw she had something for me. She took up a small stack of papers from the table near the stove. When she put it into my hands, I took it as if in a dream. Recognition sent sparks through my mind. I saw it was tied with the familiar blue velvet ribbon and my heart leapt.

"Oh, Imegine. Do you know what this is?" I raised my eyes to meet her gaze. She shook her head.

"Something of your mama's book, I'm guessing. Something I think you were supposed to have a long time ago."

"Where did you find this?"

"Well, I told you, I pulled that old travel wardrobe of hers apart, thinking it's about time it took a trip. I figured you might want it here."

"Honestly, no," I said.

"Well, I'm glad to hear it because I'm afraid I broke it," she admitted. She was relieved. "But that's how I found this. When I pulled that middle door off, the one with the mirror, the glass just fell out. Crashed to a million little pieces. And I guess she'd tucked these pages up in there for you."

"It was there? In the wardrobe, all this time?"

I thought of the awful wardrobe. I remembered that it was the place my mama had chosen to hide her ruined clothes and the sack she'd carried into the forest. My daddy had found those things before we left Evertell.

"I've thought a lot about this, and I think she knew you'd find them when you needed them, when you got ready to set out and go," Imegine said. "Of everything she could have given you from here, she sent you with a wardrobe that was supposed to go places, never supposed to sit on the side of the road twenty years like it did. And now you need to see what she had to say to you. See where it takes you, Alice."

I thought of all the times I'd walked past, afraid to see what that dark glass would show me. I let my gaze drop away from Imegine and onto the pages in my lap, let my fingertips play with the soft ribbon. I could see the faded indigo ink. The same curling penmanship from the commonplace book and Eleanor's Tale. My eyes were drawn over and over to the heading on the front page and I longed to read the rest.

For Alice
my curious girl

But now I pulled the pages up against my chest and looked to Imegine.

"Thank you."

"My place has been beside John, but he's gone now. It's time I find something of my own, Alice. I asked you to stay down here because I believed it was going to be good for you and Penn, but I really needed a little time for myself too. I needed to know what it felt like, being on my own again. It's helped me decide some things. I hope you of all people understand that."

"You don't want to stay at Merely's?"

"No, not the way it's been. I won't be needing to hire a mechanic because Merely's already has one. I sold half the business to a boy who's going to run that part of things. I'm going to keep up my part, feeding weary travelers." She briskly kissed my forehead. "Now that you and Penn are sorted, I'll be staying in Helen. Just a little rental house, but it'll be my own. You come visit when you can. And get yourself a telephone so I won't worry myself to death."

✕

When she'd gone, I ran the soft velvet ribbon between my fingers and tested the knot. It held tight, just as my mama had tied it, to bind us together all these years. When I could manage to stand, I took the whole of Eleanor's Tale and went to find Penn, high in the cupula where she watched for the sunrise.

"Look what Imegine discovered," I said, offering her the found pages. "In the old travel wardrobe Grandmama Claire wanted me to have. She must've thought I was going places, but now I think I'll stay put for a while. What do you say? Grandma Imegine says she's staying in Helen to feed all the people who'll be coming down the road when this war's over, but she'll come visit." Penn drew in her breath. She nodded. Just like that, we were home. "We'll put that thing back together again when you want to take it around the world."

Penn took the pages gingerly, her eyes darting to my face. I saw her chest rise and fall with a shudder of recognition. I sat down close beside her and opened the commonplace book to the place where the pages had been torn away. I carefully smoothed the ones I'd taken into place. "But first, let's put this back together. All right, my little storyteller, see if you can work that knot free," I said.

She hesitated. "I don't want it to end."

"This was never the end," I said. I kissed her forehead as she slipped the ribbon free. "There's a lot more to this story. There's us."

AGNES

Spanish Colonial St. Augustine
1654

Agnes Lavat was a walking miracle, or at least that's what people said. She never believed it herself.

The sickness of 1607 came to St. Augustine in the autumn. She was sixteen years old. The news saved St. Augustine from King Philip's decree that the city be abandoned, but the illness killed Agnes's parents.

The fever stole the elderly first, and then the children. Her mother remembered the old plague. She knew it lived in the shadows of this wilderness. Her father had no medicine strong enough to beat it back but made poultices from the bark of trees she couldn't name and steeped leaves from plants she knew only by the shape of their leaves. When these failed, he knelt beside her mother as she tried the prayers of her Protestant father to his God, and then to the Catholic God of this New World, and finally to the native spirits of every living thing. But it was a doomed fate that they could not change.

Her father became despondent when it was clear that Eleanor had fallen ill, for he had not noticed until it was too late. Agnes was not allowed near them then, as hard as she cried. When her mother died, her father lay down beside her and never got up. And just like that, Agnes was an orphan.

On her deathbed, her mother had called for Agnes. While Agnes pressed her ear to the door, her mother told her the full tale of who she'd been and what she'd done, of mystical visions and espionage, of loss and love and secrets and magic. Agnes was shocked to hear her practical mother spin such a wild tale of a girl named Eleanor Dare. Even more, she was stunned their quiet life had been one of lies. Eleanor promised Agnes her own future would come clear when her heart was ready. She swore a guiding vision would be hers by blood, just as surely as her blue eyes or the length of her thigh bones. But Agnes wasn't interested in such a consolation, a legacy of deception and illusions. Her heart was broken, filled with questions where once there'd been only love. And with her mother gone, she had no hope of finding the answers she needed to go on.

With so many dead, no one was paying any attention when Agnes Lavat went missing. No one thought to consider a girl might walk right out of town, wearing her mother's red boots and gray cloak, sprinkling black hellebore with every step. The people of St. Augustine were too busy digging the graves of their loved ones to worry whether the doctor's daughter lay, unaccounted for, among their dead. They set fire to the doctor's cottage and to a pyre of the dead. Agnes clutched the iron box that protected the commonplace book and Eleanor's first copper printing plate and watched the sky turn dark. The air filled with smoke and ash that made her choke as she ran into the forest.

Not a single soul imagined the girl disappearing. It was a mercy, anyway, they whispered, that the Lavats would see heaven together. Agnes didn't know if she believed in heaven, but she'd no faith left in the world. She had lost her parents and her home, along with everything she knew to be true. Worse than that, she had lost herself.

She wandered up the coast to a bay where she made a camp on the shore. For weeks she slept in the dunes and ate mollusks from the tide pools when she grew hungry. She sat with her face to the wind until her skin blistered and her hair hung in knots, but there was nowhere left to go. She'd come to the edge of the map. She'd meant to drown herself, but staring out at the ocean, she was surprised when the thought of dark water terrified her. She'd thought she was beyond feeling. Instead, she realized she was angry as the fire she'd witnessed consuming all she'd loved. So she resigned herself that if she sat there long enough, completely unmoving, she would simply burn up, leaving only her bones bleached in the sun to be discovered one day far in the future.

She might have gotten her wish if it weren't for a storm that blew a boat off course. A trio of Spanish fishermen staggered into the dunes and tripped over what they thought was a stone, but discovered it was Agnes, sunburned and half-starved. When they returned to St. Augustine with the girl, the church bells rang. But fishermen ran inside their homes, certain they'd seen a ghost. The monks in their garden genuflected as she passed and whispered she was a walking miracle. Sailors at the port repeated rumors her parents had been spies for the French. Some of the women spat on the ground and said she was a witch with her book of charms, otherwise how had she returned from the dead?

Agnes ignored it all. Her life before seemed nothing but a fever dream. Even years later, she suspected she hadn't been spared as she'd heard her neighbors say, but that she still carried the ash of all that loss inside her, a madness that would consume her and any she loved, if she looked back. She married one of the fishermen and lived a common life, although she'd never been able to get the smell of cinders out of her hair. Some things even fire and time can't destroy. When Agnes lost babies too early or when the black flies nearly carried them off in the summers or when her husband suffered a stroke that left him mute and helpless as a babe for her to nurse some long years into their old age, she calmed her fears by pressing her hot face to the cool pages of her mother's book. The practical advice she found there was the legacy she chose. She read the words so many times she could close her eyes and recite the parables or give direction for planting a large crop of sweet peas or know the precise secret to a fine squash soup. She raised her children to trust in the most solid things, the harshest truths and the hardest facts, and she kept her mother's secrets, until one day her heart began to stutter.

She was an old woman and not at all prepared when she began to see, from the corner of her eye, the finest silver flicker. At first she feared she was losing her sight, or that maybe she was suffering the same sort of attack of the brain that had taken her husband. But her eyesight was sharp as a hawk's. Even at her age, her reflexes were quick and agile. It was her heart that was the problem. She knew the constant stutter would likely soon be a full stop. Then finally, one night, in the space between two beats, the shining vision came so clear that she reached out her hands in ecstasy. She heard a song that was not a song, a language that was not a language, and just as her mother had described it, a thousand silvery mysteries trailed past her, the secret lives of those who'd gone before. Her mother's story was there among them, beautiful and beyond her reach, maybe even a lie of love. Agnes could not hold it, no matter how she tried. And suddenly, desperately, she understood the vision was not a revelation but a choice. A thing more powerful than the truth: the chance to accept what she'd never know, and choose love still.

She leapt from her bed as though she'd slipped her earthly bonds, a girl full of promise, amazed to learn the secret had been within her all along. Her mother had not failed her by living a life she'd never fully know. Her mother had not abandoned her by dying. A woman's story was her own. When the vision faded and again all she saw were the familiar surroundings of her bedroom, she curled up on the foot of her bed and wept and called for her mother like a child.

For some women, guilt over having doubted such a precious promise might have stolen the joy from this wisdom, but Agnes had never been one to waste time. Instead, she placed the copper plate atop her mantelpiece and her family complained of how brightly the firelight caught the whipping tails in the engraving. She trusted the stutter in her heart for experience rather than weakness and hurried to find a pen and ink. She opened to the front of the commonplace book, to where she'd long ago written her name just below her mother's.

Old as it was, as many names as might follow her own, there was only one woman who had carried this story so impossibly far, one woman to whom this book would always belong, the author of a life that would be remembered by her daughters, always. Agnes turned back to the very first page. In as graceful a hand as her grandfather's, she made her own mark on the story. This was Eleanor's legacy; not a stone, but a book.

The Book of Eleanor Dare

For a long while she looked at the title, then turned to the map her mother had drawn. She knew what she was doing when she gathered the girls, the younger expecting her first child. Her daughter and granddaughter wondered if Agnes was growing senile when she put the map before them. "Maps don't lie," she said when they asked for an explanation. "And stones keep all our secrets. You'll see. People will say this is where our story ended, with the stone, where my mother buried her family. But that's not true. She carried them all with her when she walked away from there," Agnes said. "They were the light inside her."

While Agnes traced the way her mother had come from the wilderness to the edge of the map, they watched the journey take shape, one she might have forgotten had it not remembered her. At last, she looked out on the view from her window, down to her mother's garden, over the port of St. Augustine with its wide steps leading to the sea. There, stepping into the surf, a girl so like she had once been turned toward the unknown future. At her feet, the dazzling light caught on the edge of every current, reflecting the mysteries of the heavens above. There was magic in such a moment. A dare.

"Some say my grandfather was an artist," Agnes explained. "An explorer to the New World. They say my family was lost. But our grand-mothers were women with vision. It came to my mama, as it came to me. One day it will come to you, the wisdom she called our Evertell. Not a revelation, but something better. A story. When your heart is ready, you'll know. And you will pass these secrets to your daughters."

She could see they barely believed her. They could not conceive of the silver flash between magic and faith. They could not trust that love is never lost but rests in stones and shells and bones, which are time's keepers. How could they imagine such things in a world so full of wandering men, of lonely shores and unmapped wilderness? What chance was there that anyone would even remember their names when the most beautiful truths are often hidden and little girls can disappear? But Agnes hoped as all mothers do that what they could not yet see with their eyes, they would one day know in their hearts. That we need not be content with simply being part of the story. That we may choose to be the storytellers.

—Claire Clerestory

Chapter Thirty

Penn

As dawn broke, Mama read Eleanor's Tale aloud, the story Grandmama Claire had left to guide them. Here's what Penn knew now: she was home. At Evertell or anywhere. Within herself, she knew what kind of girl she was—prepared, expectant, a girl who would dare to dream.

She loved the beauty of the light on the water that greeted her every day. She loved the rambling old house with its fallen chimney and the holes in the roof and the floorboards on the front porch that stuck up in all directions. She loved the great oaks that spread their arms to shade the wide lawn and the shady pond and the snapping peafowl with their long, arrogant necks, their glorious feathers drifting over everything, turning up in every corner, reminders of a whole universe of possibilities. She loved Doris La Roche and her little house that smelled like cinnamon and spice and heartbreak. She even loved Nelson and Sammy, her first new friends who had believed in her and helped her hang the bell clapper. And she loved

Sonder, in a way that did not make her feel she'd betrayed her father, but came alongside that love, safe and certain.

She looked up to search the bits of pale sky at morning's light before coming to the edge of the lawn where it met the banks of the wide gray waters of the river. From here, she could see the house behind her and, across the water, the top of the bell tower on Bell Isle. From here, she launched her boat into the mystery of what came next.

The commonplace book couldn't tell her what to do. She knew better now. She'd found it open beside her on the bed when she woke. Today she understood the entries weren't magic. They were only tips for getting by, ways to survive another day, dreams and hopes for a better crop, a secret love, a comfort for a sick child, or an ingredient for a perfect fish stew. She remembered something Mama once said, that a story matters not because it is true but because it's been told. She might never know the truth about Eleanor, but all the stones were part of her story now. Part of Penn's story and the legacy of Evertell. A myth, after all, wasn't hindered by facts but was shining through with possibilities.

That was the secret of Evertell, the silver light at Penn's center: To expect wonders, silver-scaled dragons of the air, fantastic lurking monsters in the deep, and invisible people of the wood. To know, despite the fact that the world has been discovered and lost over and again, the heart is a lover of mystery. Mystery is the mother of hope.

Penn was halfway across the water when she made out another boat.

A boy's voice called out, "Hey, what are you doing out here? Are you leaving? They're saying ole Hitler's dead. It's out on the radio. They're saying they heard it on the shortwave in Savannah. Can you believe it? Nobody knows if it's true yet. I was coming out to see what Sonder knows."

It was Nelson. Penn felt all the blood rush out of her head as he pulled his boat up alongside her. For a moment she was dizzy.

"I'm going to ring the bell," she said. Her voice hardly sounded like her own. "Will you come with me?"

They didn't bother trying to secure the boats on the other side.

When Doris opened the door, the smell of cinnamon was sweet and strong. Her eyes flicked back and forth between Penn and Nelson as she yanked an old robe together at the neck. "What trouble are you two up to?"

"Hitler's dead!" Nelson yelped. "They're saying he's dead."

"We're going to stay." She beamed at Doris and saw the light reflect back at her from the old woman's face, warm and sure as the indigo tea.

Doris gave a dry kiss to Penn's forehead. She looked between her and Nelson, who was barely able to contain himself.

Doris said, "What are you two waiting for?"

※

Penn stopped to look at the bell hanging secure and whole again in the tower. Her daddy would have been proud of her. She was proud of herself. She could see the piece of iron, carved with the marks of this community, now a part of the bell forever. She looked to her friends.

"Help me now?" Penn said, breathless.

The three of them grasped the rope together and gave it a yank, setting the great bell swinging so that Penn was startled by the resonant sound that echoed out across the island and the water. When the bell tolled again, Penn let out a long, slow breath. Maybe the first deep breath since they'd come to Evertell. With each chime, Penn called the names of her family, the nameless, too, all the people they'd found at Evertell. She called to the people she'd lost, to her pop, far away where he rested beside the stone they'd placed to remember her daddy. She called to her daddy, who was all around her and in the work she'd done on the bell. She knew the story she would write in the commonplace book, the one she'd been waiting to hear, so desperate to discover. It was her own.

Chapter Thirty-One

Alice

I climbed high into the cupola and sat at Sonder's desk. I brought the commonplace book with me and opened it there, to begin the work of repairing the damage I'd done. All I'd lost, all I'd loved, seemed so clear to me now. Take the bitter with the sweet. Guide by your mother's light. I didn't know what I might see if I dared to look into my own heart, but I lifted my eyes.

Once there was a girl who went into the forest.

The Evertell bell tolled clear and bright. Penn had found her way across the water. The sound carried high on the air, over the forest, over the marsh, out to the sea. Our neighbors would hear the bell after so many years. Evertell would have the homecomings Penn had dreamed of, friends and strangers from near and far. I could see it now, visitors—no, cousins—streaming into the yard, year after year, lingering in the shade of the oaks, pulling strings of fish in from the dock, eating Imegine's fresh corn cakes and sipping cold sweet tea on the wide porches. They would remember the days when they were young at Evertell, when my daddy had told them the secret to balancing the great burrstones of our grist mill and when ladies had sighed over the sweet scent of my mama's honeyed candles. As the daylight slipped into dusk and the shadows grew soft and long and cool, they would tell ghost stories. *"Look there, so fair, the Evertell heirs of Eleanor Dare."*

Once there was a girl who always took a dare.

My eyes stung as I searched the horizon, the edge of the map, for the shape of a man I'd dreamed of long ago. I could see Sonder then, and myself. Seasons would turn as we walked the fields, planning for summer gardens and autumn harvests. On warm spring nights, we'd listen to the peacock's unrelenting love song piercing the night, insistent and impolite, and we would dream deeply of the most brilliant blues and greens of Evertell. We'd travel to bustling cities to stare up at skyscrapers and wander through hushed museums and linger in awe at the great churches of Europe. We'd go north, into the mountains, back to the bend in the road where I'd waited for fate to find me. But we'd always come back to the farm he loved. He couldn't be gone from that river for long and I couldn't be far from him. He'd kiss me in the pigeon loft, all the birds having found their way home, and he'd say he wanted another child, a sibling for Penn. We'd have three more children, twin girls and a boy. They would run the river, free as wild things. The youngest would have his father's gift for recognizing the divine in plain sight. "Our family has always been partial to visions and charms," I would say.

Once there was a girl who went to sleep and awoke someone else.

In the archival rooms at Brenau there would be gawkers and hecklers, but they would not know the likes of us. "Who are you?" they would ask when we showed up each year on May Day, and we would laugh, Penn and her daughter, myself the loudest.

Piled in corners and against walls, lying all over the floor, there they would be, the Dare Stones. Just as the papers had described them, forty-eight rocks in all. Varied in size and shape, they'd be covered with the mysterious markings of unknown authors, so many stories, all of them ours, inspired by one girl's vision. "We love the mystery most of all," I would explain to my granddaughter. "A story matters not because it is true but because it's been told."

Penn's daughter would spread a clean piece of paper over the original stone and make an etching of the inscription with plans to paste it into the commonplace book. I would see such satisfaction on her face. But it would only be a blink. She would already be looking forward. When one story ends, another is already beginning.

"Now what?" my granddaughter would say.

Once there was a girl who could always find her way home.

)(

The river was quiet and gray. The marsh hugged its edge as the tides turned once again. The sun was pale behind high clouds, the trailing hem of last night's storm moving out to sea. The forest exhaled and the air was sharp with evergreen when I opened the commonplace book. Its wizened pages fell open to the place marked by the blue velvet ribbon. I thumbed carefully through the recorded recipes, secret poems and prayers, cures for colds and heartbreak, wistful records of moon phases and hard-won gardener's wisdom, smiling at Penn's ink drawings, marking all she had. Finally, I came to the list of Dare descendants. I did not need to read the names. I knew them by heart. I'd remembered them with every breath, with every step that had brought me here. I'd made my peace with that stone.

In my hair, pinned high on my head, I tucked two peacock

feathers so they crowned my bent head with their glowing moons, worlds of possibility. I thought of Penn as I smoothed the page, a curious girl who had waited for me to find my way, even as she taught me exactly who I was and where I belonged. I knew when the time was right, she would not hesitate to make her mark. We were the Evertell heirs of Eleanor Dare.

Beneath my mama's name, I wrote my own.

Dare Descendants

Eleanor White Dare Lavat 1568–1599

Virginia Dare 1587–1591

Agnes Lavat Marquez 1592–1657

Catarina Marquez Abreu 1615–1662

Marguerite Abreu 1639–1668

Francoise Abreu 1657–1702

Esmé Abreu Laurens 1692–1749

Garnet Lee Laurens Rutledge 1709–1757

Sally Rutledge Ribault 1729–1785

Angelique Ribault Reece 1758–1847

Bernadette Reece Telfair 1774–1822

Camille Telfair Parish 1799–? (vanished)

Delaney Parish Beaufort 1820–1894

Flora Beaufort Vaughn 1840–1908

Calista Vaughn Clerestory 1860–1914

Claire Clerestory Merely 1891–1922

Alice Merely Young 1909–

Pennilyn Young 1932–

Author's Note

It's likely that you have never heard of the Dare Stone, or of any of the inscribed stones that were discovered across the South between 1937 and 1940. But the rocks do indeed exist, though their shadowy history has been all but forgotten.

The Dare Stones are a series of forty-eight rocks chiseled with messages purporting to be those of the survivors of the famous Colony of Roanoke, who went missing between 1587 and 1590. The rocks tell a dramatic tale of the survival of just a handful of colonists, and it's a story fraught with misery and war, sickness and massacres. Most of the stones are believed to be hoaxes, and only the first stone discovered holds the tantalizing potential of being genuine. To this day, of the many historians and scientists who have investigated the first stone, none have found a way to conclusively determine its authenticity as an artifact.

Back when the stones were found, people wanted to believe. The 1930s were the heyday of P. T. Barnum, forged Indian artifacts, and fake effigies, and the decade also marked the three hundred fiftieth anniversary of the greatest unsolved mystery in American history.

Gone with the Wind had put the South square in the public eye even as the nation struggled through the economic fallout of the Great Depression. The time was ripe for a drama on an epic scale, and the discovery of the Dare Stones fit that bill perfectly. Even as scholars remained skeptical and fully expected another humbug, the entire nation buzzed with the thrill that historians might have something big on their hands: an answer to what happened to those early settlers who had vanished nearly four centuries earlier. Splashy headlines hit the newspapers. "'Lost Colony' Stone at Emory," the *Atlanta Constitution* declared. "Inscription May Solve Virginia Dare Mystery," Raleigh's *News & Observer* claimed.

The spell was ultimately broken when the *Saturday Evening Post* ran an article in April 1941 by investigative reporter Boyden Sparkes that debunked the stones, declaring them nothing but a fabulous con. The piece was damning. Soon after, academics were forced to admit they had been flimflammed. On May 15, 1941, the *Atlanta Journal* ran the headline "Hoax Claimed by 'Dare Stones' Finder in Extortion Scheme." The *New York Times* wrote, "Expert Says Some Dare Stones Are Fraud: Accuses Georgia Mason of Playing a Part."

With that, the rocks became a joke and, even worse, a source of shame. They were hastily tucked away in a basement storage room at a small Georgia university and left to molder in the genteel and Southern tradition of dealing with inconvenient relations. It is telling, however, that until his death, even hard-nosed reporter Boyden Sparkes continued to search for answers about the first stone, the one marked with the initials E. W. D., for Eleanor White Dare, the young daughter of the colony's governor and the mother of the first English child born in the New World. It was the only stone that could not be explained away or connected to the scandal.

Is the Dare Stone real? I don't know. But unlike for Sparkes or the academics and historians who have investigated the stone over the years, that was never my question. Perhaps that is why that old rock has captivated me for so long, until I conjured the message I needed in the writing of this novel. I am not a scholar; I'm a storyteller.

It has been nearly twenty years since I first learned of the Dare Stones. Curiosity initially sent me to the Northeast Georgia History Center and to the special collections section at Brenau University. But I was unprepared for the visceral reaction the stones drew from me. I wept when I saw the original stone, presumably Eleanor's first message. I couldn't help but think what I would give for a message from those I've lost, in any shape or size or form. How precious it would be, a kind of miracle, one I don't think I would call into question. I realized immediately that I hadn't made my pilgrimage to determine if the message was or was not the answer to the fate of the colony. I didn't care if the engraving was authentic. Instead, I wondered about a girl who dared to want more, a young mother who walked into an uncertain future. I wondered, what if that first stone was only part of a greater story?

That day I set out on a search for Eleanor that would last more than a decade.

To start, I began as others had before me, with theories on the stones. I read, cover to cover, Robert W. White's *A Witness for Eleanor Dare* and David La Vere's *The Lost Rocks*. In some ways, I found Eleanor in the historical facts and academic speculations, but on a deeply personal level, I remained disappointed. As the years passed, I spent hours searching through scant pieces of information about the lives of those who first visited the coast of the New World, especially Eleanor's father, John White. Little is known. Purportedly he was a man of faith and an artist who gained influence in his time, and eventually he was commissioned as the governor of the first English colony in the New World. But before any of that, he'd lost a wife and a young son. He was deep in his grief on those long expeditions as a mapmaker and illustrator, and those travels to the edge of the world might have been the escape he craved. But they meant leaving Eleanor behind.

I began to speculate about that girl, alone, abandoned, anxious for attention and love. I pored over her father's beautiful art and imagined Eleanor's wonder at the world he'd seen, and likely her bitterness too. You can see the drawings in Paul Hulton's *America 1585: The Complete Drawings of John White,* but I wonder if you will notice the thing that struck at my heart. John White was a renowned artist who had been a talented miniaturist even before his adventures abroad, yet nowhere among any of his known works is there a portrait of his daughter, Eleanor.

Records tell us that the John White family made their home on Fleet Street in London and that Eleanor was married at St. Bride's Church. Stumbling across mention of a printing press near the family's location, and the fact that John White's art was published, I thought it seemed likely that Eleanor might have recognized the power in written work. It didn't seem a leap to conceive she might have learned a bit of the trade to her advantage. The idea of Eleanor as a printer was supported by many online accounts of women taking on the running of a press, often in secret.

As I learned more about the person Eleanor, I felt I was beginning to know her and befriend her. I could see her, a very young woman, married to a man of her father's choosing and newly pregnant, boarding a crowded ship bound for uncertain shores. After all, I was a young mother. Experiencing motherhood added another dimension to my understanding of what Eleanor faced. I had followed my new husband from our hometown in north Georgia to the Pacific Northwest and only three years later, with our first child on my hip and another in my belly, crossed the country again to North Carolina and another town I had never seen. In my mind, as I aged, Eleanor aged. As my children grew, Eleanor's children grew.

Marjorie Hudson's *Searching for Virginia Dare* inspired me to consider the stories of mothers and daughters, as well as to travel to many of the places where Eleanor might have lived. I traveled with my then young children to the Outer Banks of North Carolina, to stand where Eleanor might have stood, at the edge of the map. I visited the Elizabethan Gardens and attended a performance of Paul Green's outdoor play, *The Lost Colony*, and had a royal tea with the cast members. And I thought not at all about whether any of the tales I was told might be true but rather about all that Eleanor had left behind, and all the questions she must have had for a mother she'd lost so young. Where on earth had she found answers?

When a third move brought my family back to Georgia, I landed in Fulton County. If you believe the story of those later stones, this put me only miles from the place where Eleanor's life ended. And it was there that I began to write the story that had been taking shape in my mind, starting not with the tangled speculations obscuring the message of the Dare Stone but with the loss of it. I began, not with a location on a map, but at a place with no coordinates, save these: *Eleanor was here.* Setting the novel in the years after the stones were discredited, I dreamed up a family of women on the coast of Georgia, desperate for wonders and mysteries and messages from the beyond—the descendants of Eleanor Dare.

Eleanor whispers to me, not detailing historical fact but telling a story, a shifting, shimmering tale that teaches a singular truth. It is that the mysteries of us—the possibilities in our stories, the secrets in our legends and wishes and dreams, not the facts of us—ultimately connect us all. The Dare Stone is a call, begging a response. We are all the triumphant girl setting sail for a distant shore as surely as we are often the forgotten girl, lost in the wood. The question was never whether the inscription was real—because it was and is most certainly a part of a much larger and very authentic legacy—but will we dare as Eleanor did?

As I've imagined the possibilities for Eleanor's legacy, I've tried to ensure that the narrative in *The Lost Book of Eleanor Dare* depicts many of the events inscribed upon the Dare Stones: the birth of Eleanor's first daughter, Virginia; the massacre of her husband and that child; the supposed birth of a second daughter, Agnes. My choices for Eleanor's further travels were based on records of trading trails before the British colonies were ever established, during the time when Eleanor allegedly wandered the wilderness, and drawn from accounts of pirates, prisoners, and spies among the Spanish. And while the fictional story I've conjured deliberately splinters from the story inscribed on the stones, I believe it is as plausible a fate as any. Most importantly, it is my love letter to Eleanor Dare, to my mama, to my sisters, to myself.

"We are here. We are here." I imagine the echo.

In the end, there is no one story that will ever capture Eleanor's fate, or mine. I could tell it a thousand different ways if my lifetime would allow. I've struggled greatly with this reality, right up until I composed the final pages of this novel. In some small way, I've managed to scribble my imperfect mark. Only then have I found some measure of comfort in the work I've undertaken on her behalf—on behalf of all lost, curious, daring girls—with this most unexpected revelation: I think Eleanor might like it that way.

The Dare Stone

Photos courtesy of
Brenau University

443

Acknowledgments

Years have gone into the writing of this story, and I am not the only one who has leaned close to be part of the telling of it. When I think of this book, I will always hear the voices that have joined my own, a chorus of wonder, celebrating a woman who seemed to disappear from history, but who has bound us together in search of her. In search of ourselves, I think.

My heart is in my throat as I offer my deepest thanks to those who came alongside me first and would not let me give up—Patti Callahan Henry, Joshilyn Jackson, Alison Law, Kristy Woodson Harvey, and especially Marybeth Whalen and Ariel Lawhon—who always, always said, "Tell me you're still working on Eleanor's book." And thanks to Sally Kilpatrick and Nicki Salcedo, who met me for gumbo, looked me in the eye when it was hardest, and have been sisters from the start.

There would be no book without the vision and daring of everyone at Harper Muse—especially my publisher, Amanda Bostic. You are a team who understands a book of dreams. Kimberly Carlton, my sharp-eyed editor, I'm indebted to you for asking all the right questions and for marking the path so I was never lost. I'm a better writer because of you. Jodi Hughes, Julie Breihan, Becky Monds, Caitlin Halstead, and Laura Wheeler, thank you for putting a shine on these pages and for a title that means everything. To my marketing team, Nekasha Pratt, Kerri Potts, Margaret Kercher, and Taylor Ward, thanks for your tireless work and savvy ideas, and to Patrick Aprea and LaChelle Washington for mixing virtual magic to reach readers. And to Savannah Summers for your amazing attention to detail.

Many thanks go to Benjamin Barton, Collection Development Librarian of the Trustee Library at Brenau University, for helping me sort historical details of the Brenau Academy and to Edie Rogers, Director of Communications at Brenau, for permission to use photos of the Dare Stone.

To those who open doors widest and make such gracious space for the telling of tales, I'm forever grateful to be in your orbit—Kathy Murphy, Shari Smith, Mari Ann Stefanelli, Zachary Steele, Jonathan Haupt, Orly Konig, and Laura Drake.

When I needed magic most, thank you to the women of Women's Fiction Writers Association, who danced in the desert and told their ghost stories with me—especially Amy Impellizzeri, Kathryn Craft, Christy Kyser, Jen Fromke, Nancy Johnson, and Kelly Hartog. And to Reta Hampton, instant cousin, who sidled up with a drawl like my own and whispered, "Listen, do I have the place for you . . . ," making the dream of Tinderbox Writers Workshop retreats a reality.

For the women of Tinderbox, who came when I opened the doors of a house and stood at the edge of the world, I miss you and look forward to another retreat! When I read this book, I will always feel the glow of that time together captured into its pages. I'm grateful especially for the abiding friendships of Karen Filos,

Samantha Kendig, Pam Arena, Karen Means, Connie Deerin, Connie Vincent, Kyle Ann Robertson, Gina Herron, Heather Bell Adams, and Katherine Scott Crawford Dodson (who imagined the fictional news article about the Dare Stones), early readers and dream weavers. You are gifted writers, wise women, and you make me a better person.

Amy Sue Nathan, this book exists because you said it would. I believed that then and now. Thank you for helping me find my backbone. I aspire to be as faithful a friend as you have been to me. And unending gratitude to Camille Pagan, Kelly Harm, Katie Rose Guest Pryal, Heather Webb, Amy Reichart, Eileen Goudge, Erin Celello, Aimie K. Runyon-Vetter, Ann Garvin, and all the Tall Poppy Writers—you have taught me so much about the business of publishing and the best parts of a writing sisterhood.

Danielle Egan-Miller, Literary Diviner, I imagine you seated in your office, sussing out the story within this story even before it was half written. You gave me trust, patience, and all the courage to tell Eleanor's tale. Maybe more importantly, you gave me permission to embrace the mystery that matters most of all. I'll never be able to thank you for that and for crying in all the right places. Thanks to Clancy D'Isla for a few tears too! And when, at last, we wandered from the wood together, thank you for giving me the confidence to know this was exactly the book it was meant to be.

To the entire team at Browne and Miller Literary Associates, I'm forever grateful for all the time invested and your unwavering belief in this book, for being behind me all the way. And especially to Ellie Imbody and Mariana Fisher—your ability to help me find all the best words was invaluable.

To the vast community of writer friends, both local and virtual, who have kept my boat afloat. I am lucky to have you—I appreciate your friendship and generosity. I can't name you all! But especially

Robyn O'Bryant, Pam Mantovani, Colleen Oakley, Lynn Cullen, Kimberly Belle, Signe Pike, Julie Kibler, Margaret Dilloway, Erika Robuck, Sarah McCoy, Kay Conroy, Lisa Wingate, Susan Meissner, Susanna Kearsley, Rachel McMillan, and Joy Callaway, for bringing just the charms I needed at just the right times.

Carmen Slaughter, I knew this story would mean something to you too. Thank you for sitting on a bench outside a bookstore, for helping me make this work count, and for giving Bridie Quillian a name she deserves. Special thanks to Foxtale Book Shoppe and all the kind, encouraging independent booksellers whose stores offer us a place where these meetings of the mind happen over stories. I am honored to work with you.

Emily Carpenter and Manda Pullen, sitting around a fire beneath a full moon with you is my favorite. You are the friends my soul has known since time immemorial.

To my family, thank you for making me who I am and listening to my stories the longest and best. And to Doug Norton, Uncle Duck, for bringing the books of Eugenia Price when I was only a girl and it seemed I'd already read everything else.

Thank you to my husband, Daniel, who has supported me at every turn, and to my children, Claire, Paul, and Morgan, you inspire me every day—you are, now and always, my Evertell.

You, the reader, thank you for spending time with my words, and not only for writing reviews, emails, and notes of encouragement, but coming to my talks and events. I hope you know there's a place for your name, too, in this story that is no longer mine, but ours, and that it brings you joy.

Discussion Questions

1. The theme of loss and grief weighs heavy in this book. If you are comfortable doing so, can you share an experience you've had with loss and grief? What helped and what did not?
2. How are stories passed down in your family? Is there a special book, similar to the journal the Dare descendants pass down? Or perhaps your family passes memories down through the art of storytelling?
3. What do you think is the truth of the Dare stone found in 1937? Is it an historical artifact of the Lost Colony or artifice?
4. Which character's story engaged you the most and left you wishing for more?
5. *"A story doesn't matter because it's true but because it's been told."* What do you make of Claire's words to Alice?
6. There is great symbolism in this book: Penn's quest to restore the Belle Isle chapel bell; Penn slowly removing the loose bricks from Evertell house's chimney; homecomings at Evertell. What drove Penn to do these things? What was she hoping to gain?

7. Discuss Penn and Doris's relationship and how it develops throughout the book. What is each able to provide the other?

8. The question, "Who are you?" runs throughout the book. Have you ever grappled with that question? At what times in your life?

9. Bill Hawkes said to Penn that history depends on "who's telling the story." What does Bill mean by this? How might this story change if it was narrated by Sonder, Doris, or Bridie Quillian? What other character's perspective might you appreciate?

10. How does the specter of World War II play a role in this book and for many of the characters' stories? Consider Sonder, Walter Kreischer, Alice and Penn, Imegine, Bill Hawkes, Sammy Hunt, among others.

11. What did you think of Eleanor White Dare's story, interspersed in chapters throughout the book?

About the Author

Claire Brock Photography

Kimberly Brock is the award-winning author of *The Lost Book of Eleanor Dare* and *The River Witch*. She is the founder of Tinderbox Writers Workshop and has served as a guest lecturer for many regional and national writing workshops, including the Pat Conroy Literary Center. She lives near Atlanta with her husband and three children.

※

Visit Kim online at kimberlybrockbooks.com
Instagram: @kimberlydbrock
Facebook: @kimberlybrockauthor
Twitter: @kimberlydbrock